BROKEN TIDES:

A TALE OF TWO BROTHERS

R.J Kenny

To Gill

Enjoy the read

ACKNOWLEDGEMENTS

First of all Broken Tides would have never been possible without my amazing fund raisers on Kickstarter, a list of whom can be found after the historical note at the end. I need to thank my brilliant family for helping me through the process of writing. Thank you to Tina and Chris for giving me funds for editing. Thank you to Dean and Siâna for being wonderful proofreaders. As well as that a huge thank you to Fiona for being my rock whenever I needed morale support and financial help as well.

Broken Tides is dedicated to you all.

Ryan James Kenny.

Carlnut

It was the seventh day at sea and neither the captain nor his men knew where they were. The Jarl paced the deck, his men silent but their eyes sullen with hunger. Jarl Bergi was not a wrathful man, but he was a firm one. Only three days ago, when rations were scarce and throats titillating for fresh water he had thrown a man overboard for stealing someone else's last scraps of food. Carlnut could remember the terror in Liki's eyes as the Jarl ordered him to be stripped naked and whipped against the mast. Each of the sailors was then forced to rub salt into their friend's back, sending him into screams of pain. Eventually Liki's heart gave in and his whipped body felt heavy when Carlnut and his father Hrolf were ordered to throw the body into the darkening blue sea.

That all seemed an age ago; the food ran out not long after that and the last drop of water was drunk on the sixth night. The twenty men that set off from Hordaland

"Solvi, you are the Jarl's skald, you are the one who has brought honour to our family, and you and you alone have written our names on the great watery walls of Valhalla," Carlnut said. He began to turn to the large boat where his Father was waiting, until Solvi reached out his hand to meet with his own. Solvi's hands were cold but Carlnut could feel a simmering warmth coming from within them. The elder brother looked at the younger in enquiry.

"I have spoken to Odin, I've spoken to Thor and Loki, I've spoken to every god I know," Solvi said. Father had never bothered to teach much of the gods to Carlnut but had spent many hours teaching Solvi everything he knew. "You will return to Hordaland."

***

Carlnut began coughing uncontrollably. A golden cushion lay beneath his aching back, and a lovely woman stared down at him.

~ 12 ~

Carlnut

He lay alone in the fiery night, bright colours dancing and changing before his heavy eyes. Carlnut watched the flames leap and hiss, always reaching feverishly out for him, trying desperately to grab and hold onto his fleeting shadow. Beautifully they swayed, beckoning him and enticing him, but each time he looked away, Carlnut knew they were looking back at him, calling him home.

The priest placed the torch back into the rusty holster on the mud and wattle wall. The flames seemed to subside, like he had tamed the fire and begged for its silence. He wore a simple grey robe that was tattered at his wrinkled feet where it hung between the floor and his worn sandals. Strapped around his thin and bony body was a frayed hemp rope; little material remained, but the priest wore it like a gold chain. A dull cross hung from his old, veiny neck as if it was weighing him down. The first time Carlnut woke, he rose in a fit of terror, struggling and lost in his own imagination with a thousand thoughts trying to understand where he was. He had pulled on the cross so hard that it had broken the priest's skin and caused heavy bleeding, which stained both his robes and his cross. However, every night without fail the priest would scrub both shimmering clean as he said it cleansed the soul.

"Will he live?" Selwyn asked the priest.

"He will, Sunflower, but I fear he cannot stay. The Earl of Christchurch is doing his rounds a few days from now. He cannot see this . . . this." Selwyn placed her hands on the old man's shoulders. If anyone was to hear that they were hiding a Pagan, they would be burned. At twenty, Selwyn was just old enough to remember the last Pagan burning. The entire town came to watch; food stalls lined the streets of Poole and children were dancing in the alleys; priests from as far away as Northumbria had come to see one family burnt. There were two adults and two children, Selwyn remembered; all four were tied to a huge log in the middle of a mountain of firewood that the whole town collected. Selwyn could recall the family being engulfed by the swirling inferno to the tune of cheering and laughter. She did not want the same fate to befall a man she had rescued from the unforgiving tides and certain death.

Carlnut was almost twice her size and four times her weight so it took her most of the day to drag his lifeless body from the shore to her small thatched house just on the edge of Poole. For six days Carlnut had lain in her bed and each day the priest would come in the morning, pray and do his best to nurse the foreigner back to full health, then pray some more.

Every movement sent claws of pain down Carlnut's back, and when he tried to sit up, he could only move his head. Selwyn heard the groans from the other room and came prancing in.

"The priest says you will get your strength back," she said as she gently placed a cup of water to the raider's cracked lips. Selwyn was a small woman; her face was thin but glowing, and her auburn hair was tangled and stained like old rope. Her red hair fell down to her narrow shoulders, which were covered by an old brown shift. Carlnut began to look around the dark and damp room he found himself in but could not draw his attention away from Selwyn for too long. She had breasts smaller than any of the other women he had known in Hordaland but yet he found himself enjoying the petiteness of the woman who was caring for him.

A few days passed and Carlnut could feel the cold upon him as he heard the screech of the door. Voices in a strange tongue were murmuring to each other followed by the sound of crying. With all his strength, Carlnut lifted himself out of the thin wool sheets that were stained with shit and blood. Every bit of him wanted to fall back onto the straw, close his eyes and dream of his home. He tried to walk but collapsed, sending a thud throughout the house. Selwyn and the priest came rushing in.

"He is not ready, Luyewn," she cried. "They will kill him!" As well as the pain in her voice, Carlnut sensed alarm even though he had no idea what she was saying.

"Help him up, Sunflower. We will put him on my horse, and I will keep him in the church." The priest ran outside to ready his horse as Selwyn reached her hand out to help Carlnut. The two staggered through to the door. The sunlight made Carlnut's heart burst out of his chest; he had not felt the warmth in days, weeks or months; he could not tell. But all he knew was he liked it. He could almost smell the sea. And if the sword was Carlnut's wife, then the sea was his mistress. He was born on the blessed waters of the Bjornafjorden and would wade into these waters every full moon. The cold warmth of the mysterious fjord that engulfed Hordaland soothed every pain Carlnut ever had. Ever since he was a boy he would be out at sea or in the fjords, sailing, swimming and praying. Odin was always closer to him when he was in the water, Carlnut believed.

Women carrying straw baskets full of poorly grown vegetables stopped and turned as the priest rode by on his pure white mare. The mare's powerful legs stomped into the dirt, causing dust to scatter across the road; it was a well-fed horse fit to carry a soldier. Carlnut wondered why such a skinny old man needed such a beast. Yet Carlnut was grateful for the animal's strength; he knew he could barely stand; he knew he was weak and he hated it.

They passed a thatched roofed house; from outside it didn't look like much more than a cattle shed but the space appeared to be adequate for a family, who were making their way outside to see what had caused their neighbours to gasp. Carlnut noticed that the buildings here were different from any he had seen before.

'Where am I?" he mumbled.

"Quiet, please be quiet," the priest uttered in a language Carlnut didn't understand. The thatched roofed house was soon behind them, and the horse went at such a speed that the muscles of its hind legs would continue to hit Carlnut in the face as he lay limp across the horse's back. He could taste blood in his mouth; he liked it, it made him think of war, which made him think of his home and of his family.

Carlnut's first taste of battle was when he was around thirteen and his father Hrolf had taken him on a raid. A group of thirty of Jarl Bergi's best men, led by Hrolf raided a nearby fishing village. According to Hrolf, the headman of the village had not paid his due to Jarl Bergi.

"Why do we need to attack him, Father?" Carlnut asked innocently.

"The world works in a way that you will always have a leader," his father replied. "The men of this village follow their headman who follows a chief and that chief is meant to follow our Jarl Bergi just as Jarl Bergi follows the gods. All men therefore must kneel to the gods."

"What if Bergi and the gods tell you to do different things?" Carlnut enquired. Hrolf looked at his son and tilted his head, appearing to be confused by the question, but he had no time to respond as the headman had ridden out to meet the small war band with about twenty villagers behind him. Carlnut saw old men with grey and white hair that walked clumsily with their bent backs and he saw young boys just older than himself with small patches of fluff on their children's faces. Rain woke them that day; it continued to pour even to that point. Everyone who stood on that small grassy knoll was wet through and truly didn't want to be there. But all men did their duty, just as Carlnut did his. He stayed close to his father as the massacre began, holding his spear point level. The headman ran for Hrolf with a dented old sword in his hand. His screams of self-encouragement were deafening as he sprinted like a wild beast towards one of the greatest warriors in all of Hordaland. However, his shrieks were in vain as one dodge from Hrolf allowed the headman to slip and go sprawling past him. Therefore it only took one swing. In one movement of body and sword, Carlnut noticed his father had ended the traitor's life. Carlnut had never been happier.

Priest Luyewn laid Carlnut down upon the floor next to the kempt altar. The chapel was small but grand. The glass was painted with colours from across the rainbow, each colour forming and spiralling into another. Some even appeared to tell a story. The biggest window was central and above the altar. It was perfectly round and had an ornate golden border. As the light shone through it, a woman holding a babe could be seen and somehow the light gave the woman emotion. She seemed to be looking down upon Carlnut and crying. Luyewn made a cross on his chest and kissed his crucifix.

"Dearest God, I know I have sinned for I have bought a Pagan into your home. But please I beg for your forgiveness." As a cloud passed and the light dimmed, Mary almost nodded in agreement to the priest. "This man, and he is a man for I see no physical differences to he and myself, is in need of my protection. Like the Samaritan I stopped and I listened for his blood does not make him an enemy of mine nor does his faith." Luyewn began to weep; he knew what he was doing was against everything he had been taught but he knew he had to help, for it was his duty.

The linen cloth was like the warm hands of a lover on Carlnut. The whites of the linen would soon become stained with red and browns of all shades but for Luyewn that was no worry. The bony priest hurried to the bedside every time he heard Carlnut in discomfort. He changed the chamber pot, scrubbed the warrior's muscular body and even handfed him twice a day.

That night Carlnut had a dream. He was rowing alone on a blistering cold night. He could feel the chill across his whole body and when he looked down he was naked and covered in tingling pimples. He recognised the water as the Bjornafjorden, so he continued to row to a small wooded island that lay in the middle of the grand fjord. As he dismounted the old, tattered boat, the mist descended. A raven hidden from the moon's pale light called four times.

"You will return to Hordaland!" the screams seemed to say. He turned suddenly as he felt the grapple of a man's hand upon his stiff back. A tall thin king stood there, flushed in his studded garments and fine jewellery. Then a small rotted man appeared behind him, and Carlnut instinctively rushed to protect the decorated king but both vanished. The mist grew colder and the screams grew louder.

"You will return to Hordaland! You will return to Hordaland!" Twice now the raven seemed to call this. As the echoes of the second call subdued, the ghost-like mist cleared. Carlnut found himself in a great white hall. The architecture was flawless as if perfectly crafted by the gods. The ceiling must have been about thirty feet high. Designs and patterns spiralled and danced around the room. He thought of Valhalla, and he wondered if he had died on the raiding ship and everything was just the ride to the great watery halls of Odin. Excitement grew as he walked through the hall across shining marble tiles. The two enormous oak doors at the far end of the room creaked open. Nude women of all colours circled him; some were as black as ash and others as pale as snow-capped mountains. One had an unhealed scar from her left breast to the base of her hip bone like the strap of a satchel. He glanced around hoping to see a face he recognised, but all of them were faceless strangers. The women escorted Carlnut to another king; this king was less prettied up than the last but instead this king stood straight backed with an air of power surrounding him. His armour was bright and clean but showed dents and scratches as if it was worn from battle. Carlnut went to open the second king's visor only to find thin string. Endless cords of string. He pulled and pulled, hoping to find where the string ended but as the string left the armour, it fell as fine silk to the marble floor below.

"You will return to Hordaland! You will return to Hordaland! You will return to Hordaland!" This time the screams were coming from a door behind the empty armour so he followed the screeching sound of the raven. It took all of his strength to open the doors that seemed to get heavier and heavier after every push. However, they finally surrendered and led him into a pit. The walls were steep and slippery and the door on which he had exhausted all his energy was nowhere to be seen. Carlnut could feel his heart bouncing around in his chest. A young, battle-hardened hand reached down and grabbed Carlnut. Upon this hand a black tattoo ran from thumb to each finger and a red ruby ring on his index finger pierced the skin. Seemingly, the third king had helped Carlnut out of the pit but only to push him into a larger fighting arena. The competitors didn't have faces; instead there was nothing but a blank hole of emptiness; however, they flooded with emotion. They were warriors tall and strong in leathers and mail. All of them turned in unison to face the naked Carlnut so the young Dane reached for his sword Karla at his side but the more he reached for her, the further the sword seemed to recede from his sweaty grasp. The soldiers started to move towards him; some had axes wonderfully carved into the shape of wolf heads. Others held long swords sharpened to a point, but all of them appeared to be of shimmering gold in one light and as dark as a moonless night in another. The hilts were decorated with various pommel heads; some had beasts both mythical and real, others were carved into the shapes of flowers. As the faceless men got closer and Carlnut cowered on the sandy floor of the arena, a deep loud voice cried out. The master of the voice strolled into the arena. He was a fat man, with a long ginger beard covering his multiple chins. His arms were like trunks as he painfully lifted one up and beckoned Carlnut over. He put his heavy arm round Carlnut, putting immense pressure upon his shoulders. As the fat king spoke, he spat food out of his greasy mouth. Crumbs of bread, chicken and wine covered his bulging belly and for some reason he began to poke Carlnut in his chest with his big, sausage-like fingers.

"You will return to Hordaland! You will return to Hordaland! You will return to Hordaland! You will return to Hordaland!" the big king screamed. His pokes begun to get more aggressive, each one caused more pain and as Carlnut looked down he could feel fire-red blood dripping out from his chest. When Carlnut tried to remove the king's hand, he couldn't. Carlnut couldn't move, so he stood still with his chest in agonising pain and his body became faint with his head spinning as though he was drunk.

The old stone room was cold when he jolted up like a hare's head after hearing a fox. Carlnut was dizzy and confused; he noticed the window was open and the drapes were blowing around the room uncontrollably. He tried to stand but a sharp pain in his chest caused him to look down and examine himself, he gasped at the sight of blood. His eyes darted around the room desperately searching for the fat king. In the corner of the room sat a dusty wooden chest. The lid of the chest was open, and a scream echoed from inside it. A loud banging flapped within, followed by a gentle tapping of stone on wood. A raven black as night hopped out and perched on the end of the bed. Carlnut could only stare at it and the raven stared back. Its eyes were empty but full of pain. A paralysing shock filled Carlnut as he looked into the bird's distressed soul. With a squawk, the raven flew upon Carlnut's bloody chest and began to peck at the wound. The pain was horrifying and Carlnut lifted an arm to scare the bird away. Lifting his arm sent strings of throbbing through his shoulder and as he struck the bird, the shoulder pains got worse, but still the raven screeched and flapped. Its dark ink-stained wings lifted it into the air almost effortlessly and it took off out of the open window. As soon as it left the room the extinguished candles re-lit and the five tiny fires around the room warmed Carlnut's skin and heart. He fell back into the blood-stained linen and fell asleep once more.

Solvi

"We will feast tonight!" Solvi bellowed to his enthusiastic followers as they all crammed into the warmth of one of the brothel's back rooms. Solvi ran his hand through his blonde hair, which was spiked up over the middle of his head and formed into a neat pony tail that went halfway down his straight back. Using a sap residue from the yew trees that lined the Bjornafjorden, Solvi would stiffen his hair, so that whenever he moved, it did not. It was Myrun's brothel that the men stayed in that night. Myrun was a small, busty lady who had a temper as fierce as a raging bull. Women and girls of all ages lived within the four walls of the brothel. Most of the girls treated Myrun as a mother and had grown up within the comfortable confides of the brothel ever since their mothers were killed or taken in raids. It was the only brothel in the area and every night there would be regular visitors who each had a favourite woman. There would also be travellers and tradesmen passing through Hordaland wanting a night of amusement.

The main room was awash with fine-coloured wools and soft furnishings. There were chairs and rugs from far foreign lands and incense fumes cascading throughout the well-heated rooms. A great ivory tusk that shone like a crescent moon hung over a raging hearth that spewed its flickering shadows upon a carefully varnished oak door.

"You know what day it is, Frosti?" Solvi asked his friend.

"Lordag?" Frosti responded in a confused tone.

Solvi carried on: "This is the day our life begins and we start that winding road to Valhalla; this is the day we pick up our shields and axes; this is the day we kill the Jarl." Frosti was Solvi's best friend and they both shared the same enthusiasm to kill Jarl Bergison. Frosti was tall and well-built with arms as thick as oars, whereas Solvi was slender with little defined muscle. However, Solvi was powerful and quick; whenever they sparred, Solvi would simply dodge Frosti's attacks till he grew tired. The taller Dane had a long, burning red beard that almost seemed to tangle within his chest hair that rested on him like moss upon a rock. Unlike Solvi, Frosti never needed to worry about his hair upon his head for he had none; his bald head would shine in the sun and the veins formed creases in his skull.

The thirty men that followed Solvi waited till it was dark. They had been ordered not to drink a single drop of ale until after the job was done. Eddval had been chucked out of the brothel by Solvi for drinking. As the sun hid behind the horizon the cheers and laughter subsided; in its place an overwhelming stench of nerves filled the air. It was only natural for men to get nervous before a fight but normally ale helped calm the body. However, Solvi cared more for the skill of his men than the inner tingles of a coward's stomach. The moon began to climb to sit in its sky throne and the band of men left the warmth and comfort of the brothel for the freezing uncertainty of the wilderness.

Solvi had managed to gather people from chieftains across Hordaland. Even though Bergison was the Jarl of Hordaland, he relied on chiefs to help him run it and collect taxes. There were twelve chiefs altogether and nearly all were represented. Solvi, Frosti and his younger brother Friti were all from Osoyro, the capital. Osoyro was the centre of trade. Fishermen from across the region would sell their catches in the great market. Before the sun rose they would have set up their stalls and filled them with freshly caught and salted fish. Each stall was different in its own way. One stall would provide herb-soaked cod whereas another would sell large clams bathed in vinegar. However, they were all controlled by the jarl; he would send his men around the bustling stalls to collect forty percent of all money made that day. Very rarely did anyone refuse to pay but those who did refuse were dealt with. First of all the guards would trash the stall in front of all the other fishermen. If the vender still refused to pay, the next day his boat would be burnt. And if the man was stupid enough to refuse again, then the guards would trash the vender's home, rape his wife and take any children as slaves to scrub the barnacle-covered boats clean and ready for the summer raids.

"Gisha," Solvi whispered loud enough to take her attention away from the two-handed axes she lovingly sharpened as she perched herself on a green and black stained rock. "Get your men ready; it's almost time." Gisha was from Bergen. Bergen lay many leagues north of Osoyro and by population it was a bigger chiefdom than the capital of Hordaland, but the settlement wasn't nearly as flourishing in trade. Gisha had usurped her chief position from the famous warlord Gunnar Hadmunderson with nothing more than her three men, Yuki, Olm and Higta. No one truly knew how and why she had murdered Gunnar but the whole of Bergen immediately accepted her as their chieftess, and Solvi was grateful for her presence.

Hordaland had several islands to the west coast and each island had a chief. The Isle of Blornvag was represented by Umiston, and Askoy Island was represented by Jikop. Even though they looked identical with grey beards, tied-back grey hair and a strange scar across their cheeks, they hated each other. Solvi noticed how Jikop and Umiston sat on opposite sides of the brothel sipping mead horns filled with bubbling broth that one of Myrun's half-naked girls had cooked.

Everyone knew their part in the plan. Frosti would take eight men with him including Jikop to the front gates of Osoyro. The gates were made of iron that curved and twisted like a hundred silver snakes. Two wooden towers sandwiched the iron gates in place rising at least thirty feet. Frosti shouted to the watchmen above who would have surely been huddled round each other to avoid freezing in the deep winter's night.

'Let us in, we are back from a bloody hunt!' The guard peered over the fence and disappeared only to reappear moments later with Eddval standing by his side. The drunken fool that Solvi had thrown out of the brothel now looked sober and harsh; his golden hair seemed to be the colour of ash and his skin pale from a recent sickness. The sentry disappeared back into the night leaving Frosti's neck stiff from looking up and his eyes squinting as he tried to make sense of the scene above him. Frosti wanted to scream at Eddval. His fists clenched and his round bald head began to burn red. Seconds before the pounding vein protruding out of his skull burst, however, a limp body dropped to the trodden and worn grass at Frosti's feet. At first Frosti expected Eddval.

"That traitorous bastard deserves such a miserable death," Jikop said.

"That's not Eddval," a warrior named Killig said as he inspected the crushed skull of the man who had fallen from the night above them. It was the guard. Another man screamed and fell to the ground followed by another. Suddenly like a lone bird's cry in the night, the gate began to wince open in terror. Not even the howl of the wind and the low patter of the emerging rain could hide the noise. Nervously the eight men hurried through the gate following Frosti and Jikop.

"You are most welcome, Baldy," Eddval said as he climbed down from the watchtower. He wiped his blood-stained hands on his breeches and then wiped his two bloodied dirks on Huyfrid's leathers. Frosti stared at the long-haired drunk for a moment, then shrugged and turned away towards his and Solvi's more important goal.

The party now numbered nine and the time pressure became increasing heavier on their minds. Somehow they managed to rush through the bushes and weaved past the huts not making a single sound. Then, Jikop slipped on some seal pelts that must have blown off someone's hut; he pulled at a hemp rope that was being used to hold up copper pans to dry overnight. They clattered and banged as if Thor himself had entered Osoyro to smash Mjolnir against his anvil. The village slowly began to wake up. At this point the rain fell like boulders and Frosti called for his men to run towards the great hall. Only Frosti, Eddval and an archer called Jik didn't have swords. Jik carried a large yew bow and two dozen goose-feather arrows whereas Frosti carried a giant battle axe perfectly sharpened for a slaughter. The head was delicate and beautiful with the design of the Yggdrasil fitting perfectly within it. Its shaft was oaken and strengthened by iron bars with a bronze pommel at the end. The rest of the men drew their axes and spears and continued to run with squelching feet towards the centre of the slowly waking village.

Solvi had instructed the rest of his men to split up and enter the village through the dense forest on their own so as not to arouse any suspicion. He desperately hoped they had all embedded themselves in hovels and bushes ready to pounce. Solvi trusted Frosti and his small band of men to kill those at the gate so they would not run off and alert any of Bergison's supporters. Solvi knew the village's layout by heart as he had spent many years running away from Carlnut as they played at swords together. His heart bounced like a disturbed bee's nest when he glimpsed sight of a moss-beaten well in the grassy courtyard in front of the great hall where Jarl Bergison was sleeping.

The assault was far more than a vendetta for Solvi; it was what had to be done for the people of Hordaland. When they received no word from Jarl Bergi, Hrolf and Carlnut, the people demanded a fleet to search the coasts, but Bergison refused and instead declared them dead so he could take the Jarldom off Solvi's father. It had been two years since Bergison had taken over and Solvi found himself on the brink of ending the misery for his friends and his people.

The rain smashed on the courtyard's cobbles, and small torch fires began to light up around the village as its people started to wonder what had awoken it hours before the sun had begun to show itself. Like his men, he had crept into the village from the forest like a creature from Niflhiem. Finally he was standing in front of the large looming doors that led to the great hall, holding his sword with a firm but shaking hand. Seconds seemed like hours and each breath felt like a storm. His fingers tapped the bronze hilt of his sword, Gutstretcher. Gutstretcher had been Solvi's friend since his first raid. It was a gift given to him by Jarl Bergi when Bergi made Solvi one of his swordsmen. Only a few men could afford a sword like the ones that were usually worn by Bergi's personal guard.

The yew sap from Solvi's hair began to run down his sweaty forehead followed shortly by a few strands of blonde hair that clung to him like thin slugs on a rock. As he used his shield hand to clear his vision, the doors smashed open. The sound was accompanied by a great boom in the sky, which was instantly followed by a flash that created shadows of everything on earth. Six men ran out in light leather and more than a few of them seemed to be unstable on their feet. They were tired and half-drunk whereas Solvi was ready, awake and horribly sober. None of the men recognised Solvi, but they did recognise an enemy. One of them ran stumbling towards the focused Solvi. He raised a spear and swung it like a wild thing at Solvi's head. In one swift manoeuvre, Solvi spun on the spot and kicked the pursuer down into the mud. As he was about to thrust Gutstretcher into the man's vulnerable belly, another two men ran towards him. Time seemed to slow down; Solvi smacked the taller one in the face with his sword hilt, knocked him back and parried a few blows from the much smaller man who waved his hand axe as if it had a mind of its own. Then the blood spilt and Solvi was lost to the blood rage. The small man was on the ground screaming in pain in a puddle of his own blood. The first man then had the thirsty Gutstretcher in his throat as he attempted to get up out of the thickening mud. The rain diluted the pure red liquid spurting in a thousand different directions and the tall man fell back towards the other half-drunken warriors who all stood wide-eyed and open-mouthed. Somewhere a high-pitched whistle screeched and arrows and spears flew from all directions like a flock of birds taking flight. The drunk men had no chance of escaping the slaughter.

"You are late," Solvi smirked towards Frosti.

"Maybe, but you are alive so stop bloody complaining. Now let's kill that bastard," Frosti said.

Twenty men walked into the great hall. Umiston had nine men outside Osoyro ready to butcher any men returning after a night at Myrun's or fleeing from the impending doom. The hall was plain and dull yet still lived up to its name. Stone steps that were used as seats during the great gatherings of Hordaland formed a valley to the smoothed floor. They could hear the rain falling upon the roof, which was heavily thatched with moss, mud and straw. Some streams trickled through in places, forming puddles that glistened in the only light, which was coming from the dying embers of the centre hearth. Each puddle appeared to house small eyes following them round the room.

"Where is he?" Friti asked his older brother.

"Hiding like the bloody coward he is, crying, shivering and sucking on his mother's teat," Frosti replied in a tone dense in anger. The Jarl's chair was empty but Friti walked up to it, fiddling with some of the rushes that were still adorned the old piece of sturdy furniture which had been worn smooth by years of use.

"Someone was here, very recently," he said with excitement in his voice. Friti turned towards his brother with bright eyes that were itching for a fight. Moments after his eyes made contact with Frosti, he was squealing in pain and began to shake violently on his back with an arrow sticking out through his neck. The bloodied shaft had flown from the abyss straight through the teenager's flesh. The group stood still and even Frosti had no time to contemplate what was going on. Stamping feet grew louder and louder, overpowering the noise of the rain. Jik's head was violently twisting side to side for any view of movement. Everybody had their weapon firmly in their hand, grasping them as though they were lovers.

"Pintojuk Bergison, your death is coming, fate has decided you die tonight, Thor has provided the backdrop and Odin has provided my strength. You will die, now show yourself, you coward!" Solvi shouted towards the walls. Silence replied. The stamping was gone; the hole in the floor seemed to become darker and the rain began to ease. Dark green moss on the walls started to drip with the rain water it had soaked up. The room began to grow dense with a thick burning smog. They were surrounded by small fires being lit on the bases of the large oaken beams that supported the great hall. Gisha's men Olm and Yuki ran to the doors. Sweat was pouring off their heads as they tried to shift the doors open.

"Odin's beard, we need to get out of here," Gisha yelled towards Olm. Solvi saw a fear in her eyes that he had never seen before. He took a deep breath and walked calmly to the doors, ignoring the chaos around him. On his way, he grabbed Frosti's axe. The big man stood frozen and blank-faced next to the body of his brother. Solvi lifted the heavy axe above his head and, with all his strength, he aimed between the gaps of the two doors. With one clean swipe, the barricade on the other side loosened. Eddval charged towards the door, applying all his strength to Solvi's, who was now using his shoulder to force the doors open. Jik readied his bow. Gisha held her two axes ready to throw; the blade of each was about four inches wide with a highly curved edge that would end a warrior's life if it hit the right spot. The heat started to become unbearable. They could feel their clothes starting to burn and their bare skin starting to dry like summer's straw.

The door finally burst open under the great pressure from Solvi, Eddval, Olm and Yuki's pushing. A volley of arrows greeted them. Every arrow either hit a wooden shield or flew straight past the heads of the expectant warriors. Solvi was so thankful that Gisha had quickly instructed the men to rush to the front with raised shields. Each shield was interlocked forming a perfect shield wall. At this point Solvi found himself thinking of Jarl Bergi who had demonstrated that the strength of well-built walls comes from overlapping the shields in one direction so at any point in the wall was being braced by two men. Solvi was in the middle of the wall with his shield in his left arm and Gutstretcher in his other. In the distance he heard a familiar voice scream something.

"Bergison is among them," Eddval whispered to Solvi. When the arrows stopped striking their shields, they looked like a giant hedgehog in the middle of the courtyard with the burning great hall behind them and blood-thirsty men in front. There were only fifteen men in his wall. Solvi had ordered four of his crew, including Frosti, to disappear through the night and fog. Even though the rain had abated, the smoke from the giant fire blanketed the entire village. Solvi knew Loki the trickster God would be looking down and laughing at the chaos.

A few of Bergison's men ran forward to try and find a dint in the wall, but Solvi's warriors kept their shields tight and steady. Solvi instructed the men to form a circle with their shields pointing outwards round the old well in the middle. His eyes jumped around his sockets desperately searching for Pintojuk's face. There were approximately forty men staring at the fifteen battle-hardened warriors. The fire behind them made Solvi and his crew appear like daemons and maybe that is why Bergison's men couldn't force themselves to attack. Their shadows were worming in and out, twisting and raging. It was a stalemate; Solvi didn't want to attack as he knew Frosti and Umiston would be arriving soon, and Solvi could only guess Bergison was too cowardly to make a move.

Two ravens flew between the standoff, their black wings flapping like the sound of a spear shaft on a shield until they eventually landed on the well. Solvi's heart began to beat out of his chest. To him it was a sign, a sign that Odin, as well as Thor and Loki, was watching.

"Odin is here, brothers; he is watching our victory. Remember every detail of today, for your grandchildren will wish to hear the story of how you saved Hordaland," Solvi shouted with elation. Solvi glimpsed steel flying through the shrubs and bushes behind the enemy. He knew Frosti was here. The sound of steel on steel had always excited Solvi, but the sound of steel on flesh pleased him more that day. Umiston's grey hair twisted and danced as his sword pierced leathers and skin. Frosti's roar was met with cries of pain. The shield wall broke open in a mental frenzy. Hungry wolves ran across the courtyard to face Bergison's stunned warband. It was a slaughter. Gutstretcher tore open bellies and ripped apart faces and sliced necks until Solvi was surrounded by screaming, dying men. The night had blinded him and the fire had confused him, but still he danced and chopped his way through Bergison's men, desperate for his revenge. One young warrior ran towards him with a great axe that was far too heavy for the man. Solvi parried the man's swing and threw him to the floor.

"Where is Bergison?" Solvi's breath was poison to the man and he started to wet his breeches.

"Where is Pintojuk Bergison?" he said again, this time in a smoother tone, tightening his grip around the man's neck. However, he remained silent. Solvi looked deep into the dying eyes of the strangled man as his crew slaughtered more of the Jarl's followers around them. He looked for the ravens on the well but they were no longer there. Instead the man whose neck was still being crushed by Solvi squawked and flapped like a bird trapped in a tightening net. Solvi fell back in shock. The man was gone; instead a raven lay injured and crying. When he went to reach for it, it squirmed back into the night, cowering. Standing up, Solvi became dizzy and light-headed. He looked around but could only see his friends' shadows laughing as they murdered the drunken army.

The doors to Valhalla were getting smaller and smaller as Solvi got closer. All that was left was a window that he could do nothing but peer through. He saw Frosti and Friti sharing a huge horn of mead laughing as two naked women braided their hair. He saw his father Hrolf embracing Carlnut with open arms and smiles. He saw Jarl Bergi seated on a chair proud and calm admiring the marvellous marble walls and perfectly crafted statues. Carlnut walked towards the window and looked at his brother.

"You will never enter these halls, brother," Carlnut said. "You are greedy, selfish and a traitor to your people; you didn't save them, you killed them all." Then Carlnut covered the window and it was gone.

"We have him, Solvi, we have him." Solvi woke up to Eddval slapping him across the face. "Jarl Bergison is tied to the well." He had no idea how long he had been out for or what even caused him to lose consciousness, but Solvi knew everything he saw was a dream, and dreams were lies.

The night was almost over. Most of the village had stayed away from the chaos that erupted in front of the great hall but Solvi noticed a few faces amongst the thatched roofs and the burnt carcass of the great hall. What pleased him most of all was the bloodied face of Pintojuk Bergison, the traitor jarl. Beneath the jarl lay the four bodies of Friti, Huyfrid, Omposon and Gifri, all of whom were killed in the fight, which meant his crew of thirty were now only twenty-six. Anger bubbled up inside of him. He hated Pintojuk even more now, and he could feel Frosti's eyes piercing his skin. Solvi knew that Frosti would not just want Bergison dead; he would want the blood eagle. That punishment would make even the Gods shake in fear. The victim would be knelt down in front of a large audience with his arms tied to outstretched posts either side of him. The torturer would then proceed to slice into the man's back and cut into the ribcage to force it open like a pair of wings.

"I want to see him bloody suffer for what he did to my brother and to our friends." Frosti put his hand on Solvi's shoulder. "Huyfrid has just had a son and Omposon was one of our best spearsmen. You cannot let this man die without suffering," Frosti said.

"Don't worry, he will suffer," Solvi said in response. Bergison looked up. His nose was shattered and one eye was forced shut. He went to speak but thought otherwise.

"There will be a blood eagle tonight!" Solvi exclaimed. His men roared in reply.

Solvi

The ash and bones of the great hall had been swept up by Osoyro's residents at Solvi's order; he gave each one who helped a copper coin and personally thanked them for their hard work. All that was left of the once-great structure were the stone steps that surrounded a stone platform in the middle. Solvi thanked the Gods that they blessed them with a warm winter's day; the water on the ground had all been evaporated by the wind, which was light and pleasant.

Olm and Yuki were tasked with burying the four fallen men apart from Friti. Frosti had carried his limp body through the surrounding forests and all the way to the Bjornafjorden. There he bought a small and crooked wooden boat off an old local fisherman with whiskers whiter than snow for far more than it was worth. He placed Friti inside and grabbed flower petals of all colours from around the fjord. There were pinks and reds from the thorny brambles and greens and blacks from the various weeds that lived in the shadows of the trees. Under a yew tree that must have been at least forty feet high he found a wonderful purple orchid. Somehow Frosti was transfixed on the deep swirling colour as if that flower was the most beautiful thing in the entire world. He wasn't sure why but it reminded him of his younger brother. Maybe it was the darkness of the purple, which almost mirrored Friti's eyes or maybe it was the patterns that danced around the petals that reminded Frosti of Friti's enthusiastic personality. Instead of tearing the petals from the plant, Frosti decided to dig up the entire thing. He scooped up the earth till the roots were exposed and a centipede scuttled across his fingers, which Frosti simply admired for a moment until he flicked it off. He carried the plant to Friti's funeral boat and placed it on his chest. Friti looked smaller than Frosti remembered and for a moment Frosti saw a child lying dead in front of him. His blood heated up, sweat began to drip from his forehead and his fists clenched.

"Brother, I swear Jarl Bergison will pay for this, I will shout your name and drink in your honour tonight at the feast." Frosti continued: "I wish to see you soon in Valhalla; there we will drink and laugh. And you will tell me everything about your journey." Frosti placed his mud-spattered boot on the side of the tiny vessel and pushed it into the Fjord. Bjornafjorden was different from any body of water like it as it had a current that pulled towards the sea rather than away from it and for this reason the people of Hordaland viewed it as a sacred place, the road to Valhalla. A small fire was lit on the pebbly shoreline next to Frosti. He looked into the fire for a moment and found a sense of peace. Even though the fire was small, its flames were spitting and jittering. He placed a fine goose-feathered arrow lined with oiled cloth into the fire's roaring mouth. Frosti had borrowed Jik's fine yew bow that could shoot an arrow further than any other. Jik often joked that he had stolen the bow off Skaoi the goddess of hunting in the morning after they had spent the night together. This thought made Frosti chuckle as he pulled the flaming arrow back. His shoulders twanged and his arms began to shake mildly whilst he took his aim. Tears hindered his eyesight and his heart pounded even faster than it would if he was faced with a charging enemy in a shield wall. After taking his aim and slowing his breath he loosed; the arrow made a whooshing noise as it flung past Frosti's ear. The flames looked like a shooting star breaking through the clear sky. He could hear the slight thudding sound that the arrow made as it hit the deck. The oils and plants that Frosti had put inside the doomed boat were set alight first. But quickly they grew until, the whole thing was gloriously ablaze.

"Goodbye brother," Frosti muttered as he turned his back on the Bjornafjorden and kicked sandy pebbles into the fire to extinguish it. He took one last glimpse at the burning boat that drifted off into the distance on the unusual current.

Cooks were rushing round Osoyro with carts full of fish and mutton. A huge fat cook made Eddval laugh as he struggled to keep up with the pace of the event. Solvi hit his man over the back of the head and walked over to the sweaty tired cook. Solvi reached out his hands and took the barrel off him but the fat man refused, pulling the heavy thing back into his grasp.

"Please don't help me," the cook said as his arms shook like branches in a storm. "You are soon to be the Jarl; there is no honour in speaking to a thrall like me."

"What is your name?" Solvi enquired.

"Rollaug," the thrall replied.

"Your father, what was his name?" Solvi said.

"Err Dani, I think. Yes, he was called Dani." As he spoke, the nerves in the fat man's voice bought a smirk to Solvi's face.

"From now on you are known as Rollaug Danson. You are to be my personal cook and will always have a place at my table," Solvi said. This was a huge honour for a thrall as most men needed to be highborn or great warriors to warrant using their father's name. Most of the people round the centre were watching the exchange with eyes keener than a hawk's searching for prey. Solvi picked up the barrel of salted fish that Rollaug was carrying and carried it towards a longhouse that had become the kitchen for the feast. The smell of the fish almost knocked him over until the steam from the oils and powders that were being mixed into broths and meats revived him. Most of the cooks were women, who all stopped what they were doing and gave Solvi a slight bow. One woman, however, who was huddled in the corner, made no attempt to look at Solvi as she continued to mix bright green herbs into a giant copper pot.

"Who are you?" Solvi asked. However, she still did not look up from her steaming pot. The strange women intrigued Solvi and he quickly discovered his arm had reached out and touched her bony shoulder. She jolted and winced under the touch as if his hands possessed some kind of power to twist her soul. She tried to hide her face but he grabbed both her shoulders and pulled her towards him. The young woman's face was covered in light blue bruises and her eyes were full of a deep sadness. It was then that Solvi noticed her swollen belly and plump breasts. Solvi turned to Rollaug.

"Who is she?" he asked. Rollaug stuttered in response.

"Her name is Aesa. She is . . . she was Jarl Bergison's err . . ." Solvi raised his hand to stop him speaking and studied Aesa's body.

"Rollaug, get Eddval." He turned to speak to Aesa. "You will no longer be hurt by him. He will be dead tonight and your child will be able to live a healthy life. You both have my total protection." Aesa didn't even flinch at the news of her husband's fate and instead just carried on tending to her boiling pot. Eddval came stumbling in followed by a red-faced Rollaug. Eddval's eyes widened after he saw Aesa standing there battered and shrivelled. She was nineteen years old and yet her face showed years beyond her own. Eddval took her by the hand and escorted her outside. Once they were both gone and Solvi had tasted some of the boiling liquids, he clapped his hands together.

"Carry on what you are all doing; tonight's feast will be something special." Solvi stormed out of the hut to a lighter air with no herby smells that hugged his senses but instead he was captured by the smell of blood in his mind.

Gasping from dehydration and lolling from exhaustion, Jarl Bergison was still tied to the well. Jik was guarding him smiling and holding onto a hardened tree branch that he would use to whip Bergison if he nodded off to sleep. The Jarl's breeches were covered in urine and shit. The smell was so bad that a woman with mad bush like hair had thrown a bucket of petal water at him in the morning. Some of the petals still hung from the Jarl's straw-like hair. Eddval walked past Bergison with Aesa in hand and Pintojuk sighed deeply; his eyes welled up as he followed Aesa's belly with his dead pupils. His staring was interrupted by a punch to the stomach, which caused him to whelp like a beaten dog.

"Please don't let her see what is going to happen to me tonight," Pintojuk begged but Solvi only chuckled.

"Why not, she may like it, she may like seeing the man who beat her and raped her have his back forced open and lungs flutter in the wind." Solvi found an overwhelming urge to kill him there and then.

"Jik, fetch me a hot knife!" Solvi shouted towards the archer. Bergison suddenly started to panic like a bull who knows it's about to get its neck sliced open. The Jarl tried to wriggle free of his restraints but the rope that bound his arms to the wooden beam on top of the well had already started to make his wrists bleed. Bergison was too drained to move any more but still he protested.

"You cannot kill me now, Solvi, everyone is expecting blood eagle, you must wait for the feast and the occasion tonight, they will think you weak otherwise," Pintojuk said, desperately trying to cling onto his own life. Jik ran over carrying a small knife that was burning orange with heat whilst the colour seemed to disturb the air around it.

"I am not going to kill; I'm only going to hurt you really bad." Solvi lifted the knife up to Bergison's face. He could feel the pounding heat on his cheek and started to let out a whimper. However, Solvi didn't touch his cheek; instead he grabbed his left ear that was hidden under the Jarl's dirty hair. In one swift motion the knife cut through the flesh. The bloody ear fell to the ground. The screams of Bergison could be heard throughout Osoyro. Some children had run up to the courtyard in hope they had not missed their first glimpse of blood eagle. Instead they saw Solvi holding the ear towards Bergison's mouth.

"Eat or you lose the other one," Solvi said. The blood from the hole at the side of his head was gushing out upon Bergison's already stained shirt. Bergison shook his head as he bit his curling cracked lips. "You are hungry I'm sure . . . ah I forget: you like your meat cooked well." Solvi held the still-burning knife to the loose ear and it began to crisp brown and then black, sizzling like a prime piece of meat on a stake.

"No," the Jarl said as a tear escaped his eye giving his face some much-needed moisture.

"Eat it," Solvi ordered and Pintojuk Bergison opened his dry mouth. His lips were parched and chapped and his tongue was desiccated. Bergison began to chew down on his own crisp ear. Solvi laughed and mercifully pulled away the rest of the ear, which looked gruesome with the Jarl's bite mark in it. As Bergison looked up to see if he was about to be forced to take another bite, Solvi threw the ear on the ground and walked away laughing.

Osoyro started to fill with men, women and children, all desperate to see their first blood eagle. There were people from the nearby settlements of Softeland and Sovik who had heard the news and made their way to Osoyro. Almost two hundred and fifty watchers were waiting to be fed, sitting themselves at long tables and benches that had been dragged from longhouses and huts. A large table had been erected in front of the well with Bergison and the stone steps of the great hall behind it. Solvi had ordered nine chairs at the high table. There was room for him, Frosti, Gisha, Eddval and Aesa, as well as room for Jikop, Umiston, Rollaug and Jik. The rest of Solvi's crew sat on two slightly smaller tables on either side of the higher one. They were all armed and lightly armoured in case there were any strong Bergison supporters wanting to ruin the festivities. Solvi knew unrest was unlikely because everyone he saw seemed happy and their smiles grew even more so when the first course arrived. It was mutton broth lightly seasoned with basil and dandelion, which was wonderfully light and sweet.

"I am sorry Solvi, if the mutton is overdone, I tried to–" Rollaug had said before he was interrupted.

"It's all fine, Rollaug Danson," Solvi yelled from a mead-soaked mouth. "What do you think, men?" he asked his crew who all stopped for a moment and cheered for the fat cook.

The next course was salted fish bathed in a spicy, earthy paste. Aesa barely ate anything. Eddval cut up the fish and tried to feed her himself but she only took little bites and spent a very long time chewing each. Rollaug was always the first to finish along with Frosti.

"Is there any more of this bloody fish? My belly is screaming for food like Odin screams for death and chaos," Frosti said whilst burping between words. Eventually he ended up eating five full bowls of the food and guzzling over nine mugs of ale and by the end of the feast, he was asleep with his beard full of crumbs and fish bones. Solvi tried to wake him but he was passed out and it took four men to carry him to the stables to sleep.

The stone steps were not large enough to fit everyone on, so Solvi chose who would have the best seats. He first allowed his men to sit where they liked and predictably they all sat together on the first rows either side of two wooden poles that had been put up ready for Pintojuk Bergison. Solvi then said all the cooks could choose their seats followed by Osoyro's fishermen for their roles in the night's festivities. The rest of the places were chosen by small fights and friendly arguments. The seating was eventually decided within half an hour with only four broken noses and one split wrist. The ones unlucky enough not to get a place on the steps stood around where the walls of the great hall used to be until Pintojuk had burnt them wanting to kill Solvi only the night before. Everyone cheered when Jik and a warrior called Killig untied Pintojuk Bergison and started to carry him towards the wooden posts. His feet dragged pathetically on the grass as he hadn't the strength to lift them up. Killig kicked the back of Bergison's legs and forced him down on his knees. He then grabbed each arm and tied them to the posts; it took the great warrior an awkward amount of time to tie the knot, as Killig was a simpleton. Many believed that Loki haunted his dreams because the big man would curse and twitch like a mad man in his sleep. Bergison's face was covered in dried blood and dirt, appearing more like an unwashed slave rather than a Jarl. During the feast, the children of Osoyro were allowed to throw dirt and faeces at him. Frosti almost chocked on a fish bone laughing when a big pile of horse shit landed perfectly in Bergison's mouth.

Solvi stood up and the people fell silent. He walked around the smooth stone floor where, just the night before, he was frantically trying to escape an inferno. It was much cooler today than yesterday, and the stars were all visible in the night sky; however, the moon was not. Mani the moon god must be sleeping, Solvi thought.

"Tonight should be remembered by all; go and tell your families and friends that Solvi Hrolfson is the new Jarl of Hordaland. Tell them he carved open the back of a daemon." Solvi gestured towards Aesa. "He raped her and beat her; now she is with child. I will end this daemon tonight and pray his soul rots in Niflheim." Solvi then spat in Pintojuk's face. "Do you have any last words?" Solvi said.

"Sigfred," Bergison muttered.

"What was that?" Solvi responded with a confused look on his face.

"Sigfred," he repeated. Solvi hesitated; many men had the name Sigfred but they all knew of King Sigfred, the land-hungry man stealing land down south for his vast Kingdom. Everyone else was chanting for blood eagle but he could barely hear them, instead his ears listened to the noises of the night. His eyes widened as he picked up the faint sound of marching horses. There must have been around twenty horses, which sounded like an army as they got closer and louder. He turned towards his half-dead prisoner then turned back to the large path that was still smothered in blood from the fight the previous night. Suddenly Gutstretcher was in his hand. His crew instinctively bounced up and drew their weapons as well whilst the rest of the assembly stayed silent and sat in awe of what was happening.

One horse emerged, followed by another and another. Astride them were men fully clad in shiny war armour and furs. Solvi then recognised the standard that one of the steel men was bearing. It was King Sigfred's black bear on a white background. The standard fluttered in the light wind making the bear look alive and giving Solvi the feeling of seasickness. It was then that the King emerged; he had a horned helm encrusted with jewels of all colours. Everyone knew of Sigfred's helm as many Skalds would describe it in their saga tales and Solvi thought not a single one of them had over-described the beauty of the object. The horns were made from tusks that Sigfred had found whilst observing the building of one of the many forts that lined the border of Jutland. The King jumped off his horse with a mighty thud. He was a large man with thick arms and a heavy belly, and his furs made him look even more enormous. Solvi imagined he looked just like one of the giant tusked war beasts that the Skalds also loved to talk about whilst indulging in their host's mead. As he dismounted, so did four armoured men who looked like Loki's war-band as each was crested with a splendidly different carved iron helm. They were all roughly the same size and build so if it weren't for the helms Solvi wouldn't have been able to tell them apart. One helm was made to look like a boar with tusks and ears included. The detail was immense and far better than anything Solvi had ever seen before. The other helms consisted of a snake, a wolf and a bear. The five men walked slowly towards Solvi and his crew, who all had their swords half drawn. However, they were severely outmatched by the leather-clad warriors that appeared behind the King. King Sigfred looked confused at what he was seeing, but his face changed from confusion to shock when he saw Jarl Bergison tied up and defeated like a common slave. His gaze then turned to Solvi.

"What is the meaning of this?" the King asked furiously. Solvi didn't respond. He couldn't. His mouth became dry like he had drunk an entire barrel of sand, and he felt his tongue disappear into his mouth. "Jarl Bergison invited me here for the future of Hordaland; he was expecting me today and I was expecting a feast," he said. Solvi took a deep breath and found himself.

"He is no longer a Jarl," Solvi said and the King was as shocked as a man could be. "I am Solvi Hrolfson and I am here to save the people of Hordaland from such a horrible daemon," Solvi said with fake confidence. The King took a few moments to assess the situation. He saw an average-size man with a formidable strength behind him, he saw a Jarl tied up and defeated, and he saw hundreds of people who seemed to be accepting of the fact their Jarl was about to die. Sigfred rubbed his jet black beard and sighed.

"Jarl Solvi, it has been a long journey. May you find a place for us to rest and some food and ale for our bellies and we will talk in the morning," he said with a tired voice. "Oh, and untie that man. Give him some water and throw him in a shit heap somewhere." Solvi reluctantly nodded his head in agreement. Even though Sigfred had no power in Hordaland, he did have an increasing grip on its borders and so Solvi had no choice but to treat him as his title suggested.

The people of Osoyro began to leave with haste and disappointment to their straw beds to recover from all the ale they had drunk. Eddval put his hand on Solvi's back as Umiston and Killig untied the doomed man and carried him off to the ditches in the ground that were used for thieves and criminals. Each one had been enclosed with fixed wooden planks and thick rope.

Later that night when everyone had left the feast and retired to their huts and tents, Solvi went to Bergison's cell. The man looked more refreshed and cleaner. Someone had given him a new set of clothes and a bowl of fresh water, which made Solvi scowl like a baby being dragged away from a tit. Bergison saw Solvi's disappointment and he laughed.

"You should have seen your face. You may be Jarl now, Solvi, but as long as I'm alive you will never be able to rest easy," Bergison said, keeping his refreshed eyes on Solvi's.

"You will die; I will make sure of it. It may not be today or the next day but it will be soon, and painful," Solvi promised. He then fixed his hair, which had drooped across the sides of his head and walked away towards the Bjornafjorden.

The still placid fjord gave Solvi peace; he stripped down naked and waded into the freezing cold water. He could feel the kelp brushing his feet and the small fishes swimming between his legs. The pebbles were smooth and flat and Solvi liked to grab them with his toes as if they were fingers and his feet were hands. He dunked his head into the water to try and wash the disaster of the day off his face. The wax from his hair dripped out, causing him to appear unrecognisable to the point even Frosti would not instantly know it was Solvi. He took out the twine that tied his hair together and threw it away, allowing him to drift off to sleep without a single care, with the waves slowly sloshing across his body. As he closed his eyes he heard the faint squawking of two ravens.

Carlnut

"Two crisp green apples, please," Carlnut said to the market trader. His English had improved every single day and after two years in Poole, he was almost fluent. He found the language strange and very difficult to begin with, but Luyewn was a great teacher. It was not easy for Father Luyewn to teach someone a new language when he didn't know Carlnut's native one at all. They originally resorted to pointing and naming things in the church to begin with and the first word Carlnut learned was bible. It made Luyewn chuckle the way the Norseman scowled when he was shown the words inside. He later learned Carlnut couldn't read Danish or English words at all and when he started the reading lessons, Carlnut would often be disinterested and thinking more about Selwyn. The two had formed a bond and shared each other's bed most nights, much to Luyewn's disappointment, but he was much happier knowing Carlnut was tucked up in bed rather than getting drunk and causing havoc at the taverns.

The market was bustling with traders from all across the south coast of Wessex. Carlnut noticed two traders with big green feathered hats and instantly recognised them as Wareham fishermen. Wareham was a fishing town much like Poole, and the two fought for trade as well as for space on land and at sea. Even though it took around three hours to walk between the two, they both shared a bay. Brownsea Bay was perfect for protecting the town as well as for catching fish, since the bay had a very narrow entrance that only one boat could enter at any one time. The gap was actually wide enough for four big boats to ride abreast, but the tide and the rocky coastline meant it was too dangerous to get too close to the banks. The rocks stuck out the water like dragons' teeth and the white waves made it look like they were slavering over the boats that would constantly wreck upon them. If a ship was lucky enough to make it through the passage, they then had to manoeuvre round Brownsea Island, which was uninhabited, except for one crazy monk who lived in the old broken chapel that was visible to all travellers entering the bay. If the sailor decided to steer left, they then had to avoid two smaller islands that were not big enough for anyone to live on, and then had to steer right immediately to avoid the Thumb. The Thumb's actual name was Arne but to the people it looked like a thumb and so the name stuck. Arne was a piece of land that jutted out from the mainland; it was fertile land, which meant the lucky farmers who had made their home on it benefited from great yields and swallowed up gallons of jealousy from their peers. If the sailor followed the wave-shattered coastline of the Thumb bearing left, then they would eventually find themselves in Wareham Bay. However, if the sailor turned right before Brownsea Island then it would be a nice easy sail to Poole's much busier port. The Earl of Christchurch, who owned the land Poole was built on, had ordered a blockade of a part of the bay, meaning anyone wanting to get to Poole would be able to take the easier passage and anyone wanting to get to Wareham had to take the harder, more dangerous route. His plan worked in increasing trade but it angered the Earl of Dorchester who owned Wareham. The two hated each other with a passion, to the point that Wareham traders had to wear the funny green hats to show the people of Poole where they were from.

The gulls were squawking as Carlnut made his way out of the market carrying a bag full of crisp apples, salt bread and vinegar-drowned cockles. Selwyn was roaming with the travelling music group that visited taverns and brothels across the south coast and Carlnut couldn't wait to see her again. She would often come back with a whole chest full of coppers and silvers as the patrons would throw money at her when they heard her voice. Carlnut believed that the Norse god of music, Bragi, had lent her his voice although he never mentioned it, as Luyewn had made him promise not to speak of any pagan deities. The hammer round his neck burnt a horrible scar into his chest whenever he found himself in a church, but he was determined to keep the necklace. It was a gift of Selwyn and Carlnut treasured it more than any other possession he had ever owned. If Carlnut died without his talisman, Odin would have no idea his body was ready for the great halls of Valhalla. Whenever he thought of Valhalla, he thought of his father feasting on endless meats with fallen brothers. He thought of Jarl Bergi and every man who had died two years ago on the doomed vessel that was destined for the shore of Frisia. As the leafless trees passed his peripheral vision, Carlnut thought of Hordaland and Hrolf and Solvi and Myrun and every single friend whom he had left behind in the snapped strings of his old life.

The chapel was a long walk from the centre of Poole, and the sun was glaring down upon Carlnut's head. The heat was burning down on the town and he was glad that the chapel was above it all, up on a small mound of earth at the edge of the settlement. The door to the chapel was always open, and rested beneath a stone arch that displayed strange carvings which twisted like angry snakes and curved like a fat hog's tail. Carlnut had never seen any carvings like it in Hordaland but on his raids of Frankish lands almost every church would display similar types of markings.

The nailed God confused Carlnut, as he knew for a fact that Christians celebrated the death of their god, which to him seemed absurd. There were no stories of giant serpents or wondrous eight-legged horses taking Odin into battle. These were the stories Carlnut had enjoyed as a boy, stories of heroes and sex, with enough blood to feed more than five thousand people.

Luyewn was in his normal kneeling position in front of the altar muttering some phlegm-riddled words that Carlnut didn't understand in a tongue he did not recognise. The priest turned to his friend and smiled, his wrinkly face moulded round his bony cheeks as he showed his slimy gums.

"My friend," he spoke in his soft and soothing tone which Carlnut had always found comforting. "I hope you got the apples I asked for." Carlnut threw an apple towards the priest who reached out his hands and fumbled to catch it.

"There you go, Father," Carlnut said as he walked towards the sparsely lighted altar.

"Wonderful. Oh Carlnut, I'm sorry to be so abrupt, but what do your people think of Christianity? I have always wondered," Luyewn said whilst his hands felt the apple for its ripeness. The question took Carlnut by surprise and it took him a while to think of his previous life; but he remembered an incident that had happened when he was quite young. He had gone with his brother Solvi, his father Hrolf and a small band of men lead by Jarl Bergi to Jutland to see the famous King Onegendus. Onegendus had built the great Danevrike, a huge line of fortifications that lined the border of Pagan Denmark and Christian Saxony; he believed the threat from the Christians was so large that he had ceased raiding to concentrate on the building of the Danevrike. Carlnut remembered walking through the perfectly straight streets of Ribe towards the castle that punctured the skyline with its stone towers and flags bearing the black bear on a white background. As grand as the structure was, Carlnut's only true memory of it was the fifty Christian priests hanging from the ramparts in rusty spiked cages. Most of the cages were far too small for the priests, which caused their skin to blister and crack like dried soil. Some of the cages had crows fluttering round like flies to honey. The birds pecked at the skin of the dehydrated old men and ripped at their half-decomposed flesh as they watched with dead eyes. With this in mind Carlnut put his hand on Luyewn's bony shoulder and said,

"Let's just say, old man, it is lucky you have never been to Denmark." They both chuckled and Carlnut let out an involuntary snort. Their attentions were suddenly drawn to the dirt road outside, which led from Christchurch to Poole. Carlnut put his arm in front of Luyewn's chest and signalled for him to stay. The priest took his advice, and his bare, grey-haired feet took a few steps back.

The sun made Carlnut wince and it took a few moments to adjust to the outside having spent a good while within the damp and dark chapel. There were five white, powerful stallions and riding them were four soldiers in perfectly unscratched armour, which shined like tiny suns in the winter's gleam. The soldiers were guarding a tall slender man with short ginger hair, a ginger stubble and freckles covering most of his face. His silky purple tunic, tied together with a golden belt and a fish-shaped buckle, gave away his identity, so that Carlnut secretly wished he had barred the chapel's doors and stayed inside. The man's shoes were painted black and had an opening down the instep, which was secured with purple and golden-seamed straps. Earl Cynric of Christchurch dismounted his horse and walked up the moss-covered stone steps towards Carlnut. The two locked eyes and, like prey to a predator, Carlnut felt Cynric's blue eyes try to penetrate him, but he refused to let them in. Earl Cynric was a very religious man and always stopped at a chapel if he passed it, either lighting a candle or saying a prayer. Luyewn bowed slightly when the Earl came striding into the poorly lit altar room; he was a confident man who knew that his power scared people. He knelt down in front of the plain altar, noting the tattered bible and half melted candle placed neatly on the white cloth.

"You too," he said and gestured towards Carlnut and Luyewn. "Kneel and pray with your Earl; it will be a great honour." Luyewn hastily shuffled towards his Earl and slowly knelt down; his knees cracked like broken ice as he rested them on the cold floor. Carlnut was more hesitant; however, Luyewn was looking and his face begged Carlnut to kneel. He owed so much to the man who had housed him and taught him the language, and so Carlnut hoped Odin would turn a blind eye as he knelt on the left-hand side of the Earl of Christchurch. Silently, they knelt until stinging pains rushed up and down Carlnut's legs like mice running away from a raging fire. The stained glass window above them, adorned in its wonderful colours of ruby red and sapphire blue, became darker. Carlnut looked at the window and squinted, hoping the adjustment would answer every question he had about the mysterious shape. It wasn't until the shadow doubled in size that the he realised it was two birds nestling in the window's groove. Carlnut looked down at his chest where his hammer was and it seemed to burn like an iron sword after a day in the glaring sun. All of a sudden he stood up and ran out of the chapel, much to Earl Cynric's horror, who was left catching flies with his mouth gaping open. One of the armoured guards was caught completely by surprise when Carlnut darted past him and he fell to the floor with a crash as his plates rattled against rocks and stones. Somehow the two birds had vanished when Carlnut reached the back of the Chapel; he searched the sky frantically looking for Odin's messenger birds Huginn and Muninn, but all he could see was the giant yellow sun in the sky laughing at him. The next thing he knew, he was being restrained by the Earl's guards.

"Stop struggling," one of them said as he bound Carlnut's hands behind him.

"You will pay for this," another guard shouted as he readjusted his helm. It was clear to Carlnut that this was the man he had shoved over and it seemed that had sparked some kind of anger in him. Luyewn came skittering round the corner along with the Earl whose face was still as stern as it was when he entered the chapel.

"You will spend a few days in the cells underneath my keep for your incompetence and blasphemy," he said. "For now you will ride at the back of our little party with your hands bound." Luyewn protested and waved his arms, begging for mercy, but the Earl had already made his mind up. Carlnut was prepared to spend a few days in a cell and didn't understand why the priest was so desperate for him to stay; he even resorted to making the sign of the cross as the Earl rode off with his four guards, Carlnut walking in the middle of them, arms tied like a common criminal.

There was around five minutes of silence until eventually the Earl turned to face Carlnut.

"You interest me. You don't look like you are from around here?" he said. This made Carlnut think. He knew he had a strange accent, but after two years he had practised the same routine of lies. West Saxons, as they were known, had a variety of sounds, but none sounded like him. He had even met a Pictish trader on the docks but his accent was so deep and strong that even after all of his lessons, Carlnut barely understood him. Carlnut had to pick somewhere from the map that Luyewn had introduced to the lessons a few months into them.

"Hexham," Carlnut said. "My father was born and raised there and I was forced to leave after I slept with his second wife." This made Cynric chuckle.

"Ah, from Northumbria are you? Those beasts haven't had the hand of Christ bless them as much as we have down here in Wessex. Even their King Edwald likes to stick his prick in as many women as he can, a filthy one he is," he said with a tone that had dramatically changed since they were at the chapel. By the time they had reached Poole's centre gate, Carlnut was on top of a tame mare. Poole had a small outer wall, which was merely there to give the town a border, as men were freely allowed to pass between. But the inside of the town had a wall about two metres high, with three iron gates dotted to the west, north and east side of it. A handful of Cynric's purple-garbed guards stood watch at each gate ready to collect tolls or reject any trader wanting to avoid the tax. They were at the east gate, which had two marble fish spurting out of stone water either side. More often than not, the fish became a leaning post for the guards. The wall circled the town hall, church and the market road, which led to the dock yards. People stopped what they were doing when the Earl of Christchurch proudly rode through the gates. One woman yelled like a creature of the night when she saw her earl. Every man or women or even child who looked in awe at Cynric scowled towards Carlnut, filling him with a sense of unease.

Riding through the entire town became a very boring affair for Carlnut until the Earl came across the two green-feathered hat-wearing traders that Carlnut had seen earlier that day. Cynric dismounted his horse and walked to their stall picking up some salted cod and a basket of bread. After some careful inspection, he threw it to another stall owner who wore a big tunic shirt that was sodden with salt water.

"This is yours now. You may sell it; it was the only thing on their stall worth buying," the Earl said. The stumpy stall owner opened his mouth to say thank you but the words were as lost as fleeting wind. Earl Cynric recognised the trader's genuine appreciation and waved out his jewelled hand as if to say thank you. Carlnut hadn't noticed the abundance of rings on his fingers until then; Cynric had two plain gold rings on his thumbs and a couple of ruby and emerald ones randomly placed on his other fingers. Carlnut instantly thought of the horror dream of the screaming raven that was still fresh in his memory from the day he arrived at Luyewn's chapel. Cynric was tall and thin and he had all the rings like the man in the dream, but the character in the dream had a crown and Cynric didn't. Hrolf, Carlnut's father, said that dreams were signs from the Gods and most of the time the signs were thin strands of wool waiting to be pieced together. Carlnut grew worried for the Earl; there was a rotted man in his dream who wanted to kill the jewelled King. Although Carlnut didn't like Cynric, he didn't hate him either, in fact, his constant jesting with and kindness to his people made Carlnut respect him.

It was night by the time they reached Christchurch. The night was peaceful and calm, with a small wind that cooled Carlnut's skin after a long day riding in the autumn sun. In his two years of living in Wessex, he had never visited Christchurch, and he was glad he had never wasted his time as there was nothing there but a large church, a few thatched houses, one large stone slate house and a strangely full pier. The pier was a stopping point for boats that wanted to travel up the river Avon to the town of Salisbury, which Carlnut knew had a large church that Luyewn would try and visit one Sunday a month. The stone and slate house was the Earl's, and when Carlnut was bought inside, he could see why. It had paintings hanging from most of the walls of boats, fields and fish. There were a lot of fish paintings and decorated fabrics littering the house and it was clear to Carlnut that Cynric was obsessed with fish. As well as the paintings, he sported a fish brooch and he also made his guards wear purple tunics with a golden fish shape woven into the chest; their shields even had a leaping cod painted onto them.

The bounds round his wrists were sliced apart by a guard called Arnum who Carlnut later realised was the one he had pushed to the floor. The Earl then invited Carlnut to a seat on a purple-cushioned chair that made him feel uncomfortably comfortable as he sunk into it as if the material was made from the world's softest material. Cynric then seemed to forget about the large man seated in front of him and pulled out a feather and some ink and started to scribble down some markings onto a parchment. Carlnut wished he could read at that moment but the Earl wrote it clearly in front of him so he assumed it wasn't important.

"Read this for me please, er . . ." There was a slight hesitation that filled Carlnut with dread. His hand reached for his sword, which was intuitive as he hadn't worn his sword Karla for years. He did however find the time to train with Karla in the chapel's burial grounds much to Luyewn's anger. A blonde guard named Engelhard left his position next to Arnum to read what his Earl had just written down. Like a man escaping certain death, Carlnut took a deep breath as his whole body sunk further into his chair.

"I am happy to accept the invitation to your birthday celebrations," Engelhard read with a stutter that made it very frustrating to listen to.

"In two weeks time, our King Cynewulf is gathering all the great lords of England for his birthday," Cynric said, never once taking his eyes off a parchment placed in front of him.

"Why do I care? Why am I not in the cell you spoke so highly of?" Carlnut said, regretting his tone the instant he spoke.

"What is your name?" Cynric asked in a friendly voice.

"Carlnut, my lord," he said. His use of my lord made the Earl laugh out loud and even spit a little, which he wiped off the table with his arm.

"I am not your lord, am I? You are a visitor to my lands and from what I can tell, you are not wanted in your own home and therefore I cannot allow you to return," Cynric said, as cocky as a hunting dog after finding the kill first. Carlnut jumped out his seat in anger. Engelhard rushed to restrain him but couldn't as the Norseman easily overpowered the guard and threw him to the ground. "Now please calm down. You have few options," Cynric said as he gestured towards the seat whilst Engelhard picked himself up with his hand over his busted nose. The Earl continued: "You can either rot in my cells, which I assure you is not a pleasant experience, or you can join my guard with men like Arnum and Engelhard." Behind his bloodied hand, Cynric could tell Engelhard was desperate to plead against his Earl's offer but, luckily for him, he restrained himself. Carlnut was still shocked; he looked around the room and tried to take in everything he had heard. His eyes were then caught by the field outside the window. There were pink and red glistening roses in a garden that seemed very well maintained. It was obvious if he stayed he was going to be well fed and looked after. He knew he wouldn't see Luyewn or Selwyn as much, although he could easily travel freely as long as he returned to the Earl.

"I will join your guard," Carlnut said with a sign of enthusiasm.

"Good answer, Carlnut," Earl Cynric responded with equal gusto.

Solvi

The ale and mead took its toll on Solvi that morning; cupping his tired face in dirty hands, he sighed. He stretched out his arms, expecting to hit the furs that lined his straw bed, but instead his arm slapped onto a large naked breast. Solvi turned his aching neck to see who he was lying beside. Her face was masked by a woollen blanket but Solvi recognised her mousey brown hair and tattooed neck; it was Gisha the chief of Bergen. Gisha had become one of Solvi's most important chiefs and somehow in a drunken haze they had spent the night together. Ignoring her own confusion, she went to put her hand under the sheets to grab Solvi's manhood but he pushed it away.

"I have a meeting with the King, I cannot be late; however, if I'm still alive after the meeting, then by all means we can continue," he said jokingly and she responded with a hiss and turned into the sheets to fall asleep again. He stumbled round the room looking for his clothes. His hair was loose and lifeless but he knew he had no time to brush it with his reindeer bone comb that his mother had given to him. His eyes began to water as he thought of his dead mother and he sat back down onto the bed interrupting Gisha's sleep. She got up on her knees, causing the pelts to fall and display her body. Gisha then put her arms round Solvi's neck and he could feel her warm naked skin on his scarred back. His head was heavier than Thor's anvil and his throat drier than burnt bread, but still a huge smile formed across his aching face for he was the Jarl of Hordaland. He found his shirt on the rugged floor and put it over his head but, as he did, he could smell the vomit and began to feel sick, throwing it on the ground and burst out of his longhouse in response. The sun was already halfway up the sky and the breeze was chilling to his bare skin. Lop and Ospak, who were both standing guard outside, turned and chuckled at their Jarl.

"Just in time, Solvi. The Snake has been round to see if you were nearly ready," Ospak said with his very squeaky voice. He had received a wound to his throat from an angry Geatish man during a raid with Jarl Bergi years ago. Most of the men knew better than to laugh at his voice as he was a ferocious man with huge bear-like hands that easily wielded the great sword he carried everywhere with him.

"Thank you both for guarding my sleep. Go and fill your bellies with food and entertain your pricks at Myrun's," Solvi said, slapping them both on the shoulder. Solvi walked through the village that seemed to feel twice as large as it did before Sigfred had arrived. Hundreds of tents were erected between longhouses and huts, their canvas walls flapping peacefully in the wind. He saw a few men tending to fires and fetching water, but he knew the rest would be asleep, nursing their feet after long journeys and their heads after a night of mead and ale.

King Sigfred's tent was large and red with a thousand black bears sewn onto it; it was pitched where the great hall had stood in between the stone steps. The tent was therefore protected from the wind and the only ways in were through the back and front, which were guarded by four men either side. As Solvi walked up to the men they crossed their spears, tickled their axes and seemed to judge his half-nakedness. The clash of spear heads had clearly been heard from inside the tent because the Snake pulled back the fabric doors and peered outside. Solvi wondered if he slept with the Snake helm on and whether he even adorned it when he was with a woman.

"I am here to speak to the King," he said.

"You are late and without your shirt. The King will not be pleased," the Snake replied with his deep voice that was exaggerated by the steel that he covered his entire head.

"Let the fool in!" the King bellowed from inside the tent like a thunder clap silencing a flash of lightning. The tent was very basic on the inside with furs lining the floor and a few tables full of food in the corner. Solvi could not take his eyes off the most noticeable item in the room with its sharpened horns and wonderfully polished iron gilded with a golden seam. The horned helmet seemed to look even bigger standing solo and Sigfred's head looked naked without it. His hair was a tangled black mess that made him look very much like the bear that covered most of his possessions. The King was seated cross-legged on the floor with the mail-clad Boar warrior standing behind him. Solvi caught sight of a quivering young man dressed in a black robe huddled in the corner holding scraps of crinkled parchments and felt uneasy. Solvi recognised the man as a monk from the cross that hung loosely from a chain on his neck; it made Solvi bubble in raging anger that he shared a tent with one of Odin's worst enemies.

"What is that whoreson doing here?" Solvi asked, pointing in the direction of the monk who grew more nervous.

"This is Smaragdus. I stole him along with many wonderful golden coins from a Frankish monastery that I thought was too close to my border. He interests me; he can speak our language and Frankish, along with many other dialects and, most importantly, he is from Charlemagne's court and I know that poor excuse for a King will be very angry to know we have him," the King said with smugness in his voice. Solvi accepted that the monk had some worth but refused to notice his stinking presence until Sigfred called him over to sit with them.

"So what do you want with me?" Solvi asked King Sigfred.

"I need a record of all the chiefs of Hordaland. I would very much like to visit them all and explain what my plan is for this fine land," he explained to Solvi.

"The people of Hordaland know the Jarl leads them. They have no love for a King's that they didn't choose. Or any such man who sits on their arse being fed meats they didn't catch." King Sigfred's face turned a fierce red and Solvi could see his fists clenching. Smaragdus skittered over toward them.

"I would advise you Jarl to at least give us the names," the monk said in a calming tone.

Reluctantly, Solvi recited each Chief of Hordaland and the monk carefully wrote them down upon a new piece of parchment that he balanced on a few well-read books:

Solvi: Chief of Osoyro
Gisha: Chieftess of Bergen
Umiston: Chief of Blornvag
Jikop: Chief of Askoy
Harold: Chief of Voss
Trjonn: Chief of Vaksdal
Volund: Chief of Sveio
Skarf: Chief of Sund
Oddlief: Chief of Kvam
Herbjorn: Chief of Lindas
Oddi: Chief of Fjell
Astra: Chieftess of Eifjord

The name of each chief was still fresh in his mind as he had met each one when he was travelling round to form his crew. Umiston, Gisha and Jikop were the only chiefs that were enthusiastic enough to help overthrow Bergison themselves, but the rest did offer at least one man from their village to fight with Solvi, which proved that no one liked Jarl Bergison.

"There are things that we need to discuss today Solvi, but first, we will eat. My belly is rumbling like a hog trapped in a net," Sigfred said, rubbing his stomach with a huge bear-like hand and seemingly forgetting his previous anger.

"I can grab Rollaug for you," Solvi offered, turning back to the tent door where he heard heavy footsteps.

"I couldn't wait for food, so I had the fat man up before dawn." Solvi looked at Sigfred's belly rolls and swollen neck but decided to say nothing. Rollaug came bumbling into the tent moments later, with two silver plates in his hands; the fat man was covered in stains of all colours and still seemed to be drunk. He tried to place the platters down onto the floor that separated the Jarl and the King but instead, toppled over with a crash as if a great wave had pushed his entire body. Fish went flying through the air like they were leaping out of the water. The crusty bread rolled towards the King's boot, covering the floor in a light dust of crumbs that Sigfred had started to pick up and sprinkle them into his wide mouth. Rollaug then passed out. Sigfred clicked his fingers and the Boar came to life, showing his head through the flaps and creating a deformed daemon-like shadow on the floor. Without being asked, he hurried in, picked up Rollaug and started to remove him from the tent.

"Boar, you will need your rest; I plan a long journey visiting the chiefs before winter. After all, who is going to try and kill me in this shit heap of a village," Sigfred said to his fully armoured beast while keeping one eye on Solvi hoping for some kind of reaction. "The reason I make them wear their helmets is it installs fear in the enemy."

"Well it works; they scare the shit out of me," Solvi said. Solvi wondered whether he should get his men to don beast helmets, but he knew he would have more joy trying to walk on water than trying to get Frosti to wear a fancy animal helmet.

Smaragdus, the monk, sat up after finishing his writing and started to walk back to the corner where he seemed happiest. Each of Smaragdus' movements made him wince in pain. He was not an old man but he was clearly a broken one; his left leg seemed to hobble behind the rest of his body, and his left arm hung dead next to his bony torso as he slithered around. Solvi wanted to kill him, not to end his suffering but because he hated the Christians even though he had very rarely come across any. There were, however, stories of the great Christian King Charlemagne murdering almost two thousand Pagans in Saxony and using their blood to drown any other Pagans who refused to turn to the Christian god. He had also heard that Priests would keep young Pagan boys locked away to experiment on, a crime that sickened Solvi.

After picking up what food was salvageable, they carried on their conversation.

"As you may have heard, Jarl, I own forests and lakes bigger than what you have. I think it will be in both our interests that we come up with some kind of arrangement to allow Hordaland to join my kingdom and bathe in the vast wealth the union would bring." Suddenly King Sigfred became serious, which made Solvi itch a little bit.

"I don't want to make your trip worthless, Sigfred but Hordaland is perfectly fine without your help," Solvi said trying to sound as sincere as possible.

"You are a fucker, aren't you, Jarl Solvi," Sigfred mused, and scratched his beard. "I had made arrangements with Bergiso–"

"I am not Bergison, Sigfred," Solvi shouted, shocking the King as if he had just been slapped in the face.

"Jarl Solvi Hrolfson," Sigfred said as his lips curled to try and halt himself from bursting into an anger fit. "You don't know what my people face. There are far worse things on earth than your meaningless troubles. My lands are constantly raided by Charlemagne, my people are burnt and mutilated and my-" Sigfred had to force himself to say the next few words. "-my son is his prisoner and the Gods only know what vile things those Christians are doing to him!"

"I am sorry, Sigfred," Solvi murmured.

"I want Hordaland to know they will have a generous King. I will give you to the spring to decide, Solvi, but in the meantime I have something that could ease your mind in the right direction." Smaragdus shuffled back over to their side of the tent holding a long rolled-up piece of parchment, which he then laid flat on the floor above the crumbs and fish bones. The corners of the parchment kept rolling back but they each found an item to use as a weight; the monk placed his scabby old-man-like hands on one corner, the King took off one of his giant silver arm rings that seemed to be tattooed onto his skin and placed it on the corner nearest to him, whilst Solvi took out his dagger and stabbed it into another corner. The parchment was a map, yet one that Solvi had never seen before. The detail was immense and the Jarl felt a great sense of power drifting up off it as clear as hearth smoke in a small hall. It was a map of the entire north of an endless continent spliced by sea and ice. It showed the boundaries of each country and county. Crude green shaded areas represented dense forests and thin white lines highlighted stone roads.

"We are here," the King said as his pointed to an area close to the sea, crumpling the page slightly. "Our next raids were going to be here."

"Where?" Solvi asked growing slowly sure of the path his words were taking him.

"I have more important things to do in my own Kingdom," Sigfred sighed.

Solvi glanced again at Sigfred's finger that was twisting the picture of the land known only as Britain.

He had heard of Britain, but he didn't really know where it was or what it looked like. A few traders that landed in Osoyro talked of the wonderfully carved stone buildings built by giants and the huge bursting city of London that smelt worse than a latrine pit in the heat of summer. Solvi took a closer look at the shape of the land and where the sea became narrow at its southernmost point. He had raided the northern shores of Frankia before so he was confident he could navigate his way to Britain using Frankia's shoreline.

"Even if I can sail us there, our boats will never make it, we will lose too many men," the Jarl said to the King, who shook his head in response. Sigfred signalled over Smaragdus who knew which parchment to present them with. On it were detailed drawings of a new type of boat that Solvi had never seen before; it was much longer and narrower than any ships that were moored up in the bay. The design had a shallow draft, which would be ideal for beach landings and navigating rivers. It also had large thick beams with perfectly shaped sails hung from them, which were perfect for sea navigation. The side of the ship showed spaces for oars and rowers for manual steering. Solvi's breath disappeared for a moment and his heart stamped faster in his chest like a herd of cows were running through his body.

"I will provide five ship builders but your men will do most of the work to build a small fleet of these new boats. In return I will allow you to lead the fleet to Britain to steal some riches," Sigfred said with some difficulty, as the breakfast wine began to take its toll on him.

The atmosphere was destroyed by the sound of blood splattering on the tent. Solvi and Sigfred drew their swords as quick as lightning as the silhouette got closer to the door. As the flaps were pulled open, the smell of shit and vomit was so strong that Solvi gagged and coughed. Frosti stood blocking all the light from the door; he had no weapon on him but his hand was covered in blood. The wind pulled open the door and Solvi could see one of Sigfred's guards on the floor holding his hands against his bloody face.

"Frosti, the King and I are—" Solvi couldn't finish his sentence before Frosti spoke up.

"Why is that bloody man still alive? He deserves death, he deserves pain for what he has done!" Frosti shouted as he pointed at the King with his large, sausage-like fingers. Sigfred sheathed his sword and was strangely calm and even had enough time to take another sip of his wine.

"Jarl Bergison will be punished but he cannot die; he will be heading with me to Jutland and there he will stay in my cells for life." The smoothness of his voice didn't do anything to ease Frosti's anger and the bald man entered the tent further, clenching his rock-like fists.

"If you take one more step towards me, my brother, I will be forced to draw my sword," Sigfred said, sounding a little more uneasy.

"Don't you bloody dare call me brother; I had one brother and that poor excuse for a man killed him.

Pintojuk will die even if I have to follow you to Jutland; when you are not watching him I will slit his throat and stomp on his face; I will chop his dick off and stuff it in the bloody mouth of anyone who tries to stop me," Frosti claimed. The King clapped his hands twice and from the door behind him on the other side of the tent the Boar and Wolf, marched in fully armoured and carrying their heavy glimmering swords. The bald man's eyes widened and he began to panic. Solvi had never seen Frosti so scared. They held their weapons to his neck chopping off small bits of the scatty ginger beard he so loved. There was tension in the room; no one spoke for what seemed an eternity. Frosti stood like a statue, eyes closed and palms sweaty; the guards stood just as still with their eyes fixed on the King, who was stroking his chest trying to make a decision. Solvi stood helpless, watching his best friend on the brink of death. Sigfred was the first to speak up;

"Take him to his tent, remove all of his weapons and strip him of his arm rings." He then pointed at his guards. "I want you two to stand by his tent night and day; he can't come out and the only people allowed in have to have my permission."

"Sorry Frosti," Solvi said.

"I give you three months to build the fleet, Solvi, so we are ready to set off in spring as soon as the snows have melted." The King returned to his usual calm voice as if nothing had happened. "And your fucking idiot Frosti will not be going with you, in fact I want him gone from this camp before I leave in a few days."

Sigfred waved his hands to dismiss Solvi, and the new Jarl of Hordaland left as promptly as a bird does a bush when it's disturbed.

Solvi left the tent feeling lightheaded and strange; he didn't know whether it was the alcohol in his system or the shock of seeing his friend almost die. The ground felt lighter on his bare feet and the trees around the camp seemed to start spinning. His arms reached out for any kind of stability but he found none and instead he collapsed smashing his head on the hard muddy ground below. The shock alerted him to where he was but still he couldn't get up; the Jarl let out a small groan but no one heard him. He felt as vulnerable as a child as he lay on the grass only about twenty yards away from the King's tent. As he went to close his eyes the ground began to vibrate a little bit, then he heard a quick-paced soft tapping getting louder and louder. The smell of the mud was drowned out by the lovely flowery scent of a woman; he could feel a cold hand reach out for his and he felt safe and ashamed. Aesa had come running over as soon as she saw her Jarl on the floor; she tried to lift him up but she hadn't the strength so she darted off looking for help. Luckily for them both, the first person she found was Eddval who immediately sprang into action when Aesa told him about the Jarl. They both lifted Solvi back to his feet.

"Take me to the Bjornafjorden," Solvi whispered and they both hoisted him onto their shoulders. The dew-covered grass tickled Solvi's feet as they dragged him through the forest. He could hear a few birds tweeting and singing to each other, and a nearby boar grunt as its den was disturbed. It was about midday by the time the three of them reached the fjord and the sun seemed to bring the still waters to life. A blinding glow bounced off the surface and created a beam that darted off in all directions, making it look like the sun was submerged in the water.

"Eddval, in three months' time this wonderful, peaceful, god-blessed body of water will be full of ships headed for the Kingdom of Britain. I will be the commander of the raid. When I am gone, I want you to run Hordaland in my place until I return with gold and unimaginable riches," Solvi said after finally regaining his senses.

"Jarl Solvi, I am honoured but what about Frosti?" Eddval responded, sounding confused and excited at the same time.

"Frosti is going to be leaving Osoyro on the King's orders; however, I have my plans for him. I chose you because you are a clever man as well as a great fighter and these are the qualities a Jarl needs; even if Frosti could stay he lets his fists do the talking rather than his brain," Solvi said, rubbing his head to check for any kind of lump that may have sprouted from his skull. Eddval seemed extremely happy and jumped up and ran to Aesa who was calmly skimming stones on the surface of the Fjord. He whispered something in her ear that made her stop, turn round and wrap her arms round him. It was a great honour for a man to be chosen as a stand-in Jarl as it meant he was a favourite, and favourites were given lands and large spoils from raids.

Solvi had spent most of the day at the side of the Bjornafjorden. Eddval and Aesa had left hours ago on his request because he wanted to be alone with the Gods. The past few days had been extremely tiring for the Jarl but he knew it was only going to get harder; he was both nervous and excited that he was going to be the first Norseman ever to raid Britain. King Sigfred requested six ships, and already Solvi was thinking about every single man on those vessels. He knew he would captain one but he needed five other captains; Eddval would have been a perfect choice as well as Frosti but both were important for other duties. His mind then thought of Jik the very capable archer but Jik wasn't the brightest nor did he have any leading experience unlike Jikop and Umiston, the two chiefs, therefore they slotted themselves as ideal candidates. He then thought of the strangely beautiful Gisha whom he had slept with the night before but it didn't take long for Solvi to remember her firm breasts and smooth body and his mind was quickly distracted from picking his captains.

After another restless hour passed, he decided it was time to make his way to bed; he secretly hoped Gisha was waiting for him there but he wouldn't be surprised if she was keeping someone else company or if she was sharpening her beloved axe blades somewhere. As dense as the trees were, Solvi could hear the singing of a few nearby fishermen who all must have been huddled together drinking mead and laughing about old times. For a moment Solvi waited amongst the creatures and leaves and just listened.

Oh Odin in the Sky,
I hear your Ravens fly.
You watch me when I'm born,
And you're there when I die.

You gave me strength for my arms,
You gave me seeds for my farms.
I hope you smile down at me,
When women love my charms.

Oh Odin in the Sky,
I hear your Ravens fly.
You watch me when I'm born,
And you're there when I die.

You gave me eyes so I can see,
My enemies hide and flee.
I will fight till I die.
And Valhalla welcomes me.

His father had made it a tradition to sing the song before they sailed out to raid, and Solvi wasn't going to ruin the tradition the day they rowed off to Britain. There were many more verses but their words became just slurred murmurings and he found himself heading back to Osoyro.

The dying fires on the floor suggested that most people were sleeping, but Solvi knew there was one tent where no one would be asleep and therefore he made an extra effort to pass it. He wasn't surprised to see the Boar and the Wolf standing outside Frosti's tent.

"Beasts get hungry quickly, and so does Gutstretcher," Solvi said, stroking the pommel of his sword and staring intensely at the two guards.

Carlnut

"Christ, where the fuck did you learn that?" Engelhard said as he picked himself up after another bout with Carlnut.

"Engel, all you need to do is stand up, it's easy," Carlnut laughed.

"He prefers lying down. He's a lazy sod!" Arnum said. Carlnut had only been in the guard for a week, but he had already made everyone admire his strength and skill with a weapon. The training yard was a gravel-covered floor about the size of a small field, with straw targets at one end that always had dozens of arrows protruding out of them. Uncountable amounts of blood splattered the ground from drills that became too rough or clumsy. It was in these drills that Carlnut recognised each man's weaknesses; Arnum was flat-footed and very rarely used his feet whilst sparring, which allowed his opponent to be quicker and more agile. In contrast, Engelhard was too loose, which caused his swings to lack accuracy and power. Another guard named Medwin provided Carlnut with the biggest challenge as he was the same in stature and strength, but Carlnut was far too quick for him and often managed to floor the West Saxon within a matter of minutes. Training drills had been increased in number for the ride to Merantune where the King of Wessex was having his birthday celebrations and every King on the entire island was said to be there.

The dawn of the first day of the ride was horrific. Every man had to wake up hours before the sun came up to prepare himself and the horses. Cynric had requested a party of twelve to accompany him, which included one cook, one driver, two servants and eight guards including Medwin, Engelhard, Arnum and Carlnut. The Earl had also demanded that they bring a carriage with a small jail upon it, which confused everyone including Carlnut. He said that the jail was a precaution as there were a large number of bandits on the road.

"That thing will slow us down," Carlnut said to Engelhard as they both swayed side to side on top of their horses.

"Cynric does what the fuck he wants," Engelhard said as if that was the perfect explanation for why the Earl had decided to bring a small jail with him. As they left Christchurch, the rain smashed against their heads like thousands of tiny rocks making dints in their skulls. The ground had become completely sodden after two whole days and nights of continuous rainfall, which led to the horses' hoofs getting trapped in the saturated mud, like flies' feet in a fallen pot of honey. However, Cynric demanded they continue at a brisk pace and he ordered another horse to be given the jail carriage. Unfortunately, the servant who was riding that horse got left behind in a patty-covered field halfway between Christchurch and Salisbury.

Carlnut thought to himself how much his life had changed over the past few years. Only two years ago he was preparing to raid Frankish lands with his father and his Jarl in a place he used to call home. He missed the Bjornafjorden and its surrounding flora, he missed the longhouses being battered by salty winds and, most of all, he missed his brother. Solvi often came to Carlnut's mind. He hoped Solvi had a wife and child and wealth. A pang of jealousy shuddered its way through Carlnut at the thought of Solvi preparing for the last raids before winter. Arnum interrupted Carlnut's daydreams about his home by trotting slowly backwards on his horse and signalling Carlnut to do the same.

"The Earl is meant to be heading to Salisbury to visit the cathedral but he is making a detour. Keep your eyes open, lad." There was something in Arnum's voice that concerned Carlnut. He had never ventured out of Poole so he trusted everyone else knew where they were going.

"Where are we heading then?" Carlnut asked. Arnum just shrugged his broad shoulders and rode back ahead into his place next to the Earl's horse. Carlnut was stationed at the back of the train with the remaining servant; a pox-scarred boy with a misty eye and a wry smile. They had been following the river Avon their whole journey but they had slowly begun edging away from it. The river varied in size drastically throughout the journey, at points it was so wide that it was difficult to see the farmland at the other side of the bank. Now and then, it narrowed and allowed small stone bridges to be built across it. They hadn't crossed the river at any time but Carlnut knew if they did, he would spend ages looking at the flowing river beneath them carving its way through rock and earth.

The party eventually got to a point where they could no longer see the river, and this is when the Earl deemed it was safe to stop and make camp for the night. It still looked early to Carlnut as the sun was still visible even for an early winters' day, but he decided it was better not to question Cynric's orders. The rain had subsided some time ago, but the ground still held most of the water on its surface, which made it very difficult to set up camp. Tents got wet and so did most of their sacks carrying a week's supply of food, along with whatever other things people found important to carry.

"My arse is redder than a whore's cunny," Medwin claimed.

"How would you know? I thought you only stuck your prick in pigs," Engelhard said, receiving growls from the saddle-sore man.

Engelhard and Carlnut were eventually given the task of getting a fire started, so they both began to rummage through the only wood in sight, which stood about two kilometres away from the camp.

"This task is ridiculous; all the wood is too wet for a stupid fucking fire," Engelhard said. "If we carried on straight we would all be in shelter right now and some of us would be spending our wages in the brothels." It seemed to Carlnut that no one but the Earl knew why they had taken the extremely inconvenient detour.

"The Earl knows what he is doing; he must have a favourite chapel round here or something," Carlnut said in defence of the man who had provided him with a job where he could wear a sword again, and maybe even buy a precious silver necklace for Selwyn.

"That's the thing, Carly, there is nothing round here: no farmhouses, no churches and no barns we can take shelter in. We must be at least a whole league away from the nearest bloody farmstead," the angry guard said as he picked up some reasonably dry twigs for the fire. The more Carlnut thought about why the Earl would want to stop in the middle of nowhere, the more his head started to ache.

"Let's stop talking about it, Engel. I'm cold and hungry so let's just take this stuff back." Carlnut pointed towards a small pile that they had both made, which would have provided fuel for a decent sized fire when they got back to camp.

A dark figure rushed past them in the distance, which startled Engelhard so much that he clumsily dropped the wood and ran. Carlnut instinctively pulled out his sword as another figure ran past them about twenty metres away. The sword Cynric had provided for him was adequate at best; he would have killed someone just to have Karla in his hands. Karla was given to him by his father Hrolf the day he got his first arm ring at the age of twelve. Carlnut had started to count how many men he had killed with the fierce blade but the count became large the more raids he went on. Carlnut knew the weapon was blessed by Odin himself, as Karla had survived the shipwreck and was simply found next to his drowning body. Father Luyewn had it safely stored away.

"They are heading for camp!" Carlnut shouted towards the panting Engelhard. "We must get there before they do," he continued. Carlnut dropped the firewood that he had painstakingly taken an age to find and ran as quick as he could out of the woods, with Engelhard following closely behind. The ground seemed to divot and bounce as they ran, making their step uneasy, which caused them both to constantly stumble like newly born lambs. Carlnut at one point had fallen face first into the mud, covering his whole face and body in slimy, black grime that tasted like a horse's arse. They were not even sure whether they were heading in the right direction as the surroundings seemed unfamiliar. The darker the night became, the more the wood began to twist and turn and the more the fields grew and shrank.

"Where the fuck are we?" Engelhard cried.

"That's a good question," Carlnut shrugged. The woods had all but vanished behind them and he could see no signs of life anywhere. They both spun around, frantically looking for something that looked familiar, but there was nothing, no fences and no trees. It was just muddy unkempt fields.

"We must get to camp, Engelhard," Carlnut ordered.

"How the hell do you expect us to do that when we can't fucking see anything?" Engelhard said quickly before Carlnut could interrupt him.

"We could head to the—" Engelhard tried to say.

"Argh!" The guard fell to the ground with a thump. Another arrow flew through the air and narrowly skimmed Carlnut's left leg, lightly spraying blood. Carlnut then flung his body into the mud like a wolf trying to hide from his prey. Water and dirt shot up in multiple directions as his body hit the ground.

"Engelhard, are you hurt?" Carlnut's eyes were full of acidic dirt, which he went to wipe off with his sleeve. He couldn't see anything, and found himself scraping more filth across his face whenever he tried to clear his vision. Engelhard, who was normally very vocal, didn't respond, and so Carlnut began to slowly crawl in the direction he last remembered seeing his friend. The thick consistency of the mud made crawling very difficult; his boots would stick in the saturated soil and pull him back. He was blind. He was cold. He was stuck. All the energy seemed to drain away from Carlnut and he rolled over onto his back, covering his body in more heavy dirt. As he lay there alone and freezing, he could see the full moon shining down upon him, warming his skin. Carlnut removed his wavy, black hair from his face and smiled. Then the moon disappeared out of his sight being replaced by an angry man hiding every single inch of the great white world in the sky. The silhouetted man reached to his back with one of his very long, thin arms and pulled out an arrow from his quiver. He then lifted up his right arm, which held an old bow, and pointed it down at Carlnut. Carlnut froze; he no longer had the moon's rays filling him with energy, instead death stood over him, draining him of hope and desire. The man drew his bow as far back as possible and loosed.

Cynric was tending to his beautiful white stallion when he heard his cook scream in pain. He turned round to find the limp body of Duncrid lying flat and lifeless on the ground.

"Ready your swords, men, we are being ambushed," he yelled above the screams of another one of his men. The Earl pulled out his expensive weapon; its pommel was adorned with tens of purple gems and one red ruby that formed the eye of the golden fish that had been melted into it. One scraggly-looking bandit with brown rags covering his nudity lunged towards the Earl, but he simply leaned backwards causing the untrained thief to stumble forward, allowing Cynric to thrust his sword into his back. At this point everyone, including the servant, had some form of weapon in their hand. Arnum held out a small dirk as he felt he didn't have enough time to rush to his tent and grab his sword. His dirk however was quickly lost when he flung it directly into the face of a bandit about to stab Medwin in the back. Medwin awarded Arnum with a short sword that hung unused from his belt. Arnum caught the sword just in time to parry another man who furiously thrust a spear destined for Arnum's face. The blow of sword on spear shaft sent a wooden stave flying into the air. Now the attacker held nothing but a club-like weapon, which did nothing to stop Arnum's short sword piercing his chest and ripping through muscle, fat and bone.

"Form a circle and stand with your back to middle, then we have vision all around," the Earl said with a loud but calm voice. His men followed his orders immediately and soon the attacks stopped; however, he could feel them in the dark waiting for the best opportunity to strike like a pack of wolves closing in for the kill. An arrow then flew out of the darkness and into Medwin's chest causing him to fall down backwards, holding the wooden appendage that stuck out of his body. The sound of him hitting the floor startled one of the horses, forcing it to rear up and run off in the direction that the arrow came from. A man cursed in pain and Cynric followed the call. A young man, battered and bruised from the horse's attack, was nursing his wrist that must have snapped as the great beast flew into him. Cynric picked him up and threw him back to the ground.

"Who are you and how many of you are there?" the Earl asked furiously.

"I am Kim, sir, there are nine of us in total. Please don't kill me, have mercy," he pleaded. Cynric ignored the pleas and instead asked everyone how many people they had killed. Arnum said he had killed two and Medwin had killed one, the servant said he too killed another and then the other guards told them they killed two between them.

"So there is one left," Cynric said.

"But that only makes six my lord," Arnum replied hesitantly.

"Well, I killed two including Kim," Kim's eyes widened when Cynric said this and he held his hand out in front of his face, but the Earl ignored his surrender and instead grabbed the bandit's mousey knotted hair and slit his throat. Cynric held the head up as pools of blood left Kim's body and the life left his eyes. "We have to find the other one or he will run and gather more of his treacherous friends," the Earl said.

"I need help!" A familiar voiced called just as the Earl sheathed his sword. It was Carlnut. He was carrying Engelhard over his shoulder whilst holding a sword at the bridge of a man's back. Engelhard was unconscious when Carlnut dropped him onto a tent that had been taken down to form a canvas for the injured man to lie upon. His breeches were covered in blood where the arrow had found its way into his groin.

"He needs a healer immediately if he is to live," Arnum said. Cynric was too transfixed on the man who had his arms bound behind his back. The two shared a glance that everyone else but Carlnut missed; it was a short yet deep glance like the two knew each other. It was hard to figure out how the well-dressed clean Earl knew a man who had brown stains all down his ripped pants, and a shirt that was more of a rag than anything else.

"Throw him into the cart," Cynric said before turning away to inspect his fallen men. A maddening rage conquered Arnum who took the opportunity to beat the prisoner till his nose was busted and a few ribs were cracked. Carlnut and a guard named Figih needed a good amount of strength to pull Arnum away.

"It is clear to me that we must ride to Salisbury immediately for the sake of Engelhard," Cynric said. The adrenaline in them all had waked them up completely, and their bodies had all but forgotten that they had spent most of the day travelling. Before they set off on the road to Salisbury, Arnum and Carlnut had to find two large logs to tie the canvas to in order to make a stretcher. The logs were easy to find, the difficult bit was attaching them to the canvas as they had no rope, but Figih had already started to carefully trim the horses' tails to use the hairs as a rope to tie canvas to log.

The walk lasted a lot longer than anyone had anticipated as they had to stop several times along the route. At one stop, Arnum had to take his tunic off to stop the flow of blood out of Engelhard's groin as the rag they were using had become completely saturated in his blood. The party now numbered ten; Cynric rode at the front of the train on his large snow-white stallion, with Figih and a tiny guard named Madulf. Madulf was only a foot bigger than a dwarf and he was always angry, as if he had the spirit of a wild dog living inside of him. Behind them the jail carriage was being pulled by two horses. A rather old-looking mare was being ridden by the servant that Cynric called Flea due to his nervous tick whenever he did something wrong. However, the marvellous black stallion was being steered by the hooded driver who Carlnut did not know. The hooded man had joined them the day they started their journey but not a single one of them but Cynric had ever spoken to him. The rest of the guards, including Carlnut and Arnum, rode behind the carriage and on several occasions, the bandit's eyes met Carlnut's, sending an ill feeling of unease throughout his entire body.

The sun slowly started to rise and they still hadn't reached Salisbury. Carlnut could hear a few of the men muttering between themselves and gesticulating towards Engelhard. In response, the Earl raised his hand to silence them and the train stopped immediately as if they all had reins on that could be controlled by the red-haired Earl. The jolting motion of the sudden stop caused the bandit to fall to the floor of his cage and smack his head against one of the bars. Cynric rode up and down the train staring each one of his men directly in their faces. The dew kicked up off the grass as the horse's powerful hooves skidded across the diamond-like leaves.

"Yes to answer all of your questions; we have passed the cathedral at Salisbury. Engelhard will survive till we get to Merantune; he is a strong man." The Earl then reared his horse and trotted back to his position, however, no man followed him; instead, they just stopped and prayed for their friend. "If I do not get to the King's Birthday celebration in time, I will be holding you personally responsible," Cynric warned. This warning was enough for Figih to steer his less-impressive horse to his position next to the Earl and, after this, the rest of the men fell into position.

"He won't make it, Carlnut," Arnum whispered.

"He will, he has to, I won't let him die," Carlnut said in response. It was meant to be a kind gesture but they both knew conditions weren't looking favourable for their foul-mouthed friend. It was then that Carlnut started to feel tired; he wasn't sure whether it was because of the long march, lack of sleep or the emotional trauma, but he knew he had to sleep. His steed was a young brown gelding, and Carlnut could feel him tiring too. He had named the horse Gladdy after the famous horse Odin rode to judgements. Luyewn would have disapproved, he knew, but naming the horse helped Carlnut ride it better; it enabled them both to form a bond and even after a day of riding, he could feel that they both had started to know each other's bodies. He tapped Gladdy's hindquarters and the young horse changed his light trot to a slow gallop, which enabled Carlnut to quickly catch up with Cynric at the front.

"Earl, I must get Engelhard help. Please let me ride ahead with Arnum and him to Merantune to find a healer," Carlnut pleaded. He could see the doubt in the Earl of Christchurch's face so he continued, "I can ask the patrons there to kindly provide our men with fresh clothes. It would be insulting for us to greet our King in such a basic manner."

"Very well," Cynric answered in a very dry and coarse tone. Carlnut instantly sprang into action; he directed Gladdy towards Arnum and they both took Engelhard off the two youngest guards, Jurmin and Jaenbert, who's turn it was to carry the injured man. They then took Engelhard off the stretcher and placed him in front of Arnum. The movement made the barely conscious man wince and groan like a dying child. The movement also caused the wound between his legs to bleed further, spreading across the horse, the smell mixing in with the foul stench of urine and shit. Carlnut was drained. After around twenty-four hours without any sleep, the surroundings seemed to blur into one green-blue mix in Carlnut's vision; trees became clouds and the sky appeared to be flowing menacingly like the sea.

The gates of Merantune were bland and nothing special, which begged the question of why the King of Wessex wanted to have his birthday celebrated there. However, once they trotted past the unguarded iron gates, a huge garden greeted them. There were flowers of all colours and plants spiralling into beautiful shapes that Carlnut had never seen before. Only a few metres from the gates there was a very long thin spiny plant that Arnum made the wrong choice of touching. Carlnut had expected the village to be bustling with reluctant guests and rushed servants, but instead two peacocks were the only life present. Both peacocks had large beautiful tail feathers that they waved and fluttered when the men dismounted their horses. After navigating round the red thorny rose bushes and the incredibly large bluebells hanging inquisitively above their heads, Carlnut could see the mansion between the trees. It soon came clear to them that Merantune wasn't a village at all, but rather a retreat for a very rich King. They tiredly jogged towards the oak doors of the mansion over a sea of smooth orange and brown pebbles whilst carrying their friend. Before they had the chance to knock, a woman opened the door. She was one of the most beautiful women Carlnut had ever seen, yet she was covered in dust and dirt as well as wearing rags that were no better than the bandits'. Her eyes shone a perfect blue and her hair was plain black, but very well maintained.

"You must come in, sirs," the girl said in a panicked voice when she saw the man lying lifeless in front of her. "I will take you to the women." They twisted and turned round corners and climbed and descended stairs all whilst carrying a man that had clearly lost too much blood. The woman pointed towards a room, which

Arnum and Carlnut then entered. There was a large double bed with clean bed sheets and two jugs of water sitting appropriately next to it. Carlnut barely had any time to put his friend down when three women who had their faces masked came bumbling in and began examining Engelhard.

"Excuse me good ladies, may I and my brave friends acquire some clothing so that we may not be travel stained for meeting his grace," Arnum said in a very graceful tone. Carlnut was extremely taken aback by Arnum's well-spoken tongue, but was very pleased when it seemed to work. One of the ladies stopped snooping around Engelhard's wound and left the room only to return with ten sets of comfortable cotton tunics and breeches. For the duration of the time they were in the room, the ladies never spoke, they only murmured and pointed around the wound inspecting Engelhard like a wounded bull.

"The ladies request you give your friend some space," the pretty servant said to Arnum. It was around mid-day before the rest of the men arrived at the mansion. Before they entered the house, Arnum ran around with the new clothes he had been given and politely asked everyone to put them on. Cynric dismounted his horse and brushed the dust off his boots whilst giving Flea an evil look. The hooded man nudged the young servant and he jumped off his horse knowing he had to carry his Earl's belongings into the mansion. The threshold was perfect; it was made out of a shiny green marble with darker green stone running through it like vines on a tree. The overwhelming colour was green; most of the furnishings that littered the hall had green fabrics clothing them and the marble floor even had a lime green colour to it. Carlnut had never seen anything like it; he was amazed at the houses in Poole, and then had his breath taken away when he saw Luyewn's Chapel, but Merantune Mansion was just something else. He imagined Merantune looking much like one of Thor's dwelling places and looked to the sky to try and see if the great god was watching.

"Where is the King?" Cynric asked the serving girl who still hovered around.

"My lord, he is in the garden with some other nobles. I have told him you are here," she said. This pleased Cynric but his smile didn't last long when he remembered the bandit that still lingered outside in his shit-stained rags.

"Carlnut, take him to the shack at the side of the house and whatever happens do not let anyone see him," the Earl commanded. Carlnut was quick to obey his orders and left the mansion without so much as a glance at the marvellous decorations that hung from every wall inside. Carlnut opened the bolt that had kept the sweaty man locked inside and pulled him out.

"Why did you not kill me when you had the chance," Carlnut asked as he pushed the bandit away from the front doors. The prisoner didn't respond. "You had a clear shot at my entire body; you could have killed me over and over again." His voice was rich in agitation and anger. They had to follow a pebble path away from the house that brought them to a building which made Carlnut feel more at ease. It was an old broken shed that was obviously in disrepair. Its windows were smashed and their remains were scattered across the grass, making it look like they had teeth. The wood that the building was made of wasn't intentionally green like the mansion's insides, but instead was covered in a damp bristly moss that drowned the wood of any sunlight. Carlnut had to pull at the door quite hard to get the hinges to allow it to open but when he did, he dragged the bandit inside and pulled out some rope that he picked up from the jail carriage. Within the shed there was nothing but four old wood, worm-infested beams that vertically reached top to bottom. He tied one end of the rope around the most disgusting-looking beam and then tied the bandit's chapped wrists to it as well. The bandit didn't so much as wince or complain as the rope grew tighter and tighter as if he knew it was all going to be over for him soon.

"For attacking an Earl I imagine the penalty would be death, so give me your fucking name so I can let my god know not to let you into his heavens," Carlnut said loosely. He had completely forgotten to hide his paganism but thankfully the bandit took no notice of his mistake and instead said his first words.

"My name is Cyneheard," he said, looking at the floor and allowing his hair to cover most of his bloody face and broken nose. The introductions were cut short when Carlnut heard his friend Engelhard scream in pain. As tired as Carlnut was, he started to run down the pebble path, but the loose stones jittered beneath his incredibly aching feet, making it almost impossible to gather any speed. It took him around five minutes to track down the location in the house that the screams were coming from. Before he found Engelhard, he bumped into an out of breath Arnum doing exactly the same thing as himself. Arnum's brownish hair was drenched in sweat, which appeared to drip on his neck, causing his tunic to have unsightly darkened damp patches on its collar and shoulders.

"Where is he, lad?" the exhausted guard asked Carlnut.

"I think it is coming from upstairs," Carlnut said. So they both powered up three flights of shiny wooden stairs with the most decorated banister he had ever seen. In fact, Carlnut must have seen more metres of banister in the mansion than he had ever seen his entire life. 'I hate rich people,' Carlnut thought to himself. When they reached the very top landing there was only one door, which they were almost sure Engelhard was being hurt behind.

"It is locked!" Arnum said, as he tried using his shoulders to force the door open. Their fists banged on the door until they became battered and bruised, but still no one unlocked it and the screams continued.

"I have had enough of this," Carlnut exclaimed whilst unsheathing his less than favourable borrowed sword. The first swing did little to no damage to the wood other than a small scratch, however, the more swings he made, the more scratches the sword created and eventually the door surrendered. They both used their battered and splintered hands to try and bend the wood like men trying desperately to escape a burning barn. Once the hole got a little bit wider, the screams of pain were relieved by the sound of crying.

The bed looked like a thousand men had been slain upon it. There were puddles of congealed blood all across the room and all over Engelhard's body. As his friends got closer they noticed something that made them gag. Carlnut had to rest his body against the wall when he saw his best friend's manhood was missing and replaced with an empty mound of black scarred tissue that had been awkwardly sewn up. There was nothing there at all but stitched skin and rags covered with very light red-coloured blood.

"They cut my fucking dick off, Carly!" Engelhard screamed before passing out.

Solvi

The snow formed an icy white blanket on the ground, transforming the entire camp. The tents protruded out of the soft velvet cushion like tiny snow dunes. For four days straight, the snow had fallen and, at points where the path wasn't being shovelled by the warriors of Kind Sigfred, the snow was about two feet deep. However, almost ten of them returned with black and blue fingers complaining of no feeling in them, and the blacksmith had to have his middle and index finger on his left hand hacked off to prevent what he called the daemons from travelling to his soul. Solvi saw the snow as a blessing; it made him invisible to anyone who knew his face, as he didn't look out of place wearing a hood and cloth over his head. There were parts of the camp that didn't have snow but instead had a black slush that squished under the heavy footfall of horses and warriors preparing to leave. Due to the snow, Sigfred had ordered Solvi to remove Bergison from the ground cells and place him in the King's tent bound to a pike that had been shoved into the floor. Solvi hated the fact that the dead man was being cared for and looked after; he had even seen Smaragdus the monk treat the ear wound that still made anyone queasy when they saw it.

"I am leaving in the morning, Jarl, and I see Frosti is still in camp. If he is not gone by the time I leave, I will have no choice but to assume you don't care whether he lives," Sigfred said. The large man come up behind him and he wrapped his huge arm round Solvi's comparatively small neck.

"He will be gone, I assure you," Solvi said as he marched off away from the King whom he increasingly disliked. Solvi had been planning how to get Frosti out of the camp without the captive's two shadows noticing. The Boar and the Wolf were much more disciplined than Solvi had anticipated; he never saw them eat or sleep and it had been four days since they were given the task of guarding Frosti. Last night round a dying fire, Solvi had told his plan to the three men he trusted above all else. Eddval was excited to be a part of it, while Rollaug was as nervous as a newborn lamb and Jik listened intently, accepting his role in the proceedings.

By dusk, the snow had stopped falling. It was still bitterly cold, so that any bare skin would sting and ache until it was nursed by a fire or covered in some kind of fur. Osoyro had no shortage of seal and bear pelts, which Solvi thanked the gods for. Seals happily lived and bred on the small islands that appeared across the Bjornafjorden, and there were a few men who had been trained by their fathers in how to catch, skin and treat a seal carcass.

Solvi headed back to to his tent that he had made his home. Gisha hadn't visited his tent again since the night of the anticipated blood eagle, but every time Solvi lifted the flaps that hid the warmth from the stinging cold, he hoped to find her lying naked on his bed. He couldn't get her off his mind; he needed to touch her again. He knew next time he would be sober, so he could fully remember and enjoy the moment. As he sank his body onto the furs that made his bed, a terrible gust blew the tent flaps open, allowing a pitch black raven to swoop in and perch itself upon a chest. Although all ravens looked the same, something told him it was the very bird he saw on the night of the raid.

"Odin, send me a sign. Is this you or just a bird wanting to nibble at my leftovers?" Solvi said. To his shock, another pitch-black raven glided effortlessly into the tent. He could feel the winter when the bird pulled back the tent flaps. Solvi covered his skin with the bear pelt and stared at the two birds, which hopped silently together on the chest.

"It must be you; will I return from Britain? Will I end up like my brother and father? Will I ever be King?" he asked the birds. The last question shocked him; he had never given any thought to being a King, and why would he? He was a just a warrior who became lucky and rose to the powerful Jarl position; he had no royal blood or a real Kingdom to rule. Hordaland, much to Sigfred's annoyance, was a Jarldom and had not yet been taken into the Danish influence unlike Jarldoms to the south, which now answered to a King hundreds of miles away.

"I could be King. I am smarter than that fat brute, I am quicker and could beat him in combat if given the chance," Solvi muttered to the birds that just listened without any answer. The more he spoke, the more confused he got.

"How could I be King though; Sigfred is alive and he has a son," he continued to say. At this moment Gisha burst in, along with a wind that caused Solvi's entire body to pimple. She stared at the birds that Solvi was talking to and waved her hands at them to make them fly away. They remained unruffled as if Gisha didn't even exist; they perched almost fixed to the battered wooden chest. She tried again but it was fruitless so instead she turned her attention to her Jarl.

"You must see this, Solvi," she said in a concerned voice. He therefore picked himself up from the bed that he now wished he had never lain on. Before he left the tent, he looked back to his shield chest, which had no birds upon it. He felt faint; he was sick of the gods playing tricks on him and cursed under his breath, swearing that Loki was trying to test him.

Gisha was right; he did need to see the commotion that was being made outside in the snowy courtyard. A bunch of villagers were being held back by much bigger warriors of Sigfred, who, by the time Solvi reached the angry mob, was exiting his tent. The Snake was marching in front of a beaten and defeated Pintojuk Bergison who still had enough energy to muster a smile. Behind the ex-jarl the Bear walked with Smaragdus limping slowly; every movement of the monk seemed to cause him pain, but he still managed to keep up with the large party that was leaving the King's tent. Sigfred was at the back of the group of people and purposely ignored the villagers who had stopped throwing vegetables by the time he made his appearance. The King stopped and turned his head towards Solvi and snarled; it was at this point the Jarl knew his plan had to work if Frosti was to survive. Sigfred was leaving for his boat even though he had said he was leaving at dawn the next day, which meant he would not be responsible if the Wolf and Boar killed his bald friend.

The camp seemed terribly quiet once the King had left; there was no longer a steady stream of cooks and servants flowing across the snow. Sigfred had left his bear-covered tent behind, which Solvi knew he would burn once all the King's men left. He could envisage the longhouse he was going to build in its place; he had been a Jarl for almost a week but he had not yet felt like one. It was the custom for the Jarl to have a welcoming feast and to call a Gulating. A Gulating was the annual meeting of all the chiefs in the region; they would discuss trade, disagreements and raids. Some Gulatings, however, would consist of the Jarl deposing of chiefs and instating men of his own choice. He knew, however, that he would have no time to do any of this as he had been given the saga-worthy task of sailing to Britain. Solvi had given the parchment with the design on it to a shipbuilder in the village named Thord. Thord must have been over fifty yet his body never showed it; he had arms that rivalled most warriors and a brain that trumped most Skalds. He could see things others couldn't. The day Solvi gave him the parchments, the old man wept and claimed he had never seen anything so beautiful. Even so, he ran to his larder and pulled out some paints to immediately edit the design the King had given him. Thord wasn't pleased when Solvi announced he would have five other shipbuilders from Sigfred to help him; however, the Jarl was not hesitant to assure the grey-haired boat builder that he had final say.

As time passed Solvi felt a sickening feeling of nerves. His belly ached more than the night of the raid as that night he knew he was going to succeed. Now his idea relied on too many people playing their part to perfection. Jik had left the camp before Sigfred to make sure he got to Myrun's in time and, Rollaug had been working in the kitchen nonstop to get the correct recipe. The winter sun caused his brow to sweat as Solvi put on his tattered leathers. Rollaug arrived at the tent as he did every evening with three meals. The Boar and the Wolf had been given goat's leg roasted to perfection and seasoned with basil and thyme. The fat from the goat had been added to the pot where their vegetables were cooked, which made them brown and wonderfully crispy.

"Thank you, fat man," the Boar said. His voiced sounded deep and echoed within his helm. With a stutter Rollaug responded, "This is for Frosti." The fat man handed the guard a wooden bowl of mashed oats. Behind the guard's helm Rollaug could see the large grin on his face, which was followed by a few chuckles.

"Be gone now!" An armoured arm smacked Rollaug Danson on the back of the head, causing the cook to stumble to the floor and hit his head against the cold ground. He clumsily tried to get back to his feet but the Wolf kicked him further to the floor with a heavy boot. The two guards clearly enjoyed tormenting the fat man and continued to kick him to the floor as he tried to climb back up.

"Please let me leave," Rollaug begged his captors. They must have either gotten bored or genuinely felt sorry for the cook as, after he pleaded to leave, they let him go. Rollaug Danson limped away slower than a cripple and he could hear the sharp daggers of laughter piercing his back. The dark soon hid Rollaug and the guards quickly started to pick at their food. Both helms had a hinge at the mouth so they could eat and drink when needed. The juices from the meat flowed down their stubbles and over their armour, but still they continued to feast on the goat legs like the beasts they emulated. Abruptly, the Wolf stopped eating and began to cough uncontrollably, causing his friend to remove the bare goat bone from his own mouth and smack the Wolf on his back. Each smack clearly hurt his friend, but neither of them relented; the coughing continued to get fiercer and the pounding against his back became quicker and more powerful. The last smack was the hardest as it caused the Wolf to fall face down onto the floor, but the coughing ceased. Instead it was replaced with laughter as the large guard rose to his feet holding a small bone in his mailed fingers. They both shared a look and continued to feast on their food. When the Boar finished licking the juices of the vegetables, he untied the rope that kept the two door flaps of Frosti's tent from blowing open in the wind. The guard then threw the wooden bowl of oats in for Frosti to eat. Seconds later the guards could hear Frosti vomiting and coughing, so the Boar went inside to see what was up with the big bald man. Every second was vital; the guards were stronger than oxen and Solvi felt he couldn't take them both without himself getting hurt, and so he sprang into action when the Boar disappeared into the tent. Out of the shadows a few feet away, the Jarl pounced and caught the Wolf off guard. The Wolf howled and grabbed at his waist where a dagger had been shoved in between the joints of the amour. He pulled out the bloody knife and threw it at Solvi who could only duck and narrowly avoid the flying weapon.

"Come and get me, dog!" Solvi screamed. His face was full of anger and his hair fell flat across his head, while the flames of a nearby torch created shadows that danced across his grinning mouth. As the Wolf pounced, so did Solvi's friends. Eddval emerged from behind a snow pile and Gisha flew in from the sky. The Wolf was injured and outnumbered and desperate to find the rest of his pack.

In the tent, the Boar had wrestled Frosti to the floor as the big man had tried to fight the armoured beast. Even the screams of his wounded friend outside didn't make the guard relent in his duties; he was devoted to Sigfred who had ordered that no man other than themselves were to allow Frosti to leave. Frosti squirmed under the weight of the man and his armour, plus the vomiting had not stopped, which meant they were both covered in sticky orange oat-like glop that stank worse than a corpse. The flaps then burst open and the silhouette of a very rounded man stood there with a bow in his hand. The Boar's armour was almost impenetrable, and this installed confidence in the beast man who stood up and beckoned the fat cook to make his move.

"I will give you one shot, cook. If you miss, I will kill you and your bald friend. And judging by your sweaty, sausage- like fingers pulling that bow string that is clearly too heavy for you, you will merely make a scratch in my armour, which I can assure you I will clean off with some of the flab you painstakingly have to carry around." The beast roared at Rollaug, who was petrified. It was never in the plan for the cook to come bellowing into the tent, as Solvi had assumed Frosti could take the guard by himself. Frosti reached for the

Boar's leg but instead his chest was smashed in with a giant boot. The warrior removed his helm to reveal a ferocious countenance. His face was covered in scars and he was missing most of his teeth, which Rollaug noticed when he grinned at him. Every step the scarred man took towards Rollaug caused his bladder to loosen. He had no idea what he was doing there and was certain he could do nothing but stand frozen and wait for his inevitable fate. The headless boar picked up the pace and galloped towards the fat man. Rollaug's body move involuntarily and his arms tangled into a pose he did not recognise. The bow tangled in his hands causing the string and arrow to spin into an odd shape. Microseconds later he could feel the weight of death upon him. Warm blood trickled across his chest and shooting pains raced up and down his ribs; he could barely breathe. The shock, pain and blood made the cook close his eyes and pass out.

Gisha, Eddval and Solvi were circling the Wolf, who had picked up a torch in one hand and held a long sword in the other. Solvi had never seen a man be able to wield a long sword with one hand so comfortably, which made the Jarl realise he had greatly underestimated his opponents. The fire swirled and raged as the other man swung it. Loki's eyes were following them everywhere they moved, his eyes burnt their skin and blinded their vision. The beast seemed to get slower with every step, none of them knew if it was the loss of blood or fatigue that was causing it, but they had to capitalise on the enfolding weakness. Eddval jabbed at the Wolf with his dirk and the Wolf spun to face him, blocking the attack with his large blade. Solvi then lunged forward, but somehow his movement was cut short by a burst of flames in his face. Eddval tried again, this time he leaned in one way to try and force the Wolf to block an attack that wasn't coming; however, the beast saw exactly what was happening. He cut down with his blade in an attack that would have sliced a horse's head off. Luckily for Eddval, he managed to avoid it, allowing the sword to shoot down helplessly into the snow. Gisha then swung one of her axes against his unguarded arm. The blow forced the rabid dog to his knees, and within the armour his shoulder cracked and ached.

"Any last words for us, Wolf?" Gisha asked as she kicked the sword from his hands.

"King Sigfred will kill you all for this, and he is the only true ruler of Daneland," replied the dead man. Eddval ripped the Wolf helm off the kneeling man to reveal a young well-kept man underneath, which caught them all by surprise. They had expected a horribly disfigured and battle-hardened fighter, but instead they saw a warrior no more than twenty-five summers old with a face that any women would love. None of this stopped Gisha doing what she wanted to do, and she pulled back her axes ready to take the Wolf's head clean off his neck. As she swung them forward, Solvi's sword met them in the middle and parried the axes away. Both she and Eddval looked disgustedly towards their Jarl.

"What are you doing, Solvi?" she shouted, spraying her spit all over his fire-warmed face. He muttered some words under his breath. The Wolf was the only one who heard him and he immediately began to weep and beg. Solvi whispered in her ear words that made her smile; her teeth were black and rotten, but Solvi still wished to have her. She picked the dead man up and asked Eddval to help carry him to where King Sigfred's tent used to be.

The biggest smile of the evening came when Solvi passed Frosti's tent to find his best friend standing up. He was in pain and bleeding quite seriously out his gut, but he was alive. The sight of the Boar lying dead on top of a fainted Rollaug made them both laugh. Somehow Rollaug had managed to ram an arrowhead straight into the Boar's eye and out through his skull.

"He is just as heavy as he looks," Frosti muttered as they tried to help the fat cook up.

"We will get him in the morning," Solvi said with a chuckle. "We will get Aesa to look at your wounds and I have a present for you as she does."

The rest of the evening felt like what it should have been the night of the raid. Most of the village were having a feast anyway to celebrate the King's departure from Osoyro, and Solvi's crew had set up the evening's entertainment. A huge fire raged where Sigfred's tent once stood, and red and white pieces of fabric flew through the dark sky like fireflies. A small piece landed in front of Solvi who was seated on a wooden chair facing the party and with his back towards the fire, his eyes fixed on the burning bear that had just landed at his feet. He saw it as a sign. He rose.

"I am going to Britain! And my crew will be coming too; we will bring home riches and women. And when we do arrive home, and I promise you we will, I, Solvi Hrolfson, will be your greatest ever Jarl!" The crowd roared and lifted their cups into the air.

"Jarl Solvi. Jarl Solvi. Jarl Solvi." His men screamed and chanted. The Jarl lifted his arms up to silence the crowd that filled him with so much passion and strength. Gisha emerged out of a tent along with Eddval and, between them, they dragged the Wolf, who had lost all will to fight. Solvi's eyes met those of his best friend, who was laid on the snowy grass being cleaned up by the gentle hands of pregnant Aesa. Frosti's eyes lit up brighter than the stars in the sky when he saw Sigfred's guard being tied upright on his knees with two arms spread across upon two stumps of wood.

"Blood Eagle," he whispered to himself with delight.

Eddval/Frosti

The morning after the feast was beautiful. The snow had almost melted, creating heavy dew upon the ground that sparkled as the sun rose to start its journey across the sky. The Bjornafjorden was like a flawless mirror, with the trees and the pinkish morning sky reflecting perfectly from it as Eddval rode along the pebbly shoreline. His golden hair rippled with every gallop his horse made. He wore simple brown leathers with his two dirks at his side along with a brown satchel that was heavy with victory. Solvi had ordered his vice Jarl to ride to King Sigfred's ship to deliver the helms of the Wolf and Boar. He was to also deliver the message that Frosti had broken free and slaughtered his elite guards. The King could delay setting sail to investigate, but Solvi was fairly sure he wouldn't bother.

Sigfred's ship was the grandest Eddval had ever seen. It had three masts adorned with red and white sails; on closer inspection, he could see tiny black bears sewn into it, much like the ones that had gone up in smoke the night before. His heart began to try and escape from his chest as he dismounted the grey stallion he had been given to deliver the King's gifts. A few men on the prow of the ship took notice and started to gesticulate towards Eddval, one of whom disappeared somewhere else upon the deck. The wood Eddval could see was free of any barnacles and scrapes, which was often a bad thing as it meant the ship had never been battle tested. Eddval wondered whether she would survive the beating of the harsh cold waters around the daggered Frankish coast or even being surrounded by pirate boats full of bloody-thirsty crew determined on boarding.

"She's beautiful isn't she?" The voice came from behind Eddval, who was taken aback by the fact he hadn't even noticed the man was there. The man had long black hair that fell to a few inches above his waist line; he was naked apart from a simple rag wrapped round his pelvis and covering him modestly.

"Yes she is," Eddval replied. "Does she have a name?" The naked man wasn't interested in small talk, Eddval noticed, but instead all his attention was drawn to the full satchel that Eddval carried. "Have you seen King Sigfred?" Eddval continued after having his previous question ignored. It was only then that Eddval realised who he was speaking to. The long-haired man also held a brown bag that was half as full as Eddval's.

"I will show you mine if you show me yours," the warrior said with a worrying smirk on his face. Eddval flung the satchel to the warrior's feet and the rattle of metal on metal startled a few birds that were nesting in an overgrown pine tree a few yards away from the two of them. Eddval cautiously squatted down towards the bag but kept his eyes fixed on the towering man who overshadowed him. His hands fumbled about to untie the string that kept the dirty brown bag shut tight. As he found his way into it, a beast stared back at him. The bear's polished eye sockets glinted in the early sun and its teeth looked as sharp as knife blades. A small bit of bile found its way into his mouth, and the fine sand under his feet started to spin uncontrollably until a hand found its way onto his shoulder.

""Go and tell your would be Jarl I will make sure the King sees these. You may gallop off back to your shitty huts with your shitty women," the Bear said in a calm but dangerous tone. Eddval was suddenly able to move again and jumped back up to his still-shaking feet, which were just about steady enough to carry him back to his trusty grey stallion. He took one look at the ship, which appeared much more daunting now he realised its true power. Just three ships of a similar size to King Sigfred's would be able to carry more than enough to take Osoyro and most of Hordaland. Luckily for Solvi and Eddval, Sigfred had only taken a small party with him. What worried the vice Jarl more was the fact Bergison was on the boat with the King, instead of tied to a post with carrion feeding from his rotting skull and maggots crawling through his veins.

***

Frosti knew why he had to leave the camp, but it was still heart-breaking for him to abandon his beloved Jarl and friends behind him. Solvi had spent the entire night in his tent with his best friend, talking through plans. However, once the alcohol reached their brains, they quickly changed to talk of dangerous past raids and even more dangerous past women. Frosti still felt a little queasy as he headed on the first part of his long journey to the northern camps. Thankfully for the big man, he wasn't to go alone as Jik was waiting at Myrun's for him. The morning was quite a chilly one, with frost on the ground that crushed and crumbled under his feet. Frosti decided not to take the obvious path out of the village he loved so much in case any of the King's men still lingered behind to spy and scout. He loved the fact that even though many of the plants around were brown and dehydrated, the pines that stood like a fearless army across Hordaland never faded. The greens were covered by the dominant snow, but whenever he would grab a branch to clear his route, the white power gently cascaded down to reveal the spiky, beautifully smelling pine needles. A hare bounced happily in front of him, followed by another, both ignoring his presence.

The fact that Jik had been at Myrun's nearly two days made Frosti jealous, but he was still thankful he had the archer for company. Before he left, Frosti made sure he thanked every one of his friends who had helped him escape. No one got more thanks than Rollaug Danson.

"You saved my bloody life, fat man," Frosti had said. "I owe you everything, but I have nothing to give. I could persuade a girl from Myrun's to come down here for you?" Rollaug blushed at that suggestion.

"Get him four girls, Frosti. It will be four more than he has ever had!" Eddval laughed as he downed another horn of mead. Frosti looked at Eddval and snarled. He saw Eddval's three warrior rings on his forearm and that gave him an idea. He had removed four of his own seven arms and handed them to the one arm-ringed cook, who burst into tears when he collected them.

"Four! Are you serious?" Eddval had shouted. "I wouldn't give four rings to an ant who manages to tackle a wolf."

"You don't have four to give," Solvi said, smirking from his chair. It was a Chief's or Jarl's job to hand arm rings out, and every boy once they reached the age of twelve would receive their first. The three Frosti kept all had more sentimental meaning than the others he had willingly given away. One was a very plain bronze that had lost most of its colour and shine, but that was the one he got when Jarl Bergi deemed him a man. His arm had become far too big for the arm ring so he wore it around his neck instead hanging from a silver chain he found in an East Frisian church. The other two rings did fit, however, and he wore them proudly. Many warriors used their rings as a form of currency for other valuable goods, but Frosti never saw the need as he had his own little silver coin pouch on him at all times. One of the rings he wore was made out of a beautiful twisted gold with two dragon heads at either end, that had never been damaged or scraped. Solvi had given him the golden jewellery after Frosti saved his life on some raid. A Frisian monk had somehow escaped the attention of the normally alert Solvi and was about to bring down a two-pointed fork into his neck until Frosti threw his shield, knocking both of them to the floor. The last ring Frosti wasn't unique as a similar one was also given to all thirty of the crew who joined him for the raid on Osoyro, but Frosti wore it with tremendous pride. It was not a fancy piece of jewellery, but it was distinguished: the bronze was twisted and had already started to fade, but at one of the ends, it held a depiction of Thor's hammer and on the other side, Loki's horns were unmissable.

It was midday before he could smell the welcoming fragrance of Myrun's. The brothel stood alone on the crossroads, meaning any man travelling to and from Hordaland's biggest settlements had to use the path Myrun's was positioned upon. The amazingly built longhouse was bigger than any of the buildings in Osoyro, and Frosti noticed the foundations of a few smaller ones starting to satellite the huge building in the middle. Myrun's longhouse was about fifty feet wide and one hundred and thirty feet long, and it had smoke pouring out of tiny holes spread across the roof, making it appear as if though it was on fire. Frosti found himself reminiscing about the night they had all left Myrun's to kill Bergison. It tore at his heart that the ex-jarl lived, whereas two of his friends, Huyfrid and Omposon, and his brother Friti were rotting in the ground. Frosti knew he would prefer the pain of an axe to the skull or an arrow to the balls than the ever-present thought of never seeing his beloved brother Friti again. He knew Bergison deserved death, but Frosti was angrier at King Sigfred for getting in the way of the gods' will. Frosti's fists clenched at the thought of the King and Bergison drinking wine together and laughing.

The lavender smells of Myrun's almost made Frosti's eyes water when he stepped into the warm and comfy longhouse. A short thin girl dressed in no more than a light white top that left nothing to the imagination took Frosti's arm and sat him down on a chair heaped in furs and pelts.

"Would you like a drink?" the fair-haired girl asked in a faint whisper as she slowly poured some ale into a tit-shaped cup. Frosti whipped it straight off her and drank the entire cup full in one long swallow. "You must be thirsty. Is there anything else we can do to quench your thirst?" she said as she glided the tips of her soft fingers from his knee to the tops of his tensed thighs.

"I am looking for my friend; his name is Jik," he replied trying to stay focused on the job in hand. "However, I will not complain if you cannot find him because you could join me on my bloody journey instead," he jested. The ginger girl who couldn't have been any older than sixteen summers giggled youthfully.

"I will see if I can find him for you," she said, winking in the process. As she disappeared, Frosti's mind wandered again, yet this time he thought what it would be like meeting the Greatjarl of the Northern Camps. Solvi had sent Jik and Frosti on a mission to recruit the legendary Gudrod the Hunter and his large crew for the raid on Britain. Gudrod was renowned for being the greatest warrior ever known, and had single-handedly killed seven northern chiefs to take his position. He was the King of the Northern Camps, which consisted of hundreds of square miles of ice and snow as well as horribly dense forests crawling with beasts and Loki's daemons. The Greatjarl had potentially the largest crew in the whole of what King Sigfred wanted to call Daneland, however, he had never bought them all together to fight.

The pale girl floated in a few minutes later with the slim archer in hand. Jik opened up his arms and greeted his friend into them. The size difference between the two was extreme, as Jik was average height but very thin with no fat and little muscle on his person. However, the archer's most distinctive feature was his very peculiar facial hair; he chose to wear a small patch of fuzz below the centre of his lips and nowhere else.

"Glad to see you are still alive, Frosti," Jik exclaimed as they embraced each other.

"Looks like I've missed out on all the bloody fun though," he responded, flicking his eyes towards the ginger girl who was now welcoming another client to the brothel. "How many have you had whilst you have been waiting for me?" Frosti jokingly asked.

"Just the one, but I have fucked her more than I have done anything else." They both laughed energetically knowing they wouldn't be laughing much on the harsh journey north.

Carlnut

By midday, the mansion was chaos. Servants were darting up and down the maze of halls carrying delicate silver trays and plates. The grand meal started just on time, and three rows of around ten eight-man benches were set up in the well-looked-after garden, with flowers ranging from the beautiful to the exotic. Each table was covered with a wonderful cloud-white cloth that had gold streams woven, into it reminding Carlnut of the tables the skalds would say littered Valhalla. Carlnut had always wondered why Kings would spend all their coin on such pointless objects, but he was glad

King Cynewulf had as it was the most beautiful piece of cloth he had ever seen.

Not all of the guards could sit at the banquet table, so Carlnut was lucky Earl Cynric chose him and the balding Figih to sit either side of him. There were hundreds of important people that he had no time to learn the names of, but the five men sitting on the raised table at the very end of the garden did strike his interest.

"Who are the men sitting beside King Cynewulf?" Carlnut asked Cynric, who responded with a raised eyebrow that bent like a worm on his forehead.

"The one to the far right is King Offa of Mercia; he is a great King and has never been defeated in battle," Cynric said. There was something strangely familiar about the tall thin king but Carlnut couldn't put his finger on it. Offa had greying hair, but anyone did well to notice that due the large ruby-encrusted crown he wore; out of all the crowns on display his was by far the most splendid.

"He doesn't look much like a fighter," Figih muttered to himself.

"Next to him is King Cynewulf's cousin, Ealdormen Beorhtric," Cynric carried on, ignoring his man's comments. Beorhtric didn't wear a crown nor did he wear a pretty look; he had a stern and unkempt face. A visible scar ran across his left eye, which he struggled to hold open, forcing it to squint. In the middle of the dais, King Cynewulf of Wessex sat proudly, filling his face with a rich pheasant pie. As the juices of the pie started to dribble out his mouth and onto the table, a wide-shouldered man next to him handed the King a scrunched-up cloth to wipe his hands on. Ungraciously, Cynewulf waved away the kind offer of help and carried on biting into the crispy layered pie.

"Our King is a gracious man," Figih said again, encouraging a few heads to turn his way.

"That man handing the cloth to our grace is King Aelfwald of Northumbria, a powerful king. But I suppose you know all about him, you being a Northumbrian after all," Cynric said with a hint of sarcasm. "The one next to your King is Osric; he is one of Cynewulf's most trusted advisors and ealdormen," Cynric said, accompanied with a yawn. Osric had no distinguishing qualities and, especially amongst the other four, he looked the most normal. He smiled when the servants bought his food and he laughed when the jester fell over whilst juggling some ripe plums.

Before a course of ripe plum pies could be served, the King stood up, his velvet and green cape flowing in the slowly building wind like a ship's sails curving in a sea breeze.

"I thank all the Lords and Ladies present for attending my birthday celebrations. This moment is not just to celebrate my name day but, as shown by the powerful men seated aside me sharing stories and wine, this is a celebration of peace." To this the entire garden clapped and whistled.

Carlnut had stopped eating the food after the fifth course and by the ninth he had become sick of even the sight of it, so when the sixteenth one arrived, he had to leave the table. However, by this time half of the party had left the table to either drink elsewhere or chat within the mansion. For an early winter's day, the weather had been quite calm, but the rush of the servants to try and clear all of the crockery and furniture showed that they knew the weather was going to change for the worse.

Most of the people at Merantune were guards of the Lords and Ladies who were invited to the occasion; they carried their weapons and they were all a little uneasy. Carlnut wasn't sure whether it was the impending storm that did that or whether it was just the requirement for a guard to always be anxious.

"Just to let you know, we are wanted in our room, Carlnut." Arnum's voice was a pleasant surprise and it made Carlnut feel a little less queasy.

"I can't wait to leave this place. Selwyn will be home when we return to Christchurch, I think," Carlnut said, completely blanking out Arnum's words. He missed Selwyn; he missed her knotty auburn hair, her raspy voice and her beautiful body. "Where are you, Selwyn," he whimpered to himself. She could have easily been home in Poole drinking some of Priest Luyewn's broth or still on the road singing and flirting in taverns and brothels to earn coin. Halfway through the feast, a singer had arrived, but King Offa found her so repulsive he had her scrubbing plates in the kitchen to make up for her wage; unfortunately there was no singer to replace her, so the whole proceedings missed a musical aspect that Carlnut was very much looking forward to.

"I will meet you up there, lad. I am just going to check on Engelhard," Arnum said, appreciating that Carlnut's mind was elsewhere. He must have checked on his friend more than five times a day. Every time there was nothing new to report, apart from the fact Engelhard still refused to leave his bed. The birds were tweeting and singing to each other like a tavern full of competing bards. A robin hopped from branch to branch in a thorny bush, and its dancing shape caught Carlnut's eye. The small bird bounced happily even when he tried to reach into the bush and touch it. The bird, however, flew off when a thin shadow covered Carlnut and the bush. He turned round to find King Offa standing unusually close behind him like a blind man would stand behind his guide.

"Any normal guard would have sensed me behind. Why did you not?" the King queried. Carlnut had no answer; he had never been ruled by a King before, never mind three. Before he left Hordaland, he could remember rumours of a powerful, land-hungry Jarl from the Rutland wanting to unify all the tribes and villages. He wasn't sure which King ruled him: Could he do the bidding of King Offa over the bidding of Cynewulf without consequence, and at what point over the border did the roles reverse? That is why he preferred the Hordaland's way of doing things, one Jarl, many Chiefs and even more subjects. A beam of light bounced off Offa's heavy crown and into Carlnut's eyes causing them to squint.

"How can I help, your grace?" Carlnut, said secretly wanting to do nothing but retire inside.

"This weather is most unbearable; we should really be going inside." Carlnut had never heard anyone talk so perfectly. Cynric was articulate but monotone, and Luyewn knew his words but preferred not to use them all. The King on the other hand sounded like he knew every single word ever used by man. "I saw you at the table next to your Earl, I forget his name. Nevertheless, you eat like a Welshman and I cannot believe he let you into his household. So if I were you and thank the almighty lord I am not, I would watch my back." Offa slipped away just as quietly as he had arrived, effortlessly gliding over the lime green grass.

After feasting for hours and drinking a few mugs of mead, the shelter of the mansion was most welcome. A smooth breeze ran through the open-space centre of the stately home and snaked round the winding corridors to the kitchens below the surface, all the way to the ward where Engelhard lay ashamed, which was four flights upstairs. Arnum was right, Cynric and his men were all sitting around in the room they had been given. When the Earl saw Carlnut walk into the well-lit room, he immediately stopped talking. Arnum had a worried look on his face similar to Jurmin; however, the rest seemed to be smiling and in good spirits.

"What is amusing?" Carlnut enquired more out of paranoia than interest. The short stumpy man Madulf cleared his throat.

"We are going to be breaking into the wine stores. I saw the snotty-nosed servants travel to and from them. I think it's time we show these northern Kings how much we southerners can drink!" A few faint cheers of agreement followed, but not many. The back room they found themselves in was beautiful. Roman paintings of child angels and white plump clouds covered the walls, whereas a giant yellow sunburst covered the ceiling in spectacular fashion. There must have been over forty rays coming out of the painted sun, but there were five big ones, each pointing to a window. Carlnut had seen lots of the Roman legacy since he left Hordaland, but not all of it he liked. He found there were too many naked men, which made him uncomfortable, especially as most sculptures were displayed in full detail. However, paintings such as the sun upon the room's ceiling were more amazing than the sight of any natural feature. The paintings were drawn to great detail and appeared to come to life.

Carlnut had been in the room for over three hours, and had only realised Flea was missing when the kid came running in with some news for his Earl. Flea's moppy black hair gave the servant a very youthful look. According to Arnum, Flea had been Cynric's servant for over seven years so he either started serving early when he was a child or he was a lot older than everyone thought he was. He headed straight to his Earl and kneeled down so he could whisper in his ear. Cynric was seated upon a plain wooden chair at the far end of the room. It looked nothing like a throne but he sat on it like it was one. His ginger hair was perfectly combed to the left and his purple tunic was more ornate than ever. Like the tablecloth, it had golden thread woven into it but he had two leaping fish either side of his chest looking in. Whatever Flea whispered in his ear made Cynric's face turn pale; his cheeks clenched and his eyes lost all happiness. Immediately, the Earl shot up and dropped his wine-filled cup on the floor, causing the blood red vintage to form a puddle on the shiny wooden planks like blood escaping into the cracks of the earth. The Earl of Christchurch raced out the room, not once taking his focus off the door; before he left the room, the Earl turned towards Carlnut and gestured for him to follow him out. Carlnut without question stood up and followed his Earl. As they both walked out of the room side by side, they passed Figih who was on door duty.

"Figih, come with us," Cynric commanded of the thin-haired guard. The three of them paced in a direction through one of the many halls within Merantune Mansion; like most of the halls, it was decorated with hanging paintings. One caught Carlnut's eye, and he thought he could see a drawing of Thor and his hammer but he hadn't the time to stop and look at it in more detail.

"Where exactly are we going, Cynric?" Carlnut asked his Earl.

"Well my dear Northumbrian friend, you are going to get that bandit we have tied up outside for the King and I am going home," his voice responded in a much more calm manner than his persona portrayed. Both parts of that sentence confused Carlnut. Why would he be going home and why did the King need to fuss about a bandit? "My wife has taken ill. The priests say she might not last the week, so I must ride with haste to Christchurch," he said as he ran his sweaty palm through his ginger hair. "I would like you men to stay as a big group will only slow me down." This made sense since the more horses and people there were, the more stops they would have to make.

"Earl, please take me with you. I wouldn't be able to cope if something happened to you on the road," Figih said with genuine concern. However, the six-foot-four guard was soon silenced when they arrived at the threshold as the hooded driver from the day they arrived stood outside, holding on to the two biggest horses they came with. It was incredibly strange to Carlnut that he still didn't know what the driver looked like and who he was, but the Earl seemed to trust him and that was enough. Without saying another word to the two guards, Cynric and his fellow rider pulled on their horse's reigns and rode off.

"I guess if the King wants to see the bandit we must grab him as soon as possible," Figih suggested to Carlnut. Accordingly, they headed for the side of the mansion. This part of the establishment was drastically different from every other part of the house and garden. The trees were not looked after and the floor hadn't been cleared in a very long time, to the point they had to walk through thick piles of brown and crumbling leaves. Cobwebs formed in-between the trees' branches. Some were spiralling and others were jumping from branch to branch. Carlnut flapped like a child as he walked through what must have been a newly made web, but soon regained his dignity when he stepped up to the old shed's sad-looking door. The whites of Cyneheard's eyes appeared in the middle of the shed, still and calm like a wolf's eye peering through the darkness towards their prey.

"We are here to take you to the King, Cyneheard," Carlnut let him know to try and create some unease within the prisoner but instead it seemed to form some kind of confidence within him, allowing him to lean against the beam he was tied to and stand up.

"I would sure appreciate if you could unbind me from this mouldy plank," the bandit said. Figih hurried to untie Cyneheard, but was even quicker to bind the prisoner's aching hands back together. Nothing felt right to Carlnut. The sun had been down for two hours and King Cynewulf would surely be tired from entertaining all day. He thought back to what King Offa had said to him after the feast: "I would watch your back." Carlnut's feet still pushed on towards the mansion. He could now feel how cold the night had become, as his arms began to pimple beneath his new tunic and his teeth started to chatter. A puff of breath swirled past Carlnut's face where Cyneheard was aimlessly pouting his lips and blowing. They hoped that the fire would have been blazing when they dragged the bandit into the main hall, but their hopes were dashed by the sight of a black ash mound where the roaring flames once stood.

"The servants must all now be in bed." Figih had a tendency to point out the obvious and, like always, Carlnut neglected to comment further. They carried on towards the stairs to try and carry Cyneheard to the second floor where the King had given himself the biggest chambers. Figih held on to the captive's left forearm and Carlnut held onto the right; even though Cyneheard had his hands bound behind his back, he could have still made a run for it to avoid the King's justice. Merantune was surrounded by dense forest and a vibrant garden, giving the bandit hundreds of possible hiding spots. Only half the torches on the stairs were lit and those that were had almost extinguished, but Carlnut was just thankful for even the little amount of light. As perfect as the house was, it was very easy to trip on the steep steps, and any fall would have certainly given Cyneheard the opportunity to run. As they got to the top, Figih must have lost his concentration as he tripped on the top step, causing the whole hall to shake. He was a relatively big man so his fall was clumsy and awkward. Carlnut went to reach out to help his friend, but a boot met his back. Instead of helping his companion he found himself falling down the hard wooden steps. Each bang sent a jolt of pain through his body and he suddenly remembered his weak back that Selwyn and Luyewn had helped nurture to health.

His head spun and his chest felt broken inside, but he knew he had to climb back up the steps that had almost caused his death. He looked down at his brown, rugged tunic, and it was covered in blood. Using his aching hands, he patted himself to discover where the blood was coming from but he could not find a wound. It wasn't until he rubbed his blurry eyes that he felt warm moisture. The fall had given him a nasty cut on top of his forehead, which had burst blood all down his face and chest, making Carlnut look more warrior-like than he had for a very long time. With a huge groan and a wince, he got back up to his feet. Through his blurry vision, Carlnut could make out the frame of Figih standing on top of the landing, reaching out for his fallen comrade. Carlnut mumbled out some words but Figih seemed to ignore them and instead reached for his sword belt. Instinctively Carlnut reached for his sword too and found nothing. He longed for Karla to be in his grasp. He longed for any weapon.

"Where is Cyneheard?" Carlnut asked Figih. His response was the drawing of his sword. A gleaming, well-sharpened blade emerged, glittering like dew-covered grass. Before Figih could take a step towards Carlnut, he dropped his sword and screamed. Carlnut was dazed and confused, not knowing what was going on and even whether any of it was real. The world felt light again and he dropped back onto the floor in a lump. His back, legs, arms and head needed a rest but his heart wouldn't allow it.

"Take my hand, Carly," a familiar voice softly requested. Arnum was carrying a bloodied dagger when Carlnut finally got his vision back.

"What's happened? Why did you kill Figih? Where is Cyneheard?" Each one of Carlnut's questions sounded more and more desperate; he needed answers.

"We have to protect King Cynewulf!" Arnum screamed. So, they ran away from the stairs that now were covered in blood instead of wax and the body of Figih instead of Carlnut. Arnum handed his friend Figih's sword as they turned left down a huge corridor covered in blood stains.

"What the fuck is going on?" Carlnut asked feeling the gash on his head. The faint sound of metal on metal grew louder and louder as they reached the King's quarters. Outside were two lifeless bodies of guards that would have stood sentinel as their King slept. Arnum kicked the door open with ease as to their surprise it hadn't been locked or even barricaded; the surprising lack of effort needed caused him to stumble into the chaos. Turning to face the two new arrivals to the scene were a bunch of too-familiar faces. Carlnut could see Flea, Jurmin, Jaenburt, Madulf, Cyneheard, and a few others he had never bothered learning the names of, all standing weapon in hand facing the King and his friend Osric. The manic scene must have only begun as none of them had any signs of cuts or blood. However, the entrance of Arnum and Carlnut ignited the flame. Flea took a rather weak swing at Osric, who parried with much more battle-hardened strength, so much so the servant stumbled backwards. Swords and blades started to swing all over the place at that point, like lightning spreading across a pitch-black sky. Carlnut had to duck to avoid Jurmin's attempt at separating his body from his head. His blade in turn was thrust into his assailant's stomach; Jurmin instantly fell, limp and heavy. Even though the wound on his forehead still bled heavily, Carlnut was where he belonged, in the heart of a fight.

"Watch your back!" Arnum yelled and he jumped into the frenzy when a guard went for Carlnut's spine with a wonderfully carved spear. Arnum hamstrung the man, causing a fountain of blood and a trail of flaying muscle to emerge like worms from the man's legs. As he fell to the ground, Arnum's blade struck down a death blow that would have killed any man. King Cynewulf's ability with the sword was impressive as he continued to defend himself from frontal attacks from Cyneheard and low rear attacks from Madulf. Seeing his King begin to get outnumbered, Osric kicked a chair into the knees of the struggling Flea, jumped on to a wooden set of multiple drawers and leaped down onto the short bald guard Madulf. The sound of splitting bone almost made Osric sick as his sword went straight through Madulf's skull. The angry guard became motionless and was dead before he hit the floor. Cyneheard started to become agitated, which caused the bandit to miss-time some of his blows, allowing the King to go on the offensive. They navigated round the moss green bedpost that made up one of four around the King's bed. The bedposts held up a green canvas that had already been damaged in the fight, either being splattered in blood or ripped by a vengeful blade. Flea made a dash for the door and managed to make it halfway down the corridor before

Arnum gave chase. Only the attackers were wearing any kind of protection, but Carlnut saw this as an advantage as it made slow fighters even slower, and cocky fighters even more arrogant. Jaenburt, who had somehow become disarmed, swung with a clenched fist at the once-dazed Carlnut, but he was ready and altered his body in such a way that allowed him to bring his sword underneath Jaenburt's arm and into his armpit.

"Argh!" he screamed in pain, closely followed by the sound of vomiting. The vomit was a clear brown colour that only mead would help deliver and so Carlnut thanked the gods some of these men were drunk. Carlnut noticed Jaenburt's breeches darken and then he smelt the great bowel movement of a dead man. Osric had been injured at some point, which made him have to watch the rest of the fight from the elm chest that he leaned on in the corner of the room. Cyneheard was outnumbered; he had Carlnut closing in on his left side and a tiring King dressed in his nightwear holding up a King-worthy sword that remained perfectly still.

"Do you not recognise me, Cynewulf?" The King shook his head in surprise. "I am the brother of the King you unlawfully stole the throne from," Cyneheard continued whilst looking directly at Carlnut, knowing he posed the greater physical threat.

"So? Why do I care, your brother is dead and he never deserved this throne anyway," King Cynewulf said, panting like a dog. The purposely toying words agitated the bandit, and he struck the King's chest with his sword. The King tried to bring his sword up in time but the speed of Cyneheard's attack and the power in his arm meant there was no chance. The King started to bleed heavily and Carlnut burst into a fit of rage. Numerous bodies lay dead or dying on the floor and only Cyneheard and Carlnut remained without a scratch.

"You have injured a King; you do know there is no going back on this, don't you?" Carlnut shouted at Cyneheard. He brought the sword up and down on Cyneheard's left shoulder, but just as it was about to hit, Cyneheard moved his entire body in a flash. Cyneheard spun and screamed like a wild thing, lifting his sword up towards Carlnut, and just managing to catch his hair. Carlnut pushed Cyneheard away and the bandit stumbled over the body of the coughing King. He was off balance and his sword pointed straight down to the floor. Carlnut feinted one way and then heaved his blade over his head and straight down onto the off-balanced man. Blade crushed into skull, and pieces of brain flew up into the air. Everything happened so quickly; the King lay squirming in pain and Carlnut had to yank his borrowed sword from the bandit's disfigured head. He began to feel the wound on his head again and the aches and pains across his body throbbed reminding him how much he needed rest. Carlnut suddenly felt alone; he was surrounded by dead strangers. He stumbled like a drunk man to the looking glass that hung from the wall and he could see nothing but anger and death. His long hair was matted with dried blood from the top of his forehead. It was clear the fall had taken a large chunk of hair and flesh off him, and that was why the wound hadn't stopped bleeding since. The sight of the sword in his covered with the entrails of his enemies filled his stomach with raging butterflies, and made his mouth smile uncontrollably. 'I belong in battle', Carlnut told himself.

"Carly! I managed to kill the little bastard before he escaped," Arnum shouted as he turned the corridor to enter the bloodbath of the King's chambers. By this point, Osric was still stuck in the corner of the room, King Cynewulf was unconscious and Carlnut had entered a state of delirium. Two other men barged their way past Arnum and into the red room. They were both dressed very similarly with a green tunic and a white overshirt with an oak tree at its centre. One of the men had flat blonde hair and already held his sword in his hands. However, the other much shorter and older man kept his sword sheathed. They were both Offa's guards, so it would soon be clear that in a matter of days the news would spread across Britain that the West Saxon King Cynewulf lay at death's door on the same night he had two other Kings in his residence. The blonde guard sheathed his sword and tread lightly over to the mesmerized Carlnut to try and snap him out of whatever land he found himself in.

"Excuse me, are you all right?" he asked Carlnut as he put his young nervous hand upon Carlnut's powerful shoulders. The touch brought Carlnut back from his trance and he snapped at the man who was trying to help him.

"Do I look all right to you!" he responded angrily. "Help your King!" he ordered. The older guard had already tried for a pulse before Carlnut had said anything but, after trying all the different areas where even a faint pulse can be felt, he couldn't locate one.

"The King is dead, even I can see that," Osric yelped from the other side of the battlefield. Offa's men turned to face Carlnut with drawn swords, so Carlnut dropped his own and sank to his shaking knees.

Solvi

After men from the villages that surrounded Osoyro heard of the raid on Britain, they started to flood into Hordaland's capital like flies towards rotting meat. Solvi was very open to helping as many people in through the iron gates once he had arranged for his best friend's release. He needed as many hands as he could to build the six ships he required to raid the shores of a land he knew his people had never raided before. Even though Solvi hated King Sigfred, he had been given the opportunity to make history, as well as the help of five of the King's best shipbuilders, all of whom had their uses. Solvi commanded that each one be in charge of a ship, and that Osoyro's resident boat builder Thord needed to be listened to at all times. The grey-haired man relished his role as he knew he would be richer than most chiefs off the plunder. When King Sigfred left, he seemed to have taken the horrible winter weather with him, and after a week, there was little evidence of it having snowed at all, however, it was still bitterly cold. Every morning, the Jarl would walk round the area next to the Bjornafjorden where Thord had ordered the ships to be built but after only a week, it still appeared to him to be an unorganised mess of timber and rope.

"Thord, come here," Solvi shouted rather aggressively. "I expected you to at least have the skeleton of one ship already; what is taking you so long?" Thord seemed to be accepting of his Jarl's straight-to-the-point question as he had a response prepared for him.

"I cannot get anything done. One of Sigfred's men, Yanik, I think his name is, has edited my redesigns and has started to build his ship differently to how I would like," he ranted.

"I will sort it," Solvi said. However, once Thord got his teeth into a rant, he never stopped.

"The fat one, he is useless, Punjif is worse as he sits on his fat arse all day eating our food and eyeing up our women. Don't get me started on the snotty-nose toddler who thinks he knows everything. This morning he came up to me, Thord, the great ship builder, and asked if he could be captain of the boat he builds. I am telling you, these men are not to be trusted." Solvi nodded and left the steaming man behind him. He wondered whether Sigfred had given his men orders to try and sabotage the build, causing it not to be ready by the time he returned. As he walked up a small grassy embankment a few metres above the fjord, he looked back to the chaotic boatyard that housed all his hopes.

Finally, the construction of the Jarl's longhouse began exactly where he pictured it, right between the steps that formed the old hall. Even with the excitement of his new longhouse and all the fresh faces wanting to meet their new Jarl, Solvi could not stop thinking about the raid. It was more than likely many of his friends would travel to Britain but never return; happily, he knew Eddval would not need to worry. He and Aesa had formed a special bond straight from the moment they met, even though she carried Jarl Bergison's baby. Eddval was to help raise it as his own, which was one of the main reasons Solvi chose him to govern Hordaland in his stead. Frosti would have naturally been Solvi's first choice but he wasn't sure he would even make it onto the boats, as any journey to the northern camps was full of risk. But before they could even sail, they needed ships and they were being built at a horribly slow pace.

The first of the shipbuilders poked his head into Solvi's temporary house, which was a large, bland, white canvas tent housing all of his weapons and leathers. All five of the builders had arrived with Sigfred but stayed in Osoyro with the King's personal guards the Wolf and Boar, who both lay at the bottom of the Bjornafjorden being torn apart by crabs.

"I am Huy," he said as he fastened the two tent doors together behind him. Huy wasn't old but he definitely had some years on Solvi; the wrinkles on his face said as much, yet the full mop of bright blonde hair argued against it. "You would like to speak to me, Solvi?"

"He is the Jarl," Killig growled from the corner of the tent.

"He is not my Jarl," Huy said defiantly. Solvi ignored the heated exchange and gestured for Huy to take a seat on the furs that littered the floor. The pair sat in silence for an hour-long minute until Huy had to break the silence.

"Why am I here? The boats won't build themselves," he said.

"How is Thord treating you?" Solvi said, completely ignoring Huy's impatience.

"Well. He could lay off us a bit. These are new boats and we have never built anything like them before." As the boat builder spoke, Solvi's mind continued to eye every twitch and stammer in his speech.

"Well Huy, I have seen a lot of promise in you and I think you are more than a boat builder. In fact, I think you have the skills to be a great leader." Huy looked confused, as if he had never received a compliment before.

"How do you mean, Jarl Solvi?" Killig and Solvi shared a glancing grin as they knew Huy had been caught in their snare.

"I have a spot open for a captain on one of the ships, and I'm hoping you can fill it for me. Of course, it will be on your ship that you build because it will be the best-built one," Solvi said in a genuine and kind tone.

"Really?" Huy's expression suddenly changed when he shot up like a startled dog and his feet danced on the spot in anticipation. He grasped Solvi's outstretched arm and nodded. "Thank you very much, Jarl Solvi," he said as he unfastened the tent rope that swung around like a mad snake from the clumsy touch of the boat builder.

"Huy!" Solvi shouted towards the fabric doors. "If you tell anyone, I will be treating you how I treated your King's Wolf," he said, making sure he sounded as serious and threatening as his threat suggested. "Just four more traitorous shipbuilders to deceive now," Solvi whispered to Killig, who grinned like a snarling dog.

There was no problem in deceiving the other four as, like Huy, they walked in suspicious and blank but left the tent in a joyful mood. The only thing that could go wrong for Solvi was if any of them told one of the others that they were to be made a captain; then he knew he would have a horde of angry boat builders running for his door. Solvi was fairly certain that the threat of a blood eagle would buy their silence as three of the five of them had thrown up when the Wolf's back got ripped open. That night still gave Solvi goose bumps. He remembered the howls of the Wolf as his back was slowly torn apart. He remembered Yuki pouring freezing cold water over him to wake the Wolf up before he passed out so his suffering would last. Solvi's favourite memory of the blood eagle, however, was the orgasmic feeling he got as he pulled the Wolf's lungs out from their sockets to let them flap in the wind. He knew Odin would have been watching and Solvi hoped the one-eyed God was now glancing his way every so often.

As the Jarl ventured out into the ice-cold camp, Gisha appeared from the tent across from his. The tents were arranged in four parallel lines of about thirty, and most them housed about four men. Solvi had allowed the residents of Osoyro to keep their longhouses and huts for themselves rather than to give them to the new habitants who had come storming into their settlement like ants to a bread basket.

"So, have you decided who is going to captain your ships yet?" Gisha asked flirtingly. "Well, that is if they ever get built in time. Who knows when Sigfred will come down here and steal your head from your body and use it as a shit bucket?" Gisha ran her hand through the stiff blonde tuft of hair in the middle of his head and followed it all the way down to below his shoulder blades.

"Yes I have, and I am afraid there is nothing you can do to change my mind," Solvi said sternly.

"Nothing?" she replied with an accompanying wink. Her personal guards Olm, Yuki and Higta walked round the corner with mugs of mead in their hands. Judging by their walk, the Jarl could tell they had spent all morning and probably the previous night drinking.

"Oh and you have sent these men to fight me for that precious spot on board a boat?" Solvi said, laughing like a wildcat. "Okay . . . Okay, I surrender. You may captain one of the boats, just please don't hurt me," he laughed.

Gisha brushed past him wearing a pure white fur coat and pants; ordinarily, she liked to hunt her own furs, but there were no pure white animals this far south, so she must have had stolen or won them from a northern settler. As she passed her Jarl, she slapped him on the arse and winked once again in his direction. It was true he had decided who was to lead each ship to Britain, and Gisha was going to be chosen anyway. He hoped Frosti would arrive in time because he would also be a candidate to captain a ship, as well as himself, Jikop, Thord and Umiston.

As the sun started to disappear behind the earth, Solvi's belly began to rumble, so he headed for the feast tables. He had never eaten as well as he had the past week. Every night, Rollaug Danson would somehow produce a feast big enough to feed the forty people. Sigfred's men were never allowed to join in group gatherings. Each night, Solvi's crew would talk about special shield wall formations, past raids and, after a few drinks, women would be discussed and compared like cows at a meat market. Solvi sat down on the high table with Eddval and Jikop to his right and Gisha and Umiston to his left. Even at feasts, the two island chiefs couldn't agree with each other; their followings grew week on week, Solvi had noticed, as men from their chiefdoms had been called upon to the capital. Jikop's men were all over the place and Solvi wondered whether the long-haired island chief's crew outnumbered his own.

"Once again, Danson, you have put on a wonderful spread; the amount you sweat it's a wonder why you aren't half your size," Solvi shouted towards the fat cook who was dishing out some steaming grey lamb broth to the warriors at the feast tables who were all already half drunk on ale and mead.

"He only cooks because he can't swing a sword," Eddval yelled as he signalled to a thrall to fill up his mead horn. Rollaug's apron was stained with old and new juices, which became much more recognisable once he got to the high table to serve the chiefs their food. The lumpy grey matter looked like saliva as it swirled about in Solvi's bowl, but it smelled delightful. There were hints of spice that tickled the nose hairs and sent shivers of delight and warmth through the body. Eddval hammered his empty cup on the wooden table, startling the thrall who was about to fill it, and stood up looking a little uneasy on his feet.

"I had a dream of Freyja; she has blessed me and she will bless my new wife," Eddval said and pointed towards Aesa whose swollen belly was starting to show more prominently. "I promise to look after you and that child you bear; he will be raised as my own but only if my Jarl allows it." Solvi nodded his head, smiled and raised his own horn, which was followed by a roar of cheering and applause from the rest of the men at the feast. Aesa was dressed in a long, navy blue shirt with Thor's hammer sewn at the waist line. To Solvi, she looked extremely beautiful; he had never fucked a pregnant woman before and found himself wondering what it was like. His day-dreaming was interrupted by a pat on the back from Eddval; immediately, he felt guilty and stuttered in response to the half-drunken murmurings of Eddval.

"Thank you Solvi. I promise you, if Bergison ever comes back looking for his woman, his cock will be in his mouth before he can say the words 'shield wall'." The mention of Bergison brought a sour taste to his throat, which luckily was diluted by Rollaug's next dish that was made up of roasted pheasant and earthy vegetables like carrots and potatoes. The bird was cooked so perfectly that juices ran down the chins of those who were fortunate to have taken a bite before the clouds opened up. As sudden as a flash, the rain pelted down like boulders falling from a cliff. The tables were soon flooded, and the bowls that were filled with lumpy grey matter were now overflowing with light pale water.

"This is a sign from Thor; he is cleansing my new bride!" Eddval shouted to no one in particular whilst he jogged off to his tent with Aesa.

"More like a curse from Loki warning us that we can never have happiness," Solvi whispered to the person next to him, who happened to be the chief Jikop. It was the first time Solvi had seen the chief's hair not tied up; it was tangled and extremely curly with mostly grey strands but a few white ones hiding in between.

"I don't think this is a good idea, Jarl, I fear Eddval is marrying a serpent," Jikop said.

"I am the Jarl, it is my decision to allow them to marry, and Eddval is a strong-willed man; he does what he likes!" Solvi shouted as he pierced Jikop's eyes with his own terrible stare.

"I am only saying that she is a dangerous piece in the game of Jarls and Kings. I think it would be best if you removed her from the game," Jikop said with nothing less than a smile. The words struck a chord with Solvi and he snapped, like a beast inside him had just awoken. He pushed the respected Jikop to the floor. Jikop had fallen directly into a muddy puddle that was quickly filling thanks to the storm that swirled around them. A small crowd of men who had still not found their tents or huts gathered round. Solvi couldn't see any of his crew as they must have carried Eddval off to his longhouse with Aesa but instead he saw glimpses of men he didn't recognise. He felt an unsettling feeling of nervousness and vulnerability. His blonde hair was spread awkwardly across his head where the rain had washed all strength out of it.

"Leave it, men; I am sure the Jarl is not aware of his own strength, and we must get out of this storm before the rain drowns us," Jikop said as he jumped back up to his feet and straightened his dirty clothes. An alarming number of men left with Jikop, so they must had been the new arrivals from his island of Askoy. He was thankful that hordes of men had joined his cause, but Solvi was also anxious that not all would follow him.

The cooling rain and the beautiful sounds of Thor banging his hammer Mjolnir didn't bother Solvi; he embraced it as he walked into the dense forest that surrounded Osoyro. Droplets trickled down the bark like tiny rivers cascading down rugged mountains finding themselves at the debris-covered and sodden ground, to feed the dark green mosses that neighboured the tall evergreen spruce trees. An explosion erupted from the moonlit sky, followed by a blinding flash and intense heat across Solvi's entire body. The tree that Solvi had just passed had just caught flame; the fire burnt red then orange and then blue. Its face melted as the blaze swirled rapidly round the bark and the screeching of the inferno made it seem like the tree was in pain. No words left Solvi's mouth as he just stood and watched the tree's life burn away; somehow no other trees had caught the flaming disease. His eyes burned whilst he stared at the heart of the fire, but he could not tear them away regardless of the pain. He expected ravens to come flying into the scene but there were none. Maybe the Gods were bored of playing their games or maybe the tree was simply one of the many that would catch flame during intense storms. He thought of Frosti as the fire raged untamed in front of him. They had grown up together, and he knew together they would become saga-worthy warriors. He could imagine Skalds huddled round Jarls' hearths spreading stories of how Solvi the Fierce and Frosti the Red had sailed to Britain. Then he thought of them telling tales of how they defeated King Sigfred in a huge battle to make the Gods jealous. Solvi smiled.

Frosti

"We must preserve the bloody food. We are still more than a bloody week away from the camps," Frosti told Jik as they tucked into the last piece of salted fish Myrun had given them before they had set off. After almost a week and a half travelling north, both men looked completely different: Jik's normally carefully trimmed facial hair had spread across his whole neck and cheeks. However, his short beard was nothing compared to Frosti's bright ginger one, which seemed to melt any bunches of snow that fell upon it. He had not treated it in any way since before he became King Sigfred's prisoner and it had become uneven and knotted with bits of bone and meat embedded within it.

The first two days' walking were fairly pleasant for them both, as the snow had stopped falling and was instead replaced with a cold wind, which they could cope with. However, the further north they got, the worse the conditions became. On the third day, hail fell so heavily that Frosti's bald head began to bleed. He preferred not to wear a leather hat like Jik as he said the gods cannot truly see who you are if you cover your face and head. Frosti stood with this rule in battle as well, as he never donned head gear during a fight.

Jik lived in the village of Manger, which was within the chiefdom of Voss that was run by a Chief named Harold. Only two days north of Manger was the start of the Northern Camps, and men from the camps would often raid the vast fjord-riddled lands of Voss and steal livestock and even completely obliterate a farmstead. Chief Harold was rarely seen, as Voss was such a huge chiefdom covering the entire north of Hordaland; he preferred to stay as far away from the turbulent, raided border as he could. His lack of presence and care was one of the reasons Jik joined Solvi's crew, as well as the fact Jarl Bergison once ordered half of all sheep born in Voss to be transported to Osoyro.

"We can shave four days off our journey if we travel by water, Frosti. All we need to do is borrow a fishing boat and head through the fjords," Jik said as he stepped over a small rock that poked out of the snow-covered ground. There was something about Frosti's face that showed his reluctance to take a boat to find Gudrod the Hunter. He hated the thought of rowing aimlessly north and getting trapped in some half frozen fjord. Although he did agree with Jik as his feet were starting to numb and his hands felt as cold as steel.

"If we arrive happy and dry, he is less likely to understand how important he is to Hordaland," Frosti replied.

"And how important is this self-proclaimed twat who has raided several of my brother's farms?" Jik responded angrily, stopping to make sure his agitation was apparent.

"Well I might as well bloody tell you in case I die now and you have to get on your knees and beg for the Hunter's sword," Frosti said. "Hundreds of men follow or at least listen to the Hunter. Even though he has no real borders or trading posts, he still has quite possibly the potential to have the largest bloody army imaginable. Solvi knows King Sigfred will try and take Hordaland by force if he has to. However, if Solvi has Gudrod's men at his side, he could defend against the King's large, well-trained force." Frosti continued to speak whilst navigating over a small clear stream that was meandering its way down the small mountain the duo was in the process of crossing.

They were somewhere between the great village of Bergen, which was Gisha's home, and Jik's village of Manger. The conditions were vastly different from the ones they had left behind in Osoyro; forests became larger and denser, which made them increasingly darker. They looked like the great forests spoken of in the Saga tales where heroes would find themselves and be trapped for a lifetime. There were also hundreds of small lakes and large fjords blocking any direct route north; the fjords were almost impossible to cross as the wind made them susceptible to large crashing waves. Along the banks of the fjords where bog land should have been, were treacherous ice sheets that hid within long sharp grass, like a thousand blades piercing a canvas. If Frosti or Jik were to stand upon the ice sheet, it would have cracked and sent either of them into a freezing and muddy, weed-ridden bog that would have certainly meant a drowning death.

It was midday when they spotted a small fisherman's hut watching over a huge river fjord about two kilometres wide. To get where they needed to go, they had to cross the river, or it meant another week on foot and the conditions were not getting any better. The hut was larger than most of Osoyro's longhouses and there was smoke pluming from the thatched roof.

"Someone must be home," Jik said aloud. It was only then that Frosti took a closer look at what he was seeing. He saw around seven small rowing boats moored up along the bank of the river against a wooden pier. A two-metre-high wooden palisade with sharpened edges surrounded the edges of the grounds, which led to suspicions that the hut wasn't all it appeared to be. *'Why would anyone go through all this effort to protect a fishing hut?'* Frosti thought. Then another rowing boat emerged into view, with two large men throwing ropes over to a third man who had stepped out of the hut to help them moor up. They carried cargo but it certainly wasn't fish;

it looked to Frosti like a wooden chest with iron brackets locking it shut.

"These men are pirates. Look at those chests Frosti. They must be filled with plunder of some kind," Jik whispered as his eyes never left the huge sea chests.

"We need a bloody boat, Jik, and these pirates have plenty. We need to make it back in time for Solvi," Frosti said.

"We can't just steal one of theirs; they will outnumber us if they catch us. And I don't know about you but I am not in the mood to be skewered like a rat," Jik replied pessimistically. Frosti nodded and accepted that Jik had a good point; they had no idea how many men were in the hut, what they were hiding and how well they were guarding it.

"I hope your arrows are sharp, Jik, because we are going on a mini raid," Frosti declared. They continued to move slowly across the ever-moving landscape making sure they couldn't be seen. Their leathers were covered in snow and their skin appeared a slightly blue tinge. They crouched and stalked like two wildcats as they tried to get as close to the wooden palisade as they could. When they knelt down behind their cover, the snow seemed to pull them to the ground. The white blanket reached to the top of their aching knees and numbed them, making them feel like their feet had been hacked off. Frosti didn't mind the cold and seemed to embrace it with a smile as if it was an old friend, whereas Jik's teeth were crashing against one and other.

"Stop your bloody chattering," Frosti whispered harshly and Jik just shrugged. The big warrior edged in close to Jik and whispered the plan in his ear, steam blowing out of his mouth like an angry geyser. Three of the boats were moored up separate to the others and Frosti saw this as the best place to start the raid from. He took out his flint and rumbled through the fluffy diamond-coloured layer that covered the ground for the perfect rock to help him light a spark. As he did this, Jik peeled chips of wood off the palisade with one of his arrowheads; the shavings were no thicker than a blade of grass but Jik knew it would make perfect kindling for a fire. Together, as silent as a flea's heartbeat, they gathered up the wooden clippings and began to scrape the flint against the cold rock. Each scrape sounded like a thunderclap, which made the duo wince in anticipation. But the rock was useless in helping to create a spark. Frosti looked up to the sky almost begging for help, but none came; he cursed Odin and Thor under his breath and, like a sulking toddler, threw the rock into the water, creating a loud splash. The sound acted as a good enough distraction for the men inside the huts who were asking questions of each other. One man holding a small thin-bladed sword emerged; he headed towards the pier to inspect whether the sound was manmade or just a harmless act of nature. In one quick split-second decision, Jik lifted up his bow, fletched an arrow, and fired. The shaft flew as quickly as a bird's wing and, luckily, the pierced man fell onto the snowy side of the pier with the arrow jarred into his throat. Blood trickled out of the wound, steaming as it escaped the dying man's body.

"We need to strike now!" Jik whispered as loud as he could towards the bald man who was still lying flat on one of the boats. Without any further hesitation, Frosti got to his feet holding onto his wonderfully carved battle axe.

"I couldn't agree more," Frosti said without any control of his voice's volume. Upon hearing the unfamiliar voice, two more men appeared where the pier started and the entrance to the hut was. One was holding onto a foreign spear that had a shimmering golden handle, whereas the other held onto what looked like a basic Danish sword. The two men couldn't have looked more different; one had just as much hair as Frosti, with a scar running from the crown of his head to his chin, almost partitioning his face. The other, much shorter man was as hairy as a great bear. They were both covered in layers upon layers of wool and leather that made them look like creatures from the freezing lands of Niflhiem. The unfrightened man made the first move towards Jik and Frosti but the archer immediately loosed an arrow that fell perfectly into the man's chest right between the ribs. Realising his vulnerability to Jik's long-distance attack, the man with the weirdly positioned scar turned and fled towards what he felt was safety—until one of the archer's arrows hit him just below the shoulders on his back. On his knees the man tried desperately to move towards where his friends hid inside but Frosti finished him with a terrible blow to his lower back. When Frosti removed his axe, the pelt-covered man became limp and flopped onto the disturbed, blood-spattered snow.

"Come out and face me like real bloody Valhalla-worthy warriors, instead of hiding as always like the bloody cowards you really are!" Frosti shouted towards the hut. Jik was standing with an arrow perfectly placed on his bow string.

"It must just be women inside there," Jik jested. Frosti picked up the golden spear that the brave dead man was armed with and took a moment to admire it. It was about one and a halve metres in length and had a similar thickness to a child's arm. Even though it didn't feel warm whatsoever, the sun was shining, causing rays of light to bounce off the spear's golden surface, making it look rather beautiful. Four men who were all unarmed walked out with their sea-hardened hands in the air.

"You may have our hoard and our boats but please just let us leave," begged a black-haired man covered in silver arm rings and golden finger rings. He also wore a huge necklace with a crucifix hanging below it that clearly belonged to some raided church. Frosti noticed the cross and scowled.

"Who do you pray to?" Frosti asked. The question seemed to confuse the pirate who now thought it safe to bring his arms back down to his sides.

"Odin," he replied, accompanied by nods from the men who stood either side of him who preferred to stay mute.

"Who do you pray to?" Frosti asked again.

"I pray to Odin, to Thor, to Freya. Why do you ask me these stupid questions?" the pirate screamed with an increasingly worried look spreading across his face. A moment of silence followed. The pirates looked at Frosti and Jik, who both replied with stone-faced looks of their own. Frosti slammed the spear into the ground and it landed with a thud.

"Odin does not want your bloody prayers; he does not need false men to fight with him at Ragnorok." Frosti said as he took a step towards the four unarmed men who backed up towards the wooden walls of their hut. Jik closely followed behind Frosti and never relented the bow's string; his arms stayed perfectly still and his eyes remained fixed on his target whilst his legs did all of the work.

"I pray to Odin, Odin is my god!" the highly decorated pirate continued to claim as Frosti came closer with his battle axe in hand. One of the men went to run inside out of cowardice or stupidity and soon found himself lying in a puddle of his own blood with one of Jik's goose-feathered arrows sticking out from him like a sapling. Frosti then dropped his beloved weapon, which was cushioned by the snow below him. He pulled back his sleeves and towered over the two mute pirates as Jik held his weapon against the neck of the now crying jewel-covered man. From his belt, Frosti pulled out a tiny blade; he must had stood more than a foot higher than his victims, who didn't even try and fight back. In two smooth motions Frosti's blade was covered in blood. Both men clung to their necks where they had been sliced open but nothing could have stopped the relentless gush of steaming blood.

"Who do you pray to?" Frosti again asked the last pirate.

"I don't know what to say. Please, please, I will do anything," the man once again pleaded.

"Oh well, that is interesting. Only a moment ago you were adamant you prayed to Odin, but now you are not sure; it must be that bloody cross round your neck poisoning your mind." The pirate looked down at his chest, only seeming to acknowledge then what he had hanging from his neck. He looked up with a face as white as the snow they both stood on. Frosti pulled the man by the scruff of his neck towards the entrance of the grounds and lifted him up against the palisade wall with ease. The pirate didn't even struggle as he knew any effort would surely mean more pain and Frosti's raw strength was too great. Jik was on the other side of the wall standing on a wooden chest that he had pulled out of the hut. As soon as the defeated man began to realise what was about to happen, he tried to squirm out of Frosti's hands and kick out at him but the huge figure of Frosti just knocked him to the ground with a punch straight to the face. The pirate looked up at his fate with a hand automatically clutching his broken nose. As Frosti lifted him up as far as he could, Jik appeared over the other side of the wall and grabbed the thick silver chain that the crucifix hung from and pulled it over the spike of one of the palisades trunks. Frosti twisted the pirate round completely, causing the chain to twist round his neck, he then let go of the soon-to-be-dead man. The jewelled pirate hung there trying to free his neck from the chokehold, but he couldn't and instead the chain got more twisted and locked into a position that completely strangled him. His face turned red, then blue, then white as slowly all life left him.

"Pirates are scum no matter if they are Norse or not," Frosti said as if to reassure his reasoning for killing the unarmed man. Jik said nothing in response and instead decided to focus on the hoard inside the hut. When they entered, the fire in the middle of the large room instantly filled their entire bodies with a comforting heat. Surrounding the fire were stacks upon stacks of wooden and bronze crates. Jik moved towards the one closest to the door, which had already been forced open; broken, the bronze lock seemed to glow with the reflection of the fire. The lid was much heavier than Jik had anticipated and he needed Frosti to give him a hand to raise it.

"The bloody thing has frozen shut; it must have been here for ages," Frosti claimed. But finally the hinges whistled open and the lid hit the wattle wall behind, sending a small shower of snow to fall through the thatch. Thousands of golden and silver coins greeted them. Their hearts skipped a beat. Between them, they had been on hundreds of raids and taken a lot of booty, but never had they had access to so much. Each crate and chest had similar piles of coins and pieces, and there were also a few crowns and multi-coloured stones mixed in as well.

"We should tell Solvi," Jik suggested. Frosti was fixed upon a ruby-encrusted crown, stroking it and feeling every single curve within the polished metal. "Frosti?" the archer said sternly. The crown dropped back into its chest once Frosti snapped out of the trance he found himself in.

"Yes, yes we definitely should," he said.

Carlnut

He knew why he was in the cell but hated it even so.
When the oak tree guards ran in to the bloodied
chambers, all they could see was Carlnut, sword in
hand, covered in dead men's fluids as well as the King
of Wessex lying dying on the floor. Carlnut counted the
days in the damp dim prison by how many meals he
was brought. Every day, the same guard wearing a
green tunic with an oak tree upon it would walk round
the corridor holding a torch in one hand that lit up the
entire cell room. The walls were as bland as Carlnut
expected, with trickles of water cascading down into the
cracks, emerging dirtier until they hit the stone floor. In
his other hand, he would carry a wooden bowl barely
filled with a horrible pink-coloured mush. Each time the
soldier placed the bowl on the floor, Carlnut would ask
how the King was and where Arnum had been taken but
the man refused to speak. Carlnut wasn't sure whether it
was the same man each day as he always wore a helmet,

but even so, he wished one of them spoke. The eight days he spent within the cell were the longest of his life; he missed conversation, proper food and, most desperately, he missed light. He never expected to miss it so much but he did; the cell had no windows or links to the outside, which he knew meant he was underground. The guard's torch was the only light that touched his eyes but he found that the raging fire was too bright and disorientated him more than anything. Carlnut was thankful his hands were not bound, which enabled him to get some kind of sleep.

In Hordaland, when Jarl Bergi was attacked during the night, Carlnut's father Hrolf was there to apprehend the attacker. Carlnut recalled how the attacker was bound hands and feet together and thrown into a pit for almost a week with the only liquid being the piss of the village. Bergi had ordered that all defecation was to be thrown into the pit and after a week, the attacker was starved and covered in flies that had begun to eat him alive. *At least there are no maggots,* Carlnut thought to himself with amusement.

The straw Carlnut lay upon to get some sleep had not been replaced since he was marched into the cell and had become completely useless as a bed. Luckily for him, he was given a bucket to piss and shit in, which was replaced by the reluctant guard every few days, probably for his own well-being rather than his prisoner's. As Carlnut lay on the cold stone shivering, he heard voices. The echo grew louder as it whizzed round the corridor and was then followed by the haze of more than one torch. Carlnut jumped up, his aching body forgotten about for a moment; however, his head still rang from his wound and occasionally Carlnut would catch the scab and blood would poor down his face onto his disgusting tunic. As the voices got louder, they became more recognisable. Carlnut could vaguely hear the voice of King Offa of Mercia and his faultless way of speaking. The torch that one of his guards was carrying cast a great shadow of the King on the wall. His already thin, bony figure became even more so as it twisted and bent on the dripping wall, making him appear demonic. Carlnut was suddenly reminded of the dream he had months ago. The dream of the four Kings. He wondered which one in the dream Offa was. The Mercian King wore a long dark jade cloak, which was attached round his neck by a golden oak tree exactly like the one his guards wore. He must have been wearing some kind of thick heels on his boots as his footsteps were louder than his well-spoken words. His purple eyes were fixed on Carlnut when the party eventually reached his cell. The King's gloved hand reached up and he flicked his wrist. One of his guards understood perfectly what this meant, and he passed a pile of neatly folded clothes through the bars into Carlnut's makeshift home.

"Sir, we have been made aware of your true role in the events that conspired last week," Offa said with a little nod. Carlnut had never been called Sir before and it felt rather strange to him. However, he did not dwell on it too much as the sight of a new set of clothes to change into took precedence. He was even given a brown band to tie his long black hair back. Once he got changed into a wonderfully fitting tunic and pants, which were far more comfortable than any he had ever worn, Carlnut went to speak. However, he was interrupted by a finger hugged by a brown glove to his lips. "I think it will be paramount if you just follow myself and say as little as you can," Offa advised him. So Carlnut once more found himself listening to a King's order without hesitation. After eight days of solitary confinement and slave rations, he was delighted to be leaving the moss-covered prison. He wondered if any of his prayers could be heard by Odin but then deduced that they must have been as he was still alive. Carlnut was much further underground than he first imagined. He counted over one hundred steps to get to the first set of windows, which were almost hugging the ceilings and had a view of flower beds and tree roots.

"The Romans were certainly masterful builders but the question that plagues me is, where did they go? We hear stories of their battles and my priests assure me their generals were mostly loved by the common folk. If this is the case surely they would still be living," Offa twittered on as they continued to spiral through the halls and corridors of Merantune. Offa was right, the Romans built wonderful structures; Osoyro had only one stone fixture and that was the stepped seating within the great hall but even so, the Gods created that and not men. Carlnut knew when he was getting closer to their destination as stone steps were replaced by marble ones and rotting walls were replaced by beautiful paintings. There was no way to tell there had been chaos in the mansion just a week before other than the eerie silence. Before King Cynewulf's birthday, there were hundreds of people rushing around getting drunk and generally having a good time. After making their way through the front hall, which had a roaring fire and all the green furnishings that hadn't moved since Carlnut last saw them, they reached a set of white doors. Carlnut couldn't remember visiting this part of the mansion; the doors were pure white without a mark of dirt or even a scratch. The hinges didn't make a single squeal when one of the two oak tree guards who stood either side of the doors pushed them open.

"Now, Carlnut, welcome to the very beginning of your life," Offa said as a heavenly light covered his body. He found himself in a chapel, which was much more decorated than Priest Luyewn's chapel. There were rows of benches filled with wonderfully dressed lords and ladies who all wore different garments that glittered like the night sky had dropped into the room. Four stained glass windows each depicting some scene from the bible allowed light to filter into the chapel. Two windows on the right hand side of the room had two crying ladies whereas the ones on the left showed a shepherd and a king. Carlnut remained silent as a beautiful lady grabbed his hand and pulled him to one of the front rows. She had long flowing blonde hair and wore a long white dress that hid none of her modesty as her plump breasts were clearly visible as well as a dark bush around her womanhood. Carlnut's eyes were fixed upon her features even as she seemingly floated away until a familiar voice greeted him.

"Carly, thank fuck it's you lad, I thought you were dead," Arnum said as he embraced his friend. Arnum was well dressed and the few crumbs on his tunic hinted that he had also eaten well. Carlnut could only guess that his friend had fetched King Offa's men meaning he wasn't a suspect in Cynewulf's murder.

"What's going on? This morning I was sitting in my own shit and now I've got a stiff cock in a church," Carlnut replied. They both laughed like they haven't seen each other in years. Somewhere in the chapel, a bell rang, the doors glided open and a small stout man dressed in a simple grey robe scuttled through. Instantly Carlnut recognised him as a priest as he wore exactly the same clothes as Luyewn.

"Who is that?" Carlnut asked Arnum. The soldier responded with a shrug and a look that couldn't have seemed less interested.

"That is the Archbishop of Lichfield," a raspy voice behind them said. "He is a fairly new creation of Offa's; he wasn't too happy with the Archbishop of Canterbury for some reason or another and decided to find his own. Heaven only knows why," the man continued. Carlnut became conscious of how loud he actually was being and decided to not say anything further. Once the Archbishop reached the altar, he stood silent facing the pale white doors. Had anyone not seen him walk in, he could have been mistaken for a statue as not once did his face change expression or hands even twitch forwards an itch. His minions, however, were shuffling and fidgeting behind him. One carried a golden cross that housed a single jewel in its centre whereas another one was swinging an incense ball around. A fresh scent of burning herbs filled the air. Carlnut would have hated the smell but over a week in his own filth made him appreciate any stink other than shit. The bell that signalled the coming of the Archbishop rang again, whilst the sound of a harp from the back of the room caught the attention of Carlnut's ears. With each ring of the bell, it pealed louder and more frequently until it was as common as a heartbeat, and once it finally became a permanent fixture in the chapel, it stopped abruptly. Carlnut's mind still heard the high-pitched squeal of the bell as the harp became the only sound within the hall. Each string that was plucked vibrated like a wild thing but it made the sweetest of sounds. Carlnut thought of Selwyn and her Odin-blessed, voice but his daydream was cut short by the booming tone of the Archbishop.

"All rise!" the Archbishop commanded of the entire room. His voice certainly did not match his basic appearance; he spoke with a similar accent to King Offa.

"You smell like a hog's arse," Arnum whispered to Carlnut.

"Stay risen for Beorhtric!" the priest said looking directly at Carlnut. He felt like if the Archbishop was a God he would have wanted nothing more than to seal Carlnut's lips shut. Beorhtric was clad in the finest robes he had ever seen, which still didn't make the man look very pretty but it certainly helped. Every item of clothing had some kind of shine to it, whether it was from a jewel or just the perfect cleanliness of each garment. Even his scarred face seemed to have some kind of glow to it but Carlnut was sure that was due to some kind of powder or lotion Selwyn told him Queens and Ladies kept in their rooms. As far as men go, he was certainly not weak, he had the build of a warrior and Carlnut hoped the scar could tell some kind of battle story.

The Archbishop of Litchfield stood directly behind Beorhtric upon the altar's step; however, he could barely see over into the nervous crowd, mainly due to Beorhtric's blessed height and his lack of it.

Once more the bell rang, making everyone jump a little in astonishment.

"What the fuck is going on?" Carlnut asked Arnum who was too busy trying to stifle a yawn. Carlnut was growing impatient; he was hungry, thirsty, tired and had no idea why a King had freed him from the prison to watch the proceedings that were taking place within the chapel. A small child wearing exactly the same clothes as the Archbishop stepped into the room; his head had been completely shaved, making him appear like a slave. In his hands he was carrying a plump purple cushion with golden tassels. Carlnut began to comment to Arnum that the pillow looked like Earl Cynric but thought better of it. However, unlike Cynric, the pillow had a crown upon it, Cynewulf's crown. After seeing the crown, Carlnut finally knew that he failed to protect the King. The child knelt upon one knee in front of Beorhtric and raised the crown towards him. The scarred man attempted to open his left eye to see his future that lay upon a purple cushion, but he couldn't, so instead he reached out for it. Beorhtric's hands shook furiously and his brow begun to flood at the sight of the golden spiked jewel that held the key to an entire Kingdom. Carlnut could feel a slight breeze against his neck and as he turned to investigate, he saw a glimpse of King Offa shuffling to the back row. Incidentally, Beorhtric must have seen King Offa as well as the Mercian's sudden appearance gave Beorhtric the courage to pick up the crown. Beorhtric raised it up above his own head, where the Archbishop took it off him. Lichfield eyed every single soul in the room before he began his speech.

"May God bless Beorhtric of Wessex and long may he reign over us," the Bishop begun by saying then proceeded in a tongue Carlnut recognised as the language of old Rome. However, the Archbishop's last words stood out from the rest of the horrid incomprehensible drone. "Teneat, Luceat, Floreat," which the procession repeated each time the Archbishop said it.

"Teneat, Luceat, Floreat, Teneat, Luceat, Floreat," the entire room continued. Seeing Carlnut's confusion Arnum translated for him whilst still keeping to the monotonous natter that everyone else, including Beorhtric, was fixated on.

"Let him hold, Let him shine, let him flourish," Arnum said just for the benefit of his friend. Archbishop Hygeberht, which was the priest's real name, placed the crown softly upon King Beorhtric's short black hair, which had a scalp canyon running through it, causing tuffs of hair to sprout off in multiple directions like marram grass in a sea breeze. Thunder erupted from the room as silent lords clapped their rich hands whilst their lady's soft gloved palm's barely met each other.

"I am King Beorhtric of Wessex and you will kneel," the King commanded. As harsh and sudden as the request was it was the custom for such an order to be a newly crowned king's first words. Carlnut was down on one knee and looking at the polished floor when he felt a hand upon his shoulder. A bolt of pain flew down his arm from a wound he had received in the fight within Cynewulf's chambers. "Rise," Beorhtric's voice whispered. So he did. He was standing face to face with the King of Wessex and they were the only two people in the room who were standing. Carlnut presumed Offa would not be kneeling but it was impossible for him to tell at that point. Their eyes locked. Behind Beorhtric's squint hid two eyes as brown as mud and as stern as storm clouds.

"Wessex thanks you, Carlnut of . . ." he paused, not quite knowing anything about Carlnut and hoping he would finish the sentence for him.

"Northumbria," Carlnut said, trying to hold back a wince of pain. His stomach whirled like a rushing river but the King thankfully ignored the terrible noise. The

~ 177 ~

cells had not allowed him to get much rest and he craved it like the sea craves the wind. He would have given anything to lay upon a bed of fresh straw and to be lying with Selwyn in their home in Poole. He surprised himself when he thought of Poole as his home. But after all, he had not seen Hordaland or Solvi in three long years. The last words he heard from his old home were, "You will return to Hordaland." Those words had haunted Carlnut ever since, but he could never shake the memory of the squawking Raven who repeated them dream after dream. In time though, Carlnut knew, he would return.

"Well you are no longer Carlnut of Northumbria, you are Lord Carlnut of Portland," Beorhtric announced to the entire procession. He only knew Portland as a small island a day's walk away from Poole but he had never visited and was already relishing his new responsibility. Soon enough it dawned on him that he would soon be in possession of his own land, men and household.

"I don't know what to say, Your Grace," Carlnut said with eyes wide enough to blind the moon.

"Ealdorman Osric told me of your bravery and strength in your attempts to save my cousin; we owe you. If you have any requests, please feel free to speak to me." Hundreds of things were rushing round Carlnut's head; to be made a Lord was enough for him. He felt after his efforts he did deserve some kind of reward like some gold or maybe a fine war sword. He did not expect land, and he certainly did not expect any title of any sort. It was then he noticed Arnum sitting in the front row with a smile as bright as the sun. He helped defend Cynewulf too, yet Osric must have left that detail out.

"I do have a few requests, Your Grace," Carlnut asked awkwardly. Even as a foreigner, Carlnut knew the dangers of asking too much from a superior. In Osoyro, a farmer had turned up at Jarl Bergi's longhouse begging for coin as his crops had failed. The Jarl gave the farmer ten pieces of silver, which was a big enough sum especially for a lowlife like he was. Jarl Bergi then told the farmer to yield his farm as he didn't deserve to own one.

"I would request that Arnum join me in Portland; he is a great soldier and better friend," Carlnut said before he got too lost in his old memories of Hordaland.

"Done," King Beorhtric said. "I have also sent a rider to Poole to take your Lady to her new home. Ealdorman Osric has also sent his thanks, as without you he would not be alive." Carlnut had not thought of the ealdorman much but it soon became clear to him that Osric was the reason he was no longer rotting in the horrid cell underneath Merantune. The King puffed up his chest and with one huge sigh commanded the entire room's eyes to turn in his direction. He wanted to make his first act as Wessex's King a generous one and pointed towards the huge man standing behind Arnum. "This is Sicga, Osric's eldest son. Osric would like you to let him join you in Portland." Beorhtric's monotone voice had never sounded more amazing to Carlnut. It was a huge honour for an ealdorman as respected as Osric to give his eldest son away. In a matter of minutes, Carlnut's had life changed.

After the ceremony had finished, Arnum came jogging towards Carlnut, his brown hair bouncing up and down and his face gleaming with a new sense of purpose.

"My Lord," he said sarcastically and gave a little bow to accompany the charade. '*I will have to get used to that*', Carlnut reminded himself. "I am wondering whether we could take Engelhard with us too?" Engelhard had been wounded in a fight with the bandit who would eventually kill King Cynewulf. Engelhard's body wasn't anywhere near to any kind of fitness, but Carlnut feared more for his mind, which would be all too likely to shatter into a thousand pieces after his traumatic ordeal. Not until he is drinking mead in Odin's halls with his friends would Carlnut forget the screams. It was a horrid sound that would rival a banshee's cries and Carlnut had secretly hoped his friend could be put out of his misery. However, he showed more signs of improvement than signs that he was heading for his heaven.

"Engelhard will join us," Carlnut said with some authority. Arnum smiled and gave his new Lord a sincere bow before ducking away to talk to some Lady's maid who had been giving him the eye. Out of the corner of Carlnut's green eyes he saw the Ealdorman Osric limping into a room. The room the Ealdorman had walked into was a library; hundreds of rolled-up parchments cluttered shelves, giving the room the look of a bee's honeycomb.

"Osric, is that you?" Carlnut shouted in no direction in particular. The relatively small man peered from a desk in the corner that he had just managed to sit down at. The little desk was littered with pots of ink both full and empty, as well as blank parchments sprawled out like clouds. "Ealdorman, I am glad I have seen you, I would like to thank you for . . . everything," Carlnut said.

"Ah, it has nothing to do with me although I am grateful for your service. You ought to say your thanks to God. Have you? Have you thanked God yet?" Ealdormen Osric asked whist dipping his goose feather into a black ink similar to the colour of his hair. Carlnut hesitated in response. After two years with Luyewn pleading with him to offer prayers to the Christian God, he had never done it. The Christian god was a strange one; he preferred a life Carlnut just could not adapt to as Carlnut loved fighting almost as much as he used to like whoring.

"I thought as much; you ought to pray more, Lord. Thank God for everything. He is all seeing and all powerful. I am not sure where the nearest monastery is to Portland but I extremely recommend you become familiar with it," Osric said never looking away from the writings.

"What are you writing about, Lord?" Carlnut asked not knowing whether he genuinely cared.

"I am writing about what has happened today. Look around you, this entire room is filled with years and years of events: From King Penda's death to the coronation of King Beorhtric. And now I include your appointment as Lord of Portland, of course. Talking of which, where were you born so I can record it?" Osric's question was one Carlnut knew he couldn't answer but luckily Sicga, Osric's son, interrupted the conversation. Meaning an answer was never needed. Sicga was a large man roughly the same age as Carlnut; he wore leathers fit for war and carried a magnificent sword on his belt. His face was clean shaven but stubborn and upon his cratered forehead flopped curly hair. The curls made him look younger than he was, but his evident strength and battle-hardened grin made it plain the curls were the only innocent thing about him. Something deep inside Carlnut told him he had found a very influential friend.

Selwyn

After almost four months on the road, Selwyn was glad to be back in Poole. The familiar smell of the sea soothed her lungs and the sound of the squawking gulls brought a smile to her face. She had been back in her thatched house for almost a week and was extremely surprised not to find Carlnut waiting for her there. It wasn't until a few days later when Father Luyewn rode to greet her that he had to give her the grave news of Carlnut's imprisonment. The old man tried giving her the news as gently as he could, but she still fell down upon the floor as heavily as a cow. She longed for her man, but that longing was instantly replaced with worry. He was a pagan and if his captors found that out he would surely be dead or even worse.

Selwyn was never alone; between the endless but lovely visits from Luyewn, she had the company of Bedfrith. Bedfrith was a harpist she had met as a child and they both profited from each other's skills. From an early age, they discovered a combination of his effortless playing of the harp and her light, almost angel-like voice earned them coin. Every time Selwyn went on the road to sing in the taverns and brothels, Bedfrith would come too, for which she was extremely grateful. The musician was extremely easy on the eye; he was tall, handsome and wore clothes much above his station. He had always claimed that just because he smelt poor, he didn't need to dress poor and so with that reasoning, he spent the majority of his wages on the finer garments. They were both twenty-two years old and Selwyn saw him as a brother even though she suspected Bedfrith did not see her in a similar light.

Poole had been plunged into darkness and the unforgiving sea winds had already started taking over. Buckets, straw and anything else that was light enough began to throw itself around in the street, banging into houses and causing loud thuds that meant sleep was impossible. Getting no sleep had been the norm for Selwyn since she found out about Carlnut, and she often lay flat on her bed whispering prayers until eventually her body shut down. She could hear the faint sound of a dog howling in the night and the crazy bleatings of the sheep in their pen until a loud bang startled her. She jolted up at the sound and felt a sharp pain run across her shoulders and back. Selwyn was almost inclined to give in to her body's pains until the bang repeated over and over again.

"Hello? M'Lady?" A voice cried from outside. It was raining now, heavily, to the point her roof started to drip and puddles were forming upon the floor. "M'Lady!" the banging and the shouting continued. Between the happenings at the door and the chaos swirling outside, Selwyn felt like she was suffering God's wrath. She found herself whispering Carlnut's name, begging him to save her. The door crashed open with an earth-shattering tremor, sending the wooden planks splintering across the floor. There was no fire or torch lit so the only light was supplied by the occasional flash of lightning. Two silhouettes emerged at the threshold with a backdrop of hell's fury behind them. Her heart screamed in her chest as she now found herself standing upright, back against the mud and clay walls, cold, scared and alone. One of the shadows was of a man built like an ox, arms wide and chest bulging; the other was another, much smaller man, holding his shoulder in slight pain from the force of breaking open the door.

"M'Lady, please, I beg of you, come with us," the smaller man protested. "We don't have much time, we have to leave Poole."

Selwyn froze. The men had stepped further into the house and now they were standing a few metres away from the threshold until their faces were as clear as day. A big bushy beard hung from the big man's face, which was accompanied with a blank expression.

"Come," the big man grumbled. The man must have been simple, not just from the way he spoke but the vacant look he had when he delivered the words, like his mind was lost in his own head. Still unable to move, Selwyn felt the cold and wet grip of the smaller man's hand on hers. He pulled and eventually dragged her away from the wall.

"Where am I going?" Selwyn asked the men rather timidly until she found a strange courage inside her. "I'm no Lady, I will not go with you!" she yelled, her voice growing in intensity as it grew hoarse and tired from the lack of sleep.

"But I am an Earl," the smaller man replied, shouting over the thrashing of the rain. "Earl Eafled of Dorchester to be precise, M'Lady and it is my request that you follow me now." Dorchester was a huge area of land in the south of Wessex bordering Cynric's land of Christchurch. It had brilliantly fertile lands, wonderful forests and rich seas full of conger eels, pollock and bass. Traditionally, the Earls of the neighbouring lands never got on, but Cynric's and Eafled's relationship was sour to the point neither was allowed on the other's land.

"This is Cuth; what he lacks in brains he makes up in brawn," the earl explained as Cuth reached out a hand.

"Come," Cuth ordered again. There was something about the simpleton that Selwyn found reassuring, and she found herself slowly edging away from the wall and towards the two strangers. Eafled wrapped a tattered blanket over her. It had been scrunched up in the corner but she was grateful for the slightest bit of warmth the old thread provided. They had to take a moment before they went into the raging storm. Selwyn's heart was pounding like it was trying to break free of her chest and all the words that were being said by Eafled and Cuth were so much nonsense in her ears. Poole was in chaos;

Selwyn could see a white horse fighting against the gusts, its mane flowing wildly and its head down to protect its eyes from the straw and stone that became one with the air. But upon the horse she could make out the old and frail figure of Father Luyewn, his robe trying desperately to cover his face and what was left of his hair uncontrollably pulling on his wrinkled scalp. The only thing that seemed unaffected by the wind was the crucifix he had round his neck; it stayed perfectly still, only moving with the movement of the horse. Eafled and Cuth must have had been expecting the priest's arrival and suddenly it all became easy. She had no idea where she was going but Luyewn's friendly face reassured her that it would be safe. Earl Eafled and Cuth jumped onto their tired and wind-distressed horses after they had lifted Selwyn onto Father Luyewn's horse.

"Sunflower, I am so glad you are all right," he said in a soothing tone that seemed to keep the weather at bay.

"Where are we going, Father?" she asked. Then they began to move, first at a slow pace to allow the horses to become accustomed to the conditions once more, but after a minute of a slow trotting, all three horses began to gallop. "Why won't anybody answer me?" Selwyn shouted, more to make her voice heard over the hooves that were smashing onto the sodden dirt and the rain that pelted every surface with unrelenting anguish. Every few metres, Father Luyewn looked over his shoulder searching for something or someone that could have been in pursuit of them, which sent Selwyn into more of a panic. But she didn't say anything, instead she wrapped her arms round Luyewn's skeletal frame and rested her drenched head on his back.

They had finally left the border of Poole, which was marked by a tiny earth wall. However, the horses' gallop transformed into a maddening sprint. The increase in speed was accompanied by the shouts of Earl Eafled.

"They are here; make haste towards my land. Not far to go now!" he shouted. The rain had started to lessen when they got to the open fields but the ground had become saturated and was on the verge of becoming a bog, making the horse's path almost impossible.

"Who is here, Luyewn?" Selwyn asked as she pointed behind her towards a small pack of horsemen. Then they all came to a halt; whilst Selwyn was concentrating on the pursuing horsemen, she did not see the group of about five or six riders come from the front to block their path.

"Stay close to me, Sunflower," Father Luyewn whispered, and then began to silently mouth some prayer under his breath. They were now surrounded; about twenty men had dismounted their horses and had their weapons drawn. A few carried swords but others had spears, reaping hooks and other farming equipment and one even held a flaming torch that shone like a beacon showering everyone in light. One or two more torches were lit allowing colour to enter Selwyn's eyes. She noticed that most of the men wore purple-dyed leather and one horse was even clad in a wonderfully coloured purple cloth with gold-trimmed edges. There was some kind of shape sewn into the cloth, which

Selwyn guessed must have been a fish even though she could not quite make it out properly.

"Earl Eafled, it appears you are trespassing upon my land. Is this true?" Earl Cynric of Christchurch asked. Selwyn could tell it was him because his hair was so recognisable, ginger and combed to perfection. His clothes were also a tell-tale sign but had it not been for the hair, any one of the purple-clad soldiers could had been Cynric.

"I do not want any trouble, M'Lord, just let us through," Eafled pleaded knowing there was going to be no way out other than a futile begging. "We have a man of god with us; we mean no harm." He gestured towards Father Luyewn who stayed so still he could have been mistaken for a corpse.

"Yes, Father Luyewn is a priest on my land, for which I pay tribute to his chapel. So am I to think you are stealing my priest? Or am I to think there is some other business afoot?" No one said anything. The rain was completely gone now but the wind still howled and tugged on everyone's clothes. Cynric's feet squelched as he walked past Eafled, then past Cuth till he reached Luyewn and Selwyn. "Are you being kidnapped, Father?" But before the priest could even improvise a response Cynric became more interested in Selwyn. "Remarkable. You are the renowned Poole singer, aren't you?" Selwyn nodded feebly. "I have seen you perform; your voice sounds like it was given by an angel. What is such a magnificent woman doing out riding in weather like this?" His words were in synch with a look of inspection over Selwyn's body. "Does nobody know how to speak?! Have I interrupted a party of mutes?!" The earl screamed so loud that it made Luyewn's horse whinny and another to rear up until a soldier calmed it down. "Very well, as you are on my land I have the right to detain you." He turned back to Eafled, seemingly ending his interest in Selwyn. Cuth half drew his sword when Earl Cynric threatened his master. As simple as Cuth was, the big bearded man was extremely loyal to Eafled.

"Away," Cuth grumbled. "Away!" His sword was now completely free in his hand and he was swinging it round and round maniacally, causing Cynric to fall back and stumble. Even the soldiers were so taken by surprise that they failed to even close in on the big man. It was then that Selwyn noticed her escape route. She and Luyewn, Cuth and Eafled were mounted, whereas, stupidly, none of Cynric's men were. She smacked the rump of Luyewn's horse so hard that her hand began to sting but it worked and the white mare bolted forward towards Cuth's horse, which received the message and also jolted into a gallop. Cuth was caught off guard and the shock of the horse's movement sent him flying into the mud. Cynric's men finally decided to act; they all charged towards the downed Cuth, leaving a perfect escape route for Eafled and the white mare to break through without a challenge. Earl Cynric was shouting and cursing, commanding them to chase the horses rather than to attack Cuth but they were consumed by battle hunger. Selwyn was on the brink of freedom but Eafled stopped to contemplate saving his friend.

"His sacrifice will be applauded by God, my Lord, he will be received a saint," Luyewn told Eafled.

"He wouldn't care much for that," the Earl said. Luyewn ignored that response and Eafled charged. That was the first time Selwyn had seen Earl Eafled of Dorchester fight and hoped it wouldn't be the last. He moved so elegantly and effortlessly, like he was born to war. Eafled had run into the heart of the group of Cynric's guards who all still stood a metre away from Cuth, who must had been growing exhausted from the chaotic way he swung his sword around to stop any advancing attack. The Earl dismounted his horse in a jumping motion and allowed the beast to run into a short man grasping a spear. He then weaved past two men with farmer's tools and allowed their backs to turn towards Cuth, who had already seen the opportunity. His large polished sword took a man's head off cleanly and before the other one knew what had happened, he was clutching his belly trying desperately to hold in his own guts. An old man with double the amount of years on his back than Earl Eafled came charging into the fold, desperate to make a name for himself before a straw death took him. He lunged at the Earl like a fiend but Eafled had already read the entire situation. The Earl leant to the side and pulled on the man's spear, causing the old man to slip. Eafled then allowed his sword to end the man's life, and both men smiled as the blade plunged straight into the heart. From then on it was an easy fight. Cynric had already fled with a few of his men whilst the others, who were merely boys pretending to be soldiers, either yielded or died. The Earl with his messy black hair and stern look smiled towards Selwyn. Luyewn made the sign of the cross against his chest and Cuth cleaned the blood off his blade.

"What is happening?" Selwyn whispered to herself as she mounted onto Luyewn's horse once more.

As they rode, the sun woke up. Its golden gleams shimmering across the water covered grass bringing the entire view to life. The road was less than flat with scores of hills and bogs to navigate round, but the light made that task far easier. A dragonfly wisped past Selwyn's greasy ginger hair and made its descent into the tall marram grass that Eafled said marked the border of Dorchester and Christchurch.

"So M'Lady, I am terribly sorry for not telling you why we have taken you away from your home but I could not risk doing so whilst we were on Earl Cynric's land," Earl Eafled said whilst he helped her down from the white mare that had worked tirelessly through the night to carry them to safety. Before Selwyn could answer, Eafled spoke up again, almost knowing what she was going to say. "Your man, Carlnut or should I say Lord Carlnut, has been rewarded a large portion of my land, which I so happily gave away at the King's request."

"Money," Cuth grumbled, trying to hide it with a fake cough.

"Even if that is the case, I was more than happy to give my land to the new Lord Carlnut. He saved an Ealdorman from certain death and put his life on the line to protect a King he is not sworn to. In any case, I was tasked with collecting you to take you to your new home before Cynric heard he had a Lady amongst his people." Eafled gave Cuth a slap on top of the head for his laughter but none of that mattered to Selwyn. Carlnut was alive. And she was now a Lady. Even as a little girl, Selwyn would watch the Lady of Christchurch handing out flowers to the village with her golden hair and multitudes of rings. She couldn't believe it and gave Luyewn a huge hug, which almost knocked him off balance.

"Sunflower, it is the truth. All my prayers have been answered. Carlnut is safe," he said, pulling her away from him before his bones snapped. "An Ealdorman named Osric wrote to me telling me I am to be made Priest of Portland. Oh, what an honour. Praise be to God. Praise be to God."

"Praise be to God," the other three repeated in chorus. Once the whole sun became visible from its horizon cave, so did the sea, as calm and majestic as she had ever saw it. The faint outline of a trading vessel bound for Frankia or Cornwall bobbed on the waves; Selwyn swore she could smell the goods on the ship, but that could easily have been the fresh air. Life had taken an extremely strange turn. And just then, another unusual occurrence presented itself. A horseman galloped in the distance; it was a tall horse, muscular and aggressive, as each thump of its hooves upon the soaked sandy ground sent vibrations to their feet. Cuth drew his sword instinctively but Eafled waved a hand to ease the big man's want for a fight. It was when Selwyn saw the rider's clothes that she realised who it was. He wore a lord's tunic, red and white trimmed, his short black hair was combed within an inch of its life and he carried a golden satchel upon his back.

"Bedfrith?" she shouted. "Bedfrith, is it really you?" Somehow, within the chaos of the storm and the dangers of the battle in the night, Bedfrith had found Selwyn. Bedfrith was her best friend and in a strange way she loved him. Once he reached the top of the small dune that Eafled declared they would rest on, he smiled. A toothy grin filled his face as he dismounted his warhorse; he almost skipped towards Selwyn and lifted her up into the air.

"I couldn't be happier, Selwyn, that you are alive," he managed to say after half a minute of laughter and giggling.

"How did you know where she'd be?" Eafled asked accusingly. Bedfrith snarled and decided to ignore the comment rather than respond. Eafled did not take that slight on the chin and half unsheathed his hungry sword. "I am an Earl and you answer me when I ask you something."

"Er, yes . . . Yes Lord," he stuttered nervously. "I was riding my stallion through the county when I saw your party being ambushed by Earl Cynric's men."

"You were riding in the middle of the night?" Eafled's tone had taken a sharpness to it that made the harpist wince.

"Yes Lord," Bedfrith said never taking his eye off the small reflection of light from the Earl's partly visible sword.

"Very well, if the Lady has no issues with you then who am I to judge," Eafled said calmly, sheathing his sword and clapping his hands together. However, Selwyn could tell the Earl wasn't completely happy but who could blame him, he'd been awake all night and must have been physically drained from the fight as well as the ride. After a small rest and a bite of stale bread, the five of them set off for Portland. Seagulls called in the distance and the waves crashed blissfully against the rocks. Nothing would remove the huge smile Selwyn had on her face at the thought of Carlnut being alive.

Frosti

The sight of the huge ivory bones made Frosti look twice. He had no idea how long Jik and he had been travelling but was comforted by the knowledge it was almost over. His fingers were numb, his back ached and he was almost blind from the shine of the snow. Jik seemed to be handling the cold better, but still the archer looked uncomfortable in the boat that the two of them had shared for at least three days. The boat was stolen from a pirate hut towards the south and Frosti had engraved the location of that treasure trove in his mind, for it truly was a treasure trove. He could remember the warmness of the gold and silver coins and the rivets in the pieces of precious jewellery. With that hoard, he knew he could be one of the richest men in Norway or Daneland, never mind Hordaland. Pirates never seemed to know what to do with the treasure they stole, so instead they hid it and the small group that Jik and Frosti encountered must had felt very safe. As Jik rowed the boat under the huge bones, their true size was revealed. They were as thick as a tree stump and as long as two men, with a point sharp enough to break metal. As a child, Frosti was told of giant hairy beasts that roamed the ice and he thought these could have belonged to one of those beasts, but nevertheless he only knew it marked the start of Gudrod's territory. No one knew how much land Gudrod the Hunter owned and it was impossible to tell, but for some reason everyone who lived that far north paid tribute to him.

The land was ice, thick white sheets that seemed to last forever. Frosti could only just make out where the ice ended and was replaced by gushing, freezing lakes but, once they ended, the ice continued. It had not rained or snowed since before they found the treasure but it was still deathly cold.

"How long do you reckon until we reach the first camp?" Frosti asked Jik.

"Not long, look," Jik said and pointed into the distance. After Frosti's eyes adjusted to the sun's reflection that jumped out of the ice into their eyes, he could see men. Three men were all he could see at first but then a fourth and fifth emerged, followed by a dozen other men all carrying weapons.

"How the bloody hells do they know we are here?" Frosti grumbled as he picked up his fine war axe. Jik shrugged and leant the boat towards the icy bank. Frosti imagined this place must be beautiful during the summer, before the snows fell and the plants froze. He could picture a wide flowing river that had been reduced to a trickle only five rowing boats wide, and he could see hundreds of different shades of green and yellow grass that had been covered by white, a colour that dominated winter, a colour that could kill. The men got closer, and once Frosti and Jik stepped out of the boat, they held up their hands to show they didn't want any trouble. Frosti could have put up a fight against the men that now numbered fifteen and was confident he could kill at least six before their sheer numbers alone sent him to Valhalla.

Four of the men stepped forward, holding their weapons low. Three of those men were carrying spears with points that were sharp enough to pierce the three layers of leather Frosti wore, whereas the other man held an axe. It was a crudely built thing with a head that sat awkwardly upon the dented wooden handle but Frosti was sure it could still take off a man's head with the right wielder.

"Who are you?" the axe-wielding man shouted as the small party got about ten feet away. They all had long scraggy beards and matted black hair that grew from the top of their heads all the way down to their lower backs. "Who are you?" The man asked again. He must have been the small group's leader for he wore seven arm rings, three more than Frosti and four more than Jik.

"I am Frosti and who the bloody hell are you?" he shouted in response.

"Halfdan Halfdanson," the black-haired man replied in a tone that suggested Frosti should have heard of him. "I fought in the battle of the frozen tooth where I killed

Juyfrid Bjornson and in the taking of Voss where I killed their famous Chieftain, Harold Granraude." None of this meant anything to Frosti but Jik seemed to be getting furious. Only a few days ago Frosti had learnt that Jik was from the Chiefdom of Voss, and the long-haired warrior who faced the pair had just admitted to killing his chief. Warriors like Jik swore an oath to their chiefs much like Frosti had sworn to die for Solvi. Jik must have done the same for Harold Granraude. Halfdan got closer and his size was palpable; he stood almost a foot taller than Frosti, who stood a foot taller than Jik. He wore a seal skin coat fastened together with either tiny bones or teeth. His breath stank of fish and his eyes argued with the ferocity of his body. There was some kind of joy within the deep blue eyes of Halfdan's; they portrayed an innocence it was clear he did not have.

"So, who is Frosti?" Halfdan grouched. Their language was the same but Halfdan's accent was deeper and seemed to come from the throat rather than the mouth.

"We have been sent by Jarl Solvi Hrolfson to speak to Gudrod the Hunter," Frosti said. Jik remained silent but his face shouted insults at the Halfdan.

"Ha ha, these half-shrivelled pieces of seal shit want to speak to Gudrod." Halfdan turned towards his men who also laughed at the proposal. "Listen, there is only one way you can speak to Gudrod, and that is through me. I do not care if a Jarl declares it as he is likely more shrivelled and more like seal shit than you two. So what do you whale turds want from Gudrod?" After a few moments of silence, it was Jik who first spoke.

"Men," he said in a voice that could have been missed easily had he not cleared his throat before speaking.

"Men! Fucking men! Who do you think you are? I was mistaken; you aren't whale turds or even seal shit. You are the small pieces of shit that get stuck in my arse hairs. You must have been dropped on your thick heads by your dirty slut mothers then whacked with a stone, because how dare you even want to ask Gudrod for men. Get the fuck out of the camps before I send you out. Piece by piece." Halfdan was so furious that his face had turned brighter than the sun behind him and his hands clenched over and over again as if he was about to burst. Frosti swore he could see steam rising from where Halfdan stood. He turned his back on Frosti and began to march away, spitting on the floor over his shoulder every few steps.

"We can pay you," Jik shouted out desperately, fearing Solvi's wrath if they don't even see Gudrod. Halfdan stopped but still kept his back towards them. "We have a hoard of silver and gold greater than you could ever imagine but we need to speak to Gudrod before I can tell you where that is."

"Don't amuse me, arse hairs," Halfdan said as he was just about to carry on walking.

"There is jet, amber and I swear I saw a golden crown," Jik continued. Frosti felt empty inside; he was confident all that treasure was going to be his, but in one swift sentence he had lost it all. Frosti was more annoyed at Jik than he had ever been at anyone but he was also more grateful, as Halfdan said something to one of the spear-carrying men who awkwardly hobbled over to them and told them to follow Halfdan.

They didn't spend long walking until the first tents and hovels appeared. Some appeared empty whereas others were full of families crouching round a huge fire. Frosti looked longingly at the flames, wanting nothing more than to run into the hut and cover his body in the wonderful heat. After passing the groups of clumsily built homes, they came across a small pack of hills. In front of Frosti stood two hills with icy inclines growing steeper and steeper as the hill rose. They weren't particularly big hills, but they still left a terrifying mark on the otherwise flat landscape. Between the two hills that seemed to curve once Frosti got close to them was a narrow valley with a foot-trodden path. The path was covered in light fluffy snow rather than ice, and Frosti could see a few specks of green underneath where the snow had been completely flattened from the sheer number of people that walked it. It was a horrible place to be. Shrieking birds squawked and insects crawled on the rocky walls of the path like lice in a man's beard. Jik fiddled with a bone hammer that hung from his neck and Frosti touched the Yggdrasil carving on his axe. Yggdrasil was the tree of life upon which all worlds stood, including Asgard, the home of the Gods, and the place that housed Valhalla.

"After you, arse hairs," Halfdan said and gestured Frosti and Jik forward and out of the ever-narrowing valley path. Frosti's first step was onto greenery. What he saw took his breath away. There were hundreds of tents, huts and even a few longhouses huddled together in a huge crater that was surrounded by the two hills. Smoke rose from countless fires, making the crater look alive. In the middle was a huge glistening lake, untouched by unforgiving ice and snow. It was like they had entered a completely different land. There was snow but very little of it. Grass and wildflowers grew happily, as well as thorny trees and heather. A heron flew overhead and found its way to a small rock that protruded out of the wonderfully blue water.

"The Northern Camps, arse hairs," Halfdan said, pointing his heavy axe towards the canvasses. "Come on now, I want my treasure." Frosti noticed Halfdan was in a much better mood now and whether that was because he had the potential to be a much richer man or because he was home, Frosti could not be certain. The crater, which seemed like it was handpicked from a famous Saga tale, was much warmer and the presence of this new, invisible warmth delighted Frosti, who was all but ready to give up and go back home.

After climbing down a few rocky steps that had been carved flat allowing two men to climb abreast, they reached the first set of tents. There seemed to be no division between any of the houses, and at this time, most of the people were inside huddled round cooking pots. Frosti could smell burnt eel, herb trout and fresh duck and he longed for the taste of meat in his mouth. One of Halfdan's men embraced a women who rushed out of one of the tents, and then snatched a leg of some cooked bird out of her hand. Frosti's stomach rumbled and he tried to steal some unguarded duck off a table. An elderly woman smacked his hand away with a wooden comb, causing the meat to fall to the ground and be snatched up by a shaggy-haired dog.

Finally, they reached a large longhouse that was half buried within the ground. Outside the moss-roofed house stood four guards each grasping onto a spear.

"Stay here, arse hairs," Halfdan said. The lake looked even bigger from where Frosti now stood. He could smell fish everywhere and thankfully, for the first time in almost two weeks, he felt safe.

"How many people live here do you reckon?" Jik asked Frosti.

"Five hundred, seven hundred, maybe even one thousand. It is bloody impossible to tell," he shrugged, as if right then such a question had very little importance. The door, which was made from birch, swung open and a man that was not Halfdan stepped out. He wasn't a small man, but stood at a similar height to Jik. He had few teeth and a grimace that looked permanently disgusted. However, his most unusual feature was that his left hand was missing two fingers and hooked over itself in a twisted bony mess making it resemble an eagle's talon.

"Gudrod would like to speak to you," the deformed man said and, using his eagle foot of a hand, he gestured into the longhouse. The house was filled with bursting barrels; one was filled with swords, axes and spears whereas another was filled with arrows and clubs. The most unusual thing about the house was that it had no fire. Instead, in the middle of the longhouse lay a pool of steaming water that was surrounded with blackened rocks and stones. Steam twirled to the top of the longhouse and dripped down warm droplets of water that sizzled when they landed on the rocks or just simply splashed if they fell elsewhere. Four men sat on benches round the pool, one of which was Halfdan who leant against his axe staring right into Frosti's eyes.

"Gudrod, these are the fish guts that would like you to provide them with men," Halfdan croaked without ever taking an eye off Frosti. A man with a similar build to Halfdan stood up; his face was crinkling and scowling, as though trying to read every thought Frosti had in his head. He wore at least five different pelts round his back, which made him look like a giant. His soot black beard was covered in dripping grease, which gave him a savage look and his face was almost all covered in ink depicting creatures and runes confused into each other. He looked at Jik and Frosti and then at Halfdan.

"These are the 'arse hairs' that want my men?" Halfdan nodded and then gave a half smile as if there was some hidden joke. The tattooed warrior then gave a belittling look at his man, which removed the smile in an instant. "These two are renowned warriors, Halfdan; look at their arm rings. I am disappointed, warriors deserve better." Frosti sighed a huge sigh of relief; he thought if Halfdan was a grizzled brute then everyone in the northern camps must have been the same. "Oh, aren't I an idiot, where are my manners? I am Gudrod, this here is Eric Clawhand," he said, pointing towards the man who had led them into the longhouse. "You have met Halfdan, and this is Finlit Hafgramr," Finlit hadn't even looked up from the bowl of broth he was scooping into his bearded mouth, so Frosti assumed he was just one of Gudrod's hearth men. "Sit and eat, you must be tired from your journey." At this point Frosti liked Gudrod; he had had visions of him being half man and half beast, and in many ways he was, but luckily it was just his appearance rather than his personality. The food was better than anything Frosti had eaten before but he did not know whether that was because all he had eaten for two weeks was bread or because the flavour of the duck made all his senses tingle. He could taste a smokiness tied into each bite of the food and a saltiness that seemed to pleasure his palate rather than dry it. Even if his mouth had become dry from the food, the ale was easily drunk and had a very seedy taste that went down easier than water. Jik saw Frosti gulping down his third cup of ale and nudged him in a sign to stop drinking.

"We have a job to do, Frosti, and we can't do it if you are pissed," the archer warned. So the next time the woman who poured the drinks came round, Frosti put a hand over his cup to signify he didn't want any more.

"Not drinking anymore, Frosti?" Gudrod asked of his guest.

"Ha ha, the arse hair is ready to get all serious," Halfdan burped, filling the air with his ale-stained breath.

"Finally, Frosti please do beg and grovel to me, I have time enough to spare. But I can assure you the answer will be no," Gudrod said. So Frosti told him everything. He told him that King Sigfred had given Jarl Solvi the chance to raid Britain but the King only did this so he could restore the old Jarl back onto Hordaland's seat and use Jarl Bergison to extend his own Kingdom. Frosti continued by saying Jarl Solvi needed the men to guard Hordaland whilst he was off raiding and in return the Northern Camps would get an annual tribute of a ship filled with seal pelts and food. As he described his Jarl's idea, Frosti knew it was fruitless. Solvi had greatly overestimated the Northern Camps' need for sustenance; their crater provided them with enough food and drink to last till Ragnorok so the proposal of a shipload of food really did nothing to persuade Gudrod. Although Halfdan did smile at the mention of the pelts, as they could be turned into silver and Halfdan loved silver.

"Jarl Solvi would be bloody thankful if you can help," Frosti ended his plea with. Gudrod pondered, Halfdan smiled, Eric rubbed his deformed hand and Finlit continued to scrape the last pieces of food from the bowl into his mouth.

"So your Jarl is raiding Britain?" Gudrod asked.

"Yes he is," Frosti said in surprise that he didn't get a straight no.

"Tell me more of Britain," Gudrod demanded.

"Well, I haven't heard much but the one or two traders I've spoken to say it is a land split by Kings who all have enough gold to fill this entire crater." Gudrod's inked face remained frozen even if Halfdan's smile filled his entire face. Noticing that the leader didn't even flinch at the thought of mountains of gold, Frosti carried on. "One bloody trader I met a few years back said their lands are fertile enough to grow thousands of different crops to feed multitudes of ship crews." Gudrod still didn't bite but Frosti noticed Finlit was now listening. However, Halfdan and Finlit didn't matter, Solvi needed an army and for that to be possible Frosti needed to win over Gudrod the Hunter. He looked round the steam-filled room, searching desperately for any weakness in Gudrod and it wasn't until Frosti saw Jik instinctively touching Thor's hammer round his neck that everything became clear. On almost every timber beam a god was etched; he could see depictions of Odin, Thor, Frig and Heimdallr. Frosti also noticed the pile of rune sticks upon a table near the back of the house. Rune sticks were cast by men or women who were able to read the message of the gods from the way they fell. Frosti knew Ospak, a warrior in Solvi's crew, could read the rune sticks and they were very rarely wrong. "The same man also told me that the majority of Britain no longer believes in the true gods and instead the people of that island have had their minds clouded by the nailed god,"

Frosti exclaimed in one last attempt to win over Gudrod. Eric, Halfdan and Finlit turned to face Gudrod who was pacing up and down before Frosti had mentioned the nailed God; now he stood still facing a carving of Thor. Gudrod ran his dirty fingers down each line of the carving, following carefully the hammer that the mighty Thor held.

"Do you know why they call me the hunter?" His voice was calm but stinging now.

"No, Lord," Frosti didn't know why he called Gudrod lord; he had never called anyone a lord, but there was something about the huge towering man that commanded authority.

"They call me the hunter because I have hunted and killed more Christians than you could ever imagine. I am not from here; I was born in a small village in Saxony. I saw the nailed god worshipers burn my parents, I saw them send women to the bottom of lakes with stones round their ankles. So I got my revenge. I've gouged the eyes out of their heads. I have shoved their precious crosses up so many arses I cannot even count, but I am still not satisfied."

"Well, the nailed God–" Frosti began to try and dig deeper and hit the rock underneath Gudrod's hard exterior but it seemed that blow had already been struck.

"I will come with you, Frosti, but I will not be your hounds, guarding your families. I and my men will be on those ships heading for Britain and I will hunt every last Christian on that fucking island." Halfdan cheered,

Finlit grabbed his sword and Eric smiled an evil smile that only had killing on the mind.

Jik and Frosti were ushered out of the longhouse as they heard one of them cast the rune sticks inside. The men of the northern camps were coming and that was an achievement, but Frosti was not sure how happy Solvi would be that Gudrod would want to join him on the raids. All of a sudden it had become dark. The lake was nothing more than a silent mist and the fires were left to crumbling ashes that hissed and growled as they died. Frosti and Jik were given a tent to themselves with new clothes and plenty of fresh water and bread.

"Well, that went well," Jik said as he laid his head on a small sack filled with straw.

"You think this has gone well? Bloody hells, Jik," Frosti said angrily. "We have lost our riches to a crazy fool and an even crazier fool is going to demand the world from Solvi." It was obvious Gudrod was never going to listen to Solvi, but why would he. Solvi Hrolfson was only just becoming a famous name but Gudrod the Hunter was a name known across Norway and Daneland. He was feared in Frisia and could have easily been feared in the Christian land of Frankia. "We better hope all he wants to do is captain a ship," Frosti added.

The next day they were woken by the shrieking of gulls and Frosti cursed the beasts under his breath. He scratched his bald head and pulled a few bread crumbs out of his fiery beard, choosing to eat them rather than throw them to the insects. Through the canvas, it was easy to tell the sun was directly above his head, meaning he had slept right through the morning. Small distorted shadows ran across the tent's walls. Jik wasn't asleep nor was he in the tent so Frosti peered out of the fastened door and could see no one.

"Where the bloody hells is everybody?" he said to himself. Frosti donned his leathers and jogged into the maze of canvas and timber huts. He rested his axe on his shoulder and could see only women weaving or scrubbing pottery as he lifted up about eight tent doors. He caught one woman twisting her hair into a bun and it quickly fell back down to her waist once Frosti poked his head in.

"Sorry, where is everybody?" he asked.

"They have all gone to the lake for the offering. Waste of time if you ask me," she hissed. Frosti ran to the lake, forgetting the aches and pains that still plagued his legs after the long journey north. The lake was almost as big as the Bjornafjorden, and it was definitely just as beautiful. It was the life source for the entire camp and that was where the sacrifices were being made. A giant pyre had been made from timber and bark, and on top of it was one man tied to a pole. In one hand he held a simple sword dented and bruised from battle and in the other he clutched at a few small white sticks.

"What is going on?" Frosti shouted towards Gudrod who was standing next to Halfdan at the front of the crowd.

"We are going to war, arse hair, and this man has sacrificed himself to Odin. He will cast the rune sticks before the fire takes him and he will shout our future before he is greeted like a hero in the watery halls of Valhalla," Halfdan yelled through his beard.

"This is bloody mad!" Frosti's voice was drowned out by the roar of the fire.

"What do you see?" a voice called from the crowd.

"What does Odin say?" another voice shouted.

The smoke almost became too thick to see the poor soul on top of the inferno but once a gust of wind blew the shroud away the dead man could be seen pointing at Frosti. A thousand eyes were on him now, but none of them meant as much as that one shrivelling finger.

"Well, that can't mean anything good," Frosti muttered to himself.

Carlnut

The Isle of Portland lay straight ahead and in truth, it wasn't an island, for it was connected to the mainland by a stretch of mud and sand that seemed to stick out impossibly out of the land. Carlnut could hear the waves crashing on the small cliffs below where he stood. Sicga had taken them through the fort at Wareham and towards Wessex's southern coast and since Carlnut could smell the saltiness of the sea, he felt happy and this happiness doubled when he saw his new home. It was a small land mass but it was the most Carlnut had ever owned. He could see a poorly built wooden palisade sharpened to points in the distance and knew his first job would be to repair the ruins. The small fortification overlooked a fishing village, which Sicga, Ealdormen Osric's son, said was called Fortunes Well. He then went on to describe that the name was from the Roman well in the middle of the village that some said holy water could be drawn from. Gulls shrieked overhead, searching and hovering over their prey whilst a score of small fishing boats floated gently on the winter's strangely calm sea. For a moment Carlnut forgot his burning need for battle; he had forgotten the amazing rush he got at Merantune where he killed Cyneheard the Atheling. An Atheling was the word the Saxons used for a nobleman with rights to the throne and it was discovered after a number of black-robed monks probed the body that he was in fact the brother of the King Sigeberht whom Cynewulf had deposed. Carlnut was in love for the second time, but this time with a shabby old fort, a fishing village and hundreds of mounds of mud and sand.

"Does that stretch of land flood at high tide, Father?" Carlnut pointed towards the arm that clung onto Portland almost as though at any moment it could float off into the sea.

"No, Lord," Father Osyth said in his grumpy voice. Osyth was a young priest around twenty years old; he had a full head of wavy black hair but an incurable snarl due to the fact he resented being sent away from the comforts of his church in Wessex's capital Winchester. Osric had demanded that a priest travel with them, which Carlnut had no use protesting. Carlnut hated the presence of priests almost as much as Osyth hated the presence of himself on the journey. Carlnut didn't trust their Christian magic and felt uneasy in a priest's company. The only priest he liked was Father Luyewn. Luyewn constantly pleaded for Carlnut to pray and give thanks to God but gave a blind eye to his Paganism;

however, if Osyth, Osric or King Beorhtric knew he was a Pagan he was sure he would be burnt alive.

"Father, you are more than welcome to turn back if you don't like my company," Carlnut jested.

"No, no, no Lord. I have a duty to King Beorhtric and to God. I will bless your household, Lord. Bless it in the name of God and in the name of the gracious King," Osyth said in a tone that seemingly failed to sense any hint of sarcasm in Carlnut's words.

Finally they reached the spit of land that must have been at least one kilometre long. To the right hand side of the sandy mounds lay a small sea lake with driftwood floating peacefully within it. It was a lake due to the fact that the other side of it was enclosed by a strange straight line of stones and rounded pebbles. The line was around two longboats wide and its length ran from the Island to beyond Carlnut's line of sight.

"Father, how long does the pebble shoreline go?" Carlnut asked.

"Three times the length you see here Lord and conveniently for you, it marks the boundary of your land," Father Osyth replied.

This shocked Carlnut, because he didn't know he was already standing on his own lands, and it meant the small village of Weymouth that they had stayed in the night before was also his. Something made him dismount his horse, bend down and grab the sand between his fingers. He opened his hands to let the tiny rock fragments float away into the sea wind. It wasn't a painfully cold day; the sun remained visible and the clouds did all they could to blanket them in some shade from the icy winds that hid behind them.

Now, he was on the straight beach path that led directly to the small fort from which he could almost fully see his island. Fortunes Well was hidden as it was on the southern part of the land, but the wooden palisade could be seen in more detail and looked even worse than Carlnut had feared. An earth wall looked like it had been started but then abandoned and Carlnut imagined this was either due to the lack of men, boggy conditions or even due to the fact the sandy spit offered enough protection anyway. If any land attack was to be made, the army would have to thin itself and walk carefully down the spit. Carlnut's small party found it easy enough but an army of one hundred would be slow and tired travelling down the uneven ground.

"Better than the fucking traitor's thatched house, eh," Arnum said, smiling towards the ruined fort. Carlnut smiled and looked back to see Engelhard's reaction but the wounded man had the face of a corpse. Engelhard had remained silent throughout the entire trip but no one said anything about it as they all sympathised with him. All five of them continued their trot towards the fort and Carlnut noticed the glint of two spear points on what must have been the ramparts behind the palisade. Noticing Carlnut's confusion, Sicga pulled his horse up next to Carlnut's.

"Your lady is already here, Lord. Earl Eafled has provided you with a small garrison of thirty men, half of which he said you may keep under your protection as a thank you gift for your actions in Merantune," the muscular man said.

"Selwyn is in there?" Carlnut asked as if he hadn't heard anything else Sicga had said.

"Yes Lord, she arrived a few days back," Sicga said. Carlnut couldn't believe it; he was suddenly scared and nervous, then delighted and overwhelmed with joy. He kicked Gladdy's rump with his legs and sent the horse into a gallop. Gladdy was a young grey and black stallion that Carlnut had gotten very close to ever since he rode him to Merantune.

"Lord!" a voice cried out.

"Be careful!" another one yelled. But they were just forgotten words taken by the salty wind. Selwyn was inside. Carlnut hadn't seen her in almost eight months and at one point, he believed he would never see her again. The fort had two large wooden doors that opened as Carlnut approached. Gladdy's feet dug into the sand and the ground was treacherous enough to break any horse's ankles, but he was a strong horse and instead kicked sand into a dust cloud behind him. About twenty metres before the doors the land became hard rock. A part of Carlnut wanted to dismount his horse again and fumble at the ground and thank the gods it all belonged to him, but instead he was filled with the overwhelming desire to find his woman and embrace her.

For some reason he expected Selwyn to be inside waiting for him but she was not. However, the search for her around his new home allowed Carlnut to get used to his surroundings. The fortification had a few thatched houses within it, all of which were damaged in some way and one was completely missing its roof. There was a court yard where Carlnut could envisage his men sparring and practising their swordplay. Much to his annoyance, there was a basic chapel, which displayed the Christian's nailed cross hanging from above the door. *At least Father Luyewn will be pleased*, he thought to himself. The whole complex was very circular; a round spiked wooden palisade wall surrounded the houses and the chapel was directly in the middle. A little to the left, almost touching the chapel, was the biggest building in the fort, which compared to the rest was in decent shape. There was an oak or birch door held together with iron bars that appeared to split the wood in three pieces. Two spearmen stood outside the door in amazement that Carlnut had arrived without their prior knowledge. They shuffled on their feet and straightened their backs.

"Is Selwyn in there?" Carlnut asked.

"N . . . no Lord," the guard spoke with a stutter. "I . . . I am happy that you are finally here, Lord."

"Do I know you, boy?" The guard was a very young man scarcely turned fifteen. His face was covered in bumps and pock scars.

"No Lord, I have heard what you did at King Cynewulf's gathering," he awkwardly announced. Carlnut was bored with the conversation with his admirer and decided to proceed into his hall. Drapes and fabrics hung from giant oak pillars that shot up from the floor to the steep roof, mimicking the trees they used to be. Cob-webbed benches were placed on either side of the hall and a large chair stood where an altar would have been, had the hall been a chapel. The sight of his small throne should have pleased Carlnut, and what he could see of it did, but he was far too focused on the finely dressed man seated comfortably upon rushes that were carefully set on the chair. He had short combed black hair and was stringing a golden hand harp when Carlnut walked into the hall.

"Get out of my seat, harpist!" Carlnut shouted in a fit of rage. The musician jolted in sudden realisation that he wasn't alone. Carlnut recognised the false lord as the man who followed his woman like a bird follows a fishing trawler.

"My Lord, there is no need to shout at him, he is a nice man," came the voice of a woman from round a corner where the candles were not lit. It was Selwyn, her ginger hair flowing in the small breeze that somehow found its way into the hall. She looked beautiful. Bedfrith made his way out of Carlnut's hall, sulking and holding his head down as if weights hung from his ears. Selwyn was wearing a fine dress fit for a Lady; it had a long, leaf-green cloth that tied the dress together at her waist. The colour was a striking golden design of patterns woven over each other. They both took a step forward and clasped each other so tight that Carlnut felt his breath slowing.

"Where have you been, Carlnut?" Selwyn had tears in her eyes but they were not formed by sadness but from an incomparable joy. "I have missed you so much, my love."

"I've made a life for us and our family," Carlnut said wearily. That was true. Almost two months ago, Carlnut rotted within four boring mud walls but now he had stone and wooden walls and tens of rooms to explore along with a land to govern.

"And I hope we can try and make a life as soon as possible," Selwyn said with a hint of cheekiness to her voice.

The pair stayed up all night talking and remembering what their touches felt like. In the morning, Carlnut woke up in his fur-covered bed that could have easily fit six men the same size as him. He felt like a king. A fire blazed in front of him that must have been lit by one of the servants that Earl Eafled had provided. Flames danced and the sparks sang and Carlnut hugged the naked Selwyn, her breasts pushed sweetly against his flushing skin. At that moment of bliss, Father Osyth creaked open the door. Selwyn had to grab for sheets to hide her nakedness but Carlnut made no such effort. Instead he stood, stark naked and Father Osyth blushed, held up an apologetic hand and tried to sneak out like nothing had happened.

"What do you want, Priest?" Carlnut enquired with fury in his voice.

"Er, Lord. Men are waiting in the hall ready for the oaths and appointments," Osyth said awkwardly.

"And there they will stay!" At this response the young, snarling priest ushered himself out of the room.

Carlnut turned to Selwyn, smiled and threw himself back into bed laughing. She laughed too and at that moment love was all they felt, no anger, no hatred and no responsibility.

It was around an hour later when Carlnut entered the smoky hall. He wore a warrior's garb. A red tunic, with golden waves sewn into its collar and hem, clung wonderfully to his muscled body. His long black hair was bundled with red ribbons and a silver broach clasped his dark green cloak to his neck. Under his tunic and cloak a small amulet hung round his neck. Selwyn had given him a small bone hammer to wear with her name etched into the side of it. At least that's what she told him last night as he could neither read or write. However, since she was a Christian, Carlnut saw this gesture as one of eternal unity between him and her and nothing had ever filled him with happiness as much as that gift had. The hall was full of people. Some sat on the benches and others stood leaning on the posts and upon their spears. He noticed one man scratching at his groin towards the back of the hall, moving towards the now-closed doors that blocked any more villagers from Weymouth or Fortunes Well from getting in. The man caught Carlnut's gaze and shuffled into the crowd where he became just another face in the mix.

"Today you look upon your new lord, the great Lord Carlnut. And before god you will make oaths to serve and protect him, you will lay your weapons at his feet, kiss his hands and bind your life to his. In return–" said Father Osyth, who was perched on top a small stool and looked straight at Carlnut, "–he will protect you and reward you if you please him. Most importantly, our great Lord, our blessed God will reward you." Osyth was confident and Carlnut noticed that whenever he spoke of his God he was invincible; his snarl turned to a faint smile and his step had a certain bounce to it. The men who were standing up then sat down in preparation for a long meeting. The sound of swords and axes clattering against the floor actually made Carlnut smile as he knew he was in the presence of warriors. Father Osyth pulled out a tattered, ink-scrawled parchment and was about to name the first name on his list until Carlnut waved an objecting hand. Carlnut was now seated on his Lord's chair, which was plush with rushes and carpets. Selwyn sat on a slightly smaller chair next to him whereas Father Luyewn was on a stool to his right, his back arched but face full of delight.

"You first, Priest," Carlnut said, pointing directly at a confused Osyth.

"Me, Lord?" Carlnut nodded. "I am sworn to God only and after that I give my services to our great King Beorhtric."

"I thought Priests were meant to be smart." Carlnut looked at Father Luyewn hoping for an approving glance. It had already become common knowledge the two priests did not enjoy each other's company. "The King of Wessex and his Ealdormen Osric have given you to me for one year and therefore you will swear me an oath. You must not send any messages out of Portland without letting the Grand Priest Luyewn read them. In fact you must not so much as piss without him knowing." Father Osyth looked so shocked he could have fainted but somehow he remained steady. In fact the whole room was stunned. Assessing his options, Father Osyth bowed his head and whispered some faint words. Carlnut cleared his throat and stared at the plainly robed priest.

"I swear my service to you Lord Carlnut and accept your rule as long as I am in your service," the young priest said, defeated.

"Great, now you may read from your page," Carlnut said as he flicked his hand up to signify the priest to resume his work. The first name Father Osyth read out was Arnum's. Arnum and Carlnut had become good friends and fought side by side outnumbered against King Cynewulf's attackers. Fighting alongside a man created an unbreakable bond stronger than brothers. Arnum's oath giving was easy; he knelt down in front of Carlnut's raised chair, placed his sword at his feet and pledged his life to the service of Lord Carlnut.

"The noble Sicga," Osyth announced. The great presence of the man strolled through the crowd as if he had enough confidence in him to fight one hundred battles.

"I pledge my life to yours," Sicga said whilst his knees sank to the ground and he lay his fine sword at Carlnut's feet. "I pledge my sword and my council but I ask of you one favour." Carlnut looked down at Sicga's huge hunched frame and nodded. "If my father the

Ealdorman Osric dies I will need to be released from my oath and allowed to govern his lands." Sicga looked up and smiled because Carlnut was smiling too.

"Of course, noble Sicga," Carlnut said. Before the next name was read out, Carlnut asked Arnum to join Sicga at the front.

"These men are fierce warriors and that is why I have awarded them with the following positions. Arnum is my personal guard and will be in charge of my household guard if and when I create one. And this man–" Carlnut said, opening his hands out to Sicga who looked fierce in his shining mail, "–this man is in charge of all the other fighting men on my lands." Their positions pleased both men tremendously. Some of the seated men hit the smiling warriors on the shoulder in congratulations when they returned to their places in the hall. Carlnut sat up in anticipation when the next name was read out.

"Engelhard," Father Osyth shouted, looking up from the parchment he held out in front of him at arm's length. "Engelhard!" he said again, this time shouting louder and causing two pigeons that were nested in the roof rafters to flap crazily until they found themselves perched in another corner and once again content. Unbothered by the lack of a response Osyth was about to read the next name until a figure must have caught his eye. For some reason, Engelhard had decided not to shout out to let the priest know he was here. Instead, he just slipped through the seated crowd like a fox hunting an unaware hare. Engelhard's eyes were fierce and direct as he stared straight through Carlnut, begging him to make the first move. Sometime between his injury and then he had shaved his blonde hair off revealing a scarred stubbly head that looked cracked where the dried blood had flaked off.

"Do you swear to serve your Lord?" Father Luyewn said, startling the hall with his first words during the entire proceedings. Engelhard shook his head once at Luyewn and again at Carlnut.

"You do not?" Carlnut was confused. He knew Engelhard had changed so much since his dismemberment but didn't know he would go as far as to out rightly deny him in front of a hall that was bursting to the rafters. Osyth stood silently, shocked at the defiance and Luyewn straightened his back, creating cracking sounds that sounded like the earth ripping open. "Why do you not swear your allegiance to me?" Carlnut stupidly asked, knowing full well he would only get a vacant, scarred face peering right back at him. The once talkative soldier raised a tired arm towards Selwyn, causing her to lean forward and for the first time look interested.

"Would you like to swear an Oath to me instead?" Selwyn asked. He nodded and then, after various nods and points, it was arranged. Engelhard had silently sworn an oath to protect Selwyn till death and Carlnut accepted that. The rest of the meeting was long but easy enough. Men came to the high chair, kneeled and swore their lives to their lord and in return Carlnut would reward them with a smile and nod and a few were given positions. A blacksmith named Ordmaer had been given the task of forging a sword for every soldier in Portland. He originally hesitated at the order but after a small pouch of coins was laid at his table the following night, he began his work.

Other than Carlnut's treatment of Father Osyth and Engelhard's sheer stubbornness, the most surprising bit of the evening was the appointment of the snotty-nosed, spot-covered stutterer who had greeted them into the church. Carlnut's hammer amulet burnt a hole in his chest every time he looked at Osbert, and so Carlnut believed the gods were sending him a sign. As a lord, Carlnut wanted to be seen as generous and therefore gave Osbert the role of Portland's Steward. This meant whenever Carlnut was away he would be in charge of the settlement and lands surrounding it. Normally a lord would reward his most trusted advisor and experienced man with such a position, but Carlnut didn't know anybody and the people he did know were needed for other positions.

"Lord, may I offer my council?" Osyth had said after the meeting was adjourned. "Osbert is just a young boy; he has no skills to be noted. Might I suggest the fine Beric who did tend to this establishment before you were given it by our great King?" Carlnut stopped and signalled for Selwyn and Luyewn to carry on to their rooms without them. The fact that Osyth didn't like Osbert made Carlnut want to stick with his decision even more.

"Is Beric the fat man who couldn't get up after he knelt, or the old man whose skin drags across the floor like a boat's sails when it is being pulled to shore?" Carlnut asked, getting uncomfortably close to the priest who was becoming increasingly annoying. Osyth saw the amulet hung round Carlnut's neck and gave him an inquisitive look. His eyes bulged in their sockets like foxes in a hen coop and a wicked smile spread across his face that twisted into a terrifying scowl.

"Very well Lord, you know best," the Father said and then spun round and tottered off back into the hall to presumably head towards the chapel. The plentiful torches fluttered as Carlnut walked down the narrow corridor that adjoined his quarters to the hall. He saw a mouse scurry into a hovel and felt a drip of moisture fall onto the back of his neck. His mind was stale as he walked down the hall; he knew he might have made a terrible decision in appointing Osbert but he trusted his Gods, and Odin or Thor saw something in the pus-covered boy. Light from inside his quarters emerged from the bottom and the sides of the closed door and a few rays of light penetrated the door as well. Selwyn must have somehow sensed that Carlnut was on the other side of the door as she opened it as soon as Carlnut was about to knock. She still wore the fine clothes, which originally confused Carlnut who expected her to be in her night clothes. He noticed a few shadows floating in another room.

"Who is here?" Carlnut asked.

"Luyewn and Earl Eafled," Selwyn replied with a hint of shame in her voice.

"Eafled is in there? For the sake of Odin, I wasn't expecting him." Carlnut desperately tried to wipe the dust off his red tunic whilst Selwyn straightened his cloak's broach. A huge man ducked through the gap in the wall from one room to the other and stared at Carlnut and then tugged at his big bushy beard. He then walked across the room towards the window, which at this point was useless as it was pitch dark outside other than the dim, mysterious light of the stars. Earl Eafled was nothing like he had expected. Selwyn did describe him as a kind man with a lovely face, but the huge man who was fascinated by the window looked none of these things.

"Earl Eafled, I owe you . . ." Carlnut began, trying his best to sound like a lord. But this effort was in all in vain when the big man turned round, smiled and then laughed.

"Over there, Lord," the hairy man said. The actual Earl Eafled was leaning against the mud and wattle wall, smirking.

"M'Lord, I see you have met my oath man, Cuth," Eafled said. Cuth was huge enough to scare any man and even Carlnut was slightly nervous in his presence. "I must admit, I really did not expect you to mess up on your first day. Nevertheless, you are new to this, you will soon learn how to run a fort, own land and control people," Eafled spoke with a calming authority to his voice. His words were calmly said but well chosen. The

Earl wore a dirt brown tunic, and tied to a wonderful lace belt was a fine sword that hung from its scabbard, which Carlnut could not take his eyes off. "This is a fleeting visit but I suggest we dine with each other as much as we can and discuss the certain land and neighbour issues we both currently face."

"Yes, Earl, whenever you want. I will ride to yours immediately," Carlnut said.

"We can also see how well the child steward fares whilst you are visiting my fort," Eafled said with a wink as he turned and signalled to Cuth to start leaving. Cuth left with the Earl; the huge man had to bend down through every single threshold, whilst even if the Earl had jumped, he would have only just touched the worm-infested beam on top of the door.

The day had been long and he felt it, but Carlnut was saddened that he hadn't even seen daylight that day. *I will ride tomorrow and search my lands,* he thought to himself as he took his breeches off. Selwyn appeared like a Valkyrie in the bedroom, carrying a scabbard. It was a fine leather scabbard with tassels and threads hanging off at seemingly random areas. The man in Hordaland who made it told him that it signified the threads of life everyone lived. Three Norns sat at the roots of Yggdrasil threading the lives of men and would at any moment cut the thread to end a man's mortal life. Carlnut found himself wondering whether at this point the Norns who sat at the base of Yggdrasil, the tree of life, continued to spin his thread even if he was surrounded by Christians. Regardless of this, Thor and Odin must have been smiling down at him from Asgard as they had reunited Carlnut with Karla, his sword. Karla was Carlnut's first sword and was the only thing he had from his old life; it connected him to his Gods and to Hordaland. As he unsheathed Karla from her bed, she awoke in a glimmering whistle of glory. She was beautiful, with waving rivets gliding though the steel and upon the pommel was a silver raven's beak, which felt as good as a woman's body as Carlnut stroked it.

As beautiful as Karla was, Carlnut knew she would look like a goddess when she was drenched in Earl Cynric's blood.

Solvi

"He took a quarter of our men, Solvi; some of them weren't even his followers," Eddval said.

"That's why we should rip the bastard limb from limb," Umiston added.

The embers of the fire were beginning to die and men were starting to head back to their longhouses, tents or shelters. Solvi sat silent with his most trusted warriors who all offered their advice on what to do about Chief Jikop. Eddval was there sharpening one of his dirks with a whetstone whilst his wife Aesa, who was pregnant with the Pintojuk Bergison's child, messed with Eddval's long, bright blonde hair. Rollaug Danson sat swaying on a tree stump, like a branch in the wind. His gut, which stretched out bigger than anyone's around the fire, rumbled like an untamed beast as the ale swirled around it. The grey-haired Umiston, who was the Chief of Blornvag, scratched at his scar, which almost partitioned his face, and poked the dead fire with a mossy stick. Gisha, Solvi's favourite Chief, sat next to him. She was dressed in a real warrior's garbs with a leather jerkin and brown paint in the shape of a hand covering her face. She was nonchalantly picking at her yellowing teeth with one of her axes, unaware of the blood trickling down her lips from the point on the axe's head. She had short brown hair that didn't get in her eyes and face when she fought.

"Umiston is right; we need to kill the traitor," Gisha muttered with a mouthful of axe.

Solvi finally spoke. "We need to find him first and when I see the bastard I will let my sword; Gutstretcher sing." Solvi felt Gutstretcher calling for blood; it had failed to kill Pintojuk Bergison, and it longed to slice King Sigfred open, but now it sung and begged to kill Jikop. In the early hours of the day when the sun hadn't touched the land and the birds slept in their tree nests, Jikop had left the camp. Around fifty men followed him with horses, swords, spears, shields and food. Jikop had raided some of the storehouses, stealing salted meats, barley and ale.

"Eddval, send some scouts ahead to see where the fuck the grey-haired piece of worm shit has gone. Umiston, double the number of men on sentry duty. Gisha, I need you to ride with the scouts and if you see the bastard, follow him at a distance and see what he is doing; he couldn't have gone far," Solvi said, and his instructions caused everyone to leave the fire and head off to prepare for their duties. Solvi stood up and wiped the dirt from his backside. The weather had improved incredibly since the great snowstorm, which meant the new boats were no longer skeletons on the beach. Instead, each stood like a proud warrior waiting to be dressed.

It was dark, terribly dark. The lingering light was obliterated by the rapidly falling night. The once salmon and purple sky transformed into a vast expanse of jet-black that engulfed the entire settlement. A canopy of luminous stars materialised amongst the ocean of blackness. Some were dull, merely flickering into existence every now and then, but there was an adequate number of shimmering stars to faintly illuminate the dark, moonless night. Solvi waded into the shallows of the Bjornafjorden, being pulled back by the dark green weeds that grew miserably in the pebbly ground. The fjord glistened, mirroring the dazzling assemblage of glittering stars. The faint wind brushed against the water's surface; the ripples ruffled the stillness of the deep purple liquid and shattered the reflection of the trees that hung like creatures over the shallows. Solvi clutched onto a small leather pouch, which bulged unevenly with its contents. He opened the pouch up and took out the pure white rune sticks within it. For a moment, he seemed not to know what to do with the sticks and just stood motionless, looking at the ripples in the fjord. At each ripple the stars would flash and Solvi knew the Gods were with him, which meant then was the perfect time to throw his rune sticks. He released the white sticks and they flew through the sky glistening and swirling almost as if they were being carried by a hidden spirit. Each of them landed individually, and each of them floated upon the surface, spinning and jittering. Solvi threw them towards the shore as the waves were being sucked back in towards the centre of the fjord so the sticks floated calmly back to him. A murder of crows flew overhead shrieking crazily at the patterns the rune sticks made. Solvi knelt with the freezing water up to the bottom of his neck with strands of his blonde hair fanning out where the water washed away the wax. However, he felt nothing but elation.

"It is my fate," Solvi whispered. "It is my fate," he said again a lot louder, scaring a heron that perched on top of lichen-covered rock in the middle of the fjord. He saw his future, he was certain, he saw himself leading a fleet of over twenty ships. He saw Frosti laughing so hard he was clutching his chest. He saw a group of warriors standing behind him holding pointed blades; one looked like Gisha and another man with an otter pelt round his neck was smiling.

"The Gods can present you the future but it often can be distorted," his father had said whilst he showed Solvi how to read rune sticks. A warm salty tear ran down Solvi's face at the thought of his father, but he wiped the tear with the knowledge that he would one day meet Hrolf again in the watery halls of Valhalla. The night was peaceful. The strange creatures that dwelled in the woods at night danced and scuttled about, desiring to curse Solvi but the power of the Bjornafjorden kept them away. Water poured down Solvi's body as he walked out of the fjord, giving him a shiny appearance. He could see far off in the distance, on another shore of the blessed fjord, the five ships that would help his fate become reality.

One of the strange night creatures was rustling through the thick brambles and thorny leaves, stomping and panting. Solvi reached for Gutstretcher, which rested on top of a round rock, and he released it from its scabbard. The sword, like the lake, glistened and almost came to life with the dim reflection of the stars. As the panting grew, so did the beating of Solvi's heart, but he was confident. How could he die now? His fate was shown to him and he would live to see it with his own eyes. Bumbling out of the woods was Rollaug Danson and not one of the grotesque daemons that were meant to hide within the stumps or disguise themselves as tree snakes hanging from branches. Although, Rollaug the fat chef did almost look like a daemon; sweat ran down his rounded face only to get trapped in the layers of fat under his chin.

"Jikop," he said trying to beat off his breathlessness to be able to form words. "He is in the village," Rollaug finally managed to say before he had to lean against a mushroom-covered tree. Solvi's eyes widened. He sheathed Gutstretcher and ran off into the dark-drowned woods. He wore only his trousers, which were dripping sodden and uncomfortable against his body. Thorns whipped against his face, scratching and splitting his skin. A tusked boar saw Solvi running and charged off deeper into the woods. His feet stung and were bloodied from the jutting rocks and knotted roots that littered the muddy floor, but still Solvi kept running. Gutstretcher was tight in his hand and seemed to swerve about almost on its own to avoid being lodged in a thicket or trapped within some brambles. Solvi could feel the night becoming thicker and pressing down, suffocating him slowly as he ran chaotically though the thick maze of woodland. The densely packed trees loomed high above but remained still despite the icy breeze that continued to flow high around them. He was blind but was able to follow the faint sounds of men shouting. Whether it was Solvi's men shouting in triumph or Jikop's men gloating, Solvi did not know, but he needed to, and that need kept him going through the sharp, hateful woods.

Finally, Solvi could see the clearing. However, he did not feel the relief he wanted to when he got there. He wanted to see Jikop's men lying on the damp ground with spears deep in their chests, but instead he saw the back of a shield wall. From what he could see, there must have been around forty men all bundled up in around four thick layers of flesh, bone, steel, leather and shield. To the left of the shield wall was a steep embankment that dropped down to a small stream, and this provided the wall with cover towards its flank. Solvi tried to peer over the wall to see the other wall forming, but had to stay hidden and quiet as he had no idea whose wall he was looking at. He hoped to see a familiar face but he knew all his brothers would be at the front of the wall ready for the enemy to ram into them. Solvi had been in many shield walls and not one he would like to repeat, for a shield wall was a terrible place that stunk of piss, blood and sweat. A shiver of unease ran down his spine as he thought of the hundreds of friends he had lost in the chaotic stabbing and thrusting that occurred at the heart of the wall, where shield boss touched boss and blades whistled blindly underneath and spears thumped into the oak of the shield hoping to catch flesh. It was at this moment that Solvi caught a glimpse of a familiar face. Sadly for Solvi, it was Chief Jikop; his hair was untied and its grey strands lay freely on his back. Most of the men with him wore leather helmets that covered their heads and faces but the fact Jikop was there made it obvious that Solvi was on the wrong side of the battle. Solvi's stomach wanted to find the floor and his bladder wanted to loosen. There was no way to get to the other side without being spotted by one of Jikop's men. He could try and sneak round, but he risked being outnumbered and slaughtered or captured and then most likely tortured. Solvi muttered a small prayer to Thor to give his men strength and then wondered who would be leading the line. Umiston or Gisha would have been the best candidates to lead the shield wall, but it was Eddval that Solvi could hear.

"You are a bastard traitor and your mother should have kept her legs shut," he roared followed by a chorus of other jeers as one man would shout to his opposing number.

"I can't wait to use your women as a horse," another man cried. When the two walls were preparing for the clash, you could always see the small glints of eyes peering through the enemy shields and you knew they would be the men you would have to kill.

Solvi was then startled by an uncomfortably loud noise that surely could have awoken a sleeping drunk, but luckily none of the men in Jikop's wall even stirred. A man came stumbling through one of the twisted thickets in the wood, rubbing his hands. Solvi did not recognise the drunken soldier, but he did see his opportunity. Everything seemed impossible and Solvi thought he would never be able to kill the man without surely alerting someone. It had to be one quick invisible motion. And that is how it was. Solvi did not let the man leave the woods; instead, he stalked him, checking every step and using every deep shadow the night provided. As the man stopped to scratch his arse, Solvi moved. Quicker than lightning and quieter than a dead man, Gutstretcher sliced the man's neck. Blood made black from the night burst out of him like an autumn waterfall. He went to grasp his neck but Solvi had already covered his mouth and eased his fall. After a few desperate jerks, he was dead. His leathers were covered in blood, but Solvi was confident that no one would notice it as he dressed exactly like the dead man. He wore one arm ring, a stained leather helmet and carried a battered sword that would have been only good enough to cut bread. Solvi left the man's worn sword in his hand so he would be welcomed into Valhalla as a warrior. He then hung Gutstretcher from the simple brown belt that he also stole from the dead man. The only thing of any value that the man carried was a bone-handled short sword; it was not valuable in terms of silver but for the fact a shield wall was such a tight space that it was difficult to be able to swing a longer sword around.

After donning the dead man's clothes, Solvi became hidden; he was just another warrior with a thirst for battle. An angry beast rose inside of him and he did have the unquenchable thirst to kill. The fear he originally felt was not the fear of dying but the feeling of helplessness, but now he was a wolf amongst sheep, a silent raven amongst mice. He shuffled into the ranks, annoying the man next to him who was a muscled hulk and had great beard tied into knots round his rotted teeth.

"We are going to spill their blood and rape their women," the bearded man grunted. Solvi only nodded. They were in the second row of the wall and Jikop was nowhere to be seen. People in the second row of a wall had the job of blocking high axe blows and flying spears from hitting the man in front but Solvi didn't even have a shield or a true idea what he was doing. At first it seemed like a simple plan; disguise himself, find Jikop and then kill him. But now in the tangle of men he was a warrior amidst warriors. Everyone there wanted to kill and there was a slight part of him that did just want to stab at the faceless men in the other wall.

"Forward," Jikop shouted.

"Forward!" Another voice yelled. And the wall moved forward. Step by step, until Solvi could smell the men who hid behind the shields opposite.

"This is going to be a fucking fight; let's kill the bastards," the bearded man said. He was holding his shield into the gap that Solvi should have been covering, and in his other hand he held a war axe. An axe was both a terrible weapon in a shield wall and a terrific one. It could splinter the enemy's shield until it was only shards of oak on the ground, but it was horribly slow and took a lot of effort to swing. There were men who knew exactly how to use the axe; the bearded man was one of those. Three arm rings pinched his skin, almost snapping from the enormity of his muscles. Solvi could hear stomping feet and knew that Eddval's or Gisha's or even Umiston's shield wall was slowly marching toward them.

"Who are you?" Solvi asked. He had no idea why and could only put it down to the sympathy he felt for his neighbour.

"Hundi," he said as he adjusted his shield to ready for the impact of the charging shield wall.

"I will feast with you one day," Solvi said as he buried the bone-handled short sword deep into Hundi's chest. No one noticed the trickery as at that very same moment the two immovable wooden walls crashed into each other. Oak splinters flew up in the air. Curses flung from side to side. One man far to Solvi's left screamed as his arm got crushed by the impact. Solvi had stolen Hundi's shield and was now blocking an axe that swung down mercilessly. At one point the metal broke through the wood and Solvi could see the blood dripping from the hungry weapon. Fearing death, Solvi firmly clamped onto his short sword and thrust it into the back of the man fighting in front of him. He screamed like a woman giving birth and he turned round to look at his killer only for Solvi to relax his shield arm and allow an axe to freely swing onto the man's head. Not even an iron helmet could have stopped the almighty blow and Solvi now stared into the soulless eyes of a man with a blade embedded deep within his skull. Luckily, a man on Solvi's right who had filled the gap Hundi had made then danced into the vacuum Solvi's next victim had created. Somehow Solvi was surrounded by five new neighbours who were all cursing and swinging steel aimlessly. Solvi had to climb over a dead man's body as the wall advanced slowly. Somewhere along the line of blood-soaked men, Jikop screamed.

"Push, you dirty maggots, push." The axe that wildly swung ahead had now stopped and when Solvi climbed over the body of the wielder his heart sank. It was Killig; Killig was a huge man who had helped Solvi take Osoyro; he was a good friend of Frosti's and a great warrior. He was also terribly cursed by Loki the trickster god, so there was relief that that curse was not going to follow him to Britain. Killig's death was a sign that Solvi had to find Jikop. If he could kill the Chief, then Jikop's men may lose heart and no more of Solvi's men had to die.

"Where is Chief Jikop?" Solvi asked the man to his left who was wincing from an axe blow that was harassing his shield. He didn't speak in response but instead whipped his head to the left, signalling that

Jikop was somewhere along the line. A singing blade sliced through a gap and caught Solvi on the arm. Another narrowly missed his neck. Blood trickled out of his fresh wound and dripped onto the already blood-stained ground. Men put their entire body weight into the back of Solvi as the men at the front put all their strength against their shields trying desperately to push the other wall back.

"Push, push, push," Jikop shouted again. As everyone pushed, Solvi did not and instead he found himself in the third layer of the wall. A stinking fellow turned and scowled at Solvi, not knowing who it was but hating his cowardice all the same. The wall was no longer as dense with bodies. Instead, there was a saddening deposit of men behind. On the next shout to push, Solvi pulled back so that he was at the rear of the wall. His arm pounded like a drum but he smiled as there was enough room to freely move left and right along the wall. Solvi tried to spot Jikop's grey hair swishing wildly as the Chief's sword stabbed and swung, but it was just too dark; instead, he saw a tangle of men who all looked identical. Being in the wall had filled his body with so much adrenaline that it made him run forward back into the mass of bodies. He shoved a person out of the way to ram into the back of one of Jikop's men who was engaged at the heart of the fight.

"Fuck," the man screamed as the force of Solvi caused him to move slightly out of line. A tomahawk that was thrown from somewhere saw the gap and danced straight through it, embedding itself into the disorientated man's neck.

"You clumsy bastard," a voice bellowed from Solvi's left. It was Jikop. He had blood running down a broken nose and half of his ear was missing. Solvi turned away ignoring the Chief's anger as he had to parry away some searching spears that peeked through the tiniest of holes within the wall. He had no idea what to do. He could have stabbed Jikop then and there, but surely someone would have seen it. The other men Solvi had killed were just faces in a crowd, whereas Jikop was their leader and all men looked to their leader for inspiration and courage. Instead, someone in the other wall helped Solvi make his decision. A giant war axe came hammering down upon Jikop's shield and he staggered from the blow. Dazed and confused, Jikop tried adjusting his shield but blows with similar if not more force rang on it again.

"The Chief has taken a knock; we will fall back for a moment, keep pushing, you stinking arses," Solvi shouted and to his surprise the men followed his order. Jikop was kneeling down with his head spinning and Solvi just stared at the traitor. They were surrounded by bodies and Solvi could not tell whose side they had been fighting on but hoped they all died with a sword in hand so he could feast and talk with them about this battle in Valhalla.

"Now let's kill that bastard upstart," Jikop said, tugging optimistically at Solvi's wounded arm. Solvi stayed put and pushed Jikop's hand off his. As confident as a bird committing itself to the air, Solvi took off his helmet. His hair, having been completely drenched by sweat, now stuck flat to his scalp and Jikop looked as if he had seen Nidhogg, the dragon who gnaws at the roots of Yggdrasil. His bruised and battered eyes looked in astonishment as he tried to speak but the words would not come; instead, all that could be heard was the ringing of swords and crashing of shields behind them.

"Stand up and die like a warrior," Solvi said finally, ditching the bone-handled short sword and unsheathing Gutstretcher. Jikop fumbled about for his sword and found nothing; he was lost and naked without a weapon, but Solvi wanted a fight; he wanted his men and Jikop's men to see who the right man to follow was. Solvi did not care for Jikop's trip to Valhalla but knew if he slaughtered the unarmed traitor he would be branded as a coward.

"Pick it up," Solvi said, pointing Gutstretcher towards a dead man's body. Some men in the fighting shield walls saw the standoff and ignored it until they could properly see who stood there. However, whichever one of Jikop's men turned to see their leader was shortly punished by swinging steel. Jikop was tired, battered and weak. The injuries he had sustained in the wall made him wince as he bent down and picked up a dead man's sword. Solvi darted forward, and ran the very edge of Gutstretcher against Jikop's shoulder. The slice was just enough to draw blood but wasn't enough for Jikop to feel much pain. Jikop levelled his dented sword and straightened his vision; he was now in another world, the world between life and death. He knew he would have to kill Solvi and Solvi saw this determination in the Chief's eyes.

"You could have been rich from the raid on Britain!" Solvi shouted to the tired man who was trying to build the energy for an attack. "But instead you decided to kill yourself and most of your men!" That fact was true; most of the dead bodies were of Jikop's men. He was outnumbered and out-skilled. Solvi lowered Gutstretcher, enticing the attack and Jikop fell for the bait. As Jikop charged, Solvi danced out of the way. He sliced Gutstretcher against the Chief's hamstrings and again drew blood, but this time Jikop was affected by the blow. He fell onto the frozen ground. Solvi admired the man's determination to continue fighting as Jikop used a tree stump to help himself back up. "I have one question before I kill you. Why?" Jikop darted forward hoping to find an unguarded leg or thigh but Solvi was too quick and took a few steps back whilst lowering Gutstretcher to defend against the lunge.

"You are not a man worthy of following. You make deals with fat arse kings and allow your men to marry the enemy. You will destroy Hordaland," Jikop said, desperately clutching his sword.

"You can't believe that, Jikop," Solvi laughed.

"You are cursed, Solvi Hrolfson, cursed. I have seen it, my men have seen it; following you will mean nothing but death and failure." Those were Jikop's last words as Solvi had grown tired of dancing and tormenting. Gutstretcher burst straight through Jikop's chest and bathed wonderfully in his blood.

The yellow shining sun started rising from the ground. It filled the sky with the mighty colours of red and splashed the clouds with endless rays of pink. It was bright and mesmerising as it invited Solvi to stare, deep into the horizon.

"I'm sorry, Chief Jikop, I have seen my fate and it is grand," Solvi said as he gave one last twist of his sword, churning the flesh and mangling the organs within Jikop's body. Solvi hadn't noticed that the fighting to his right had stopped and all the men, regardless of whom they followed that night, watched Solvi's victory. A piercing cheer echoed through Hordaland as three quarters of the men lifted their spears and shields up in the air in triumph. Around twelve men, who must have been Jikop's hearth-men, looked sullen as they had known they had made the wrong choice. Solvi turned and watched as ribbons of golden sunlight spilled into the woods that had left his body bloodied. The trees were a black silhouette against the brilliant gold sky. The dew drops, adorning the forest, seemed to glow with their own golden radiance. After the horrors of the night, daybreak brought a glimmer of warmth that ignited the birds into a wonderful chorus of high-pitched tweets. After admiring the innocence of the once-harsh woods, he turned to the scared traitors. He wrenched Gutstretcher free from Jikop's body and rested one foot upon the tangle of flesh and bone.

"Kneel! Kneel to your Jarl you gutless worms that decided this man-" Solvi squished his foot down upon Jikop's unrecognisable body "-was fit enough to lead. You have one chance; if anyone wants to fight me they are welcome to try but prepare yourselves for a trip to Valhalla." Solvi could see a few men stirring, one man who was adjusting his grip upon his spear looked at Solvi like an eagle looks at its prey.

"Who are you?" Solvi said, noticing the small signs of hatred in the man's face.

"I am Flickr Jikopson!" He charged towards Solvi in a fit of rage, anger spilling out from his eyes and mouth. For a moment Solvi laughed but then he became a little nervous for there is no one worst to fight than a man with nothing to lose. Solvi levelled Gutstretcher and readied himself for the impending spear thrust. However, all this was unnecessary as Flickr fell dead a few paces away from Solvi with an axe jutting out of the back of his head. Solvi looked around for the man who threw the blade with such deadly accuracy only to see Gisha, unmarked and unfazed, strolling up to reclaim her throwing axe. As she knelt to pull it out of Flickr's blood-mattered hair, she winked at Solvi.

She must be the woman in my fate, Solvi thought to himself as he wiped the blood clean off Gutstretcher with Jikop's leather jerkin.

Frosti

The oars soared into the white, wave-washed sea and glided out of it like the wings of a great sea bird. Droplets of water that orbited each stroke shone like stars in the afternoon sun. Rotting planks creaked underneath Frosti's aching feet and the salt from the beautiful sea stung his eyes. He and Gudrod were the only ones not rowing whilst forty other men heaved and pulled against the enormous force of the water. Halfdan was at the steering oar at the back of the boat, his face red with effort and his arms bulging as he struggled to navigate the strong current.

"She is beautiful, isn't she," Gudrod said as he rested against the dragon's head that fronted the boat. It was a wonderfully carved beast that warded away the demented, deformed sea spirits. "She is mine; Finlit owns most of the ships but Dreki, Dreki is mine." Dreki meant dragon and Frosti was mesmerised by her. The forty oarsmen seemed to be moving with one heart and two joined arms. Dreki didn't just sail, she flew. Frosti could see the fifteen other boats far behind them in the distance and all of them wore spectacular beast prows that made it seem like an army of creatures was heading to Osoyro. There was one with a swan's head, which Frosti found out was Finlit's ship, and he could also see one with a terribly long snake curling round, which was Eric Clawhand's vessel. Finlit and Eric had both reluctantly followed Gudrod to Osoyro and as both of them were renowned northern warlords, they had their own men, ships and ambitions.

"Why doesn't Halfdan steer his own bloody boat?" Frosti asked Gudrod, whose tattooed face seemed to crinkle at the question.

"We have always sailed together; our father said we were born on the seas," Gudrod said.

"You two are brothers. Is he from Saxony as well then?"

"Saxony, what in Odin's name are you talking about?" Gudrod snapped and headed down the boat to take the oar off his brother. Frosti was confused; he was certain Gudrod said he was born in Saxony where the Christians murdered thousands of pagans. There were at most five hundred men sailing to Solvi's aid. A feeling of immense pride should have filled Frosti with confidence, but instead he was nervous, terribly nervous. Solvi had only asked for Gudrod and not his chieftains and certainly did not expect the sheer number of people to be heading to Osoyro. Also Gudrod the Hunter was meant to be a mercenary, paid in a small amount of gold to protect Hordaland whilst Solvi was off raiding but instead, Gudrod wanted to raid and so did his chieftains. Out of all the chieftains, it was Finlit that worried Frosti the most. He had stayed quiet during the discussions, never once saying a word to Frosti. Finlit owned the boats rather than Gudrod. This meant most of the captains were his men and that fact gave Frosti night terrors.

Unlike most boats Frosti had sailed on, Dreki had a small wooden hut at the base of the mast that housed Gudrod's family. There was a tangle of ropes growing from the hut that hung the sail in its sleeping position. Gudrod said he preferred to row as it made his men stronger and that pleased the gods. Within the hut were four people. There was Asa, Gudrod's prize wife who clung onto a newborn child wrapped in furs. Asa was fair haired and very easy on the eye. Her slender build made her look weak and frail but her eyes held her strength. Asa's eyes were an impossibly bright blue that searched and roamed almost as though she was looking for something that could not be seen. One of the crew men had told Frosti of her story. She was the Chief Harold of Voss's daughter and as Halfdan had killed her father, Gudrod took her to be his woman. Asa didn't seem to hate her life but instead she looked like she had adapted to it. She was seated on a chair that incidentally rocked with every beat of the long oars either side of her, and resting on her lap was a toddler named Olaf. He was around two years old and had the same fair hair as his mother but seemed to have the stern face of his father, Gudrod. Most surprising to Frosti, the last person he saw in the hut was Jik. He had shaved his facial hair back to its normal well-trimmed style once again, keeping only the little tuft that ran from his chin to his bottom lip. Jik was talking to Asa like they were long-time friends, but in truth the only thing they shared was they were both from the chiefdom of Voss. Asa's father Harold was Jik's chief and that seemed to grant Jik a strange confidence. Enough so that he could talk to the dead Chief's daughter freely without fearing Gudrod's wrath. Occasionally, between drinking his ale and thumping his men to row quicker, Gudrod would look into the hut and offer Jik a disapproving look but he wouldn't ever do anything. The thrill of sailing was far more important to Gudrod than a quarrel at sea with his wife.

"That arse hair is going to get himself killed hanging round with that witch," Halfdan said, almost startling Frosti who was too engrossed in the gulls that shrieked overhead and the wide variety of other birds that nested in the cliffs the boat was passing.

"Witch?" Frosti asked, not really paying attention to the serious tone Halfdan was trying to pull off.

"Yes, are you thick, arse hair? She is a witch and her whelp is a scary child that I dream of throwing overboard. It's their eyes, those things can scare a raging bull to death," Halfdan warned Frosti. The two of them had bonded quite well ever since they met and out of all the northern chiefs, Frosti respected and liked him far more than the others.

"The great bloody Halfdan Halfdanson is scared of a child!" Frosti laughed. Halfdan wrapped his meaty hand round Frosti's comparatively thin neck, weighing him down just enough to encourage a shot of cramp to run up his thighs.

"I tell you now, the blonde-haired little shit is going to lead an army twice as large as this one day and who knows who he will march upon," Halfdan said

"He will die of the pox, I wager," Frosti said.'

"He is not the worst. That screeching child who shares my name has the blackest eyes I have ever fucking seen. You should see them. Halfdan the Black they call him. A child, with a fucking bi-name; it's unheard of." Halfdan looked towards the hut and quickly returned to the steering oar when he saw Asa looking back at him. Looking over the edge, past the row of painted shields that hung from the boat's curved strakes, Frosti could see where Dreki was slicing the water. It was a marvellous mix of crystal white foam and dark blue eddies twirling happily, only to be swallowed by the wave-like ripples from the long oar sweeps.

"Ship!" a voice bellowed from one of the rowers' benches. The man who noticed the boat must have been the only man truly paying attention to the open ocean to the right of Dreki. The mysterious vessel looked tired; it had its sail out, desperate to catch a wind that just didn't want to come. Strangely, no oars were seen and the boat seemed to just bounce up and down, following the sea's orders rather than its captain. Its sail was a large white and red piece of cloth that bore the Christian cross.

"What are these otter turds doing in our waters?" Halfdan roared and spat in the direction of the lost boat. The hairs on Frosti's back stood up as he remembered the pirate he had killed who stupidly wore a golden cross round his neck, and now he looked at a vessel that would surely carry more Christians.

"Gudrod, steer up to that bloody ship," Frosti shouted almost amazing himself with the authority he had assumed. Dreki curved round in one swift motion as easy as a baby would turn in its crib to stare the lonely boat head on. As Dreki turned, Frosti was glad Gudrod had listened to his order, but in truth, he had no idea whether Gudrod had already started to pull on the steering oar to kill whoever flew a Christian sail.

"What about Eric and Finlit?" Frosti asked Halfdan.

"The bastards know where we are headed; they will carry on. Besides, Dreki can anchor for four days and still catch those fat shit lickers." They were now close enough to see a scramble of robed men dancing around the boat waving their bony hands to the sky and shaking their tonsured heads vigorously while muttering to themselves.

"Oars! Oars in!" Gudrod yelled. And in one well-trained move, the long, heavy oar shafts were heaved out of the water on the right hand side where the mystery boat bobbed. The men on the port side had to adjust their positions to avoid being smacked by the sheathed oars. Dreki must have been twice the size of the Christian vessel and much better manned. Gudrod's men didn't even wear any leather helmets or carry any shields as they boarded the Christian boat whilst the two vessels hugged each other like new lovers. Frosti climbed aboard. The robed men were on their knees pleading and begging in some ridiculous tongue that sounded like they had a mouth full of food. One of Gudrod's men lifted up a small chest and cheered at its weight.

"You will find nothing in there, heathen," one of the monks said in the Norse tongue. The monk had a gloomy face that tried desperately to hide the terrible pain he was in. His nose was crooked from an old injury and spots clung to his face waiting to burst. He walked with a limp and an arm dangling down that only moved as his body moved as if he had no control over it.

"You speak our language, where are you from, monk!" Frosti demanded of the man who had assumed the role of leader. But the monk didn't respond, he just knelt and began to pray in his own tongue.

"We kill them all!" Halfdan said as he pulled a bony older man to the deck and searched his wretched robes for some kind of gold. However, the boat was empty; there was no plunder, no gold and strangely enough, no food. It was an impossible boat full of squirming skeletons that lived in the service of the nailed God. There were around fifteen of Gudrod's crew on board, outnumbering the ten monks in size as well as number. Gudrod had decided to remain on Dreki and allowed Halfdan to take charge of the incredibly easy assault. "Who the fuck are you and what are you doing here?" Halfdan asked with a voice like grey thunder clouds.

"I am Brother Athelstan and we have been sent here to spread God's light to lands it has not yet reached." Halfdan spat at the feet of one of the pale men who had been stripped naked to deflect the strange magic the robes apparently gave him. Another warrior fumbled at an amulet round his neck whilst Frosti stared into Athelstan's eyes. There was something about the cripple that looked familiar. His newly shaved head was a canvas of blisters and brown spots that appeared randomly around his scalp, ranging from the sizes of small pebbles to that of shiny golden coins. The soldiers were hungry for plunder, yet instead they found nothing but slithering monks, and so they wanted to settle for the next best thing: death. One man pointed his hand axe at the chest of one of the smaller monks, who feebly tried to lift his hands in the air in a desperate attempt to plead for mercy. Halfdan nodded. And the small monk fell dead to the depths of the ocean.

"He is a man of God! May Christ strike you heathen down and give your souls to the eternal fire pits of hell," Athelstan hissed. The monk was now at his feet. His confidence was spilling out of his skinny young frail body and was enough to fill the seas below the rocking ship that still clung to Dreki like an unwanted wart. Frosti was shocked that for the first time he had a slight admiration for a Christian. Athelstan had shouted and cursed men who had his life in their hands but he didn't care, he felt that his nailed god would protect him from a steel blade to the gullet.

"Kill the bastard!" Halfdan yelled.

"He is bloody mine!" Frosti stubbornly said, grabbing Athelstan by the collar of his robes and scrunching them up in his clenched fist with strength enough to tear the fabric like a wet leaf. Halfdan was dumfounded by the sudden show of mercy towards a Christian but took one look at Frosti and decided better than to disagree.

"The bald man has gone soft; kill the rest!" Halfdan commanded of his other men. The killing was easy. The monks were undefended and Halfdan's warriors were craving blood. One man continued to stab at an elderly monk minutes after he had been slain by another man's sword.

"Save that one," Athelstan whispered and tried to lift his lame left arm in the direction of a huddled mess hidden amongst some upturned wicker baskets.

"Don't push your bloody luck, priest," Frosti replied.

"He is a very rich man," Athelstan said firmly. Frosti instantly thought of the fortune he had lost to Halfdan, all thanks to Jik's big mouth.

"How rich?" Frosti asked. Having figured out that Frosti had fallen for his words, Athelstan rewarded him with a faint smile that seemed to cause him more pain.

"He is a King's bastard son, but still worth a great ransom," Athelstan said, keeping his voice low enough for just Frosti to hear, even though he could have screamed the words and the raging men would not have heard anything. Blood-thickened water sloshed under Frosti's feet and the winter sun felt surprisingly hot upon his head. Two terns flew overhead, weaving and swirling around each other as if they were in a drunken dance. Dreki bounced back and forth against the Christian ship, making the planks curse with pain. The Christian vessel was a poorly built one with holes in the deck and lichen sucking at the keel, and Frosti wondered what a King's son was doing on board such a sorry excuse for a boat. One of Halfdan's men had spotted movement around the pile of empty wicker baskets and began to stroll over wiping the blood off his spear as though it was a bit of mud on his shoes. The huddled man appeared to be more crippled than Athelstan. Under a black hood he wore a multitude of dirt-clotted bandages that were stained with blood and sweat. Once the warrior saw this, he stepped back in fear. Soiled bandages meant disease and he quickly found himself on the other end of the boat to avoid the possibility of the illness touching his own skin. His eyes widened as though he had seen a beast of Niflhiem – the Norse hell.

"This man is mine as well, he is bloody cursed, the monks were taking him to the far off lands to be cured," Frosti improvised and was fairly surprised it worked as everyone including Halfdan turned away and started to climb back aboard Dreki. On closer inspection, Frosti knew why his words were so believable. The cursed man was a horrific sight; his bandages didn't just stop at his face but covered his hands into stumps and his neck was completely covered in stained linen.

"He is a bloody King's son?" Frosti asked, inspecting the faceless man again.

"A bastard son. He was burnt in the fires in the cleansing of Saxony a few years back and still bleeds like an animal. He is worth his weight in gold though Lord," Athelstan said.

"Don't call me Lord, unless you want me to slice your bloody throat. Get on the boat and don't say another word," Frosti commanded. "You as well, bandage man,"

"Tojuk," the bandaged man muffled in response whilst his eyes studied his new owner.

Frosti was given the job of cutting Dreki free so he took out his splendid war axe, stroked the bronze hilt and released it with a huge swing that made him grunt. The rope came alive and twisted into the air, seeming happy at its freedom until it splashed into the icy cold water. Much like the first rope, the second and third snapped off with little difficulty and the Christian boat drifted away into the horizon, carrying the bodies of eight slaughtered monks. Gudrod stood at the steering oar commanding his and Halfdan's men to sit on the benches and start rowing again. There was a slight air of tiredness in the men, which meant one or two dropped their oars as they fumbled to get them back into the water. The clumsiness infuriated Gudrod the Hunter and he appeared as if he was about to smack the unfortunate man who rowed in front of him until Asa, his wife, appeared out of the hut. There was an unmissable beauty about the slender woman whose walk could have put the Valkyries to shame. She seemed to glide with a soft touch down the deck of Dreki towards her tattoo-faced husband who was still bellowing orders but now in a more relaxed tone. Jik took his place next to Frosti with his hands resting between the string of his bow and his chest.

"Isn't she just a gift from the Gods?" Jik said, not once taking his eyes from her straight back. "He should not be able to have her, he –" Jik's tongue seemed to become lost within his loose mouth "– beats her," he finally managed to say, making sure his voice was masked by the once again pounding oars.

"It is not your bloody business; get on an oar and we will get home faster!" Frosti said, losing patience with Jik. Even as Jik picked up one of the ownerless oar shafts, he could not stop turning back to stare at Asa who was perched willingly on top of Gudrod's knee. The two surviving monks huddled under their blood-stained robes as far away from Gudrod the Hunter as they could get. Every man aboard Dreki eyed them up, spitting curses and touching amulets to protect them from the nailed God's curse. Athelstan was massaging his left arm, trying uselessly to get it working again but eventually he gave up and looked down towards Dreki's water-splashed planks.

The day was getting old when Dreki caught up with Eric Clawhand's and Finlit's floating beasts. Their sails were tied up and every ship was relying on manpower rather than the Gods-sent winds. There was a rhythm beating into the water as each shipmaster navigated the island-infested stretch of water where the sea became the fjords. Frosti noted the wild island of Sund, which he knew was governed by the grizzly old Chief named

Skarf. Frosti himself had never visited Sund, but he had heard stories of its people's fierceness. Trickles of light seeped into the darkening world from small fires that were keeping some of the inhabitants of Sund warm. Orange and purple bars filled the sky like newly forged swords being plunged into the blacksmith's oven. A star shone wonderfully bright and that seemed to invite other stars to flicker into the night once again.

"We will anchor here tonight, and arrive in your home by the morning light," Gudrod grumbled. That night the air was a blistering cold and the fjord shimmered in the moonlight. A couple of otters played in the water, slapping their pawed feet against one another until one submitted and swam away in a sulk. A horsefly zipped about until it landed upon Frosti's shoulder where it was crushed.

"What is your village like, Lord?" Frosti flinched at the sound of the word. "I have never been to this part of the world before." Athelstan's accent was thick and hoarse and sounded similar to a Frisian man, but then again the only Frisian Frosti ever heard was the last cries of dying men pleading for mercy or sputtering some poem to their god.

"I thought I told you to bloody shut up," Frosti said.

"And I have not truly thanked you for sparing mine and my friend's life," Athelstan said and rested his working hand on Frosti's shoulder on top of the horsefly's remains. "Thank you, Frosti, you will not regret it." There was something hidden within Athelstan's words, sarcasm or ungratefulness or some kind of Christian magic but Frosti was too tired to care. The gentle fjord tide rocked Dreki as though it was in its mother's crib; the rocking motion had subdued the drunkenness of Gudrod's men and sent most of them to a deep sleep. Only Frosti and Halfdan remained awake although the reasons for their alertness couldn't have been more different. Frosti assumed Halfdan stayed awake to keep an eye on Tojuk and Athelstan as his striking blue eyes never relented. But Frosti was worried. He was worried that he had made a huge mistake; a large part of him wanted to run into the abyss of the darkness, find the pirates' treasure and retreat to some land far away from Jarl Solvi's disappointed looks.

Something stirred under one of the rower's benches where the men slept and dreamt of women, riches and power. Tojuk the bandaged monk turned to face Frosti like a cat being startled by a banging drum. The night was thick but there was something about his bandaged face that gave Frosti a familiar feeling of sourness within his belly.

Carlnut

After three weeks, Carlnut thought he would have visited all his lands but each time he left to visit a farmstead, he found himself engrossed in their stories of Portland. One man named Gethelred, who lived in a tattered barn and tendered to a few cows and suckling pigs, had the most interesting stories to tell. The farmer, who seemed infinitely old, told Carlnut of a man named Arthur who often rode round the lands of Portland in his heaven-white armour.

"There has been no greater man than King Arthur, milord," Gethelred would say before beginning a tale of how Arthur had saved a kingdom from a traitor king called Mordred. But Carlnut's favourite tale was that of the round table. According to the white-haired, hunchbacked man, Arthur had a round table in his fort, which sat the best twelve knights in the long-since-lost kingdom of Camelot. Carlnut would sit and listen to Gethelred all day until dusk grew closer and the two guards who were requested to stay with Carlnut at all times grew impatient. Arnum, who was one of Carlnut's closest friends and now went by the title Captain, had six warriors in his training ready to be Carlnut's personal guard. According to the Captain, two had to be with Carlnut at all times but when he could, Carlnut would ride away in stealth so he didn't have the burden of riding with two bumbling shadows.

One morning Carlnut was determined to see a farmstead to the very north of his lands but before he was about to leave, he was interrupted by Bedfrith, the harpist and stalker of Carlnut's Lady Selwyn.

"Er, Lord. May I ask you for a favour?" Bedfrith said in his normal snivelling tone. The harpist was dressed in finer clothes than even Carlnut; he wore a wonderful oak green woollen cloak that was fastened with a carefully patterned golden harp broach. Bedfrith was a few inches taller than Carlnut but dreadfully thinner, due to the fact he had no muscle. Carlnut reckoned him a coward but had no proof so decided to keep his normally loose tongue behind bars.

"Go on," Carlnut said exasperatedly.

"If it pleases my Lord, I would like a safe passage back to Poole," Bedfrith's voice became higher as if the request was already a doomed one. Carlnut sighed and was about to roll his eyes until Selwyn appeared round the corner with her beautifully combed, fire-red hair and infectious smile. Growing impatient at Carlnut's distraction, Bedfrith was about to plea again but Carlnut just raised a finger to shush the harpist who meant nothing to him compared to Selwyn.

"Are you all right, my Lady?" Carlnut asked the love of his life.

"I am fine, my Lord. Father Luyewn has told me news that I know you would love to hear," she said whilst her grin grew larger and more infectious. "Father Osyth rode off in the middle of the night and told no one where he was going." Bedfrith was extremely lucky to be there at that moment as Carlnut felt like he was ready to share all his wealth with the poor and run as naked as he was born through the mud roads of Portland. He hated Father Osyth and his crinkled face and his constant preaching to the Christian God and now he was gone, gone far away and Carlnut knew he would never allow him back in his fort.

"Thank the Gods!" Carlnut announced carelessly. "I will ride with you, Bedfrith, to the border of my land and there you will make your own way. Is that clear?"

"Er, yes Lord," Bedfrith said. The fort was awakening by this point; women muttered as they waited to be let out the newly built wooden gate to Fortunes Well, which was the village that was shadowed by Carlnut's Fort. An oven roared awake, signalling that Ordmaer the blacksmith was carrying out his duty in making swords for every soldier. Swords were expensive to make but Carlnut found himself with more coin than he knew what to do with; a distant cousin of Cynewulf had sent a chest with fine golden amulets to thank Carlnut for his role in trying to save Cynewulf. Boys wanting to be men appeared in the courtyard rubbing their eyes after a drunken night's sleep in a stable somewhere. Sicga was running drills in the courtyard that was littered with straw and old blood stains. The Ealdorman's son looked grand in his freshly scoured mail that shone like a new sun. After noticing Carlnut leaning against the threshold to his hall, Sicga told the training warriors to spar until he came back.

"Do I have any men fit for the shield wall, Sicga?" Carlnut asked sullenly as he watched a young boy swing his practise sword like it was a whip.

"I am doing what I can, my Lord, but I fear none of these boys will ever be warriors," Sicga admitted. The swords, which were mere wooden sticks, tapped together, drawing a small crowd of older men all wanting their child to beat the other. One child struck another in the head, drawing blood. His father cheered, only to anger another man who must have been the defeated child's father.

"I would like you to accompany me to a farmstead to the north of my lands; it will do them good to see a real warrior like yourself," Carlnut said.

"You do me a great honour, my Lord," Sicga responded dutifully. The tall, muscled man was always dutiful and in many ways he was the perfect man to stand beside in a shield wall, and for that Carlnut could have not been more thankful. "Who will be joining us, my Lord? Do I need to get one of the stable boys to ready Lady Selwyn's mare?"

"That will not be necessary; it will be me, you and Bedfrith," Carlnut said, knowing Sicga would raise an eyebrow at the last name. But contrary to his belief, Sicga was more worried about the lack of guard. "I will need Arnum and his men to guard my Lady."

They had decided to have breakfast before the ride. Lady Selwyn forced them to sit and eat the food she and her maids had lovingly prepared. The meal consisted of sticky oat porridge that was sweetened by apple skin, which annoyingly got stuck in between Carlnut's teeth.

"Do you have to go?" Lady Selwyn broke the silence as the seven of them swirled mead round their mouths to try and force apple peel from hidden crevasses.

"He will return, Sunflower, God be praised he will return," Father Luyewn announced from a mouth that must have ached tremendously from a smile that couldn't be shifted after hearing of Father Osyth's departure.

"I would highly recommend you take me as well," Arnum said angrily.

"Lord," Bedfrith said, reminding the Captain of Carlnut's new position.

"I thank you for your thoughts, Captain," Carlnut said. "I should be safe with the fine Sicga by my side and besides, you are needed to guard the steward." The whole table turned to Osbert the Steward of Portland who was sucking on a meaty bone before he noticed everyone's attention on him. Osbert threw the bone over his young shoulder for a couple of dogs who pounced onto the small scrap of meat. A ravenous, shaggy black dog won the fight for the bone and he grasped it in his slavering jaws as he ran out of the fort, clearly satisfied with his hoard.

"Yes, M'lord. Yes, I will be happy to run the household in your absence if it is only for a day," Osbert said. Sicga made a quiet groan and Arnum shook his head but Bedfrith gave Osbert a look of gratitude and for that gesture, Carlnut almost changed his negative opinion of the harpist. The morning was getting old and a few servant girls came scuttling in to the feasting room. They wore simple brown shifts and had their hair tied back in one manageable knot that looked like a horse's tail. Each of the girls, who looked no older than ten, wore a silver bracelet as a gift from Carlnut for their service to Portland. However, one girl wore a cluster of bracelets that rattled as she tried to pick up Arnum's wooden bowl that still had the remnants of oaty porridge sloshing around.

"Good morning, young lady," Carlnut said in his most Lordly like tone.

"Lord," she said.

"The Lord Carlnut would like to know where you got those bracelets from," Bedfrith said, after seeing Carlnut struggle with the right words to use. The serving girl blushed, her red cheeks going brighter than the rays of the sun that were blasting into the hall. Whether she blushed out of embarrassment or after being spoken to by Bedfrith, who was a very desirable man according to most of the women in Portland, was impossible to say. She crossed her legs and went terribly silent; her blushing cheeks were then washed clean by a flood of salty tears.

"My dear child." Luyewn tried to comfort the girl by lightly touching her hand but before his wrinkled palm could even get close she pulled away as if she had put it in a burning red fire. At this point her face was scrunched up and she was panting uncontrollably; the other girls had made themselves scarce and even Arnum and Sicga had left the room, not out of rudeness but they probably thought their presence would not be much help. Suddenly as if she woke from a dream, the girl darted off for one of the doors. Selwyn pulled away from the table causing a copper tumbler full of water to spill onto the floor but she neither cared nor even heard it. The chair screeched as she jumped up whilst lifting her dress about her knees so she wouldn't fall. Like a dutiful Lady, Selwyn disappeared to comfort the crying girl. *My beautiful Selwyn,* Carlnut thought to himself.

"Anyway, no time to waste. C'mon Bedfrith. I will see you all in a few days," Carlnut said. In response, Bedfrith mopped a few crumbs off his freshly washed tunic. Osbert just waved a hand whilst devoting all his attention to a mouse that whipped about in the corner and Father Luyewn bowed his balding white head.

Gladdy, Carlnut's grey and black stallion, was waiting for him in Portland's courtyard. Sicga rode a horse worthy of battle. It was black, a dark black, blacker than a fireless sky, and for that reason Sicga named him Deapscua, which meant death shadow. On the other hand, Bedfrith rode a nameless brown horse that looked uncomfortable being ridden. Carlnut nodded to one of the sentries at the gate who was almost asleep after a long night watching into the blindness. After finding what he wanted, he shouted to another man, who heaved the heavy bar that locked the gate.

Carlnut's first three weeks in Portland had flown by and he was extremely happy that everything was going to plan. The blacksmith Ordmaer had given all of the household guards a sword and engraved into each sword was a small depiction of Thor's hammer, which Carlnut had requested. Ordmaer didn't know the meaning for such a request, which Carlnut was thankful for, but it made him feel comfortable that every weapon in his service was blessed by Thor. Rebuilding the fort was a much bigger job than he had anticipated, but it was still coming along nicely. The broken parts of the palisade were being fixed, the oak spikes had been reshaped, moss scraped off and a new layer of grass rushes was placed on the palisade. As much as it needed doing, Carlnut, like the past owners, had decided not to bother with the earthen ditch surrounding the fort, which was a relief for most of the men.

Water broke white around them where the sea was trying desperately to rip apart the pebble and sand beach that kept Portland from snapping off the mainland. Carlnut gave one last turn to his home and sighed. He had fallen in love with the place and fallen in love with all the land he owned. He would often wake with visions of his land's future, a future that was peaceful with crops growing in masses and all the people of Fortunes Well and Weymouth happier than any in Wessex. New buds were starting to appear on the apple trees that were plentiful in southern Wessex, and the promise of spring blossom began to show. From the once-barren soil, the faint glimpses of crocuses, daffodils and tulips started to appear. The air, instead of being horribly cold, positively vibrated with the first bird song as they began to find their homes in trees again after disappearing to wherever they go over winter. The sunlight now flooded the land with its warming golden glow, giving its heat to the greening grasses. They passed a small flock of ewes, which were visibly fat from the young growing inside their bodies ready to emerge into a world reborn again.

"What is the farmstead called that you are visiting, Lord?" Bedfrith said after he had gotten bored with the repeating sights of the countryside.

"I am not sure; this is why I am visiting," Carlnut said.

"I don't know why you bother; you should be inside your fort eating, sleeping and fu–" Bedfrith's speech trailed off after the thought of the woman he admired most being with another man stung him.

"You should shut up," Sicga said, ending a brutal argument before it had begun. A falcon hovered overhead, waiting and searching for the perfect time. There was a sudden movement that was almost impossible to see with the eye. The marvellous bird raced down to the ground at such speed, Carlnut could almost hear the impact. Later, after another ten-minute walk, they spotted the same falcon perched contently on a thin tree trunk with blood covering his plump feathers.

"My father has always said we must follow nature's advice if we are to become stronger as a nation," Sicga said.

"I can't grow wings," Bedfrith laughed sarcastically. Sicga looked at him disapprovingly.

"We just saw that falcon, waiting and waiting. Waiting for an opportunity to strike and take its enemy down. And when it did go for the kill, it did so in one swift motion. I think striking as quick as you can and by using surprise but also patience is the best way to crush your enemies in battle." Carlnut nodded in approval and even Bedfrith appeared to have understood and admired the answer. "So, the Lady Selwyn told me you are a harpist, Bedfrith. Where is your harp?" Sicga asked. The harpist's fine clothes started to blacken with sweat and his hand shook violently as though it was possessed by some spirit.

"My harp!" Bedfrith shouted. "Oh dear God, my harp. We must turn back. We must!" His voice lacked passion and instead felt forced. Carlnut had dismounted from Gladdy to speak to Bedfrith, holding on the shaking man's horse's reins.

"Where is your harp?" Carlnut asked.

"Portland," Bedfrith said. They were in a small wood that had grown over the Roman road that led from Portland to Wareham. The trees were thick with skinless branches and the trunks all seemed to have a berry-loaded bush guarding them. A barely grown blackberry fell to the floor as one of the bushes rustled. Ignoring Bedfrith but still holding onto his horse, Karla was freed from her leather prison. The sword glimmered and shone in the first spring sun and the light that bounced off Karla met Sicga's sword, which was a finely made riveted object that looked both well used and well maintained. Carlnut's heart thumped in his chest as the rustling became more intense. But then, as if the Gods were playing some cruel joke, a shaggy dog with matted hair and blood-sucking fleas ran out. Sicga jumped in surprise at the friendly beast's appearance and sheathed his sword whilst he knelt to give the lawless rogue a pat on the head.

"If and when I am feeling generous I will get one of my men to bring you your harp," Carlnut said, looking at Bedfrith whilst he restraddled Gladdy.

"Thank you, Lord," Bedfrith said tonelessly. Carlnut was about to slap Gladdy's hind with his leg when arrow whizzed through the wood, catching dew-covered leaves but never adjusting its course from Carlnut's ankle. Luckily for Carlnut, the head only just scraped the skin but unluckily for Gladdy, the arrow made its way in between two of his giant rib bones. He reared back and whinnied in agony. Carlnut was flung to the ground, smacking his scarred forehead against a tree's root. Sicga's sword rang again followed by a scream, and then another and then another. Men fell with thuds around the injured Carlnut. He managed to get back to his feet as two more men arrived carrying spears. They both charged, aiming for Carlnut's chest but he parried one of the blows and grabbed the spear shaft from the other. Using the shaft Carlnut pulled the inexperienced soldier towards Karla's tip. She tore through flesh easily and drank the man's blood. The smell of sweat and blood mixed in with the smell of urine lingered in the air. Sicga was cursing and shouting. Carlnut was panting and feeling the bump on his head and beginning to limp from the arrow wound to his ankle. Four more men appeared, and then another six followed by two horsemen. Carlnut instinctively looked for Bedfrith but in the chaos he had managed to run away, and Carlnut hoped, for Selwyn's sake, he had gotten away to safety. Deapscua, Sicga's horse, stayed unmoved by the fight and even started to gnarl his teeth in the direction of another horseman who seemed to float towards them like mist descending upon a swamp. He was a hooded man, a strangely familiar hooded man. The memorable stranger descended on Carlnut and Sicga slowly, almost teasing their deaths. He had a straight back and wore a cloak as dark as Deapscua but that was all Carlnut could see as he kept his face well-hidden and all his other features sheltered within the thick woollen material of the cloak.

"I am shocked, Lord Carlnut. We only met a few months ago and you do not remember me. How odd. And here's me thinking I am one of a kind," the hooded man said as though he was addressing an old friend. His voice was odd enough for it sounded like no other Carlnut had heard before. It was thick and phlegmy and he pronounced nearly every letter of every word he spoke. Carlnut searched his memory but found nothing. His mind was flooded. His hands became water and his bowels churned like those of a gelded bull.

"I can pay you to let us leave, my father is one of the King's most trusted Ealdormen," Sicga said, pushing his curly hair out of his eyes. In a normal fight he would have worn his shining mail but in truth they had not expected to come across any issues, so instead he wore simple war leathers, as did Carlnut.

"I do not want your gold, Sicga son of Osric, nor do I want you dead. As long as you listen to me no one, including your lord, will get hurt," the mysterious man said.

"Welsh prick!" Sicga screamed but another threatening spear thrust managed to persuade him to sheath his sword.

"I have my orders, Lord Carlnut; I am to bring you to the council of Wessex." Carlnut turned to Sicga, obviously confused by the statement but Sicga was just as confused himself and looked back at Carlnut blankly.

"And for what crime is my Lord being summoned to the council?" Sicga asked dutifully.

"All in good time, Sicga son of Osric, all in good time." Both Carlnut and Sicga were forced to give their swords to an ugly, wart-covered man who buckled both swords on his belt and saddled his dishevelled horse once more. Carlnut almost wept as he passed Karla on to such an ugly man but the thought of revenge kept his tears from becoming free. The hooded man dismounted from his ordinary mare and strolled over towards

Deapscua. His cloak was all worn and tattered to the hem and it looked older than some of the spear-carrying men that surrounded the Lord of Portland. "I am taking this horse," he said, stroking the unaware face of Deapscua. Carlnut could only imagine that Sicga felt like he had when he had to give Karla up. But then his mind turned towards Gladdy, his own horse. He had become wounded from the first blow in the ambush but galloped off without once hesitating. Carlnut, the Lord and Sicga, the highborn were then made to ride on poorly built horses that belonged to inexperienced spearmen. After complaining that this was an insult to Wessex, Sicga was made to shut up by a spear butt that sent him into an unconscious sleep.

The smell of squished berries was extremely potent as the party rode slowly through the thickening woods. They passed a white-washed stream with water cascading over tiny waterfalls, feeding the fungus on rotting tree stumps that surrounded the splashing stream. A light wind stirred the trees and for a few curious seconds no noise could be heard until the sound of snapping twigs and rustling roosting birds overcame the silence. Out of the corner of Carlnut's eye, he could see a small trail of blood which sprayed over ferns that spewed like green fountains. A large puddle covered the purple spikes of a fireweed that looked even scarier with the blood upon it. Somewhere in the wood, a horse screamed its last breath and then fell silent.

Solvi

The Bjornafjorden was choked full of moored boats that seethed with rushed activity. A few of the fifteen boats caught Solvi's eye. Firstly, there was one that had a twisted snake-like beast at its prow. However, as to not anger the land spirits, the snake had been taken off before the boat reached the shore. Solvi watched the snake slither through the early morning mist and felt a horrible feeling of unease. Next to the snake was a boat that was around two oar shafts longer and had four extra oar holes; the longer boat did have a swan at its prow but like the snake, the beast was sleeping somewhere on board, waiting to guide the ship over ominous open waters. The most striking boat caught Solvi's eye like a beautiful girl would. He hadn't caught the huge boat's beast prow as it must have arrived a little later than the others, but he assumed it must have been as splendid as the boat itself. It was the only vessel that had its sails up even though it was moored up like the others, and upon those cream-coloured sails was a red dragon that had legs thicker than felled oak trees and teeth sharper than spear points.

"That must be Gudrod's boat," Eddval said whilst he admired the grand ship with wide, luminous eyes.

"This means Frosti and Jik have managed it," Solvi exclaimed. "I knew they would. Eddval, I think we are all going to be very rich men." The sun was rising in the sky and the long jagged shadows of the fleet, which darkened the fjord, shrunk, and the water came back to life again. Swallows looped overhead and a kingfisher skimmed the water as it tried to find its first catch of the day, and in a blinking moment, it had a beak full of unfortunate fish that flopped in a pointless attempt to escape. A fresh morning wind swept through the fjord's sentinel-like forest, carrying gritty fragments of sand and broken weeds through the air. Solvi could see a trickle of men clad in furs and great animal hide coats leaving a few of the boats, but he knew that most of the men would still be on the craft waiting for the day to get older before going ashore.

"Fifteen ships, Eddval. What's that? Around four hundred, maybe five hundred men?" Solvi said with hint of worry in his voice. "We don't even have that number of men; they could trample us, and how do we know Frosti is even with them?"

"Look!" Eddval said. Solvi glossed over the men who looked like ants at that distance. "There, Jarl," Eddval said and put his right hand under Solvi's chin, pinching and then twisting his head towards the dragon-sail ship. A huge man with a fiery red beard and a head that reflected the sun's light was being escorted off by two men who appeared to be just as huge as Frosti. Following them was a woman carrying a babe in one arm and trailing a toddler by the hand.

"Eddval, I threw the rune sticks the day Jikop attacked," Solvi said. "I saw that I was going to lead a great fleet; maybe this is that fleet. I saw thirty boats in my prophecy, but this is only the beginning. Frosti, I owe you so much," Solvi's whispered as Eddval walked off to prepare the camp.

It took around an hour for the men of the northern camps to make their way round the expansive shoreline of the Bjornafjorden and through the knife-like leaves of the bordering forest. They all met in the clearing that had been the site of the recent fierce and bloody battle. There was still evidence of the mayhem that came with Jikop's revolt, as dried blood had crusted into sandwort plants and there was a great patch where Solvi had ordered all the men who died in the fight to be burnt. The night of the burning was a grand occasion, as men from both sides of the fight drank together and grieved for their friends. Solvi had even allowed Jikop the honour of being burnt on the pyre that roared in the sky and could probably be seen far off into the depths of Hordaland. Solvi now stood at one end of the clearing with Eddval, Gisha, Umiston and Thord the master boat builder. However, the small greeting party was dwarfed by the masses of men who clumsily climbed through thickets, heather and brambles. Solvi noted how they clumped together in three groups. One group, who were the first to appear, were led by a tall thin man who wore a carefully looked-after beard that looked brown in one light and black in another. He wore an otter pelt that clung round his neck like the beast still had some life inside it. There was something about the man that told Solvi he was a sailor, a warrior at sea and those men are priceless jewels in an army. The sailor looked very similar to the man he had seen when he threw the rune sticks, but he could not be certain. Next came a horrid figure with his back hunched and a strange deformity in his hand that made his bones twist and spiral like a tree's roots in the crumbling soil. In the same way the dragon ship had taken Solvi's attention away from the rest of the waiting boats, so did the last group of men. They were huge towering beasts covered in layers upon layers of fur. Most of them scratched at great beards full of lice, crumbs and ale. A giant man with a black face and more hair than skin growled an insult towards another. His friend was adorned in enough arm rings to fund an entire war-band. Frosti stood like a great oak next to the pair whilst their followers carried sharpened spears that rested on their shoulders. Before any words were said, Solvi opened his arms and Frosti strolled towards his Jarl, gripping him like he would a long-lost brother.

"I owe you so much," Solvi whispered in Frosti's ear as his grip got tighter round Frosti's body.

"No, no you bloody don't; consider it a gift from your best friend," Frosti said back. "Oh one more thing, don't ever send me to the north again, it's bloody freezing!" They both laughed and finalised their skin-grabbing hug with a final squeeze and a thump on each other's back.

"Two pieces of worm shit embracing each other like a pair of women," one of the giant men said.

"This, Jarl Solvi–" Frosti said, using Solvi's proper title to try and solidify his position in front of men who thought very little of it. "This is Halfdan Halfdanson, one of the greatest warlords in the northern camps,"

"One of?" Halfdan said, sounding genuinely offended. "I've been killing men like you before you even sprouted out from your mother's cunt."

"And this man is Gudrod Halfdanson or Gudrod the Hunter, and he is the leader of the fleet of five hundred men who have come to your aid," Frosti said. Gudrod's thick eyebrows raised themselves a little and his ink-stained face grimaced. The ink depicted dragons fighting each other like an entire story upon his face. After Solvi saw the fighting dragons, teeth bared and fire swirling, he knew that the magnificent dragon-sail-wearing ship must be his.

"I have heard tales of your greatness, Gudrod the Hunter, and may I say I think I am in love with your ship," Solvi said.

"Dreki," Gudrod grumbled. "My ship is called Dreki."

fighting men would be decided. Unfortunately for Solvi, all he saw in Gisha's tent was a white fur coat screwed up upon a tattered hay pile that formed her bed. A bird hopped and shrieked outside the tent, its shadow deformed and twisting as it was fed by a newly lighted fire. Too drunk to find his own bed, Solvi collapsed onto Gisha's and wrapped himself up in her prized white fur coat.

Solvi was woken by Eddval, who was dressed in his war leathers with his two dirks hanging from his belt like great fangs.

"The Thing is going to start soon, Jarl," he said. Solvi's heart pulsated and his palms became sweaty, but he knew his duty was to lead the unleadable. It was Solvi's first Thing as a Jarl; he remembered attending a few during Bergi's time. All powerful men would attend followed by any free men that would like to be present. Anyone could speak at the assembly which is what worried Solvi, he hated the thought of one of Gudrod's men undermining him and sending his fragile leadership into a horrid downwards spiral.

The new morning was calm and free of breeze. Somewhere in the forest, a family of swallows squawked to one another and a wild boar grumbled. Gudrod had chosen the stone steps in the middle of Osoyro for the location of the Thing, and Solvi was grateful for that fact even though the Hunter didn't know it. This was because the steps were where he had ripped open one of King Sigfred's men, and he felt a sense of strange power when he stood near the layered mossy stones. Jik followed Jarl Solvi as he left Gisha's tent.

"Where is Gisha, Jarl?" Jik asked with an accompanying smirk.

"Hopefully where you should be, at the Thing," Solvi said as he picked up a worm-ridden apple off another man's table and proceeded to bite into it. As they walked past one of the many longhouses that were being built in Osoyro, Solvi grabbed Jik and pushed him against the damp wood, causing the archer to grimace in pain.

"Jarl?" he said in horror.

"I can see what you are doing, Jik, and I don't fucking like it." Solvi's voice was harsh and hoarse from a night's drinking. "You are trying to get in between the legs of Gudrod's whore." Jik pushed against his Jarl and punched him across the face, forcing a trickle blood to escape from his nose.

"She is a Queen! Not a whore!" Jik shouted.

"I will put that fit of rage down to your harsh travels up north, but if you ever strike me again I will personally feed you to the fucking pigs and feed their shit to the whore," Solvi said furiously. Jik wanted to fight back, his fists clenched and his eyes flashed, but before he could react, Solvi threw him to the ground and spat at his friend's feet. Clusters of men were already standing around the courtyard and Solvi had to push through them to claim his spot. Gudrod was already there, his inked face twitching and his many pelts covering the rest of his body. Solvi could smell the stench of shit, grease and blood as he passed the great towering man but refused to even give him a glance. Next to Gudrod was Finlit who was madly scooping some of Rollaug's porridge, causing drops of honey-flavoured oats to spew out. Halfdan was talking to some of his men when Solvi arrived but stopped when he saw the Jarl take his place next to Gisha and Eddval. The sun glinted off raised spear points and more men gathered round to hear the great council of war discuss the first-ever raids of a fabled land called Britain.

"I am Jarl Solvi, and I welcome all men to speak," Solvi said, raising his arms into the air. He looked at the crowd and for a moment saw only warriors he did not recognise. After a few more fleeting glances, he saw his men who all seemed to huddle to the right hand side of the crowd. "In a matter of weeks, we will sail to Britain and, thanks to these men," Solvi said and pointed towards Gudrod, Halfdan and Finlit," we can travel knowing our wives and sons are safe." Cheers rung out from the right hand side of the crowd, but the rest of the men kept as silent as corpses. Unperturbed by the strange silence, Solvi went on to thank the northern men for their help and promised them some of the plunder from the raids. The sound of a mouse pissing in a nearby thatch was louder than Gudrod's men after the promise of gold and silver. "Have your men lost their tongues, Gudrod? I promise them riches and all they can do is fart and cough." Eddval snorted but was soon silenced by a punch to the ribs from Gisha.

"No, Solvi. They have not lost their tongues, but they do not listen to a single word you say," Gudrod grumbled. Solvi's men thrust forward in anger to avenge the dishonour to their Jarl but were met by a strong wall of muscle and shields. Gisha's eyes darted round the Thing and Eddval unsheathed his two dirks ready for a fight, but Jarl Solvi remained calm.

"If I have somehow upset you, Gudrod, please let me know," Solvi said.

"Well as I told your man Frosti, I am not being a fucking guard dog. Why don't you use your own men whilst we raid Britain," Gudrod said, stepping forward and drawing his sword. "I am Gudrod the Hunter. I am the greatest warrior this land has ever seen, and he wants to have me guarding women!" He roared and so did his men.

"Gudrod, I–," Solvi went to speak, but the dragon's roars were greater than his own.

"I was born in the cold north, raised by a bear as one of its cubs, and when I grew big and hungrier, I killed that bear with my own fucking hands!" His men roared again at the story and Frosti, who was sharpening his great axe at the back of the crowd, shook his head. The crowd was getting rowdier as more drink was passed around and thrown down thirsty gullets. Gudrod seemed to enjoy getting his men to roar insults at Solvi and enjoyed even more when some of Jikop's old warriors joined in the taunts. However, Jarl Solvi absorbed all of it and sat upon one of the steps, picking maggots out of his apple. Halfdan rested one of his gloved hands on Gudrod and the crazed man seemed to calm down and take his place back in front of his people. The Thing had already been going for about an hour and it had achieved virtually nothing. The sun was high in the sky but it was masked by a sullen mass of grey cloud that rolled in like a stalking cat. The warlords were all discussing the best way to raid and how many ships to take but throughout, Jarl Solvi remained silent, instead choosing to listen to all their views. One man from Finlit's crew shouted that they should take all their ships so they could take more plunder while another man from Halfdan's crew suggested that they should send only three because the journey wasn't safe, and it was too risky to take the entire fleet. Some men stamped their feet in approval to both ideas whereas others grunted disapproval.

"Silence!" Solvi demanded, finally getting the full attention of the crowd. "You mock me, but still you can't decide the best thing to do. Have you lost your wits?" he said with a strange hint of humour to his words. The clouds began to separate and a ray of sun seemed to bounce off Solvi's waxed hair, which still ran straight through the middle of his head. "We have five ships and our good northern friends have fifteen; I say we take all of ours and seven of Gudrod's–"

"Finlit's," a man said behind a cough, which bought him nothing more than scowls and curses. However, Solvi continued:

"The boats not travelling will be crewed by both mine and north men. These men will guard the coast to protect from King Sigfred but will receive a share of the plunder." Nobody argued and for the first time there was general calm. Murmurs from the front of the crowd flooded down to the back until all men heard Solvi's plan. "I do not care who captains Gudrod's ships; that is for him to decide."

"Eric Clawhand!" Gudrod cried from the tree stump he had rested himself upon. Eric's men howled like rabid dogs pushing their spears, axes and shields up into the air calling their warlord's name. "Summarlid Edgarson, Torfi Hafsson, Thorberg Thorinson, Torsten Hrappsson and Hitig Hrappsson." Each name was greeted with shouts and the hugs of friends embracing each other in congratulations.

"That is six of your ships, Gudrod, and you still have yourself, Halfdan and Finlit Hafgramr. Who, may I ask, is steering your final ship?" Jarl Solvi asked.

"I will," Gudrod said, and every single man in the courtyard including Solvi's stamped their feet in applause of such a claim. "And the great Finlit Hafgramr will lead the fleet that stays in Osoyro." Even Solvi was surprised at that, as he hadn't expected Gudrod to give up one of his best warlords. Judging from Finlit's reaction, he wasn't expecting it either. The sea lord growled a curse and left the Thing followed by about thirty of his loyal supporters.

"The men who will captain my ships!" Solvi clapped his hands together and a leather-bound drum echoed from the back of the crowd. "Myself, Gisha, Umiston, Ospak and Thord!" There were no surprises in Solvi's announcement, and the rest of the council was made up of people congratulating friends and discussing the next few weeks

The Thing ended shortly after the announcement, and the drinking didn't end there. Osoyro became a hive of drunken punches and fights. Myrun the heavy-breasted brothel owner had sent over fifty women to Osoyro and none of them returned without pouches heavy with coin. The night was one of the best Solvi could remember. Rollaug had prepared a huge feast with the leftovers from the winter stores, which contained venison roasted till it was crispy, golden vegetables stewed in meat fats and crunchy crusted bread that could be dipped in the gallons of ale that Gudrod had provided. Men mixed at the feasting tables that held the carved oaken bowls and the few silver plates that had been taken during Frisian raids. Aesa and Eddval laughed over some joke that Finlit had made whilst Frosti and Halfdan traded insults. Even though new friendships were being made, Solvi's blood still boiled as the only two people that were not at the feast were Jik and Gudrod's wife Asa.

"I will kill that archer if he ruins this," Solvi said to Eddval who was having his hair twisted between Aesa's fingers. "Asa will travel with Gudrod and I will have Jik on my ship. Let's hope the Gods can end this unfortunate partnership somehow." Eddval held his ear to Aesa's belly and smiled, showing his yellowing teeth when he heard his adopted baby kick. "Have you got a name yet, my friend?" Solvi asked, trying desperately to forget Jik.

"I know it's a boy. I have prayed for one, and I know it will happen, so if my prayers are answered he will be called Solvi Eddvalson," he announced proudly. Eddval's smile grew till it almost reached both ears whereas Solvi's eyes began to water out of tears of happiness, but a small glimpse of unease flashed across Aesa's face.

"And what if it's a girl, Aesa?" Solvi said, thinking she hated the boy's name. But she only shrugged and rubbed her belly.

"It is a boy, Jarl, and he will give your name honour," she said dutifully. Then something caught Solvi's eye; two shadows shuffled from one tent to another holding heavy wooden buckets that were sloshing with water. Solvi shot up and ignored whatever other words the happy couple were saying. Like a cat hunting a mouse Solvi almost glided to where he had seen the two cloaked men. A blur filled his vision as the alcohol started to clog up his mind, and the night seemed to become instantly cold. In spite of his clouded sight, he could still see the two men floating into the woods like a descending mist. He felt Gutstretcher at his side, gliding his sweaty palm across its plain iron hilt. Twigs snapped and branches cracked in the dark wood where the spectres were walking. Following the sounds, Solvi pounced from tree to tree. He could almost taste the blue moss that clung so heavily upon the trees' trunks. He could see the figures much more clearly now as they must have had been only a few feet from him. One was completely bald, and his walk wasn't a graceful float but a horrific limp that made his whole body twitch at every awkward step. The other man reached clumsily for branches and trunks with a bandaged stump. Solvi's heart returned to its normal beat, and his senses became clear again. The sight of the two cripples made him feel safe, but for some reason Gutstretcher still yearned for blood. Solvi pounced like a wolf scaring both men so much that they tripped over twisted roots.

"What in Odin's name are you two?" Solvi joked whilst the two cripples picked themselves gracelessly back up. The bandaged man slipped on a mushroom clump that grew at the bottom of a great pine tree, and Solvi laughed. The limping man spoke first.

"I am Brother Athelstan and this is Brother Tojuk. We are slaves of Frosti the Red," he said between sniffles and a horrible constant clearing of his throat.

"You are Christians?" Solvi asked, shocked at the thought that Frosti would even keep their company.

"Yes, yes we are, Jarl. The great Frosti the Red spared our lives because God willed it so," Athelstan said. A flicker of anger flashed over Solvi's face; he hated Christians and a preaching Christian was even worse. Before he reached for Gutstretcher, he remembered he owed Frosti and decided to ignore the burning hatred for his sake.

"Go back to your master then, and don't let me even hear you again," Solvi said to Athelstan. As they hurried off, Solvi thought for a moment. His world was changing every day; it all seemed so simple months ago. He thought he would be the Jarl of Hordaland and that would be that, but now he had a powerful King threatening his borders, he had a great host to lead to the unknown kingdom of Britain, he had two snivelling monks preaching their weak religion and he had a crew he had to keep happy. As he contemplated his life in the lightless wood, the answer seemed easy: he could just run, run away from all his responsibilities and start a new life elsewhere. He tried to build up the courage to let his legs spring into a retreat, but he couldn't move. Darkness crept in, suffocating him, grabbing him and rooting him into the soil. An owl hooted twice, then flapped its wings as it dived towards an unfortunate mouse. Solvi could hear the tides of the Bjornafjorden splashing against the five ships that sat finished on the shoreline ready to be crewed. The thought of the ships was a comforting one; they were great beasts made from the best wood in Hordaland and built by one of the greatest shipmasters in the land, and they were a part of Solvi's first fleet. Then he remembered what the Gods had shown him the night of Jikop's revolt. He was to lead a great fleet of thirty ships, and this raid of Britain would just be the beginning. So he turned away from the abyss of forest and decided to head back to camp.

"Where the bloody hells have you been," Frosti said as Solvi emerged from the thicket, the bald man's fire-red beard looking marvellous in the flames of a nearby torch.

"I've just met your pet monks. I hope you tie them up when we raid, Frosti," Solvi said. They both laughed and picked up a full horn of ale from a warrior who had passed out and shared it between them.

"Hold this, baldy," Solvi said to his friend as he passed the horn to him and climbed onto a vomit-covered bench. "In two weeks' time, the moon will be full in the sky and when its light touches our ships, which fill the belly of the blessed Bjornafjorden, we will sail for Britain!" he shouted. Frosti and Umiston embraced. Eddval kissed Aesa. Halfdan, Eric and Gudrod dropped a drunken Finlit to raise their clenched fists in the air. And somewhere at the roots of Yggdrasil the three Norns who spin the fates of men, laughed.

Selwyn

It had only been two nights, but Selwyn hated waking in a bed that was empty. She craved for Carlnut to return and had sent scouts out on both days to search for him. Although Selwyn wasn't worried, as she suspected Carlnut was being enticed by more stories from Wessex farmers who felt honoured by his company. Throughout the night there was a clinging rain in the air that dripped relentlessly through the heavily thatched roof, which left muddy puddles that became drinking bowls for stray cats. As Selwyn made her way to the feasting hall, she had to lift up her blue dress that was lined with silver thread to her knees to avoid the dress being spoilt by the brown water. The breakfast was being served by the same nervous girl that had acted so strange around Father Luyewn a few days back. Her name was Athelhild, and she still wore the cluster of bracelets round her arms, but whenever Selwyn would question where she got them from, she would burst into tears. As on every morning thus far, Father Luyewn was at the breakfast table as well as the steward Osbert. Athelhild had grown accustomed to serving them and also accepted that old Father Luyewn was nobody to be scared of. Sometimes the little girl was even happy to listen to him tell her many stories of Christ.

"Did you know young lady that the great Christ once fed five thousand poor men with only two fishes and five loafs of bread, and here we are now barely managing to feed three," he chuckled, clearly amused by his story and continued to pick at a salted herring that was drenched in lemon juice.

"That's impossible," Athelhild said stubbornly.

"Darling girl, nothing is impossible." Luyewn had started to become frailer and his last remaining white hairs had all but escaped his head.

"How did all those people share two fish?" Athelhild asked, still bemused by the priest's tale.

"Sunflower, will you please pass me the bread; my fish juices need to be soaked up," Luyewn said, allowing the serving girl's mind to lose all interest. As Selwyn reached for the plate holding small pieces of crushed loaf, Osbert patted her hand away.

"You are a Lady; why don't you get your mute dog to do it? After all, he is your sworn protector," he said, pointing towards Engelhard who stood fixed like one of the wooden beams that held the thatched roof in place.

His look was as grim as it ever had been, and he seemed to have more scars across his newly bald head towards his sullen face. Osbert clicked his fingers towards Engelhard, and the bald hound stepped forward as though his mind wasn't his own. "Pick up the bread and give it to our priest," Osbert said. Engelhard grunted in acceptance as he clumsily grabbed the plate and passed it to Luyewn who tried to offer thanks but Osbert interrupted. "Do you thank a dog for barking? You have a sermon today; you need to save whatever breath you have left." Selwyn frowned and Father Luyewn's head dropped. For the rest of the breakfast, no one spoke. Osbert used the silence to stuff his face with the salted fish and the last of the winter's ale.

The afternoon brought heavier rain that was accompanied by screeching horse whinnies and the piercing sound of howling dogs. Selwyn had decided to spend most of that day in the shelter of the great hall with Arnum, Athelhild and the silent presence of Engelhard. Trickling streams of water dripped from the roof where the wind and nesting mice had torn holes in the thatch. A once-hidden pigeon flapped wildly as a crashing sound emerged from outside, along with the unmistakeable screams of women. Arnum and Engelhard drew their swords whilst two spearmen cried aloud from outside the great hall's doors. Selwyn felt faint. Her heart tried to escape through her mouth and not even the presence of her personal guard made her feel safe. Suddenly, a bloodied horse charged into the hall. Astride the beast was Bedfrith, who had a wicked grimace on his face.

"Lady, I bring you horrid news!" he screamed. It took an age for him to dismount his horse. The stallion was distressed and shuffled about its feet as if the floor were covered in flames rather than puddles.

"What is it? Where is Lord Carlnut?" Selwyn looked at her friend with a face full of hope but a heart heavy with impeding grief.

"It's the Lord Carlnut, my Lady; he has been taken," Bedfrith said, "taken by armed bandits." Arnum sheathed his sword and grabbed Selwyn before she went limp. He dragged her over to one of the many benches that littered the hall, his sword rattling in its scabbard. One of Selwyn's trailing legs knocked over one of the rusted iron plates that had been placed to catch a leak. The motion sent muddy water splashing in all directions, which soaked into the legs of her fine dress, and it turned from a beautiful blue into clinging brown.

"Are you sure, Bedfrith? What about Sicga? Have they both been captured?" Arnum spit out the questions as if they were burning drops of fat on his tongue. "How many of them were they? Where are they now?" Arnum started panting like a thirsty dog until Bedfrith tried to console him with a hug. Arnum winced at the harpist's open arms and quickly turned away in disgust. Carlnut hated Bedfrith and that was enough for Arnum to hate the finely dressed prick as well.

~ 296 ~

"I did all I could. They were waiting in the forest for us, all teeth and steel. I didn't see any badges or banners so they must have been outlaws looking for a prize ransom. Carlnut fought bravely, but I am afraid he may have taken a wound to the leg." The harpist shuffled nervously in his clothes and turned harshly towards the doors, which were busy with activity. Men and women started to filter into the hall to see what had caused the commotion. Most of the people were just glad to be inside to shelter from the never-relenting rain. One woman began sobbing like a child when she heard the news and another sank to her knees in a fit of rage and distress. Next to her a brave man stated that he would be willing to slaughter the bandits who took his lord, whilst another man joined him and called Bedfrith a coward for running.

"Why do you survive when our lord could be rotting in a cell somewhere?" the man yelled. Bedfrith looked astonished at such an insult, but two more men joined in until a whole host of people were screaming for justice. Selwyn regained her senses and stood to find herself between a retreating Bedfrith and a spit-throwing mob. Water fell off the mob in streams, filling their leather boots and saturating some of the rushes that were strewn on the floor. A pale sun attempted to creep through the rain clouds, but it was shunned away as quickly as it tried to appear. Selwyn could smell the breath of the mob, a stinking sour smell of ale and mixed meats.

"Stop!" a young voice cried from a threshold that was drenched in mistletoe. Regardless of the voice, one man pulled out a heat-treated knife and lunged forward at Bedfrith. Like a striking snake, a shadow flew from one of the pillars and the attacking man's arm was flung across the room. Women screamed and the wounded man shrieked like a dying goat clutching onto his bleeding half arm. Engelhard kicked the man into silence and wiped his blooded sword against the twitching man's back. "Stop this madness," the voice shouted again. "I am the steward here and you threaten a man from another earldom without trial; this simply cannot do," Osbert said. Even though he was only fifteen, he had a wonderful gift for words. When Carlnut had first met him he was a snotty-nosed, pock-covered boy and somehow in a matter of weeks he commanded the great hall and managed to get a vengeful mob to heel. Osbert clicked at Engelhard who was still smirking as he stared towards the puddle of crimson red blood that was leaking through the floor boards. "Get these vermin out of my hall," Osbert commanded, and with that command the mute Engelhard snared at the mob. They scampered like a bustle of mice from a fierce cat into the pounding rain. As the doors closed, a gust of air blew out a number of torches that were hung in rusty iron sconces upon the walls. Shadows replaced light and the smell of smoke filled the hall like a visible spectre circling over their heads.

"Are you alright, Sunflower?" Luyewn came scuttling past Osbert into the hall, holding his plain robe up to his wrinkled knees and trying carefully not to catch a worn sandal on one of the raised floorboards.

"They, they have taken Carlnut," she said behind a wall of sniffs and coughs.

"Who has?" Father Luyewn asked.

"Some bandits saw our horses as we got to Earl Cynric's borders and ambushed us as we rode through the woods," Bedfrith interrupted.

"I do not need your help, harpist. You will do well to hold your tongue whilst your lady is speaking." Father Luyewn snapped his few teeth together, which glared like razor-sharp knives. Bedfrith was taken aback by the sudden burst of anger from the usually calm man, as was everyone else in the darkening room. The pigeons fluttered in the roof's skeleton, sending showers of dust down, which glittered like newly formed snow. The room was silent; Selwyn's tears were drying up and the birds' flapping wings seemed to quieten by one look from Engelhard.

"We need a plan to save our Lord," Arnum finally said to silence the silence.

"Agreed," Luyewn added.

"With your permission, my Lady, I will take a party of around fifty men and search the land for Lord Carlnut, and I will not return without him and the noble Sicga, for that matter," Arnum said.

"Agreed," Father Luyewn added once more.

Selwyn blushed at the thought of Arnum's bravery, and her heart fluttered at the thought of her man having such a loyal friend. Her legs were numb from a pain she had never felt before and her hands felt clammy, but somewhere from within her, she knew she had to be strong.

"Yes, Captain Arnum, you may go. Please save my husband," she begged. Arnum was about to rush into the rain when a bloodied sword blocked his path. It was Engelhard's blade that stopped the captain from gathering his men. Arnum could see his own reflection in the flat steel and tried to force his way past its gleam. As he pushed it aside, Engelhard brought it up to bury the hilt in the arch of Arnum's nose. Selwyn covered her mouth in horror whilst Arnum held his bleeding nose to helplessly try and fix it back into its place.

"I do believe that it is not your decision, Captain," Osbert said. "If you were to leave Portland with the whole guard, how on earth would we protect ourselves? Do I order straw men to be built on the ramparts? Do I ask Ordmaer to forge us metal walls? Tell me this, Arnum, I do not think one man, whoever he is, is worth hundreds of lives."

"Agreed," Bedfrith said, mocking Father Luyewn's earlier words.

"I don't fucking follow orders from a child," Arnum bellowed as blood poured uncontrollably from his face. He went to push past Engelhard, who for the first time, had a look of doubt on his face. "You are my friend, Engel, and Carlnut is our friend; let me through." Engelhard looked towards Osbert then back at Arnum. In one motion that made Arnum feel like he was about to receive a blade to the throat, Engelhard sheathed his heavy sword. The soldier helped Arnum back to his feet with a hand that was cooled with sweat and simply walked away, each step an extra knife in Osbert's back.

"If you leave Portland I will have no option but to arrest you," Osbert said, trying desperately to sound confident and full of authority again.

"Steward, if you do stop me, I will have no option but to kill you," Arnum replied as he lifted up the wooden beam that had locked the hall's doors. After the two warriors had left the hall, a sad calm air started to seep in carrying a strong taste of worry and disappointment. Father Luyewn cradled Selwyn, but the Lady's tears had dried up and her eyes were instead filled with a horrific determination.

The noise of the crashing sea was deafening, but it was like a mouse's heartbeat compared to the horrendous echo of the sweeping thunderstorm. Black clouds sprawled across the sky, billowing in from the raging waves. With the ominous clouds came a wind that picked up as it hit land, crying and howling like a wolf into the night. Selwyn tossed and turned in her straw bed desperate for a sleep deep enough to forget everything, but every time her eyes closed, the harassing storm forced them open again. Athelhild had run into Selwyn's room at the first sound of the thunder and the lady hugged her tight to protect her from the furious world. After an hour of interrupted periods of sleep, Selwyn decided to listen. Listen to the bleating sheep and the tap of rain forcing entry into every building. She listened to the patter of running feet from men skidding to their homes and the high-pitched shrieking of a baby who lived somewhere within the fort's walls. Between the distinct noises, Selwyn could hear low-pitched voices and the dragging sound of spear butts against a wet floor. Then suddenly a man cursed and struggled until an audible thud silenced him. Selwyn assumed it was her guards dragging a drunken fool away from her home, and with that thought she finally gave in to her body's weariness.

The next morning's breakfast was a sullen affair as only Lady Selwyn and Osbert were present.

"Father Luyewn has gone down to the small chapel in Fortunes Well," Osbert said as he adjusted the tightness of his tunic. "He says the priest there is only a novice and he would like to lead a few sermons to the folk who are normally deprived of a brilliant man of God." Osbert made the sign of the cross and continued to stab at his food, which was a large grilled cod and fresh asparagus. Selwyn looked up from her fish in horror; she knew something was wrong, as Father Luyewn would not leave her without a goodbye.

"Did he travel at first light?" she asked the steward.

"Deep into the night, actually. Ridiculous; a frail man like that could have been swept up in that weather. Nevertheless, he wasn't the most stupid man to leave Portland last night," Osbert claimed.

"No?" Selwyn said, trying hard to mask her anger at the steward's insult to a man she loved deeply.

"Arnum stole a horse and rode out of Portland; I think he wants to play the hero. Ridiculous; Carlnut is a strong man and if he got captured, then surely Arnum will." Osbert laughed and a fish scale flew out of his mouth onto the blackened crust of some burnt bread. He gave the bread a distasteful look and swept it off the table, forcing a cup of water and a bowl of ripe apples to go sprawling across the floor. One of the apples was stopped in its tracks by the congealed blood puddle from the man who had lost an arm the day previous. Selwyn tried to smile towards Osbert, but in truth she was scared and even more alone now. Arnum had ridden off into the night, Father Luyewn had travelled to Fortunes Well without so much as a kiss goodbye and Engelhard, the man she could always trust to be at her side, hadn't appeared since he walked out of the great hall after being locked between orders and a friend. All Selwyn could do was pray, pray for her friends and pray for her man.

Carlnut

Merantune's cells were like a grand palace compared to the one Carlnut now found himself in. It was a hollow cube of stone with one way in and no windows. Carlnut had no idea how much time had passed or even if it was night or day. The only thing from the outside world he had heard was a great storm an unconceivable number of days ago. By design, the cell was totally disorientating and, given enough time, Carlnut sensed a man could forget his own name within the cube. The isolation was total and the stimulation was zero. No sound, no light, no furniture or cloth of any kind. All Carlnut could do was feel the cool walls, but even they were sanded smooth. His clothes were drenched in his own waste and the only food he had eaten were the scraps of mouldy bread and a spoonful of water that were passed underneath the flat iron door that barred his exit.

He was determined to survive; he had too many people counting on him, and if he was to simply rot away in a cell somewhere in Wessex, his name would also rot away with him. After all he was a Lord; he had a fort, a wife, men, women and children who all relied on him. The thing that puzzled him most was why he was within the confines and who would want him trapped. The familiar hooded man had told Carlnut that he was being summoned to the council of Wessex, but his lack of seeing anyone made Carlnut seriously doubt this. During the first two days he had screamed for Sicga to see if he was in a cell near him, but his only reply was the sound of his own voice echoing off the tight, damp, dripping walls and once or twice a spear thrust from under the door.

Carlnut had taken a strange comfort in counting the meals he had been served. Most of the time he was handed a lump of bread that even the mice would have been unsatisfied by, but out of necessity he ate it anyway. The thirteenth meal was different from all the rest; instead of the usual paltry fare, he was given a cup of water, warm bread, freshly caught fish and also a damp cloth infused with jasmine. At first Carlnut only stared at the dark outlines of the plate and recoiled when he felt the texture of the cloth. Out of sheer need he scoffed down the fish, not caring if it was laced with poison. A few moments after the last fish bones fell to the floor, he felt sickeningly full to the point of almost vomiting. A clicking sound then reverberated round the cell. It bounced left to right then from the floor to the ceiling, and Carlnut was certain that that would be the last sound he ever heard. A wild howl followed by a dazzling light appeared next. Words formed clumsily in his dry mouth as if he had completely forgotten how to speak. In front of him was a silhouette set against the blinding firelight that reached for Carlnut's soiled rags.

"You will sleep in a bed tonight, Lord Carlnut of Portland, and tomorrow the council will decide your fate," the shadow said. Like everything else in the room, the man was a blur of red and orange, but in spite of this, Carlnut could still make out he was wearing a hood. He went to punch the hooded man but realised his muscles had failed him. He had no energy, and that thought terrified him.

"Get him into a bed; I cannot wait to be rid of him," another man said. This man wore a plain robe and had a full head of wavy head that sprung from his scalp like a thousand tiny snakes. "Close the door, and I will see you in court tomorrow," he said as he shook the dungeon's clinging dust off his person.

"I am not going to be in court tomorrow, Father Osyth of Winchester; my King has asked to see me," the hooded man said. Then the door closed and the dark rushed in again to comfort Carlnut's stinging eyes. His head whirled and his stomach churned at the thought of the traitor Priest. Osyth's presence begged more questions than answers. Carlnut decided that all would be answered the next day, so he crawled to the lice-infested bedspread that had been shown to him before the doors were closed shut. He could still smell the stench of his cell, but the bed felt like a lover's hands across his body. Carlnut fell into a deep sleep for the first time in days.

A black-haired girl woke him the next morning holding a pile of clothes fit for a lord. Carlnut noticed that the small, frail-bodied girl wore a bunch of bronze bracelets that would have been a decent hoard for a warband. Athelhild, the slave girl in Portland, wore a similar set of jewellery, and a tear almost hit his cheek as he thought of his home. The bracelets rattled like the scurrying of tiny mice as she handed him a bucket of warm water. Furiously, Carlnut scrubbed himself, making sure every last morsel of dirt was scraped away from his dirty body. He attacked his own skin like a beast until it was covered in scratches and rashes but no dirt. Then he used a fine-tooth bone comb to untangle his long, knotted hair and to try and take out as many lice as he could. Finally, after three cloths, five buckets of water and two combs, Carlnut felt ready to face his fate. The slave nervously held out the pile of clothes that were folded to perfection and turned away in either embarrassment or politeness. She had given him a wonderfully fitting maroon tunic and a pair of black trousers that were the most comfortable he had ever worn. His boots on the other hand were clearly second hand and worn but still fit Carlnut's feet perfectly, and a cheap golden broach was provided to clasp a dark woollen cloak round his neck. Out of all the great clothes he was given, Carlnut was most thankful for the return of the crude hammer that Selwyn had made for him. It was the symbol of Thor, and Carlnut felt protected whenever he wore it.

"Where am I to go?" Carlnut asked with a voice scarred from the effects of isolation.

"Up the stairs, Lord, then straight down the hall until you meet a guard; he will take you the rest of the way," the girl said before gathering the rags and dirty cloths together and skulking out of the room. The spiralling stairs were wonderfully made out of waxed timber and hard iron but each step was an effort on Carlnut's aching thighs. For an eternity the steps seemed to curve, but at the point that Carlnut felt the dizziest, they levelled off and fed into a thin but direct corridor. The hall was about as wide as Carlnut was, which made it difficult to move forward. Every step was an effort, however, the lordly clothes seemed to have given him a new burst of life, and he was determined to make it out of whatever situation he was in. The slave girl was correct, and in the light of a small lantern that was placed in a stone hovel, Carlnut could see the guard. He wore a purple cloak and held a spear as straight as a corpse. The spear appeared to have a tiny fire sprouting out from the head, but as Carlnut got closer, he could see it was the reflection of the tiny candle that hid innocently within the glass lantern.

"Lord," the guard said. "I have been asked to escort you to the council room." His voice was teeming with anxiety, but as he turned his back on Carlnut to lead him away, his apprehension disappeared like water down a drain. "I must say, Lord; you are a hero amongst some of us soldiers."

"A hero?" Carlnut said in shock.

"Yes, we all dream of saving a King," he replied.

"King Cynewulf died, though; I didn't save anyone," Carlnut said, not wanting praise that was not due.

"Maybe you didn't, but you did slaughter ten people with your sword, and for that I can only admire you. So it is a shame for this to be your fate." The guard realised he had said too much when Carlnut prompted him on that statement, so he decided to remain silent for the rest of the trip. It took an uncomfortably long time to navigate the plain rock walls, which were eventually replaced by wonderful stone walls that were dressed in fabrics of all colours. Amazing forged iron baskets protruded from the walls every couple of feet, which were clearly made for burning torches. "This is where I leave you now, Lord. Enter through this door and I can assure you will come out a different man," the guard said almost with a hint of excitement.

"I didn't catch your name?" Carlnut asked the tall, well-built soldier.

"Coenred," he replied with a smile on his face.

"Farewell Coenred," Carlnut said. At that moment the youthful guard turned away, and Carlnut stared at the birch wood door that was held together by three parallel rusting iron brackets. "My fate awaits," Carlnut whispered to himself. "Odin, I beg for you to watch over me when I enter this room, I beg for you to lead me on the right path and if that path is death, let me die with a sword in my hand so I may dine with my friends in Valhalla." Thinking of Valhalla made Carlnut reflect on the men he might see again. He longed to dine with his father Hrolf, and he desired to speak to Jarl Bergi again and hoped if Solvi had ended up in the watery halls, that he might see him once more.

With one almighty push the door swung open, and Carlnut walked in, only to have the door slammed shut behind him and bolted. He had expected to walk into some kind of snake pit or a room full of blood-hungry soldiers wanting revenge, but instead he was in a huge church. Carlnut was led towards a small pulpit that was placed in front of the altar by a priest no older than himself. The altar held a giant golden cross tipped with rubies and sapphires as well as other finely jewelled objects. A candle was lit in the far corner of the church that flickered and danced in the dark, then another followed its example until soon the whole church was ablaze in candle light. The church was made of Roman stone that crumbled into useless rubble the higher it got. However, many restorations had been made so that new oaken beams and walls stood in the place of decayed bricks and stone. After Carlnut became accustomed to the marvellous structure, he finally noticed how full it actually was. Scores of priests huddled together behind him held back by a few soldiers who levelled their spears to form a thin wall. In front of him and behind the altar he saw a row of chairs neatly set up like a dais. His palms became sweaty and a ringing sounded within his ears as a door opened somewhere behind him.

Muttering and cheers erupted as five men parted the crowd as if someone had just stretched out a huge ball of dough. The first man carried a swinging lantern that produced strange-smelling vapours which stung the nostrils whilst the last held another ornate cross on a grand golden pole. But it was the men in-between that stunned Carlnut. He saw the wavy-haired priest, Father Osyth, who smirked as he passed Carlnut. Earl Cynric followed closely behind with his red hair combed perfectly to the left and a blushing red face that complimented his bright purple tunic. But the most surprising of all was the stern-looking man who took his place on the centre chair that was raised slightly so he could see every face within the crowd. It was the Ealdorman Osric, Sicga's father and the man Carlnut had saved from certain death some months earlier. Father Osyth and Earl Cynric took their places next to Osric and ordered a slave to serve them drink. It was the same girl who had given Carlnut his clothes, and she carefully poured Cynric some water causing her bracelets to jangle. As she shuffled over to Osyth, he tugged on her stained rag and whispered something in her ear that made her face change in horror. Either in fear or determination she continued to pour wine into his silver cup.

"Are you Lord Carlnut of Portland?" Ealdorman Osric asked.

"Yes Lord," Carlnut replied.

"Therefore you are here to answer the accusations regarding your faith." Carlnut's heart sank; he knew what Osric was going to say and hated the overwhelming feeling of helplessness. "You stand here today before God and the King. You are accused of being a Pagan. You are accused of living your life in the eyes of false deities and minions of Satan himself," Osric said. The hall gasped but Carlnut suspected they all knew why he was there for none of them had even a glimmer of remorse on their faces and one or two even looked excited.

"Excuse me Lord, but I do not see the King here?" Carlnut said not even flinching at the accusations.

"King Beorhtric is not well, and he has sent me to judge over the proceedings. So do you plead guilty to the accusations, Carlnut?" Osric said. Carlnut blinked blankly and ran his hand through his hair. He caught a louse in-between his knuckles and proceeded in crushing it between his black fingernails.

"What proof do you have, Osric?" Carlnut spat on the floor and the score of priests hissed curses like a bunch of angry snakes. Ealdorman Osric winced at Carlnut's lack of manners whilst Cynric rested his feet upon the altar, much to Osyth's disapproval.

"I do have proof," the Ealdorman said, inviting Father Osyth to rise. The priest had just finished his second cup of wine, and he fumbled slightly as he tried to stand. His black robe caught on the side of the arm of his chair, and it smacked on the floor as it fell.

"He is a Pagan! He is a dirty man and he does nothing but pollute the minds of all around him. He must die. He must!" Osyth's voice was loud and shrill and sent daggers flying through the air in the form of insults. "The fiend wears a pagan insignia, a hammer that is a symbol of one of his disgusting false Gods. He must die!" Carlnut felt uncomfortable on his feet as the priest's words cut deep into him. He felt himself grabbing onto the small pulpit to stop his anger bursting out in a flurry of fists and blood; one of the soldiers, a tall brooding man, saw Carlnut's building rage and stepped forward.

"Is it true, do you wear a symbol of your false Gods?" Osric asked. Carlnut fought against the instinct that told him to reach for the hammer that hung wonderfully round his neck. "Hold him down!" Osric shouted. Two men rushed to follow Osric's orders, they both clasped onto old spears and quickly grabbed each of Carlnut's arms. Earl Cynric jumped down from the altar and strode towards Carlnut with confidence enough for three men. Within his hand he held a short knife that was sharp enough to cut bone and used it to snap the string that tied the tunic's neck together. He clutched the hammer talisman and pulled it off Carlnut's neck then held it aloft. Once more the crowd gasped and the priests hissed and Carlnut knew he had lost. So he decided there would be nothing wrong with trying to stand his ground.

"I wear a hammer round my neck; that doesn't make me a Pagan," Carlnut claimed, removing his hands from the iron grips of the Christian soldiers. "If a woman wears a golden chain with a bird upon it that does not make her an eagle." One man laughed from the back of the church whilst another hit him over the head to silence him. Earl Cynric climbed into his chair and poured himself another cup of water. "So, Osric, is there any other false evidence you can provide these wonderful servants of the all-mighty god with?" Carlnut said, gaining a new energy from his eventual death. Cynric crunched an apple in his bright white teeth and Osyth whispered insults between sips of wine.

"I do, Carlnut," Osric said. "I have a witness to your practices and a man who can swear on his oaths that you Carlnut are in fact a Pagan." A strange shadow of doubt filled the air at the sound of the mystery witness and even Father Osyth looked puzzled but smiled at the thought of Carlnut's doom. The door at the back of the room opened once again, and Carlnut turned at the sound. A large man with curly black hair moved into the room agonisingly slowly, but Carlnut wished he had never entered the room at all. It was Sicga, whose face showed no emotion but an eye that was fixed shut from the blow he had received a few days back in the woods or maybe a fresh blow he had taken from a soldier. He walked past Carlnut without a glance and took his spot in front of the altar and in front of his father.

"For the court could you please say who you are," Osric said.

"I am Sicga the son of Ealdorman Osric and a captain of Lord Carlnut's garrison in Portland," Sicga said, only now choosing to look at Carlnut. For some reason Carlnut felt no anger towards the big man; he was after all a devout Christian and an Ealdorman's son.

"Noble Sicga, you have spent a lot of time with the Lord Carlnut. Is he a Pagan?" Osric asked as he fiddled nervously with the arms of his cushioned chair, picking at the wood and causing it to splinter slightly. Sicga remained silent and for once Carlnut saw fear in the man's face. His eyes were dark and carried purple sacks below. He looked absolutely drained. "Is he a Pagan?" Osric asked again nervously. Earl Cynric leaned forward in interest and Father Osyth stood up demanding Sicga tell the truth.

"You will rot in the fires of hell if you break the oath you have sworn in this church!" the priest spat, forcing droplets of wine to spill upon the white cloth that draped the altar. Sicga still said nothing. A stream of fresh sweat poured from his forehead until he used his leather vambrace to wipe it off his face. The crowd whispered insults at the silent witness whilst priests said prayers and made the sign of the cross in his direction. Butterflies fluttered uncontrollably inside Carlnut's belly. Even though his death was all but sealed, he still felt his fate could somehow be worse. He saw Sicga being torn into pieces from all the oaths he had made and Carlnut looked at him and nodded.

"Sicga, you are released from any oath you have made to me," Carlnut shouted before he was threatened with a spear thrust from a restless soldier.

"I ask you again, son, have you seen this man practice any Pagan rituals? Is he a Pagan?" Ealdorman Osric was now standing and leaning over the altar to stare at his son.

"No," Sicga said.

"Coward," one man shouted.

"Pagan," another screamed.

"His mind has been warped by the Pagan; his statement is invalid. Carlnut is a Pagan!" Father Osyth howled. A frenzy had begun rising behind Carlnut as the crowd stomped on the floor and pushed each other. They were hurling curses as if they were spears all hoping to kill Carlnut and some even spat in the direction of Sicga.

"Silence, I demand silence, in the name of King Beorhtric I demand silence!" Osric said, smacking his hand against the table. "It is clear to me that Father Osyth is correct; my son's mind has clearly been meddled with by the scum Pagan, and that in itself is unforgivable. Would someone please escort my son out of here and have a monk see to his wits." Three priests burst through the spear barrier that was getting increasingly harassed and ran with their robes trailing on the dust-plagued rushes towards Sicga. For an instant, Carlnut wanted to run towards him to thank him for his unwarranted loyalty but instead nodded again and that seemed to be alright for the captain of Portland. Without so much as raising a fist, he allowed himself to be taken out of the church by the three old men. "Father Osyth has given me enough evidence to prove this man's Paganism. Is there anyone else who can provide me with more?" Osric asked the room, his plain eyes squinting to correct the glare from the hundreds of candles.

"I do," Earl Cynric said. "Lord Carlnut of Portland used to be my guard. Whilst he was in my hall I saw him spitting on a figure of the great Christ that I have hung up above a blessed shrine."

"Lies!" Carlnut called.

"The accused will be silent," Osric bellowed. The ealdorman leant back in his chair and seemed to contemplate the extra evidence and after a few pointless minutes of thinking, he stood up. Carlnut prayed to Odin and his heart was louder than Thor's anvil. He thought of Selwyn and Arnum and he thought of Luyewn and Sicga but most surprisingly to him he thought of Valhalla and how he would do whatever he could to die with a sword in hand. His eyes darted around the church. He knew he could easily disarm one of the guards and go down doing something he loved as he was swamped by a multitude of other armed men. At that moment his previous thoughts of his family and friends for some reason stopped his desire for battle. Carlnut looked at the altar and saw the two men he hated the most laughing and grinning to themselves; one behind a fish lord persona and another behind a cup of wine. *You will die before me,* Carlnut thought to himself but these thoughts turned into speech.

"I vow upon my place in the other world, that you two will die before my sword," Carlnut said and pointed towards Osyth and Cynric. "I will make sure Karla sings in a bath of your blood and your skulls are used as flagons for my Lady's wine." Carlnut cleared his throat. "I swear it upon whatever Gods rule this Earth that as long as I live, your lives will not be safe. I swear that if I die your souls will be mine to torment in the other world." Only Father Osyth seemed scared by the threats, and he made a dramatic show of storming out of the hall. His chair was flung to the floor again, and a half cup of wine spilt across the altar making the white cloth look blood stained. The slave girl rattled as she stooped to pick up the misplaced chair and tottered closely behind the drunken priest.

Two rats nibbled at breadcrumbs in a cobwebbed corner of the church whilst an owl hooted from somewhere outside. Osric stood up and the whole church came back to life; the sleepy onlookers straightened their backs and gave out a chorus of yawns. The Ealdorman signalled for another priest to replace Osric and a terribly fat man, who seemed to be the only one looking at the time, almost rolled out of the crowd. He wore large, ill-fitting robes that were the colour of rotted cow's milk and held a perpetual smile that didn't falter at the sight of Carlnut. From one of the many groves that hid in the waving shadows of the church, he pulled a large candle out of a wicker basket. The fat priest, who was almost twice as wide as Carlnut and a foot shorter, slammed the candle down upon the pulpit, causing flakes of wax to scatter like stars across the stand's shining wood. He pulled an already lit torch from its rusty iron holster and lit the candle's wick. The torch's flames seemed to pull away from the candle as if they knew its meaning, but still the wick burnt and soon Carlnut could feel a slight heat close to his skin. Osric at this point was standing almost next to the fat priest, who by this time had commanded the eyes of every single man in the room, and even the rats seemed to have stopped scuttling about. Earl Cynric was leaning intently from the middle of the altar with a colossal grin on his face as if he were peering into a giant hoard of gold. With one enormous effort, the priest lifted his hugely plump arms and held them aloft towards the sky. His robe was far too big for him, and it hung like wings underneath his armpits that were stained in puddles of sweat. Behind him, upon the wall of the church Carlnut could see a giant shadow bird being cast from the tiny light of the candle. The bird encased Earl Cynric who now sat smirking at the centre of the altar. Then Osric spoke:

"Lord Carlnut of Portland," Osric said using his proper title. "You saved my life many moons ago and for that I have decided to spare you a burning." Jeers rung out from every corner of the church and a dog even joined in from somewhere inside of Wareham. "However, for your crimes of being a Pagan, you shall die tomorrow. You shall die from the executioner's axe!"

"Odin will save me," Carlnut said, focusing only on the giant raven that was darkening the entire altar and was swallowing Earl Cynric.

Solvi

The Bjornafjorden looked wonderful. Its soft waves caressed the side of the five magnificent boats that carefully bobbed in the ice blue water. A school of silver-scaled fish swam round the sleeping vessels whilst a kingfisher perched itself upon one of the five masts, searching for its next meal. Skeleton trees that had shed their skin for winter had started to get their new bloom, and all of the pine trees that surrounded the great lake began to become greener and more vibrant. A pulsating echo reverberated through the woods from one of the many trees Gudrod had ordered to be cut. The vibrations sent small waves dancing over the surface and one even caught an otter that was bathing in the warm sun. Thord, Osoyro's master boat builder, had spent a whole week carving amazing beast head prows for each of Solvi's boats. Each boat had its own beast chosen by its master. Ospak, one of the men who fought alongside Solvi the day they had taken Osoyro from the hands of Jarl Bergison, had asked for an owl's head. He had an unusually high voice and thus decided the screeching owl was a perfect symbol for his ship. Gisha on the other hand had asked for a beast like no other. It was shaped in the form of a screaming woman with hundreds of snakes sprouting out from her head. Thord had said that he couldn't even look at the beast as it made him feel as cold as stone. The beast head ship and the screeching owl sat next to Umiston's great tusked boar, Thord's own spouting seal and Solvi's raven head. Like something out of a nightmare, they rested and stared off towards salt-washed rocks where the sea met the fjord and beyond. Solvi hoped the beasts stared towards Britain, but he could not tell.

That night, hundreds of logs were thrown onto a great pyre that towered higher than the height of a man. There were rotting planks, mossy pieces of bark and all sorts of different chunks of kindling that were waiting to be burnt. The full moon's light burst down onto the pyre, reflecting off the sap-covered leaves that still clung desperately to the wood. There were five stakes as tall as trees shoved into the middle of the pile. Into each stake a god was carved meaning that Odin, Freya, Thor, Balder and Loki all watched the feasting tables that were carefully arranged all across the settlement. Solvi could see the deep-set eyes of Odin staring at him and felt an overwhelming warmth within his heart.

"How do we like the mutton?" Rollaug Danson shouted from one end of the table, lifting aloft a cup filled with brown ale. The rest of the tables cheered in reply as most were too drunk to formulate a proper response.

"Too burnt for my bloody taste," Frosti said as he furiously tore at a sheep bone.

"I will have yours then, arse hair," Halfdan said as he grabbed Frosti's plate, which caused the big man to lash out like a disturbed wolf. The blow smacked Halfdan across the face sending him flying off his seat and onto the dry grass. For a moment the drinking stopped and every man turned to face the commotion. Even Finlit, who was entertaining a woman with striking blonde hair, stopped to look at his humiliated friend. Halfdan picked himself and straightened his seal skin coat. The pelt was fastened with a pointed wolf tooth that broke off as he patted the dirt off the garment.

"For a piece of worm shit you have quite a fist," Halfdan laughed, and the rest of Osoyro laughed with him. "Now who will give me another piece of fucking meat?" An owl hooted from somewhere in the trees as if it was crying from seeing some of its home torn down as a sacrifice to the Gods. Gudrod emerged from one of the longhouses holding the hand of a brown-haired slave girl until he pushed her away and threw her some form of payment.

"These women sure know their trade," Gudrod bellowed then let out a huge belch that was mirrored by most of the drunken warriors.

"Myrun's girls are some of the best, I can assure you of that," Solvi said, picking at some meat that was annoyingly stuck within his teeth. "Although I have never tried any of them myself, my men often come away with smiles on their faces and empty purses," the Jarl chuckled. Suddenly there was dancing and music. Aesa was leading a procession of free women towards the tables, her swollen belly looking huge in a torch's light. The women weaved in-between the feasting tables running their soft hands teasingly against the wood. One woman who looked around fifteen flirtingly ran her hand across the shoulders of some of the drunken warriors, and soon she had a choir of whistles and howls directed at her.

"Should she really be doing that?" Gisha asked Eddval regarding Aesa's dancing.

"I have no idea, but she does look good so I don't mind," Eddval said with a smirk on his face. Eddval was rocking on his chair and looked as white as gushing water, but that didn't stop him filling up his mead horn. Gisha raised her eyebrows and turned towards Solvi as if she was bored with Eddval's happiness.

"When are the guests arriving?" Gisha said.

"Soon, maybe after the oaths. I am not sure," Solvi said with a mouthful of food that formed strings around his teeth and tongue. He cleared his mouth with a swig of the winter's last ale. "Are you going to be swearing an oath to your Jarl, Chieftess Gisha?" Solvi took another drink of ale. "Because if you do not I will have no choice but to reinstate another Chief to Bergen. Frosti maybe?" Gisha laughed at the thought of Solvi removing her and then winced when she saw Frosti eating his food like a bear devouring the carcass of a great boar.

"You better shut your mouth, Solvi," she laughed.

"Oaths!" Solvi shouted at his loudest across every table. Jarl Bergi, who had died almost three years ago, once told Solvi that the best thing a Jarl could do is make his men swear an oath. Oaths were the law, and if one man broke their sworn oath to another then it would be the other who had the precedent to punish the oath breaker. Solvi had seen it hundreds of times; men deserting from their chief or Jarl, women being unfaithful to their man and merchants using false weights. "I am your Jarl, and I want you to make me an oath of loyalty. You will obey my orders regardless and follow me into battle. In return I vow to protect you, I vow to be a fair ruler and I vow to make you all rich!" Cheers rung out from across the courtyard, which was now littered with spilt food, splatters of blood, hunting dogs scavenging and ale-caused vomit. Solvi noticed that two people perched under a tree near Frosti's tent were the only two people not to cheer or show emotion of any kind even after Solvi had promised to protect them. It was the monkish figures he had met in the woods the other night. The bandaged monk looked grotesque; his rags were even dirtier now, and Solvi swore he could smell him from where he stood. However, the other one, Athelstan, had much more life in him now than the night they had met in the wood. Even though half his body still walked with a terrible limp, his hair had grown out of its tonsured restraints and had begun to curl slightly.

"My men have already sworn oaths to me, Jarl Solvi," Gudrod the Hunter said with an unusual amount of decorum. He then raised his voice so most of his men that were at the feast could hear. "You have all sworn oaths to me, and for that I am fucking grateful. However, I will not deny you the chance to swear your swords to Jarl Solvi and after the raids, we are more than willing to release any man from their oaths to join the other." Solvi was astonished, much to Gudrod's amusement. "We are going be rich from these raids, Solvi, and I owe you thanks," Gudrod said as his dragon tattoos danced in the flame's light. After his speech, scores of men lined up to swear their oaths to the Jarl. Gisha was first, and she laid her two small, battle-hardened axes on the ground and swore to die for Solvi and from then on the procedure flew through. Men carrying axes, spears, shields and a few with swords all knelt in front of Solvi. A few shield maidens also pledged their lives to the Jarl. Solvi was most surprised by the presence of Gudrod's warlords. Halfdan, however, was still as ungraceful as a new-born deer, and he just stood in front of Solvi.

"I will fight for you, arse wipe," he said.

"I will count that as an oath then, Halfdan Halfdanson," Solvi said, tipping his head in response. The few clouds that were hiding the moon skated away when they saw the beauty of the moon's light reflecting off the fjord. It was a huge moon that night, and it almost filled the entire sky, drowning it with more light than the sun does at dusk. Two bats twirled overhead as the last man swore his oath to Solvi, who had almost dozed off due to the sheer longevity of the oath swearing. "Thank you," Solvi addressed the sobering men. "Now I have a gift for you," he said and signalled at Jik and Ospak who were both standing near the Christian monks. The archer and captain of the owl-headed boat walked straight past the looming shadows and towards the pits that acted as prisons in Osoyro. A few moments later the sound of hoarse voices could be heard from the trees where Jik and Ospak had disappeared.

"Who the fuck are these turd wipes?" Halfdan bellowed when a few bodies emerged from the bushes.

"I present to you the men that have made our wonderful boats for us," Solvi proclaimed as Huy the older boat builder strode into view. His grey hair had become a painful white and his arms were covered with scratches and blisters from his work. He was followed by Punjif the fat man. His extreme belly, which was bigger than Rollaug's, still defined him even though Thord said they had been living off fish for the past few months. Punjif waddled like a duck in front of three other builders whose names Solvi had never bothered to learn. Huy turned to face the giant pyre behind him then turned to look at Solvi. His eyes were as sharp and bright as arrow heads. He turned back to look at the pyre and sighed as he had truly recognised what was about to happen.

"You can't do this!" Huy said, finally alerting his friends to their coming fate. "King Sigfred is a vengeful man. He places a high price on our heads."

"What price?" Halfdan shouted. Huy hesitated. "What price does the slug-faced Sigfred place on your mole-arsed head?" Huy recoiled in shock at the question.

"We are boat builders of extreme quality–" Halfdan waved a hand at Huy to silence him, and the great warlord began to pick at a bone on his plate evidently bored with the discussion. "Jarl Solvi, I beg you. Ah, I know things. I have lived in Sigfred's land all my life, I know his weaknesses." He was clearly getting desperate. A lonesome bead of sweat trickled down his wrinkled face. The others tried to talk but were silenced by a smack on the head from Ospak or a bow string pull from Jik.

"Would your King pay his weight in gold for him?" Gisha said, pointing one of her axes towards Punjif. The others laughed. Huy turned as red as a piece of raw beef whilst one hand clenched into a fist and the other reached for an amulet hung around his neck.

"To whom do you wish to be sacrificed?" Solvi asked.

"Loki," Huy said, surprising everyone at the feast and even Gudrod looked up. The Hunter had perched himself behind the high table and had decided to stay out of the entire proceedings.

"You southerners are crazy pieces of shit," Halfdan said.

"Are you sure?" Gisha said.

"There is nothing I would want more than to be offered to the great God Loki," Huy bellowed with an astounding confidence. Loki was the most feared of all the gods and most men believed that anyone or beast that was to be sacrificed to him would be his to use or torment for the rest of time.

"Bloody fool," Frosti said. "What about you, fat man?"

"Baldur," Punjif said to Frosti. "Baldur, please Lord." He now looked at Jarl Solvi who nodded in amusement. Men keeled over in bursts of erratic laughter and one man almost chocked on his mead until his friend smacked his back. Baldur was meant to be the most beautiful God to have ever lived whereas Punjif was fat, boil ridden and stunk of rotting trout.

"The world's gone mad," Eddval laughed as he stroked Aesa's long brown hair.

It didn't take long for Solvi's men to tie King Sigfred's mix-matched team of boat builders to the freshly cut timber. The stakes had been buried in the rocky mud, which was surrounded by the mounds of fire wood. A mass of grey and black clouds rolled over the thousands of blinking stars on a chilled west wind. The ropes that bound them were tight horse hair thongs that burnt rashes into the builders' thick wrists and swollen ankles. Punjif looked the most uncomfortable as he hung from the pole squirming and panicking. His breeches were soon stained in his own urine, and the stench made the man next to him scrunch up his nose in disgust. All the tables had been returned to their longhouses and scraps of bread crumbs and fish bones lay strewn across the ground like a miniature battlefield. The people of Osoyro and the northern camps gathered round like a drunken swaying forest. All of them were preparing for the burning. The night was cold, so most of them wore thick layers of fur that gave the procession a beast-like appearance. Gisha donned her magnificent, pure white bear pelt, which made her look like a goddess, whereas Halfdan and Gudrod wore layers upon layers of seal skin that stunk of rotted fish and dung. One by one, the onlookers brought their own offerings to the Gods. Straw baskets filled with food as well as hundreds of vibrantly coloured flowers were placed onto the kindling. Rollaug carried a huge cauldron to the pyre and began to empty its contents onto the pyre. Various meats slaughtered just for the sacrifice fell to the ground, and men rushed to stuff the flesh into whatever gaps were left between the wood. The richer men amongst them brought great gifts; Jik placed a quiver of goose-haired arrows and Asa, who followed closely behind the archer, lay a wonderfully knitted scarf onto his quiver. Unmoved by his wife's closeness to Jik, Gudrod threw in an old axe that almost struck Huy's swinging legs. Then Finlit and a few of his men dragged in four oars, which made for great kindling as well as a worthy sacrifice to the Gods. After the last of the gifts were given, Solvi pushed his way to the front and addressed the crowd.

"Odin! I offer you this man in hope you will provide us with the wisdom to reach and raid Britain." The crowd started to make noise but were quickly silenced by Solvi's raised arm. "Baldur, in return for this sacrifice-" the Jarl shouted and pointed to the unconscious Punjif, "-all I ask for is the light to guide our ships to the shores of Britain. Freyr, please accept my sacrifice whilst I pray to you to give us excellent sea-faring weather." From the corner of his eye, Solvi noticed Athelstan whispering to Tojuk, but the Jarl carried on regardless. "Thor! Mighty Thor, give us strength, and I beg for you to protect us on our perilous raid. And finally, Loki, I give you this man, this ship builder named Huy. Please accept him as worthy of your almighty power." Solvi seemed breathless after his words but nevertheless, the hundreds of people who had crammed into Osoyro that night under a full moon were in awe. It was at that moment, with around four hundred people listening to him, that Solvi truly felt like a great Jarl or even a King.

Frosti picked up one of the many torches that surrounded the crowd and slowly walked up to Eddval. As drunk as he was, Eddval did manage to carry a piece of broken oak covered in pitch-smothered cloth towards the stakes. The tips touched and the flame looked joyful as it gave birth to another. Gisha came forward with another naked torch until that as well burst into life. Moments later twelve tiny flames encircled the waiting pyre. It was desperate to be lit. Solvi could almost hear the wood pile crying helplessly out for the heat to touch it, or maybe that was the screams of the boat builders pleading for mercy. One by one the torchbearers lowered their prancing flames until their sentient shadows polluted the twig-covered ground. Invisible waves displaced the once-calm air, blurring Solvi's sight and filling his eyes with water. The first spark caught a piece of dry yellowed straw whilst another whistled into a pile of dark green leaves. All twelve of the tiny fires spat at the kindling in unison until there were a dozen spots on the pyre starting to burn. The boat builders were squirming like fish caught, in a net as small trickles of smoke swirled upwards catching in their nostrils and forcing their eyes to squint. The fires soon caught more pieces of timber, dry thatch and leaves until they were bigger than the torch's flames. A great burst of light frightened the darkness into submission until the night was brighter than the day. Within the cascading smoke, Solvi could see the changing faces of the struggling men, and he felt joy. Their screams were like the laughter of small children and the sound of their constant pleas of mercy stimulated Solvi. Gudrod was laughing an almighty laugh as they all stepped back to avoid the falling burning timbers that jumped from the fire's heat.

"Can you see their flesh burn? It's fucking wonderful. The smell is better than sex!" Gudrod laughed as he smacked his war axe onto the pyre, sending a firestorm fountain into the air. At that moment, the deep grey smoke was disturbed enough for Solvi to see the melting flesh of Huy. He looked like a daemon, with skin bloodied and overlapping other hanging scabs of more loose flesh. Blood dripped furiously from where his eyes once were whilst one of his feet was completely bare till only a charcoal-coloured bone remained. Somehow from the depths of death before his soul was claimed by the Gods, he managed to raise an arm. It was a hideous, impossible thing that looked more like a piece of meat upon a stove than anything else. But stretching out from the flame-covered appendage was a single finger as the others must have been claimed by the laughing fire. This one finger that was about to lose all life pointed past Solvi towards Frosti, who was blissfully unaware of the deadly curse. In one last attempt at drawing out the last miserable seconds of his life, Huy turned his empty eye sockets towards Solvi, and the Jarl grimaced at the sight of the burning man's wild toothless smile. Solvi looked back towards his friend, whose beard looked magnificent in the engulfing fire light, and swallowed deeply.

The next morning was beautiful. There was the stillness in the air that always preceded a wonderful day. Three birds hummed to each other from their crudely built twig nests in the trees that looked down on the pile of blackened embers. A score of wild fowl gracefully made their way from one thicket across an opening to another that was stuffed with black and blue berries. Two dogs chased each other carrying sticks in their pointed teeth. One was panting wildly whilst the other was jumping up and down as if it was ready to begin some new aspect of their game. Luckily for Solvi's grumbling stomach, Eddval and Rollaug woke him that morning with a cup of thick oat porridge.

"Jarl, I have so many questions," Eddval said whilst morsels of wax still gripped Solvi's eyelids together.

"Eddval, my brother, you will be fine. I would advise you to stop drinking so much. We will bring back riches, gold and silver to the point you can no longer carry it by yourself. As I said before, I will grant you a chiefdom of your own for your great work towards my cause," Solvi asserted.

"Thank you, Jarl," Eddval said before he embraced Solvi. Rollaug Danson was still standing awkwardly at the door with his large figure blocking the new morning light trying desperately to get into the tent.

"Jarl, I need to. . ." The fat man looked down at his feet as if some kind of shame was weighing him down. "I need to thank you. If you for some reason don't return from Britain, I will wait in anticipation to serve you when I reach Valhalla. Which I am sure will be soon if you do die." Rollaug quickly excused himself, and as he turned away, he took one last look at Solvi and waddled out of sight. The void however was rapidly filled with the huge silhouette of Frosti.

"I see you are here," Frosti said, looking surprised and disgusted by Eddval's presence. "Why are you here? You are not raiding with us so you don't need to be bloody here. Get out!" Frosti bellowed. Eddval without hesitation left, but Solvi suspected Frosti would have gotten some pleasure out of trying to humiliate Eddval.

"There is no need to be so harsh on him, brother," Solvi said. "He is after all your vice-Jarl." Frosti laughed at that comment, and Solvi was quick to join in. The great bearded man was dressed in his war leathers and had his magnificent war axe strapped to his back, which gleamed in the sun's fresh rays. The thought of Huy's burning curse was still fresh in Solvi's memory, and he desperately wanted to blot out everything he had seen within the churning inferno.

"Finlit sailed off last night with his ships and some of our best men," Frosti informed Solvi. That made Solvi happy as his plan was finally coming together. Finlit and his ships, which were packed with both his and Solvi's men, were charged with protecting Osoyro. The great sailor had only agreed to do that on one condition: that he could do it from the water. At first the entire war council had argued, but he actually had a compelling argument. This was because King Sigfred would only ever attack Osoyro by sea, and Finlit's sails should be enough to defeat any threat.

"Well, my brother, it is time to raid Britain," Solvi said.

"May the bloody Gods bless us," Frosti shouted.

Only a few hours later, a fleet of twelve full ships sailed out of the wonderfully calm Bjornafjorden towards the isle of Britain.

Frosti

All twelve of the ships looked like a gathering of fluffed white cloud floating peacefully across the expanding deep blue water. Frosti could see the towering sails of Gudrod's ship, and he recognised the twirling mass of ropes that Gisha had on board hers. However, the most beautiful vessel on that subdued sea was the one Frosti was standing upon. Its planks were made from the finest pine and birch trees that had once stood so proud next to the still presence of the Bjornafjorden. He could see small holes where woodpeckers once hunted and winding cracks that once acted as great walkways for tiny ants. For the first two hours of the journey, hungry gulls flew overhead desperately searching for fishing nets and traps, but the only thing the Raven Head had on board was warriors ready for battle. On either side of Frosti there was a plethora of rowers. Overall, there were twenty rowers at any one time, their gigantic shoulders tensing and sweating with the weight of the pulsating water. However, there were another ten men sleeping, eating and bailing water out of the Raven Head's busy hull. Jarl Solvi was at the steering oar at the right-hand side of the boat towards the back. The oar was shaped strategically to catch the power of the underwater tides and had a much bigger shaft than usual oars, with a thicker blade. It was a perilously difficult task to navigate the steering oar as it took extreme strength and stamina, so Frosti was amazed at Solvi's ease at using it. Next to the Jarl was Jik, who was annoyingly trying to win his favour again. Even Frosti could see that Jik had become more of a nuisance than anything else, but his wild skill with a bow was sure to be useful on such a raid.

"Where is the Princess?" Frosti asked abrasively.

"Asa and Olaf and the babe have decided to stay on board one of Finlit's ships. She thinks she's pregnant, you know," Jik announced. Solvi turned in horror, his face showing no emotion but anger. A bead of sweat ran down the side of his forehead, showing Frosti he was starting to at least feel some struggle from the steering oar.

"Jik, please don't tell me that it's–," Solvi tried to say but Jik interrupted.

"No, never. Impossible we haven't even fucked. The whelp will be that fat bastard's," he said and pointed towards Dreki, which looked magnificent in the sun's reflection. "Although he most likely had to beat it into her poor body. She is covered in bruises, Jarl. You must see he is a monster."

"Silence!" Solvi bellowed, causing all thirty men to turn in a sweaty confusion; for a heartbeat, only the God's wind was driving the Raven Head. He let go of the oar to reveal blistered hands that probably stung in the sea's saltiness. However, those hands were strong enough to shove Frosti out of the way and grab around Jik's thin, scrawny neck.

"Gudrod the Hunter is our ally and without him we would not be raiding. So for once please stop thinking with your shrivelled cock and think with your head. She is a princess and you are a farmer's son; you have no hope of ever being with her. I need you to swear to me that you will never see her again." Solvi's grip still didn't loosen and soon Jik's normally bright face started to lose all colour. "If it were not for your skill in battle, I would take full pleasure in throwing you overboard to be swallowed by the tides." The Jarl let go of Jik who fell to the sodden planks below and began to pant like a bitch in heat. Then like a wounded wild dog he scurried away to one of the rowers' benches to try and hide his shame.

"You should have not have bloody done that, brother," Frosti said as nudged Solvi away from Jik. They then both took the steering oar bench and sat in a consoling silence for what seemed like an age. Solvi seemed content in the slight movements of the oar but Frosti hated his Jarl's blank expression. Tired of the dull atmosphere, Frosti leapt up and screamed at the men.

"Take a break, men! Man the sails and keep them strong. Any dip in the wind and you run to the bloody oars like they are your wives' open legs." Frosti had been on a hundred raids before but most of those were to the small Kingdom of Frisia and a few to the most north-western point of Frankia where the seas were rough and the cliffs steep and formidable. He was certain it was the Frisian shoreline that he could see on the horizon. The fleet had decided to follow the coast for as long as possible so they could never become lost. Frosti could almost make out the shingle beaches and winding rivers that swirled out of the land. Frisia was a wet and horrible place; it was terribly flat, which meant the land was flooded for half a year. But nevertheless it was a Christian kingdom rich with churches that were fat in shimmering gold and ornate silver so the raids always reaped decent rewards. Suddenly, a ship with raging white sails and perfectly strumming oars that sung in the water, obscured Frosti's sight of the lowland kingdom. It was Dreki, Gudrod's amazing ship. Frosti could see Gudrod sitting at the steering oar, laughing wildly at some joke one of his oarsman had made. Halfdan was also on that boat, and Frosti was sure he was screaming ear-piercing insults at some of the rowers, making them row like men possessed. Behind Dreki, and being carried by a powerful westward wind, was another one of Gudrod's ships, which had a snarling dog at its prow. Its captain was helping some of the men bail water from the ever-flooding deck whilst another group of men pulled ropes and heaved sails and sung the songs of the sea. They were singing Solvi's favourite song, and Frosti could see the Jarl's face trying its hardest to withhold a smile. But the squinting of his eyes and the slight glare of teeth betrayed its presence. Soon after a few lines of the old song were carried through the wind towards the Raven Head, its battle-hungry crew also started to chant:

Oh Odin in the Sky,
I hear your Ravens fly.
You watch me when I'm born,
And you're there when I die.

The words seemed to complement the sound of the white-washed waves upon the freshly carved hull. Frosti had lifted his great war axe off his back and smacked its shaft onto the deck in an attempt to mirror one of the war drums that echoed through the air from another vessel.

You gave me strength for my arms,
You gave me seeds for my farms.
I hope you smile down at me,
When women love my charms.

That line was the warrior's favourite as most replaced the word *charms* with something of their own, even though most shouted the word "cock." There was an incredible atmosphere upon the maiden voyage of the Raven Head as everyone pulled their tiring, heavy weight to stay on course for Britain. All of a sudden, Solvi was standing on one of the rowing benches whilst his wet and muddy leather boots caught on another cheerful man's cloak.

Oh Odin in the Sky,
I hear your Ravens fly.
You watch me when I'm born,
And you're there when I die.

He bellowed each line as if he was making one of his rousing battle speeches. Frosti knew that this battle song was Solvi's father's favourite as well, and that explained the strands of tears that fearlessly escaped the Jarl's delighted face. Whilst the last verse was being sung, something caught Frosti's eye. Something felt wrong. First, he checked to see if the coastline was still visible and that in their joyous singing they hadn't somehow strayed off course. Frosti could hear the gulls shrieking at a fishing boat that was frantically rowing back to the shore, which was like a chalk line drawn upon the horizon. He then darted over to the portside to see if the rest of the boats were still with the Raven Head. He saw Gisha's daemon-headed boat and he even saw the shield maiden looking wonderful in all her leather war gear. Dreki and Umiston's boat were still rowing like furious beasts swimming atop of the waves. After a quick flash of panic forcing warm blood to shoot round Frosti's body, Ospak's crammed boat came into eyeshot. But still even after seeing twelve fully operational and happy ships being manned by twelve powerful fit crews, Frosti felt a damning air surrounding him. Solvi and Jik didn't seem to notice a change and neither did any of the rowers, but he was adamant that something had changed. So Frosti decided to check everything again. Frisia was definitely still visible and if anything they were closer to the land than they had been all journey. Then he counted the boats again. But there were no longer twelve rowing boats all panting in unison towards Britain. There were thirteen.

From the depths of the vast ocean an ominous lonely vessel bobbed and ebbed towards them. Frosti dropped his war axe and stepped back in terror until his feet caught in a water pail. He began to fall but one of the rowers caught his weight and propped him back up again as if nothing had happened.

"No! This cannot be bloody real," he bellowed.

"Have you gone mad, brother?" Solvi said, laughing at the pale-faced Frosti. Two things at that point had made Frosti feel like his world was crumbling into one giant pit. There was nothing wrong with sailing with twelve ships and it was even better to travel with fourteen but thirteen was a terrible omen. Thirteen had been terrible ever since the banquet of the twelve Gods. A great feast was held in celebration of the wonderful feats of the powerful God Baldur. However, during that feast Loki the trickster God had shown up as an uninvited thirteenth guest. It was at that magnificent meal that invincible Baldur was to die from a spear thrust provided by Loki.

"Loki is with us, Jarl," Frosti tried to say under his breath. Then after ignoring Solvi's pleas to repeat what he just said, Frosti thought of Huy's pleasure at being offered to Loki. "What a bloody bastard!" Frosti shouted, causing a shower of spittle to cover his fiery red beard. As the boat bobbed closer, the rest of the men understood the terrible omen, which caused them to fiddle with amulets and pray to whichever God they thought could overthrow Loki's evil. As the rowers prayed and Solvi steered the oar away from the thirteenth ship, Frosti could see the boat's sails. They were battered from terrible winds and fierce waves, but they still portrayed a red cross upon a pale white backdrop. *Athelstan's boat,* Frosti thought to himself.

"It's a Christian boat!" Solvi shouted and immediately spun the oar round with all his might causing the boat to turn in one powerful motion. One of the rowers was thrown from the bench but he immediately climbed back up wanting desperately to keep his eye upon the Christian boat. "Get ready to raid it men!" Solvi barked.

"No bloody use, it is going to be empty." Frosti said sounding like a sulking child. He looked towards the Dreki and Halfdan, who was also rubbing his eyes in amazement.

"How do you know it's empty? The crew might be hiding. There might be treasures," Solvi asked.

"Because that is Athelstan's boat. Myself, Gudrod and the entire crew of the Dreki have already stripped it. But that was weeks ago; it should not be here," Frosti whimpered.

"Neither should they," Jik said staring at a whole flock of thousands of birds flying like the Gods away from the boat. It only took Frosti a few seconds to understand the real reason the birds were all travelling as fast as they could. Just as he suspected, he saw the world change. A black mass of clouds like no other forced its way through the once calm sky, following the Christian ship. The clouds were ready to pounce as if they were alive. Frosti knew the brewing storm must have been one of Loki's many sons, for the trickster God had spawned some of the foulest daemons that were ever known. Loki is the father of Fenrir the monstrous wolf with razor-sharp fangs and powerful legs that is chained up within Yggdrasil. He also fathered the great serpent Jormungandr that has twisted its body round the entire world and gnaws at the tree of life. Jormungandr must have been proud of its storm brother. In a matter of nail-biting moments, the entire crew was running round in a mad frenzy as if the world was about to end. And maybe it was.

Jarl Solvi paced the decks, swerving and dancing round the men who frantically tried to heave as much water out of the deck as they could with their cracked wooden pails.

"Row!" Solvi screamed. "Row you bastards, row!" The watching thunder-clad powerhouse in the sky drew ever closer. Frosti could almost smell the clean air that lingered in the central chaos of a storm. The sound of a nearby upsurge filled with flapping fish and shrieking gulls alerted the entire fleet of the arrival of the storm.

Solvi pulled ferociously at the steering oar, hoping to steer the Raven Head away from the doom that had already taken its first victim. Frosti saw the timbers break into a million tiny fragments as a wave ripped a boat in half. He had no idea who the captain of the unfortunate vessel was, but Frosti still muttered a prayer to Egir the god of the sea to rescue their souls and carry them to Valhalla.

"Unless you want to end up like those unfortunate souls, row! Steer towards the shore," Solvi ordered at the rowers whose arms were a bulging mess of aches and sweats.

"Jarl," Frosti muttered. But the Jarl was trapped in a daze that only leadership could cause. "Solvi, where is the bloody shore?" At that point the Jarl seemed to snap out of whatever world he found himself in and started to search the darkening horizon. They were lost. The winds had picked up so that the sail roared like an untamed beast and the ropes hissed like a thousand wild snakes. Again, a ship was torn up as another great wave came crashing down upon it. A flapping sail flew through the wind and curled round Gisha's beast-headed ship. Frosti could see the chieftess order her men to tear down the tangling canvas that must have obscured their already blurred vision.

"Pull the sail down!" Solvi ordered, much to the confusion of the men at the rower's benches.

"Listen to your bloody Jarl" Frosti screamed, pulling on the leathers of one of the warriors. The sea roared and screamed for the men's souls and the waves tried their best to overthrow the Raven Head's screeching hull. Dreki was still visible and so was Gisha's ship. However, Frosti could see no sign of Eric Clawhand's twisting snake figurehead. The great warlord was a well-renowned sailor, and Frosti knew he would surely be handling the storm better than anyone else. Rain started to slam down upon the heads of every warrior, causing their scalps to throb like a hundred tiny bees were stinging at the same time. Their clothes became sodden rags, which thickened and grew uncomfortable on their red-pimpled skin. The weight of the saturated cotton made even the simple duty of untying a rope tiresome. A flash pierced the sky, lightening up the entire sea like a single God's blink. Frosti took a deep breath from the sight of broken timbers, torn sails and dying men. For a moment, he was sure Solvi had been thrown overboard from the last tumbling upsurge.

"Have you seen the Jarl?" Frosti yelled at a man who trembled like a falling leaf. The man shrugged and was tossed to the floor by a wave and Frosti's strength. Luckily, he saw his Jarl with his sodden hair bailing water from the deepened cracking decks like the rest of the crew on every single ship in that storm.

Suddenly a great crash of wood on wood rivalled the echoing sound of thunder. Ospak's vessel, which had already been half destroyed, had headed straight for the Raven Head's starboard side. Splinters flew into the rain-soaked air like a thousand tiny darts. One scraped past Frosti's cheek, causing warm blood to trickle down, but he was more concerned by the deranged faces of terror on Ospak's warrior's faces. It was then when the screams got horribly deafening that Frosti saw his friend Ospak. Or what was left of him. He swung like a wild thing upon a timber plank that jutted out from his ship's deck. Blood ran like a waterfall down the splintered piece of timber that had made its way through his chest and out of his smashed back. Men heaved the broken vessel away from the Raven Head with weakening oars, but eventually the skeleton ship relented and it floated off to cause chaos elsewhere in the carnage. A forceful wave flushed over the deck pushing Frosti back and stinging his eyes with its terrible saltiness. Most of the crew were now in disarray. Solvi lay dazed on the floor, Jik tried desperately to control a wayward oar and Frosti managed to pick himself up from underneath a creaking rowing bench. Frosti's cheek was now relentlessly pouring out blood, darkening the swirling water that filled the deck. He thought of Athelstan, the priest he had rescued from the ship that seemingly brought doom to the entire fleet. There was nothing abnormal about the Christian monk but there was something familiar. He had a terrible limb that Frosti knew he recognised. As the sea grew angrier and the storm started a new wave of fury, he could see the crippled Christian laughing.

"When we get home, remind me to bloody kill those two monks," Frosti told Jik who had managed to grab onto an oar. The archer's efforts were making no difference as it was the sea and the wind that determined which way Raven Head was going.

"If we survive this," Jik said pessimistically.

"We must be coming to the end of the storm now; the thunder is running away from the lightning," Frosti claimed. But, as soon as he said this, the Raven Head was almost flipped over. A broken shaft flew from one end of the boat to the other to embed itself in the guts of an unfortunate warrior. The man was still alive and screaming as the Raven Head was blown straight past a timber graveyard. Frosti counted four sails that floated like flat swans on the water. The sight of around six masts protruding through the waves proved more ships had succumbed to the God's fury. A few men were still alive in the water, clinging helplessly onto bits of broken wood. They all tried to grab onto one of the Raven Head's loose ropes that drooped down into the water like a dying vine plant. No one managed to climb up the frayed piece of horse hair without being swept away by another upsurge or tossed aside by another broken ship. In all the chaos, Frosti was glad that the Dreki still remained afloat as he had started to make good friends with some of the men from the northern camps, especially Halfdan. Frosti could imagine the great warlord clad in his thick layers of seal skin bellowing orders as if the men were simply navigating a slow current. Even though Gudrod the Hunter was their leader, Halfdan was just as feared and loved. He possessed a calmness that his brother didn't have, which was valuable in such disastrous circumstances.

Frosti was right; after what seemed like an age, Loki's storm passed over, leaving a thick mist hovering over the confused water. The mist clouded the horizon and

Frosti searched frantically for a silhouette of some sails but saw nothing. Dreki and the Raven Head were alone in the still sea, lost and depleted. At least ten of the thirty warriors on board the Raven Head were missing and Frosti knew their bodies would be floating amongst the graveyard that the storm had carried away. Jarl Solvi still lived and so did Jik whilst the other men rested their aching bodies wherever they could on the boat. Frosti hoped that there was land beyond the mist. Any land would do, as he was no longer concerned about raiding Britain but instead more interested in fixing the damage that still threatened the boat. He turned to his Jarl who sat by his steering oar. Solvi was tying a dead man's jerkin to a wound on his left arm.

"You all right, brother?" Frosti enquired.

"Yeah, just a scratch. What about you?" he asked, pointing towards the dried blood on Frosti's cheek.

"I will be bloody fine," Frosti laughed. Jik had joined them at the steering oar, and there was something about his presence that irritated Jarl Solvi.

"What?!" Solvi snapped.

"The men are wondering what the plan is," Jik said.

"We go home, obviously," Frosti said as he crossed his bulging arms. Now it was him that Solvi was angry at.

"Home? Why would we go home? We have two ships with some of the greatest warriors of our lifetime. If we turn back now, Frosti, then all the men who died in that wrath will have died for nothing. I am not having their deaths hang on the strings of my conscience." Solvi cleared his throat. "We will find Britain," he screamed, making sure every man on both ships knew his intentions. Moments of silence complemented the stillness of the mist, but suddenly men were roaring from the benches on Dreki. The Raven Head's crew echoed the roars until soon every man roared their approval of Solvi's crumbling dream.

"Britain!" they screamed over and over again to help guide their oars into an even thicker mist.

Carlnut

"Does Lady Selwyn know I am here?" Carlnut asked Father Osyth who was one of the four men who were charged with escorting him to the courtyard. The priest remained silent. Instead, he saw something wrong with his golden cross that hung from his young neck and proceeded to clean it with his sleeve. The three other guards that were leading Carlnut through a multitude of Roman walls were Earl Cynric's men. Each one of their purple cloaks was secured with a fish broach. None of the broaches were as ornate as Cynric's, but they all portrayed their loyalty to a traitorous Earl.

The stone walls that must have been an amazing sight when the Roman's lived in the manor house had all fallen into disrepair. There were cracks running through the bricks, which were covered in wattle to try and keep them from cracking further. A vast amount of cobwebs formed a layer of twinkling silk on the corridor's ceiling and the sound of the soldier's boots against the floor made the spiders scuttle into their hovels. Eventually the five of them reached an open pavilion that must have served as a wonderful garden for whichever Roman general used the manor for his home. Around ten pillars that held up a crumbling brick roof surrounded the garden. Each pillar had its own network of moss and cracks that formed unintentionally appealing patterns. Flowers had sprouted ready for the spring from their patches in the garden. There were bluebells, daffodils and flowers that Carlnut had never seen before, not even in the magnificent garden at Merantune. The thought of Merantune brought a smile to Carlnut's face, but his smile was soon washed away. It was in Merantune that Carlnut had become a lord and his lordship had gotten himself and Selwyn in great danger.

From two pure white cloths that covered a threshold into one of the many rooms within the palace, the Ealdorman Osric emerged. He was dressed in all his splendour. As one of Wessex's greatest men he could afford to spend large sums on golden rings, tunics laced with golden thread and a whole host of other finery. Today he wore a brownish tunic that was dressed in red and green jewels that must have made the garment uncomfortably heavy. Carlnut noticed his hair was greying around his ears, and his limp had gotten worse. He had received the limp during a fight to save his best friend, the now dead King Cynewulf. He widened his arms with a look of embrace towards Carlnut. Carlnut felt sick; Osric had just sentenced him to death and there was nothing Osric could do to make him embrace him.

Noticing the empty arms, Father Osyth met the Ealdorman's embrace. The priest laughed as he was hugged and Carlnut felt even sicker.

"Am I interrupting something?" Carlnut said growing bored of the longevity of their embrace. As Osyth pulled away he looked as if he was finishing a sentence, and it was then Carlnut realised that they were really whispering to each other.

"Lord Carlnut, I don't suppose you know where my son has gone?" Osric said.

"If I did I wouldn't fucking tell you," Carlnut replied in anger. One of Cynric's guards struck Carlnut across the face with an iron glove causing Carlnut to sprawl awkwardly on the floor. Even though blood trickled from his nose he felt a twang of happiness. Sicga must have somehow escaped, and Carlnut hoped he would be heading to Portland to see Selwyn.

"Very well Lord," Osric said, still using Carlnut's title. "I will give you one chance to save your life," he announced. Carlnut's heart missed a beat in his chest, and he had to let out a small gasp to find it again. "I judge from your silence that you will listen to my request without being such a–," Osric hesitated a second before he found the right word, but Father Osyth spoke up before he could:

"–Pagan," Osyth said, almost bouncing with joy at Carlnut's demise. There was something deep inside Carlnut that told him Osric's request would be almost impossible, but he was desperate to see Selwyn again.

"I will give you your life back if you follow these simple orders: first, you must bow down in front of our King and apologise for your falseness. Then you must release all your lands, men and wealth to the church." Carlnut was about to burst out in curses and fists but thought better of it. "You must also renounce your Gods and Father Osyth will baptise you." Carlnut looked towards the priest who was happily smiling behind Osric. "And after you have bowed to your King, donated your wealth and pissed on your gods, you, Lord Carlnut, must allow Father Osyth to marry the Lady Selwyn as it is my understanding you have never married. And if you have had some kind of ceremony it would not be a binding one in the eyes of the Lord Jesus Christ." Carlnut tasted the sharp bitterness of blood in his dry mouth and caught a glimpse of a purple butterfly fluttering carelessly amongst the flowers that swayed in a slight spring breeze. The insect perched itself upon a bright orange flower that reminded Carlnut of Selwyn. It remained there until a hairy guard with deep set eyes squished it under the weight of his thick spear shaft. The Ealdorman's last request had almost made Carlnut sick. Although the rest of the requests were extreme, Carlnut was prepared to do them all in the blink of an eye if it meant he and Selwyn could live happily together. But the thought of the snivelling weasel with Selwyn was too much, and Carlnut was prepared to die to protect his love from ever falling into his traitorous hands.

"The answer is no," Carlnut managed to say whilst struggling to hold back a forceful tear.

"Well I can't say I didn't see that coming," Osric said with a hint of amusement. The sun was halfway up in the sky now, and its beating rays caused beads of sweat to seep across Carlnut's skin.

"I would like to prove my innocence via a trial by combat," Carlnut whispered as though he had no faith in what he was saying. Ealdorman Osric looked at Father Osyth, and without hesitation they both burst out in fits of laughter.

"You are a filthy Pagan! You must die!" Osyth uttered with an exuberance of annoying desire.

"Pagans cannot ask for the same laws as those who are bathed in the blessed light of the one true God. You are nothing more than a beast. You don't see beetles asking for justice after half the group is crumpled under a boot. You are a ridiculous thing, Lord Carlnut, and I will get extreme pleasure from seeing your head rolling across the floor," Osric said as he gestured towards two of his own guards that had entered the garden which was now alive with bees and flies. "Take him to the block!" Osric demanded, and the two guards came rushing towards Carlnut. He could do nothing but back into the pointed spears of Cynric's men and be grabbed by the reaching hands of the spearmen. Their iron grips proved too much for Carlnut whose body felt weak and drained from practically being starved during his time in captivity.

The men, who both had swirling black moustaches and breaths that stunk of ale, brought Carlnut to an overcrowd courtyard. Thatched roofed mud and wattle halls surrounded a ground of stomped dirt, which had thousands of hoof prints dug into it. If the day had been a rainy one, the ground would have surely been too treacherous for one man never mind the hundreds who all crowded round a simple rock in the middle of the open space. Oak trees loomed over a spike palisade where spearmen had stopped their sentry duties to look at Carlnut being dragged down a reasonably steep grassy slope. Wareham was the second largest town in Wessex mainly due to the fact it was built by two civilisations. On top of a grassy mound that pierced the skyline was the Roman-built part of the town, which had long since fallen into a crumbling mess, but still a few villas and buildings stood. Outside the Roman-built walls and at the foot of the knoll stood the Saxon-built structures. Carlnut turned back to see the Roman villa disappearing over the horizon and wondered how they managed to build such amazing structures all over the world. There were many villas, fountains and bridges all across Frisia and Frankia, as well as Wessex, but the marvellous builders had never reached Hordaland.

Most of the people who lived in Wareham had squeezed themselves into every nook and cranny to get some kind of view of the lone rock that was now being cleared by a few spearmen. Men spat at Carlnut from toothless mouths whilst children hurled sharp stones and snapped twigs. Some were even brave enough to push to the front of the crowd and try and throw a punch. One man who was roughly the same height as Carlnut but much more slender managed to push aside one of the guards who clasped onto Carlnut's arm. The guard went sprawling across the ground like a maimed horse, whilst the attacker prepared to swing at Carlnut. He could see a powerful fury on the man's face, and his jerkin was stained in dried vomit and blood giving the man a horrifying smell. However, Carlnut managed to duck under a flying punch and throw his own. The strike hit the man just under his arm and into the ribs. Carlnut swore he could hear the wonderful sound of bones snapping like the simple crackling of a fire. The drunken assailant found himself coughing in pain upon the ground, and he was quickly dragged away by some other less-brave onlookers.

"Don't worry about them, Milord. Most have been drinking since last night. A lot of attention is given to a Pagan's death, Milord," the new spearmen said as he took the place of the disgraced man who allowed a farmer to push him over. Much to Carlnut's surprise it was Coenred, the man who had led him to the court where he was sentenced to death.

"At least I will see a friendly face before I die. Am I still a hero to you, Coenred?" Carlnut asked, as the spearman had told him of his admiration for him a few days before.

"Milord, you will always be a hero," Coenred said but was silenced by a stare from his colleague who helped position Carlnut upon the stone. Around twenty deep cuts had been made into the rock and Carlnut found himself praying that the cut would be clean. It was then when his knees touched the hard ground and his face felt the coldness of the smoothed rock that Carlnut saw the world. The large thick oak trees had tiny buds on the end of each stalk that looked pink in the day's sunlight. Each tree spawned an entirely different shadow that twisted and cracked the ground wherever it landed. A flock of starlings flew overhead to presumably find their nests again after the long winter where they had vanished from the world. One of the birds trailed behind with a wing that flapped uncontrollably and one that barely moved at all. The bird fell further and further behind its flock until a kestrel darted from nowhere to end its miserable life in one sweep. His mouth began to salivate from the smell of freshly baked bread that glided from a stone oven that was hidden in one of the halls. Then a huge puddle of spit landed right next to Carlnut's head, which was being pressed down by one of Osric's men. From the puddle Carlnut could smell fresh vomit, which made him want to gag, but luckily his insides stayed where they were meant to. The rock wasn't as hard as it had looked. Thick moss clung to the surface, which acted like a poor pillow for Carlnut's face. An insect of some kind had crawled into Carlnut's boots and begun to bite or scratch at his toes. Suddenly all he wanted to do was itch or stamp his feet, but any movement would surely have meant a thump or worse, a nonlethal stab to some part of his body.

A cheer came from the back of the crowd so Carlnut predicted that it was either the Ealdorman Osric or the executioner. But another cheer followed soon after meaning both must have been only metres apart. All this was coming from the opposite direction that Carlnut was facing. His neck strained to lighten the hold from the man who was still trying with all his might to hold Carlnut down. Reluctantly he let Carlnut turn, thinking it would do no harm for him to face Osric. The executioner was a huge man who wore a black leather cloth over his face to hide his identity. He wore no shirt or jerkin and his body was covered in hundreds of scars making him look like the cracked bark of a willow tree. The huge man turned slightly to reveal a small tuft of curly black hair atop his head. Ealdorman Osric nodded, and that seemed to be a signal for the scarred man to take a few more steps closer to Carlnut. Carlnut knew that in a few moments, he would be dead. He hoped the man was as skilled with the blade as his confidence denoted. Carlnut had seen far too many executions where the executioner had missed and instead cleaved into the back of the poor man's head sending skull fragments and cries of pain into the air. The pressure on Carlnut's neck was finally released, but it still felt like a man's weight was pressing down upon him. Coenred leaned towards Carlnut and adjusted his jerkin so the blade could make a perfectly clean cut without being caught within the material.

"Thank you Coenred, you are a good man," Carlnut managed to say even with a giant lump in his throat.

"I am glad you think so, Milord," the lanky man replied before disappearing from Carlnut's vision. From nowhere a shadow covered the rock and Carlnut closed his eyes and tensed his entire body ready for the blade that was about to end his life. He found himself still breathing and he looked up towards the figure that blocked the sun's marvellous rays. It was Father Osyth. He had the most perpetual smile as if he were the richest man in the world. He leaned down towards Carlnut so that he would be the only person who could hear him.

"I don't normally take pleasure in people's deaths, but yours, Lord Carlnut, will make me ever so happy," he whispered. When Carlnut went to respond to the taunt, Osyth spoke again. "So how does your woman liked to be fucked? From behind like a dog, or does she prefer to ride like a whore?" Osyth stood up before Carlnut was able to spit in his face and the sad-looking glob of salvia landed feebly on Osyth's robes. The priest straightened his back and turned to address the crowd. "I have just asked the Pagan whether he will renounce his Gods here and now so that he may stand a chance to let his soul rest in heaven. But he simply spat on my offer. Would you believe it, he refuses to be saved. May Lucifer have mercy on your soul," Osyth exclaimed whilst making the sign of the cross on his chest and smiling a hidden smile down at Carlnut.

"Do you have any last words?" the executioner asked.

"May-" Carlnut said with emphasis to mirror Osyth's taunts. "-May Thor flatten you between his anvils and hammer. May Loki feed your soul to the great Fenrir. And Father Osyth, may your God laugh as mine uses your soul to wipe his shit on." Osyth looked genuinely scared by Carlnut's words but appeared to recover himself when he remembered that Carlnut was to be dead in a matter of seconds.

This time the shadow was the swinging axe and Carlnut's life flashed before his eyes. He remembered his mother and father cradling his fair-haired baby brother in their arms whilst playing swords with Frosti and some other children. Then he remembered what Solvi said before he left for a raid a week before the great storm that changed his life:

"You will return to Hordaland, brother!"

***

The three monks gladly took pleasure in keeping Sicga awake. All his body wanted to do was melt into the bed and disappear. Whenever he did feel himself drifting off, Brother Geoweld would creak open the door and shove or push him until Sicga thrust up and awakened. The room itself wasn't terrible, but its confines were starting to grind down Sicga's soul. Two days ago he remembered his delight when Brother Finrif escorted him out and around a Roman villa. However, all that was turned to despair when he ended up between his father and Lord Carlnut. It would have been so simple to announce in front of Ealdorman Osric and the other delegates that Carlnut was a Pagan. But in truth Sicga had not seen any evidence that Carlnut wasn't a Christian so he certainly couldn't lie under the watchful eyes of God. Once Carlnut burst in a fit of rage before he was sentenced to death, though, Sicga knew. Not only did he know that he had broken his relationship with his father, but he also knew he had unwittingly chosen a side.

He wasn't sure how long he had been allowed to sleep but it certainly did feel a lot longer than he had all night. He could see outlines of furniture around the room and the brass door brace had a certain gleam to it.

"Milord? Milord, are you awake? Hurry, we don't have much time," a voice whispered from the corner of the room.

"Brother, please let me sleep. I am a noble, I can pay you, just please let me sleep," Sicga said rubbing his eyes and discovering thick wax balls in the corners of his sockets.

"They will be here soon, Milord, I am sure. Please, just follow me." So Sicga picked himself up out of the furs and stretched his back feeling a terrible twitch down his spine. "C'mon now. This way, Milord, this way." The door was wide open, and Sicga was ready for an ambush or a trick. Each step was taken with immense care and his neck darted from left to right almost expecting a hidden knife in the darkness.

"Where are we going? And who are you?" Sicga asked after a few moments of silence that was more terrifying than the thought of his voice carrying to a nearby guard.

"My name is Coenred, Milord. I am one of Earl Cynric's men. A member of his personal guard whilst he stays in Wareham. Anyway, please, Milord, follow me." A fresh breeze touched Sicga's face, and it felt as good as any touch from any woman he had ever been with. After the cool caress of cold air Sicga saw the unmistakeable light of dawn. An orange tinge filtered from underneath an iron-bracketed door. Sicga had gone from drained to elated in one moment, and it was all due to Coenred.

"I owe you much for this, Coenred," Sicga said as he placed his hand on the young soldier's shoulders.

"You do not owe me anything, Milord. Like you say, you are a noble and I am only doing my duty. There is a horse outside. I am afraid I didn't have the time to provide any supplies, but I'm sure you'll be okay, Milord." Sicga went to embrace the soldier who could have given up his life for him if he was ever to be found out. Nerves shot through Sicga again before he found the energy to push the door open. He still felt like there was some kind of foul play afoot. It was all too easy for an escape. He braced himself for a bunch of arrows to rip into his flesh when he managed to open the door, but there was nothing there apart from a ready saddled horse. The mare wasn't even tied down to a stump, which told Sicga she would be a good ride. The rest of the escape was just as easy. Most of the men on sentry duty didn't even blink an eyelid as Sicga rode past them with all his youth and confidence. There was something about confidence that could mask any kind of lie. Sicga had learned from an early age that if you looked like you belonged then you could quite simply breeze from group to group without so much as a notice.

The sun hadn't even reached a quarter way through the sky when Sicga stopped his horse and turned back to the town he had just escaped from. Wareham was still clearly visible and maybe he wouldn't be too late. Sicga gave the horse a pat on its thick neck and laughed to himself.

"Well, I guess I have picked a side," he said, encouraging his horse into a gallop.

***

Carlnut felt a powerful jet of blood splash across his face accompanied by a chorus of deranged screams. However, he still couldn't open his eyes in fear he was simply watching his own death and he was on the way to the other world.

"Come on Lord, we need to move now," a familiar voice bellowed. When he heard the voice Carlnut opened his eyes to see the twitching body of a priest at the foot of the rock. Father Osyth's neck was spewing blood in all angles like one of the Roman fountains in Merantune's gardens. For a moment Carlnut couldn't move, but the man who once was the executioner was pulling him away from the priest's flailing body. Men charged from all angles with lowered spears. The crowd soon turned into a babbling mess of hysteria. Somehow Carlnut had a sword in his hand. Its hilt felt right within his sweaty palm and without even looking he knew it was Karla. He had no idea how she had found her way back into his grip, but he was ultimately grateful. All his energy rushed back into him as if Karla were the source of all life. Coenred charged ahead of the crowd of spearmen with legs that would rival a horse's power. For a moment Carlnut thought the young man was about to catch his heels and felt at ease that it was Coenred who would kill him. Coenred had built a huge lead in front of the other men so that he was at least two horse lengths away. Feeling confident in his advantage he turned and threw his spear straight into one of the pursuers' chests. The unfortunate soldier fell backwards onto the dirt where he was trampled by another four charging men. From imminent death it seemed like Carlnut's luck had begun to change.

"Milord," the soldier shouted. "Milord, watch out!" Coenred, who had for some reason decided to help Carlnut flee, pointed frantically towards a shield wall that barred any possible escape. The wall of wooden shields painted with the purple leaping fish of Earl Cynric was parked in-between two stone cottages. Behind the fugitives were the spearmen who had formed their own less-impressive shield wall.

"Kill the fucking bastards!" the commander screamed from inside the wall. Even with the command they didn't charge but instead both walls closed in slowly as if they wanted to crush the executioner, Carlnut and Coenred. Coenred was unarmed after throwing his spear earlier, but Carlnut and the hugely built man who had killed Father Osyth held their swords ready for a battle. No nerves shook Carlnut's body nor did any sweat blur his vision, but instead he felt ready to die. Death during a fight was far more honourable than being beheaded, and he silently thanked Odin for hearing his prayers. In a matter of moments both walls were just a few feet from being able to pierce their bodies with their lowered, shaking spears that gleamed in the sunlight.

"No, don't move, don't kill them," a panicked voice screeched. "Please, I order you to stop." It was Ealdorman Osric who was waving his arms furiously as if he were trapped inside a small storm. Osric was no longer protected after every single soldier had charged towards the escaping Carlnut. This had allowed a huge beast of a man with a jet black and uncontrolled mess of a beard to grab Osric and hold a knife to his neck.

"I did good!" the bearded man yelled in triumph. Even at that distance he was the most recognisable man in the entire land of Wessex for Carlnut had never seen a man so huge. It was Cuth, Earl Eafled's champion. But what he was doing holding Osric captive Carlnut did not know, nor did he have time to learn as the executioner led Carlnut straight into the shield wall. Luckily the men stood aside but scowled at the escaping prisoners as they passed them free of harm. As Carlnut appeared behind the wall the men at the back spun on an axis and closed in, blocking Coenred from escaping with them. Carlnut imagined the young warrior pissing his breeches and regretting every single step he had made to end up in such a dire situation. In that thought he felt a twang of guilt for the man.

"Osric!" Carlnut shouted up towards the sweaty old man who now had a war axe held to his neck. "If your men kill Coenred then my man will chop you into a thousand pieces and feed them to the dogs." Osric was defeated. He had no choice but to command the two walls to spread apart like grains of sand in a gust of wind. All the faces of the men revealed eyes full of hatred and snarls that could as well have been from dogs. They were desperate for the traitor's blood.

The rest of the journey out of Wareham was easy. Not one person stopped or even hindered the three of them as by now every spearman, butcher, farmer and fighting man knew Osric was being held hostage. The gate was a huge impregnable thing about three logs thick. Two looming towers stood either side of it and both were crammed full of men who spat down gobs of bile all wanting to catch one of the three men leaving. One man inside the tower even started to urinate, but the masked executioner must have given him a terrifying stare through the cute out eye holes, as the pissing man found somewhere else to drain his body.

"And here we wait, Lord," the executioner said with his familiarity being muffled by the mask.

"Wait? Why are we waiting?" Coenred whimpered nervously. His question was drowned out by the pattering of hooves, which coincidently gave him an answer. Four horses galloped towards the gate, and for a moment Carlnut thought Karla was about to sing in his enemies' blood. Three nervous women rode the first three horses whilst Cuth and Ealdorman Osric were astride the rearmost one. All four of the beasts were war horses, which had huge powerful hind legs and a strong muscular body that comfortably held Cuth's massive weight.

"Open," Cuth commanded Osric in his heavily accented voice. Osric obeyed and ordered his men to open the gates. The three women were long gone, which allowed Carlnut and his small band of followers to take the horses. He could still see one of the slave women who had delivered the horses shivering behind a cart filled with dry straw. He nodded towards the slave woman, but she hid her spotty, pock-scared face out of fright. The next step seemed far too easy. An open gate enticed them out like a woman revealing some thigh. Spears rattled on the ground as men preferred to drop them rather than risk their master's life by trying to play the hero in some mad thirst for blood. A blinding sun welcomed them on the other side where an endless green expanse began. At first the horses took slow anxious steps, but as they passed the great arch that held the two towers the riders turned the movement into a trot. As soon as Wareham was a hundred metres away, Carlnut turned his horse to face it. His back sweated due to a mixture of tension and the heat bouncing off his back. He rolled his shoulders in their sockets, and they made a horrible cracking noise that for a moment startled the horse. At least five score spearmen lined the ramparts and around ten riders gathered in front of the gate waiting and readying for a pursuit.

"I am so sorry, Ealdorman, for your discomfort during this event, but we had to save our Lord. We have oaths to keep after all," the masked executioner told

Osric. Just then Carlnut knew who had saved him from his death but decided it was best to maintain the secrecy until the job was done. Cuth threw Osric to the ground and smacked him with the face of his war axe. The Ealdorman's nose cracked into pieces as he screamed from a blood-stained mouth. The scream told the riders to charge, but it also told the four of them to kick their rides into a fierce gallop. A breeze turned into a mighty wind against Carlnut's face and his eyes began to water from the dust that was being thrown up by Coenred's horse in front of him. The four powerful beasts rode past giant oak trees and grazing sheep that were surrounded by hundreds of tiny newborn lambs. However, the pursuing riders were always on their tail. Every time Carlnut turned his head he could see at least one horsemen bearing down on him.

"We are never going to lose them," Carlnut said to Cuth who was riding beside him.

"Fight?" Cuth asked. And Carlnut nodded.

A simple farmstead with a tiny thatched barn was where the party stopped. The farmer whose land it was, was either tending to his recently thawed fields or even dead as there was no sign of life anywhere inside. The fire had not seen light in years it seemed, and cobwebs obscured the expanse of tabletops.

"They might not even know we are in here, Milord," Coenred said optimistically

"Horses," Cuth said. He was a simple man but a fierce one and Carlnut owed him and presumably Earl Eafled his life.

"So Sicga, why on earth did you save me?" Carlnut asked whilst running his hand through his long tangled hair.

"You are my Lord and I have an oath to you and without oaths we are nothing but beasts," Sicga replied proudly.

"You killed Father Osyth. Would your God not condemn you for killing a holy man?" Carlnut said.

"I cannot argue that my guilt will always weigh heavy on me. But Lord, I have killed hundreds of men so I am never afraid of killing another. Besides, Osyth was a prick; he was no holy man, and for that reason alone I am glad my axe sank into his stinking neck." Sicga picked up a small cup from the floor and looked disappointed not to find even a drop of water. "Maybe I betrayed my father, and for that I do hold genuine guilt, but he was going to allow that corrupt bastard to marry lady Selwyn and that is disgraceful." Carlnut welled up and embraced his friend.

"I owe you my life, Sicga, and I owe you two the same," Carlnut said, inviting Cuth and Coenred into the embrace. "Coenred you are a hero," he said as Coenred joined the clasping of arms and the patting of backs. However, Cuth remained standing at the door with his axe in his large, bear-like hands. He had to stoop to allow his body to fit into the one-roomed hut but he still seemed determined to carry out his duty as a soldier.

"They're here," he said as he tightened his grip on his axe. He was right; the rattling sound of mailed men dismounting from horses was unmissable. It normally sounded like rain falling onto glass or a coin purse falling onto stone but then it sounded like nothing but death.

"Lord Carlnut, I ask you not to make this difficult for yourself and your friends. Come back with us, and our Lord will happily make your death quick and painless," one of the horsemen shouted towards the hut. Carlnut recognised the voice as the same man who had commanded the shield wall.

"You are one of Earl Cynric's men?" Carlnut asked through the mud and wattle wall.

"I am, Lord, I am his commander Feolugeld," he replied.

"Your renown is well known, Feolugeld," Carlnut lied. "I suppose you know what your so-called Earl did?" Feolugeld refused to answer. "He conspired in the murder of King Cynewulf," Carlnut confidently said, trying desperately to avoid a fight where he and his friends would be outnumbered. For a few moments the only noise was the jingling sound of mail surrounding the hut. Suddenly a spear point broke through the cracking mud wall. The once-shining metal was now covered in the worm-infested dirt but luckily no blood. Another spear was thrust just in front of Coenred's face and soon another three followed until beams of light flooded the dark hut. Sicga put his mask back on. He had no reason to but Carlnut supposed it made him look fierce and at that point they needed any extra advantage they could get their hands on. Sicga unsheathed his sword whilst Cuth stepped away from the door he had just silently unbolted. Two men, thinking the door would be barred, charged towards it, but the hinges broke free with little to no resistance, and they tumbled onto the floor. Cuth drew his axe behind his scarred head and sliced open one of their backs as if he wasn't even wearing mail. Coenred instinctively picked up the dead man's spear and lodged it in the other man's neck. Blood and screams filled the room, but no one had time to even think as the rest of the dismounted horsemen charged into the room hoping their numbers would win them the fight. A man with a dented iron helm was the first to charge into the room and also the first of the new bunch to die. It was Cuth again who used his axe to such devastating effect that he almost hacked the man in half. Another soldier who instead chose not to wear a helm charged past Cuth who was still recovering from his last mighty swing. The helmetless man swirled his spear in the air and was about to strike down onto Cuth's exposed hamstring, but Carlnut had allowed Karla to do her devastating work. She stabbed through his back and was twisted inside him so flesh and bone and blood became one disgusting mess. Suddenly every one of the horsemen was inside the hut. Cuth was engaged in a fist fight with one man whilst Coenred and Sicga tackled four between them. However, a tall brooding man with lime-washed white armour and a purple cape headed straight for Carlnut. He presumed that the lanky man who was dressed in Cynric's rather feminine colours was Captain Feolugeld. Feolugeld was the only man out of the horsemen with a sword, and it was a fine one indeed. Its steel glittered and glinted in one of the sun beams that still found its way through one of the spear holes that penetrated the hut. He was extremely skilled with the sword and danced around Carlnut as he helplessly swung Karla through the air. Behind Feolugeld, Carlnut saw Cuth hammering a man's face until it was just a congealed mess of skull and brain. Feolugeld continued to dodge Carlnut's attacks, stepping back when Carlnut would swing and swaying left when he would lunge. Carlnut knew he had met his match so decided to annoy Feolugeld like he was annoying him. Both men stared at each other with unrelenting eyes knowing that one of them was about to die. Sicga was now defending himself against only one person as Cuth had taken the other off him, but Coenred was still struggling to continuously parry two men's spear thrusts. Spears were horrible weapons to wield in close combat, and Carlnut was infinitely grateful he had Karla in his hands.

"You are a horrid Pagan, Carlnut, and I will take immense pleasure in slicing your stomach open," Feolugeld teased. Carlnut backed away from his taunts and slipped on a damp cloth that was strangely placed on the dusty floor. For the first time, Feolugeld saw a weakness in Carlnut's defence and decided to profit from it. He raised his sword over his head hoping to unleash a terrible striking slash that would have surely embedded itself deep into Carlnut's neck. However, Carlnut's fall was not an accident. He knew the only way Feolugeld would attack was if he knew he would win. As the Captain's sword started its powerful descent towards Carlnut, he leapt like a coiled viper. Karla found an area just above his groin and below his breastplate that was shielded by nothing but leather. Feolugeld dropped his sword, and it clanged onto the floor, disturbing dust that became visible in the sun's peeking light. Carlnut held Karla deep in Feolugeld's body as the captain feebly tried to pull it out. All his muscles were failing, and soon his stern chin was drenched in blood that still leaked out of his mouth.

Eleven bodies lay dead or dying in the tiny hut. Ten of those were the horsemen that had pursued Carlnut for miles past calm lakes and thickening forests, but the other was Coenred. He was still alive but barely. He had received several wounds that all competed for the amount of blood they could spurt out. The fatal wound looked like the one he had taken from a spear to the inner thigh. Sicga was holding the spearman in his arms and seemed to cry as Coenred's life was drained from his body.

"Milord," Coenred whispered and pointed towards Carlnut. "Thank you for allowing me to fight alongside you; you are truly my hero, Milord." Coenred was quickly growing weaker as every breath was an effort for him.

"No Coenred. You have saved us; you are the hero," Carlnut said with a reluctant smile. These words appeared to fill the dying spearman with more pleasure than anything else could ever have given him.

After Coenred had died and Sicga hurriedly dug a grave for him, they all rode off as far away from Wareham as they could go.

"Where do we go, Lord?" Sicga asked of Carlnut.

"We go home, Sicga, we go home," Carlnut said, thinking only of Selwyn.

Selwyn

Osbert the youthful steward had ordered that no person should leave the fort without his knowing, but a few spearmen had helped Selwyn disappear. It didn't take long for Selwyn to head down to Fortunes Well, the small settlement that lay at the other end of Portland. She had received a letter from Father Luyewn demanding her presence immediately, and she did not hesitate to leave. When Athelhild bought her the rolled-up parchment written by the shaking hand of Father Luyewn, she had originally hoped it was from Arnum who was still out looking for Carlnut. The serving girl had become slightly more confident since Father Osyth left Portland and seeing her blossom made Selwyn think of having her own children.

Fortunes Well was a strangely built settlement that seemed as impossible as the island itself. Somehow, on a land that ended in steep rocky cliffs to the west and shell-scattered beaches to the east, people had managed to settle and create a lively fishing village. Most of the settlement nested on the south of the island where there was a flat, bowl-shaped cove that sheltered it from the most terrible storms that would often sweep across the ocean. Selwyn thought that, if she were a bird, she would surely see that the island of Portland would look like a piece of bread that someone had taken a bite of. It was a relatively small fishing community in size, but it teamed with buzzing activity. Children ran happily in and out of crudely built thatched homes whilst women weaved fishing traps and sails. The smell of the sea was dizzying, but the sight of the shore was perfect. The newly rising sun gently skimmed its reflection across the white-washed water, surely obscuring the vision of the dozen small fishing boats that bobbed in the tide. Luyewn's chapel was not hard to find, either. It was a small thing built in between two slightly larger buildings. The only thing that presented the hut as a chapel was the simple stone cross hung at the gable. An old door was slightly open, and Selwyn awkwardly navigated her feet across the moving shingle towards the house of God. She made the sign of the cross against her chest as she passed the threshold into the chapel. Inside was completely plain, and the only light came in naturally from a window hole just behind the altar. Selwyn walked past three lines of benches that were covered in sand and crushed shells towards the bright light of the window. There was a thick piece of driftwood underneath the hole, which she used as a step to get a view of the shoreline beyond. The chapel must have been one of the closest buildings to the sea, as all she could see was a stony beach being revealed by a retreating tide. As the tide escaped away from Fortunes Well, a few children ran onto the beach to collect whatever gifts the cruel mistress decided to give. One child celebrated as he grabbed a large pile of dark green seaweed that would be perfect for thickening thatch whilst another sulked after discovering all the shells were empty of meat.

"Hello, the service for today has already finished, but I will still be happy to help you," a voice said from behind her. Selwyn turned to find a short, black-haired man who appeared to be the local priest. A long chained cross hung from his neck and he wore only a brown shift similar to those that Luyewn or Athelhild would wear.

"Oh I am terribly sorry, my Lady. I did not see it was you, please forgive me," the priest said as he realised who Selwyn was. She could not remember ever meeting Fortunes Well's priest so she guessed he knew her rank from the fine clothes she wore. Today, Selwyn chose a light blue dress and a darker blue cloak that guarded her from the chilling sea breezes. Athelhild had made a crown of the season's first daisies that Selwyn proudly wore like it was made of finely crafted gold.

"It's fine, Father; do you know where Luyewn is?" Selwyn asked as she dismounted the timber step whilst lifting her skirts up so she would not fall.

"Oh yes, yes I do, your Ladyship. He is with the Earl in the tavern," he replied. The priest was an awkward man not much older than Selwyn herself and seemed to have a small twitch whenever he spoke.

"Thank you . . ." Selwyn hesitated, leaving a pause for the priest to reveal his name.

"Oh yes, yes, I am Father Wilthald, your Ladyship," he said after a long and tedious silence. Selwyn left the young priest sweeping the sand off the benches with the sleeve of his robe. She stepped across the shingles once more and followed the sound of laughter where she presumed the tavern would be. Selwyn wondered which Earl could possibly be in Fortunes Well and why on earth he would be talking with Luyewn. A flutter of nerves descended upon her at the thought of seeing Earl Cynric. So she prayed that it was in fact Eafled the Earl of Dorchester, who had saved her life a few months back.

The tavern, like the chapel, was a simple thing but much bigger than the religious building. It was built towards the back of Fortunes Well with the rear end of the building erected against a grass-covered cliff face that must have been around thirty feet high. A pile of split barrels sat next to it with drops of moulding ale dripping through the cracks in the shingle. A mouse scuttled between the barrels and then disappeared somewhere in between the tavern and the cliff. Selwyn took a deep breath and ducked into the comforting warmth of the tavern. There was no fire burning to produce the heat, but instead it came from the many bodies that crowded round wobbling tables and half-broken stools. The deafening laughter and drunken natter ceased as soon as Selwyn walked in, so much so that the only sound that could be heard was the gulls shrieking above the fishing boats. Selwyn was no stranger to taverns as she and Bedfrith her harpist would travel across Wessex performing. She had even been in much worse places. She remembered one place named The Bull having congealed blood stains on the floor and vomit that provided bony cats with some kind of nutrition. A hand touched her shoulder and she instinctively pulled it away as if the hand was made of burning metal. She turned and took a step back thinking a drunken man was trying to claim her for his own.

"No," she snapped.

"M'Lady, I am sorry to have made you jump," Earl Eafled said. "I just thought you would prefer to sit in the back room with myself and Father Luyewn." Suddenly she felt safe again and decided to follow the Earl, and once she turned her back, the laughter and drinking continued again. She was taken through a side door, which was guarded by a tall lanky man holding a spear. The man nodded as Earl Eafled opened the door and then stooped to give Lady Selwyn a small bow. Towards the back of the room was a small fire that was flickering in a stone fire pit, which was being tended by a bald man with his back to the door. Father Luyewn sat on his own at a round shiny table that appeared to be much finer than any of the tavern's other possessions. His white wispy hair produced worm-like shadows on the wall whilst his golden cross glinted like a thousand suns around his neck. Eafled pulled up a chair next to the priest and gestured for Selwyn to do the same. Dust littered the wonderfully heated air as the chair was moved, causing Luyewn to cough furiously. Just before Selwyn was about to accept Eafled's offer of a seat, the bald man pounced like a coiled viper. Selwyn flinched like a kitten expecting him to strike her in some fashion, but instead he simply pulled out the Lady's chair. Her heart bounced around like a tiny bird between her small breasts when she realised that the bald man was actually Engelhard. After a week of loneliness, she found herself in the company of three of her best friends. Engelhard's scarred brutal face showed no emotion as he slithered back to the corner of the room, but Selwyn hoped he was secretly pleased to be guarding her again. She had last seen him the night that Bedfrith had rode to tell her Carlnut was captured. That was the same night that Arnum, the captain of Portland, had ridden off to look for Carlnut and also the night Father Luyewn had left for Fortunes Well.

"Thank you, Engel," Selwyn said courteously. "I have so many questions, Father; please explain to me what is going on." Father Luyewn cleared his throat and wiped a piece of bubbling salvia from the side of his mouth.

"Sunflower, please forgive me," the priest replied. A tear floated its way down his cheek followed by another, which landed onto the freshly polished table. "I had to leave as soon as I found the letter."

"What letter?" Selwyn asked.

"Sunflower, I am terribly sorry; let me explain. I found a letter written between Osbert the Steward and that horrid Father Osyth. The words on the paper made my heart sink, and I knew I had to leave straight away." Luyewn was getting out of breath and Earl Eafled cupped his own hand round the emotional priest.

"What did it say?" Selwyn demanded quite harshly. The harsh tone in her voice surprised everyone in the room including the hissing fire, which seemed to quiver when she raised it.

"It spoke of how once Carlnut was gone, Father Osyth would marry you." Selwyn was about to burst out in anger, but Earl Eafled raised his free hand to silence the rage before it began. "It also listed a bunch of other names that were important to their plan. I think my name, Arnum's, Sicga's and Engelhard's were written down. I remember reading that each of us should be removed from Portland by whatever means necessary. " Luyewn sniffled up the last of his tears and sank in his chair as if a great weight was lifted from his panting chest.

"He contacted me immediately," Eafled said. "I sent Cuth, my greatest warrior, to find Carlnut, and I travelled as fast as I could to get Luyewn and yourself." Selwyn didn't know what to think. Her mind jumped from one horrible eventuality to another. "I fear who Osyth has managed to win over. My men tell me that Earl Cynric has been sending horsemen out each day, to come to Portland, maybe; I do not know." A gallon of foul-tasting bile poured into her throat, and she would have gagged on it if it not for the water that Engelhard bought her. Carlnut was somewhere in Wessex alone and frightened, and Selwyn longed desperately for his strong embrace.

"Arnum also travelled to find his Lord; maybe he and Cuth will meet and prevail," Selwyn whispered optimistically.

"Sunflower, Engelhard was on the gates that night and he never saw Arnum leave," Luyewn admitted. Selwyn turned to her personal guard whose eyes widened at the sound of his voice. Once her desperate eyes met his he nodded to confirm Luyewn's grim news. A spider innocently spun a web within the rafters and a ray of sunlight escaping through the thatch highlighted a pile of half-dead flies it had caught.

"If Arnum never left Portland, where in hell is he?" Selwyn finally asked. Engelhard simply shrugged, Luyewn turned away avoiding her pulsating gaze and Earl Eafled struggled with a lump in his throat. "Well, where is he?" she furiously asked again as she slammed her hand on the table sending her empty cup spinning to the floor.

"We haven't been able to get into the fort since Osbert ordered the doors to be locked shut, M'Lady," Earl Eafled said as he fiddled with his tunic's collar. "We are here to discuss what we are going to do, M'Lady," the Earl added.

"We are going to kill Osbert, obviously, and then Osyth. Then we will ride to King Beorhtric and demand Cynric to be removed as an Earl." Her proclamations caused a thick cloud of discomfort to cover Father Luyewn who made the sign of the cross against his chest.

"Sunflower, I think it may be safer for us to live in the sanctuary of Earl Eafled's household until we find out if Carlnut is –" the Priest hesitated for a moment until Eafled finished his sentence for him.

"– alive. I am sure in a week's time, Cuth will ride home to Dorchester with him by his side," he said and smiled after finally finding the position of his collar in which his neck was comfortable. Selwyn thought about that for a while. She had only recently become a Lady and was determined to hold onto the title. But she wanted Carlnut back; she missed his long black hair, his huge body and his general presence.

The chair she sat on screeched like a wild cat when she stood up. There were no windows in the room, and all of a sudden she felt very claustrophobic. The timber walls felt like they were getting closer and closer and the floor felt as though it was shaking furiously. She was desperate for fresh air and decided to burst out of the room, which was thick with smoke and swirling sparks. Engelhard remained in the furnace-like room, but Father Luyewn and Earl Eafled followed her through the ocean of drunken sailors and into the sea-scented outdoors. They found her sitting on one of the empty barrels that still stunk of stale ale as flies buzzed happily around her.

"This is no place for a Lady," Eafled shouted over the competing sounds of laughter and the sea.

"Please, Sunflower, let's pray with Father Wilthald in the chapel and we can also visit the well that the town is named after," Luyewn pleaded. "I promise you, Lady, with God's help Carlnut will be saved." Selwyn gave him a knowing look and the priest's face turned red in embarrassment but luckily for both them and Carlnut, Eafled didn't discover the hidden meaning.

A number of hours remained before the night's darkness destroyed all light, and the creatures of the abyss walked within the shadows. The cliff made the whole fishing village look dark, as the sun started its descent behind it. A fat man drenched in sea salt carried a heavy basket past the tavern, and the stench of freshly caught fish filled Selwyn's nostrils. The fisherman treated Selwyn to a bow when he realised it was his Lady sitting within the graveyard of tavern waste. A huge wave hit the beach, catching a few children who all ended up being violently thrown backwards. However, they all got up unscathed and gathered their things after the sea informed them of her intention to return back to the land. After the stench became too much, Selwyn decided to dismount the barrels and navigate the shards of curving timber towards her friends. The doors beside her swung open and Engelhard stormed out of the tavern, fixing his heavy sword belt to his waist. He gave one look towards his Lady and then stomped ahead in the direction of the path to Portland.

"What are you doing?" Luyewn yelled after him. Engelhard turned and smiled. It was an evil-looking, yellow-toothed smile that gave away every single intention he had at that moment. "Oh dear God," Luyewn said sullenly.

"Where is he going?" Earl Eafled asked, confused at the priest's understanding of one simple smile.

"He is going to do what we are all too afraid to do," Selwyn interpreted as she brushed away the remnants of muddy sand off her dress. They watched the warrior climb up the stone path that was lined with newly blossomed daffodils and bluebells and buzzing with horseflies. They continued watching until he disappeared out of sight as the path curved over the top of the rock cliff that started to become dense in sea birds. Luyewn led Selwyn into the chapel whilst Earl Eafled followed. The novice priest Willibald was still working tirelessly to remove the sand from his chapel floor when the three of them walked in.

"Oh, Father Luyewn, yes, I tried to acquire some bread for tomorrow's sermon but sadly the vendor had none. I'm sure we could use something else," Willibald said in his awkward twitching tone.

"Willibald, for centuries we Christians have served bread and wine during mass, and if you start making replacements, you will be seen as a bloody fool," Luyewn said and wagged his bony finger towards the fidgeting man who took the joke far too seriously.

"Oh, yes, yes, that's right, Father, I will try again," he said whilst blinking rapidly, which caused his pupils to dilate to the size of stones. Luyewn shook his head as the young man ran outside, grabbing his robes to avoid sprawling across the floor.

"So, Father," Selwyn said. "What should I do? Should I lock myself up in Portland and be helpless to whatever changes Osbert is making, or should I do what Engel has decided to do and fight?" Luyewn coughed up a piece of phlegm in surprise as if he had choked on a lump of air.

"Sunflower, the Earl has offered you safety in Dorchester, and it would be wise to accept his offer." Earl Eafled nodded silently in the corner as he rooted through a pile of dust-covered scrolls. "Get your handmaiden to pack your things, and we will leave in the morning." Luyewn had a sudden harshness to his voice and Selwyn noticed a grimace from under his stern exterior. Selwyn took a few steps towards the gap in the wall where the sea could be seen gushing onto the land. A huge cloud of dust blurred her vision, which was already poisoned with tears. She turned to find Eafled fighting with an unrolled scroll to stop the page coiling back up again in defence.

"M'Lady," he said whilst brushing the remaining dust off the page and onto the newly swept floor. His gloved hand was hovering over a seemingly unimportant list of names. It wasn't until Selwyn wiped the sandy particles out of her eyes and dried the salty tears that she recognised her own name. Selwyn could write a few words and read a few more but she had no gift of reading, unlike Father Luyewn who explained the list to her.

"This piece of parchment that the Earl Eafled has found details the owners of the fort going back at least two centuries, it seems." He examined the page more closely to make sure he was revealing its story truthfully. Father Luyewn then looked away sharply towards Eafled who was waiting for the shocked response. "This explains everything," he said, finally turning back to Selwyn who was still in confusion about the priest's reaction.

"What is it, Father?" she enquired.

"Sunflower, before yours and Lord Carlnut's name is a man named Frigrith, who was presumably the previous Lord." Luyewn looked towards Eafled to see if his findings were correct. Eafled nodded. "And Frigrith is said to have died a few months before Lord Carlnut arrived."

"A horrid disease, M'Lady; he was covered in black spots and coughed blood. His entire family succumbed to the disease. God rest their souls," Eafled said as he crossed himself.

"Why is this interesting? How does this help me?" Selwyn sighed.

"Look," Luyewn said and pointed towards a part of the restless parchment. "Between Lord Carlnut and Lord Frigrith is another name that has been crossed out, presumably because King Beorhtric gave you Portland instead."

"Whose name is it?" Selwyn asked, having finally become engrossed by the priest's tale.

"Father Osyth," Eafled said from one of the sand-covered benches. "The priest was a favourite of Ealdorman Osric, and I remember him recommending Osyth for the seat of Portland." It took a few moments for Selwyn to realise what Luyewn and the rolling parchment were trying to tell her. The snivelling Father Osyth must have felt usurped after seeing Carlnut given his promised seat, and Selwyn knew he would have hated Carlnut for it.

"You don't reckon he seriously has anything to do with Carlnut's capture, do you?" she asked both men, who just gave her reluctant looks in return.

"I am afraid, Sunflower, it may have everything to do with it," Luyewn said.

The air became suddenly chillier as though the world had descended into a flash of winter again; the nesting birds in the overlooking cliffs all began to take flight. Their flapping wings rained white and grey feathers down onto the shingles and created a pulsating clapping sound as they soared back towards the swollen sea. Selwyn had walked outside to witness what had caused the birds to act so strangely and Eafled joined her. Luyewn remained in the chapel as the novice Willibald had returned with a basket full of old stale bread. Five war horses were galloping furiously down the slope where Engelhard had disappeared just an hour before. One of the men astride the horses was carrying a large banner, which bore the insignia of a purple leaping fish. A tear escaped from Selwyn's eye as she recognised the men were Earl Cynric's. Earl Eafled quickly ran into the tavern and emerged just as quickly with a few of his own men that must have been enjoying cups of mead and ale for their steps were awkward and clumsy.

"Hide, M'Lady!" he shouted from the tavern's door as he unsheathed a fine-looking sword. Selwyn could not move; she felt as if two chains had fixed her feet to the floor. Eventually, her first step, moved her backwards towards the chapel, but during that one step the five horses had gained a lot of ground. Soon, the great war beasts were trotting slowly across the loose rocks and broken shells that formed the majority of the ground of Fortunes Well. Selwyn still hadn't made it into the chapel despite Earl Eafled's screams, which fell upon deaf ears. Seeing her helplessness, the Earl ordered his half-drunken men to form a shield wall. The wall was crude and stumbling, but the presence of Eafled stabilised it and must have unnerved the horsemen who had stopped just twenty metres away. The man carrying the striking purple banner had thrust the shaft into the ground and allowed the wind to showcase the leaping fish to the entire settlement. He was one of the three horsemen who had dismounted. All five of them wore purple cloaks and held painted shields, which showed the same picture as the flapping banner that competed with the sound of the thickening sea.

"Who is in charge here?" one of the men shouted towards the shield wall that hid Selwyn from their view.

"Who wants to know?" Eafled shouted back from behind the cover of his own shield.

"I am Rahere, one of Earl Cynric of Christchurch's captains."

"What is your business here?" Eafled said after failing to recognise the name.

"Portland's gates are locked shut and I need to speak with whoever is in charge," Rahere replied. Selwyn, who was crouched behind Eafled and underneath the threshold of the chapel, listened to the captain's words with a great deal of interest. She knew that the captain would have heard of Lord Carlnut's appointment and should have been asking for him instead. Once again, more confusing strands of one great plot twisted together and fogged her mind.

"The doors are locked because Lord Carlnut is not receiving guests," Eafled lied. "He will be most displeased you have laid your banner on his land." Rahere turned towards the flag that waved proudly in the brisk sea air.

"Who do I speak to?" Rahere asked, growing bored of the entire event.

"The Earl of Dorchester! And I order you to get that flag out of my soil," Eafled had stormed out of the wall, which closed almost instantly, proving to Selwyn that the men inside the wall knew their duty regardless of their drunkenness. Rahere looked shocked and his heavily marked face grimaced at the sight of a man far above his rank.

"I am very sorry, my Lord, but we have been charged to find a fugitive," Rahere said and lowered his head in respect. The top of his head was balding, and Selwyn could now see a number of wrinkles crinkling the captain's face. He must have been at least forty, and still his frame which was burly and thick, showed no signs of old age.

"Fugitive?" Eafled asked.

"Lord Carlnut of Portland has escaped his sentence, which was agreed upon in the eyes of the King and God." Rahere had no worries in relaying this message and even had an air of cockiness to him as a King's sentence was final and no man, regardless of rank, could overturn that. "Have you seen Lord Carlnut . . . Lord," Rahere said as he slowly moved his hand towards his sword's hilt. Eafled's men stepped forward in one synchronized motion and Rahere's men's spears sung as they were violently whipped through the air in alarm.

"There is no need for violence, captain. Please could you ask your men to stand down," Eafled said nervously whilst his grip grew tighter on his silver sword pommel.

"Is that the Lady Selwyn I see behind your wobbly shield wall?" Rahere said. Selwyn froze at the mention of her name; Rahere was now backed up by all four of his large, well-trained spearmen. Earl Eafled hesitated and found no words as he recognised the strength of Rahere's warriors. He turned to see ten of his men with lowered spears and tight shields, then saw a circle of the townspeople watching on with open mouths and wide eyes. There were around fifty men, women and children, who had all put down their drinks, food and sewing needles. Instead, some held makeshift weapons such as small carving knives and pieces of timber. A few men even carried reaping hooks that were freshly sharpened from a day at sea. Earl Eafled was suddenly a little bit more confident at the sight of the townsfolk. Regardless of that, he still felt a small twang of unease as he found himself rather far in front of his own shield wall, which had subconsciously backtracked to keep Selwyn as safe as they could.

"Lady Selwyn is in my care," Eafled said after getting a new bounce of confidence. "Now I will give you one more chance to leave my land." As the Earl said those words, all four of Rahere's men dashed forward in one fluid motion and grabbed the Earl before he could draw his sword in defence. Suddenly, Eafled was on his knees with two spear points pricking his back. Rahere addressed the anxious crowd:

"We have no quarrel with you, nor do we have any issue with the Earl," Rahere adjusted the thin battered golden fish that held his purple cloak over his mailed chest. "If anyone has seen or heard from Lord Carlnut, we need to know." No one spoke and instead Eafled's shield wall limped slightly, giving Selwyn a better view of the defeated Eafled. In a matter of moments, Eafled had gone from a confident Earl to a defeated one, and the look on his face had already sunk to a sullen one. "The Lady Selwyn will know where her man is, I am sure. Before I demand you to hand her over, I will tell the good people of Fortunes Well why their lord was sentenced to death."

"No!" Selwyn pleaded from the diminishing safety.

"Yes," Rahere smiled and revealed a mouth full of stained green and broken teeth. "Carlnut is a Pagan! He refused to acknowledge the one true God and instead worships terrible false idols that are known aliases of the

Devil!" he shouted so that even the men dragging their boats back from the sea could hear.

"Lies," one man yelled from the tavern's threshold.

"You are the devil," a woman carrying a newborn baby yelled. Earl Eafled looked up towards Selwyn, and she gave him a nod to confirm Rahere's absurd claims. The Earl dropped his head ashamed that he had been supporting a Pagan and then crossed himself. Selwyn thought she also saw him crying, but she couldn't be certain as everything she saw was fogged up by her own tears.

"Get out of Fortunes Well!" a fat fisherman screamed as he waved his gutting knife furiously.

"Our Lord is not here," another said, choosing not to believe Rahere.

"Boat!" a man shrieked from the sea.

"You are a piece of sheep shit; let my Earl go or I will have no choice but to hang your head and your men's heads from spikes," one of the soldiers in the wall shouted in a vain attempt to tempt Rahere or one of his men into single combat.

"Boats!" the far voice shrieked again. This time, enough people heard the cry, and even Rahere had his attention diverted to the young fisherman. He was pointing towards three great sailed ships that were headed straight towards Fortunes Well. Selwyn could see nothing as she was between a wall of shields and a chapel, but luckily, Luyewn pulled her inside and towards the gap above the altar. Willibald was already perched on the black wood that acted as a step, but

Luyewn pushed him aside. All three boats had oars that swept through the air like marvellous seabirds and then dived into the water as gracefully as a diving kingfisher. There must have been around eighty oars between the three ships and they showed no sign of turning or slowing. The biggest boat was slightly in front of the other two and it appeared like a daemon from hell. Its flagging bleached sails looked blood splattered and roared against every wave the sea threw at it. Selwyn rubbed her eyes twice to try and remove the image of a snarling dragon that felt more alive the closer the ship got to shore. After squinting, she noticed all three boats were adorned by beasts and she instinctively crossed herself, which Father Luyewn and Willibald mirrored.

"Who are they?" Willibald asked as he started to gather the dusty scrolls into a wicker basket. "Franks?" he guessed.

"They are not Franks, Willibald. Franks normally fly light blue sails," Luyewn snapped. Through the small window, Selwyn could see Rahere carefully treading over pieces of sand and shells towards the creeping tide line.

"Merchants?" Selwyn suggested. The three of them seemed content with that suggestion and simply watched in awe as the three boats were carried to the shore on a gentle sea breeze.

Solvi

After what seemed like days in the never-ending expanse of water, land finally showed itself. Solvi's heart exploded in his chest and he rubbed his eyes as if he had seen a miracle of the Gods.

"Is this Valhalla?" Jik asked his Jarl as the archer struggled to keep his mouth closed.

"No," Solvi said, astonished he was about to utter the next few words. "This is Britain." The three ships looked like tiny throw board pieces compared to the huge, towering, pure white landscape that cast them in a vast shadow. The ships numbered three as nine vessels had been destroyed in a furious daemon-sent storm leaving only Gudrod's, Solvi's and Gisha's afloat. Nesting sea birds poked their thin necks from a multitude of twig nests that had somehow been made upon the jagged chalk rocks. A horrible reflection that bounced off the crystal white cliffs stung the eyes whilst the terrible smashing of sea on rock irritated the ears. Solvi looked to the Dreki, where Gudrod and Halfdan were in awe of the impossibly high island jutting out of the white-washed waves. Gisha and her men had all stopped rowing to fully immerse themselves in the beauty of what they could see before their eyes.

"Dubris," Solvi muttered under his breath.

"What in the Gods' name is a bloody Dubris?" Frosti asked, seemly uninterested in the view. Frosti now bore a strange-shaped scar on his cheek from where a splintered oar had cut him. There was something about the big man that had changed since the storm, but Solvi had decided not to probe deeper until they were both back in Osoyro.

"The map that King Sigfred gave me labelled these cliffs as a place called Dubris," Solvi said.

"So what are we waiting for? Let's bloody land and plunder and go home. And before we do go home, I want a bloody woman." Frosti then begun to sharpen his great axe with a cloth-wrapped stone. Even though the water near the cliffs ebbed crazily and swirled in giant whirlpools, the Raven Head was far enough away to settle in a patch of wonderfully calm water. A family of giant fish jumped out of the sea. Their grey oily skin sparkled as if they had an entire constellation on their backs.

"Delfins," Halfdan yelled from the Dreki, which was slowly beginning to make its way towards the Raven Head's port side. In a matter of seconds, the two boats would have smashed together and caused an almighty clatter that would have surely devastated either one of them. However, both crews were so well trained that every man knew their duty without even needing to be told. The rowers on Dreki's starboard side and the ones on the Raven Head's port pulled in their oars and laid them flat upon the creaking deck. Next, Frosti tossed over a rope thicker than a man's arm, which was caught by the huge hands of a man on board the Dreki. Soon after, more ropes were caught and then tied down until both boats practically hugged each other. Gisha had decided to still her boat on the steady waves allowing her followers some much needed rest. Two of the gracious Delfins swam so close to the conjoined boats that Solvi could smell their pungent saltiness. The sound of Gudrod's huge boot hitting the Raven Head's plank made them scatter and make the most unusual sound that seemed to mimic a laughing child. Halfdan followed his brother but the rest of the men remained on board their own boat, instead choosing this precious break to rest, eat and pray for the dead. The two bothers' eyes were saturated in tears and their faces had falling stains across them where the streams had cleaned the clinging dirt. Somehow Gudrod's dragon tattoos appeared to be weeping as well, but Solvi was sure he was simply seeing things from exhaustion.

"I suggest we pull the sails down and row to the nearest shoreline," Solvi said with confidence.

"You don't suggest anything," Gudrod grumbled as he washed away Solvi's idea like it was some dirt on the bottom of his boot. "I have lost over three hundred good men to the seas and most of my boats," he said, as bubbling spit gathered in the corners of his mouth. "I am sailing back home and away from this hell that has been cursed by the Gods." A lump forced its way to the back of Solvi's throat as he felt his dream slipping away. Gudrod clambered back on the Dreki and shaded himself in the crudely built shelter that normally housed his wife Asa or child Olaf. Halfdan, however, stayed on board.

"We won't be going home, Solvi," Halfdan said as he adjusted his many seal skin pelts to shelter away from a growing wind. "My brother will land with you, but I do think it's right for us not to raid. Everyone is too fucking tired. Let's row down this channel and allow our survivors to get some rest." It was the first time that Halfdan actually sounded sincere, for normally he was often drunk and extremely sarcastic. Solvi turned to look at his crew. One soldier had fallen asleep at the oar whilst another looked at red raw blisters on his hand where sweat and wood had chafed painfully. Even Frosti looked tired. There were black bags that sagged under his dark brown eyes, and his shoulders hunched so much that they must have felt heavier than a ship's anchor to him. Solvi had decided it was actually best that the crews rested, so he ordered Jik, who was at the steering oar, to bring the Raven Head closer to the Dubris shore line. Before Jik could steer the oar away, the ropes that tied the two boats together had to be cut. Frosti took out his giant war axe and sliced through the twisting strings as if they weren't even there. Soon all three boats sailed individually and Solvi wondered what the channel would have looked like if the twelve original boats had survived the storm. He pictured the slashing oars whizzing across the water and could imagine the almighty cheer that would have erupted once they saw the white cliffs of Dubris. Solvi hoped those fallen men were now feasting in Valhalla, and a part of him felt a twinge of jealousy.

For around a full day, the Raven Head followed the coast of Britain. From the sea, the island looked like a marvellous place. From the distance they were sailing at, they couldn't see what was going on at the shoreline, but Solvi did see dozens of grand forests and the smoke of even more fishing settlements. They had passed a marvellous island of gleaming cliffs and large sea birds that had for an instant, enticed Solvi, for it had a beautifully shaped channel that would have provided a perfect bay to dock the boats. Solvi thought that if he still had the fleet, he would have ordered them to sail down the channel. There he would have then ordered them to land on both the white island and the isle of Britain on the other side.

"Are we just gonna bloody sail round this bloody place or what," Frosti said as he made his way to the steering oar where Solvi sat admiring the gorgeous cliff faces of the white island.

"Frosti, I am happy to land anywhere that has gold and I am confident Gudrod will make the right decision," Solvi said diplomatically.

"You are the Jarl, Solvi, don't forget that," Jik added from his rower's bench. The sail fluttered up above them as the wind reminded everyone of its presence. "Gudrod is a good warrior, that is all. You are our leader and I follow your orders. If you want to land, then you land. After all, we don't want another storm to hit us." Jik had no love for the warlord of the northern camps as all his love was dedicated towards Gudrod's wife, Asa. Solvi had overheard the archer boasting that he was going to find a golden necklace for the princess. Solvi had then decided he would send Gudrod and Asa away once they got back home. Jik's relationship with the princess had the potential to ruin everything. If Gudrod found out, he could want revenge and Solvi dreaded what that revenge would entail. A pesky bug landed on his shoulder but soon buzzed away as Solvi slapped at it. The day was getting hot, which led to most of the rowers taking off their shirts to avoid the horrible grip that sweaty leathers can leave on the skin.

"What is your plan when you get back, Jarl? King Sigfred is not going to be pleased that you burnt his men, and I am sure that Gudrod will stick around till his brother receives his payment," Jik had said when he and Solvi were alone.

"Payment?" Solvi asked with a puzzled look. "I have not paid them anything as their payment is whatever they plunder."

"Oh, he hasn't told you, Jarl." Jik hesitated. "It's just that–"

"It's just what! Who hasn't told me what?" Solvi shouted, waking up a tired warrior who swiftly closed his eyes again out of exhaustion.

"Well, me and Frosti found a pirate's hoard on the way to find Gudrod, and Halfdan has been offered it," Jik said.

"You got me worried then, fool; he is more than welcome to a pirate's treasure." Solvi accompanied his laughter with a sigh of relief.

"No, Jarl. This hoard was a collection of treasure from a whole host of captains and I dare say it was the biggest collection of coins and jewels I have ever seen." Solvi remained silent and simply stared off into the distance. "Frosti has given away a possible fortune in return for you being able to have the likes of Gudrod the Hunter with you and also to allow Finlit to guard Osoyro." Jik left his Jarl once he realised he was done responding. Frosti lay asleep at the front of the Raven Head with the dying shadow of the beast prow shading him. As Solvi stared at him, he felt an overwhelming desire to weep from happiness. Frosti had given away treasure that could have bought him a Jarldom, it seemed, so Solvi made the decision to give Frosti more land than he could ever hope for. The land would come from Sigfred, Solvi hoped, and in his head, the future of Hordaland unravelled like the map of Britain that Sigfred had given him. Solvi knew he would give Eddval Jikop's old chiefdom of Askoy and then give Jik the recently dead Umiston's seat. As well as that, he would persuade Gudrod to allow the northern camps to be a chiefdom of Hordaland and then Halfdan could be the chief of that whilst Gudrod was the chief of his wife's chiefdom of Voss. Solvi blushed at the thought of all the chiefdoms being run by friends that could assemble a huge army to destroy King Sigfred. The sight of a falling star interrupted his thoughts. A thousand blinking lights filled the sky, unobscured by the thick mass of clouds that usually blocked their dim light. A dying trail of embers followed the dazzling shine of the falling star that was Frey's chariot racing through the night's sky across the realms of Yggdrasil. Frey had a golden chariot that shone in the dark and lit up the sky as it flew over the earth; the chariot was pulled by a magic boar made by dwarves. Solvi thought of the boat builder who had been sacrificed to the great God and was glad his sacrifice for clear weather had finally been listened to. Solvi looked at every one of his men who were either sleeping on the sodden deck or rowing gently, lost in their own minds. A great sense of pride suddenly struck him. If the raid was to be a success then everyone who survived would become a richer man, all thanks to him.

Frosti had only slept for an hour or two before he was awoken when a rogue wave breached the deck and drenched him. The crewmen who were awake laughed as a kelp blade lodged itself in his dripping beard. Solvi noted their spirits were returning after the horrors of the night before, and he hoped soon they would be high enough to pluck up the courage to raid. Men were always nervous before a fight, their bowels ached and their heads spun with every possible eventuality. However, a different type of nervousness brewed in a man's guts before a sea raid. Normally, the terrain and opposition were scouted out by horsemen, who then brought the information back home so tactics and strategy could be carefully planned out. However, on a sea raid, this could not happen and instead men stormed in as if they were wearing blindfolds in a darkened room. On most occasions, the first men off the boat were drunk and their courage spilled out onto the other crewmen who would splash into the shallows undefended and full of a burning desire to pillage. If the defenders had ample amounts of archers, then three boats full of hungry crewmen would be turned into two boats and a mass of bloodied bodies floating in a crimson sea. Solvi prayed to Odin that the place Gudrod the Hunter chose did not have a large supply of bows and arrows waiting to be loosed upon them.

"When is the bloody Hunter going to choose his precious spot?" Frosti said between mouthfuls of crusty bread.

"He will eventually. Our men needed their rest anyway," Solvi replied. "You need your rest. You have bags bigger than fists under your eyes."

"Just muscle waiting to be tensed," Frosti defended himself.

"Your cut is turning yellow," Solvi said.

"Just a bloody scratch. I've seen worse scratches on women's thumbs after a day on the weaving web."

"I am worried about you, Frosti," Solvi admitted.

"Worrying is for bloody women. Don't tell me your bloody cock fell off in the storm, Solvi. That's the last thing we need, a female Jarl or at least a Jarl with no cock and balls." Frosti laughed and pulled himself up.

"Anyway, Solvi, there is no need to worry about me. The Gods visited me in my dreams before we set sail for Britain."

"Really? What did they say?" Solvi became excited as he often was at the thought of the Gods sneaking down into the minds of men.

"They told me that I will avenge my brother's death," Frosti said, smiling. Friti, Frosti's younger brother, had been killed the day that Solvi had taken Osoyro, and Frosti had sworn not to rest until Pintojuk Bergison, the orchestrator of Friti's death, was killed. "I saw my war axe swinging down upon his head, and then I saw it take another swing at him until every piece of him was wiped off the earth." Frosti then clung onto his beautifully crafted axe and flung it into the air and caught it again as if it was made of feathers.

A copper mist started to edge its way across the sky, adding light oranges and dark reds to the grey backdrop. A white cloud shaped like a sword glinted bronze as if it was being newly forged in a blacksmith's roaring fires. The colours seemed to become brighter and almost vibrated as the sun started slowly to rise. Solvi wondered how much of Britain's southern shore was actually left to explore, as for the past two days all they could see was her jagged cliff faces and dotted shingle beaches. Gisha's boat with its ripped sails and cracking oars was to Solvi's left and the Dreki, Gudrod's mighty vessel, was between the Raven Head and the isle of Britain.

"Today we raid!" Halfdan yelled across the sparkling water that came alive in the new dawn.

"Say the word and we will follow," Jarl Solvi shouted over in reply. Gudrod wasn't at Dreki's steering oar, instead he left that job to his younger brother Halfdan. However, the Hunter did walk up and down the deck encouraging rowers and calling for the Gods' help. Solvi had on several occasions wished that Halfdan was the leader as he seemed to have a comforting calmness to him as well as a furious attitude. Whereas Gudrod the Hunter was like a charging bull; he was unpredictable, and Frosti claimed the man had lost all his wits. But in spite all of his uncontrollable flaws he was a great warlord, and his men would follow him to death and beyond. Jik was at the steering oar, which allowed Solvi to greet Frosti under the shadow of the calling raven that stood proud in the rising sun.

"Why did you give up all that treasure?" Solvi queried, fearing that he would never get the opportunity to ask again. Frosti sighed and itched at some lice that thrived in his beard.

"Barely enough for a spearhead," Frosti snorted.

"Jik tells me it was a great pirate's treasure and when it comes to coin that idiot doesn't lie," Solvi said.

"Has that bastard being spreading lies again?" Frosti said. "Look, yes there might have been a lot of treasure. I could have bought this fleet and its crew five times over, but what would have been the point? I vowed to stand with you, and a man who breaks those sacred oaths will be mocked in Valhalla. And believe me, Solvi, there are much better things I would like to do in the great watery halls." He then thrust his pelvis a couple of times to make sure Solvi understood what he was trying to say. "I am your friend, Solvi, and if I had taken the hoard you would have had to kill me. And look at it this way; I have spared you a beating." Frosti laughed but Solvi could not. He had a huge lump lodged in his neck, and the bald man's honesty almost brought tears to his eyes. "You haven't gone soft on me, have you? I know where that hoard is and I can quite as easily change my mind." The pair laughed and shared a nervous embrace.

It was mid-afternoon when Halfdan signalled to the Raven Head. Every member of Solvi's crew fiddled with their own personal talisman or muttered silent prayers to their Gods. Solvi ran from the steering oar that had caused his muscles to ache and his hands to throb toward the bow. He could see perfectly what land Halfdan had signalled towards and felt a little bit sick by his choice. Far off in the distance in the foreground of a backdrop of slowly moving clouds and spring strong sunlight was an impossible island. He could see high cliff faces that dipped in a spiral round a graveyard of lichen-covered rocks. But Solvi also noticed a dip in the land that appeared to host a thriving settlement. The island was like nothing he had ever seen before. It seemed to cling onto the mainland by a thin strand of shingle and sand that looked as though it was being flooded by a rising tide. They were still at least an hour from the island, but Solvi already felt nauseous from nerves; however, he showed none of that to his men. A small fleet of around ten rowing boats fled towards the shore carrying mossy fishing nets squirming with the day's catch.

"A fishing village?" Jik asked from one of the rowers' benches. "What treasures do fishermen own? Right, men, get ready for a few rotting oysters and hundreds of stinking scales!" he yelled so that everyone on board the Raven Head looked towards the island to try and find some glint of wealth to prove him wrong.

"Shut your bloody mouth." Frosti gave him a smack round the back of the ears to make sure his head stung and then stood next to his Jarl.

"The bloody archer might have a point; there doesn't seem to be much here," Frosti whispered in Solvi's ears.

"Yes, he is right; however, look past the village and just beyond the ridge." Solvi pointed to a thatched tower roof that hid behind the rocky curvature of the island. "There is more. If I am not mistaken, that is a church, and we all know those priests are like women, they love their silver!" This time it was Solvi's turn to raise his voice and his men were made much more confident from their Jarl's self-belief. "We will be rich men tomorrow, rich and soaked in ale and women!"

Soon, all three boats were lined up, facing the shadowed beach of the island. The Raven Head's prow as well as the roaring dragon on Dreki and the snake-haired beast on Gisha's boat had all been removed so the spirits of the land would not be frightened by the snarling beasts. Jik had replaced the raven on the prow and desperately searched the shoreline for an estimate of their defences.

"I would say from a village this size, no more than twenty fighting men, but I don't think many of them will be fighting fit," he guessed.

"We will take no chances," Solvi said. "Gear up, men!" And on that order, the once organised boat became a confused chaotic mess. Men peered under rowers' benches, lifting up sodden rags and ripped fabrics to find their helmets and shields. After the ferocity of the storm, nothing was where it should be. Two men smashed heads as they both bent down to pick up their rusting axes whilst another few men brawled for the use of one of the only iron helmets. Solvi looked towards the Dreki and he noticed exactly the same thing going on. He could not blame his men; the voyage was one of the worst they had ever been on and nerves can cause confusion like the kind Solvi and Frosti were forced to watch. Finally, just minutes from the shore, everyone seemed content with what they clasped onto. Most of the crew had shields but only a few had any headgear. Luckily, they had all found some kind of weapon, even if one man had to be content with a snapped oar and a broken nose. Gisha was bellowing out encouragement whilst Gudrod smacked his shield to create a violent drumbeat. Solvi felt pressured to say something to the men who anxiously heaved the oars through the murky shore towards the beach. However, he froze; when he needed words the most, they would not come. He found himself holding the hilt of

Gutstretcher that slept in its scabbard, but he could do nothing else.

"Those men on that shore have bloody gold that needs to be stolen," Frosti shouted to hide Solvi's muteness. "They have priests that need to be slaughtered and ale that needs to be drunk. But most importantly they have women that need to be fucked!" The crew roared in reply seemingly unaware of Solvi's terrible nerves, and soon the crew of each boat smashed their fists against their shields to create their own thunder, which was loud enough to champion Thor. One man towards the back of the boat vomited a horrible brown liquid overboard whilst another pulled back his long, salt-stained hair to stop it becoming matted with the sick man's vomit. Solvi wanted to throw up too, but he needed to be strong. He wondered how his life had come to this one moment, and started to envy those who perished in the storm over the great North Sea. Jik was stroking the feathers of his arrows whilst Frosti stared towards the shoreline as if it were covered in a thousand naked women. A splash sounded from the left, then another, followed by a bunch of large splashes as men poured off the Dreki screaming Thor's name. Halfdan and Gudrod looked tremendous in their layers of seal pelts, and Solvi could see a lone warrior on the beach walking towards them with his arms spread open in greeting.

"Go, you bloody fools, go!" Frosti screamed as he threw himself overboard. Solvi followed his friend's orders and found himself waist deep in sand-swelled water. The sea was instantly cold as it soaked into his leathers, but Solvi's heart was pumping so hard that he was sweating. His shield felt heavy as he heaved it against the tide towards the soldier, who started to tread backwards when he saw floods of men heading in his direction. Before the man could make three paces backwards, Gudrod was upon him. The soldier tried to say something in his own language, but Gudrod had no patience for nervous stutters. Gudrod's huge axe head buried itself into his neck before the soldier could even turn round. A fountain of blood shone in the sun as it burst onto the sand below, quickly followed by his twitching body. Even before the body fell, chaos erupted on both sides of the water. The three tired and hungry crews continued to pour out of the ships as if they were alight with burning flames. They charged forward like a demented pack of dogs, thirsty for their own taste of blood. Gisha was leading her crew to where Gudrod had slain the first British man and soon all three crews were huddled round the lifeless body.

"Little cunt," Gudrod grumbled as he released his axe from the dead man's neck.

"If they all die like that then we can hope for an easy fight," Halfdan said.

"It won't be easy; look at them," Jik said as he took another step forward onto the beach to try and get a better look at the small force of men that were forming into a wall on top of the beach. Solvi was horrified. He hadn't expected so many armed men in a fishing village, and he certainly didn't expect men who managed to form a wall of shields within moments. They appeared chaotic at first, but it was evident that they all knew what was required of them. A line of around twenty soldiers all with huge long shields and pointed spears gathered together with still more men falling into place, although these men carried farmers' weapons and most of them didn't even have a shield. Solvi noted how their shields were tightly fixed and their glinting spear points remained as still as stone.

"This is going to be harder than we thought," Jik said as he too noticed the looming wall of frightened men.

"Gisha, you take your men round the wall when we engage. Do not turn back. Head to the church we saw as we were making port and wreak fucking havoc," Solvi ordered. She nodded and the Chieftess signalled to her men their new orders. Gudrod stormed towards Solvi with his tattooed face scrunched up like a pile of old rags.

"Why the fuck do you want to divide our crew?" he said making sure Solvi was drenched in his spit. "We can crush these shit buckets and whoresons easily with Gisha's men as well." Gudrod the Hunter's eyes were blood red and bulging giving his face a daemonic appearance.

"There is a settlement behind this one; I think that is where we will find the true prize of the raid. Women and silver, Gudrod, women and silver." Gudrod turned to look at the fishing village behind him. "Look around you; there is not going to be a lot of gold and silver in those huts," Solvi admitted. "But churches are a bee's nest full of sticky honey." The hunter snorted and grouped his men into a shield wall. There were around thirty men in that wall but unlike the one that loomed ahead of them, Gudrod's was huge. Each man in the wall was easily bigger than six foot and they all had bulging arms that grasped angrily onto axes and painted shields. Each shield had a red dragon painted on it, much like the beast that adorned the sails of Dreki.

"As the two walls lock, stick your spears in their guts and shit on their corpses," Halfdan yelled to his men in some sort of speech that was meant to get the men rallied up, but Solvi still felt the horrible uncertainty of nerves. Then, as if every man was using one brain, the shield wall stomped forward. Frosti, Gudrod, Halfdan and Solvi spread themselves out on the front row. Each of them made sure they were next to a man that they could trust with their lives. Frosti took one look towards a bony-looking man to his right and instantly pushed him back into a deeper rank, allowing a powerful beast to take his place. All of them would have dreamed to have a famous warrior next to them, but once the walls started moving there was nothing that could be done. The air smelt of salt and fish and sweat, but Solvi knew it would soon smell of death. Usually shield walls could look upon each other for hours before any of them had built up enough courage to charge. However, circumstances were different; Gudrod's men had seen their friends die and their ships destroyed so they wanted nothing more than British blood. Leather boots sunk into sand and cracked shells as they stamped forward without a single second of hesitation. Not even the strong stench of the gutted fish could mask the smell of urine and ale that was fresh in the air. Solvi dug his feet into the ground, making sure the incoming impact of the two walls would not knock him down.

"Stand!" Gudrod shouted from the centre front of the wall. "Stand!"

"Get your fucking shields up," Halfdan said to make sure the men were ready for the crush. The opposing captain was yelling in his own language, and his men appeared to gain a new sense of energy from whatever he had said. For a moment, there was a slight silence. Solvi saw a few white gulls circling overhead, then noticed how the sun shimmered peacefully, casting spiny shadows on the beach where its light was obscured by the beached boats. Then, as if two worlds were crashing into each other, the two walls met. Shields cracked and men cursed as both sides pushed each other for an inch of space. Solvi felt his shoulder crack and his knee buckle but thankfully he stood. The breath of the man in front of him stunk of fresh ale, and Solvi realised he must be drunk. The space was too tight for Solvi to wield Gutstretcher so instead he pulled out his small hand axe that normally hung unused from his belt. He caught the shin of the stinking man, and he fell in a fit of screams and blood. For a moment Solvi thought about splitting from the wall and pushing into the space he had just made, but another soldier filled the gap. Whilst the man built up the courage to strike, Solvi had a heart beat to look across the wall. One of Gudrod's warriors was clutching onto a stump hand as he cried for his mother. His screams were muted when a spear found his throat, but from which side Solvi did not know. Somehow, Frosti was next to Solvi, pushing furiously at the man in front of him. A pile of dead and dying bodies had already started to build up between the two walls, causing a natural barrier against downwards strokes and making advancing in any direction extremely difficult. Solvi caught a glimpse of Gudrod swinging his great axe wildly down onto a man's shield, almost splitting it in two. There was a crack that sounded like smashing bone and Solvi was certain the British soldier must certainly have shattered his wrist into multiple pieces.

"What's the bloody plan, Jarl?" Frosti said whilst his eyes bulged and muscles flexed wildly

"As soon as we break this fucking wall we raid the village and head to the church," Solvi replied.

"We have lost a few men already; we are too few without this shit. What if there are more British cunts guarding their fucking church?" Frosti asked, unusually pessimistically.

"We fight." Solvi had a smile on his face at the thought of allowing Gutstretcher to sing and dance in British blood. A mad man that Solvi did not recognise managed to ´lunge himself over the wall but was immediately flung back, holding onto a bloodied throwing spear. Now and then Jik would be lifted up by one of his friends to see over the wall to fire an arrow or two. One of the arrows skidded past Gudrod's head and buried itself into a British man's eye. The Hunter turned to Jik who offered him a small bow and a wink. Halfdan was yelling like a wild thing whilst his men hacked down with blood-soaked axes and danced back to avoid the searching blows of spears at their feet. One man squealed like a wounded pig as his ankle was torn open by a British spear, and another roared in triumph after finally downing his enemy. A few seconds took an age and every blow sounded like it was strong enough to end the entire bout, however, nobody relented. Solvi began to feel the ache in his shoulder, and in a moment of shameful weakness, his shield flopped backwards. The soldier in front of him in clean mail and a maddening fury swung a great axe down on Solvi. He closed his eyes, expecting the next time he would open them was when he greeted his father in Valhalla.

"Put your bloody shield up, Jarl," Frosti yelled as he pulled Solvi back to his feet. Frosti was grinning like a wolf whilst another soldier filled the space where Frosti had split a man's skull perfectly into two mangled pieces. Another arrow whistled overhead and throwing axes were tossed into the British wall. Soon, sand became tangled in grass and then mixed with broken shells, and Solvi realised that they were pushing the enemy's wall backwards. As each member of Solvi's wall heaved the dwindling British force towards the village they were protecting, Solvi had to be careful not to trip on the broken bodies of mailed men. Gudrod was signalling across the line like a wild thing trapped in a net. His arms were waving, and he appeared to be screaming. It was then that Solvi realised he couldn't hear anything. The world was silent. He looked round to face Frosti who was also shouting then and looked back at his men who were all pushing and swinging spears into gaps between shields. A club of some kind, that looked to be a farmer's tool more than a weapon, caught Solvi's attention. He raised his hand axe to stop the blow, but his left knee buckled again. Suddenly, his entire shin was being scratched by shingle and his head was being pounded till Solvi's own hands became blurred and his neck felt like an anchor. Each blow stung furiously and after the fifth or sixth strike a ringing started to happen. But that ringing revitalised Solvi; he could hear again. The man struck once more, but Solvi was quicker. He struck upwards with the axe and caught the loose flesh under the soldier's arm, chopping if off completely. The limb was sent spinning into the crowd of men whose yells and curses were like music to Solvi's ears. Gudrod was still flailing, trying to get Solvi's attention, but this time he could hear what he was saying.

"Now, Jarl! Go now!" Gudrod screamed at the top of his voice. Solvi took one deep breath and checked to see if Gutstretcher still hugged his waist.

"Ease maggots! Ease!" Halfdan shouted and, as if they were waves on the beach, the entire wall stepped back. British men who were all putting every single bit of their own energy into the great push fell forward. Some smacked their faces on their own shields whilst others became squashed under the weight of the men behind them. Solvi even saw one unlucky soldier pierced to the ground after one of his friend's spears buried itself in his back.

"Go, run to the village," Solvi ordered, and his men did not disappoint, even though each footstep was an effort of courage and strength as Solvi's crew ran straight through the unorganised enemy ranks. Frosti managed to swing his axe into a kneeling man's face whilst Jik stabbed another in the neck. Eventually, they found themselves behind the enemy shield wall, which was finally reforming itself. The British originally tried to stand back to back so that they were ready for an attack from both sides. However, a mixture of too few men and Gudrod attacking again meant they had to focus on Gudrod and Halfdan rather than the crew of the Raven Head. Solvi imagined the paralysing fear in every man in that wall as they must have known the havoc that was about to explode in their village. However, if they turned and ran towards Solvi then they would be butchered by Gudrod. A laugh found its way into Solvi's throat even though his head throbbed and his shoulder protested its every movement.

"To the village, men," Solvi ordered.

"Take anything you bloody can!" Frosti said, throwing his axe into the air and catching it perfectly in hands covered in sweat and blood. Once Solvi's crew hit the fishing settlement, the slaughter began. Men poured out of thatched houses, brandishing anything they could as a weapon. One huge man with a few strands of hair and even fewer teeth charged at Solvi, wielding a fishing hook. Its point still dripped with scaled slime as if it had just been used to gut the day's catch. He ran straight for Solvi, whirling his terrible weapon around his head, screaming what sounded like curses. However, his life ended just as quickly as his bravery flourished. Solvi had unsheathed Gutstretcher instinctively and allowed the man's huge weight to carry him onto the blade's point. Gutstretcher screamed in orgasm as it sunk deep into his guts and then laughed as the fat man's insides trailed desperately out of his large belly. Jik was pouring arrows into young men who were trying feebly to be heroes. A woman with soft blonde hair went to bury a small dagger in the archer's back, but Frosti destroyed her with one almighty swing of his axe. Solvi found himself inside one of the small huts. There were a few chairs, a table with half-full bowls of crushed watery oats inside and a small child cowering in the corner. He had soft brown hair and a face redder than the new morning sun. His nose and cheeks were riddled by horrible pox scars, which gave him a look similar to a ploughed field. Ignoring the young boy, Solvi kicked open wicker baskets hoping for some kind of treasure but instead found only lined sheets and dried bread.

"Where is the gold?!" Solvi screamed at the child. "Gold, treasure, silver," but the boy did not understand Solvi's language or was too scared to answer. Solvi pulled off one of his arm rings. "Treasure," he said waving the ring about in the air. The child froze for a moment and then scurried like a dog on all fours towards a pile of loose straw. There he reached in with his small, mud-covered hand and pulled out a wooden chest that was strangled by a small wooden cross. A shudder ran through Solvi's body at the Christian sign, which seemed to light the entire room until Frosti walked in and immediately crushed the cross in his hands. Solvi used a small knife to break into the chest but was disgusted when he found one single gold piece.

"Is this everything?" he shouted towards the petrified child and let the knife rest at the base of his neck.

"Jarl, there is a small church in this village as well. We should go there before we meet up with Gisha. I think that's where the bloody treasure will be," Frosti said. Solvi flicked the knife round and caught the boy under his chin producing a flash of blood, but contrary to the boy's screams, he would not die. As they left the hut, the two furious shield walls were still hammering at each other, having not moved a single pace between them. A littering of bodies filled the sand-covered shingle, where some were still shivering from fresh sword wounds. Solvi counted at least six of his crew lying dead on the ground whilst another two cradled leaking cuts, groaning. Jik had taken a few men to higher ground, where ransacked homes housed crying women.

It took a few moments to find the chapel, but once they had, there was no mistaking its eerie presence. Suddenly, the battle cries of the pillaging warriors and the clanging of sword on sword dissipated, leaving nothing but the timber creak of the chapel. The chapel was sandwiched between two large buildings that still boasted bolted doors, and Solvi silently wished he had more men with him. Gutstretcher gleamed in the sun, as did Frosti's axe, and both dripped happily with the blood of many now dead men.

"It's just another building, Frosti," Solvi said trying to comfort the big man who was clenching his free hand.

"Odin will not be with us in there, Solvi, he will be blind, Thor will be blind, even Heimdallr will be blind. We fight in there as blind men, Jarl," Frosti said, showing the uncharacteristic turn of nervousness he had been displaying ever since they had set off from Hordaland. "We should bloody get more men, who knows how many bastards are running around in there." Solvi looked around for some kind of inspiration but was distracted by the large number of drunken men flooding out of one hut carrying various metal tools.

"We are going in and trying to save this fucking disaster," Solvi ordered. "How could there be so many soldiers in this shit excuse for a village? Odin is not with us anyway, Frosti, out here or in there."

"Yes, Jarl," Frosti muttered. It didn't take long for the chapel door to swing off its hinges as the old oak quickly surrendered against the mighty force of Frosti's axe. The broken splinters of wood crashed to the floor in a pile. As soon as the sun's light flooded into the chapel, a spinning blade flew through the air like it had wings and caught Frosti in the shoulder, forcing him to let out a great boar-like grunt. Another knife followed the same path, but both Solvi and Frosti were aware of the danger and managed to avoid the blade that landed softly in the sand behind them. Solvi expected to see a fine hall like all the churches in Frisia he had raided and a whole host of priests carrying gold as if somehow it held the answer to life. Instead he was greeted by a small rabble of varying characters. Three soldiers draped in purple stood huddled around a finely dressed man who had his hands bound together in rope whilst two priests tried to hide a woman behind a terribly dusty pile of parchments.

"Let's kill the bloody bastards," Frosti screamed as he yanked the blade from his bleeding shoulder and gripped his axe as if it was his lover. The three purple-cloaked men read the situation perfectly and lunged forward with searching spears and horrifying battle calls. One spear brushed Frosti's leg, causing his leathers to tear but not breaking the skin at any point. The wielder yanked the point back towards him, this time catching behind Frosti's knee. The big man appeared not to feel anything as he shoved the attacker across the chapel. A sword flashed through the air, glinting sunlight as it whistled past Solvi. Solvi jumped backwards to avoid having his face slashed open but then lunged forward immediately in a huge burst of unimaginable energy. Gutstretcher screamed again and again as it was forced to hit steel rather than flesh. Every time Solvi tried to outmanoeuvre the soldier, his blow was anticipated and parried. He tried aiming for the man's ankles with a lowered sweeping motion that would have left an untrained man crippled, however, the soldier saw this and danced away from each sweep.

Frosti faced two spearmen who continuously jabbed their points into every available gap in the bald man's stance. His great war axe created ripples through the air. His shoulder was still bleeding furiously and he limped whenever he moved, but that did not stop him completely decapitating one of the spearmen where he stood. In that one mad moment the man had made the terrible mistake of pausing for a single breath. His body fell to the floor and his red-pointed spear excited dust as it skidded across the ground towards the bound, Lord-like figure. The other spearman hesitated as he looked towards his friend's separated head and into Frosti's eyes that were so aflame with rage he could have melted ice. Both Solvi and the purple-clad soldier stopped for a fleeting moment as they assessed the dire situation of their friends. The man Solvi faced was about his own height but had at least ten years on him and muscle that tensed and bulged whenever his sword swung. Solvi hoped he would tire first as his chain mail appeared heavy, but not one single bead of sweat escaped his forehead. A dreadful realisation struck Solvi worse than any blow he had received that entire day; he was facing someone with far greater skill than his own. An age at sea had caused his entire body to ache as if it had been in a deep sleep. His shoulder was throbbing and his head spun, so that now and then his vision would flutter and his world spin. His hands were blistered from the shuddering steering oar whilst his hair was awkwardly spread across his head after a whole week without the tree sap he used to fix it in place.

"Argh," Frosti grunted from his side of the chapel as a spear caught the top of his head. Blood and skin splattered across the image of the nailed God, which brought an unwilling smile to Solvi's face. The two priests crossed themselves and continued to whisper their magic chants. That slight loss of concentration from Solvi allowed his pursuer to gain the upper hand, until he felt his back stiffen against the damp wooden walls of the tiny church. There was an overwhelming amount of anger in the sword swinger's eyes and Solvi's heart shrank a hundred sizes.

"Pagan! Pagan! Pagan!" the soldier screamed over and over again as he tried to strike a finishing blow to end Solvi.

Suddenly, in a matter of moments, Solvi's entire life became a trodden mess in his pulsating brain. The bound man was no longer bound and instead he carried the headless soldier's bloodied spear. Frosti was already in mid-swing when his right hand side, was crushed by a charging spear thrust. Ribs cracked and smashed whilst he let out a giant roar that could have been heard all the way to Valhalla. Despite the force of the weapon obliterating his entire right side he managed to complete his swing. The axe head embedded itself in the spearman's face, entangling his skull and the iron helm he wore in one disfigured mess. The Lord twisted the spear, mangling Frosti's insides until he could no longer stand.

"No!" Solvi screamed from behind a curtain of rage and an unrivalled flood of tears. He twisted away from the soldier's next blow and swung Gutstretcher across to hack into the soldier's leg, cracking bone and causing him to fall into an unconscious heap. Then without any care for his own life, he charged like a madman towards the Lord-like figure, who continued to force his spear deeper into Frosti's waist. Frosti was coughing gallons of blood and shaking like a newborn lamb, but still he gripped onto his beloved axe. After one long duel with the soldier who still groaned behind him, Solvi did not expect an easy fight. But he desired one; he wanted nothing more than to disfigure the man who still tortured Frosti whilst he tried desperately to cling onto his last collapsing breaths.

"Eafled, behind! Behind!" a woman yelled from her poor hiding spot, but it was too late. Solvi had already thrust Gutstretcher through his back and out through his chest. Not once did the Lord flinch or scream, but instead fell silently onto one of the driftwood benches, smiling slightly as all life drained out of his body. Instinctively Solvi dived onto Frosti trying helplessly to stop the masses of stinking blood pouring out of his side. Solvi knew his best friend had only moments to live.

"My dream was wrong," Frosti choked. "I will never avenge my brother's death. Bergison still lives."

"I promise I will kill Pintojuk Bergison, and I swear to you upon my place in Valhalla I will destroy King Sigfred," Solvi whispered as he lay on his friend cradling him in his final seconds.

"Valhalla better be bloody worth this," Frosti breathed moments before he begun to choke on his own blood. As his friend became limp in his hands, Solvi turned to face the three remaining people in the chapel. A loud cheer erupted from somewhere outside and Solvi prayed that was the sound of Halfdan and Gudrod breaking the shield wall and looting every single piece of treasure on the island. It took an age for his knees to allow him to stand again, but something within forced him forward to the sorry-looking group. One of the priests was old and wrinkled and appeared as though he could be carried away by a single draft of wind, whilst the other had a gormless look and a black, ash-coloured pile of hair that circled a bald spot on his head. The most striking member of the trio was a red-haired woman with a face as if it was carved by the Gods. Solvi's heart pounded in his chest and he felt his breeches stir a little, and for the first time that day he felt no tiredness. He sheathed Gutstretcher and reached a hand for her shivering chin but instead was met by the bony chest of the old priest.

"No," the priest said as he crossed himself. Solvi was astonished. He had never met a priest so brave. He was used to seeing them squirm into little hovels like nymphs, carrying more gold than food. As easily as he would a child, he shoved the old man out of the way and reached for the fire-haired woman once more. She stayed perfectly still, but her eyes flickered to somewhere else in the room. The old priest had either pulled out a knife from his stained white robe or picked one up as Solvi felt its cool steel rip into his hip, scraping the bone underneath. The priest must have known his fate then because he begun to chant like a wild thing screaming for his God to take him. It wasn't until Solvi pulled out the blade that he realised it wasn't a knife at all but instead the sharpened edge of a golden cross. Vomit filled Solvi's mouth as the thought of Christian jewellery being embedded in his skin, and with that vomit came a mad moment of frenzy. He leaped on top of the defiant old man and stabbed him again and again until there were more holes in his chest than untouched skin. The priest died after the first few thrusts, but Solvi was filled with so much hatred for the Christian that his senses swam and his veins pounced around his body.

A shuddering horn brought an end to the furious stabs and to the woman's deafening cries. The other priest had managed to escape, but Solvi couldn't have cared less. He pulled Gutstretcher out of its sodden sheath and smacked the beautiful lady across her skull with its hilt. The flowers that were woven into her hair like a crown separated and broke into crinkled petals as she went floppy in Solvi's arms. With a great deal of effort, he heaved her over his shoulder, took Frosti's war axe and honoured his best friend with one last look before he left the chapel that had become a scene of slaughter and chaos.

Carlnut

Nothing could have prepared Carlnut for the horror he saw from the spit leading to his fortress. A wild hoard screamed at Portland's gate trying desperately to break down its large oak doors. In the distance, plumes of smoke drifted into the cool summer air from Fortunes Well. They swirled and danced, forming clouds that shattered the sun's light into diamond-like sparkles. Cuth and Sicga's mouths were wide enough to swallow a flock of birds, and their eyes failed to blink even though the salt spray stung them mercilessly.

"Go," Carlnut said as he kicked his heels into his horse's side. It was a great mount with instincts far better than the average horse, but he still missed Gladdy and cursed the hooded man who had killed her. The three of them charged down the spit of sand and shingle towards the group of around thirty men who still hadn't noticed their presence. A loud horn sounded from somewhere behind the spiked palisade that heralded

Carlnut's arrival, and for the first time, he saw one of his men poke their heads over the wall. Carlnut squinted, hoping to see the face of Arnum or Osbert, but the smoke was too dense, and his eyes were suddenly filled with tears.

"What is going on? What the fuck is happening? How, in the Gods' names, has Osric managed to get here quicker than us?" Carlnut asked helplessly as he found himself staring fixedly at the panic and chaos unfolding on his land. Another ten men on Portland's walls stood up, all carrying bow and arrows. A sense of unwelcome pride filled Carlnut as he thought of the young steward Osbert commanding his household troop. Carlnut turned to Sicga who looked as white as the gathering clouds above.

"They are not ready," Sicga muttered under his breath. Before Carlnut could smack Sicga for stuffing him with more nerves, a volley of darts rained down onto the raiding group, killing a few and sending the others into retreat. They left the gate momentarily, and the archers ducked their heads back into shelter, completely ignoring the presence of Carlnut. Carlnut's mount was dancing on the spot, kicking up broken shells from their sandy hiding places. The crazy rabble had already started to reorganise itself ready for their next attempt to breach the walls. But this time they spotted Sicga, Cuth and Carlnut and made note to shift their single force into two ready to meet their attack.

"What is this?" Cuth asked, confused with what he was witnessing.

~ 428 ~

"Appears to be a raid; maybe Cynric instead of Osric got here before us?" Sicga suggested. "He lives a lot closer, the fucking traitorous bastard." Carlnut was fixed in place and felt one of his arm rings burning his skin underneath his shirt.

"They are not Cynric's men," he managed to say after inspecting the men more closely.

"Ah yes, no purple. To be honest, Lord, I've never seen anyone like this before. They look barbaric," Sicga said, crossing himself but being the only one of the three to do so.

"I have," Carlnut muttered from underneath his breath. The two walls of shields moved independently. One headed towards the battered gate with their shields raised above their heads rather than in front of them to stop any archer's arrow from striking them from above. Carlnut looked again for his men to do something other than hide behind the walls. A small wall of around seven men had somehow managed to align themselves at the end of the spit without a single arrow in their backs. They stood in the very same place that Carlnut had once touched the ground of his new home. That all seemed an age ago. The world had somehow turned on its head and back again sending everything into a mad pandemonium that could only have been created by the Gods or even the nailed God. At that moment as his home was being raided and his people being murdered and raped, he hated every single God. He hated Odin and Thor, he hated the nailed God and regretted every single sacrifice, prayer and thought he had ever given them.

Cuth grunted like an animal, and Sicga unsheathed his fine sword. The three horses shifted around awkwardly, ready either to charge or to run. The seven warriors looked fierce in their mud and blood-stained leathers and iron helms. Most of them carried round shields painted in various colours and lifted small axes in their right hands. Two of the shields were similar. They both bore a red dragon on a white background, and the sight of such a ferocious creature made Carlnut cross himself. He had never crossed himself before and doing so felt strange. His heart burnt, and Carlnut looked into the sky expecting Thor's hammer to strike him down or one of Loki's spears to whistle through the air and split him in half. But he could not care; he would covert to Christ there and then if it meant everything would revert back to normal again. He thought of Selwyn trapped inside the walls of Portland and hoped desperately Arnum was doing everything he could to stop his fellow Northmen from breaching the walls. A wave of sickness flushed around his stomach at the thought of what they would do if they got into Portland. He had raided before and knew what warriors do if they succeed. The seven Northmen nervously shuffled forward whilst behind them axes and hammers rang against a creaking gate.

"We can't let them get in, no matter what," Carlnut said and both men nodded as if they knew what that meant for their own lives. As the Northmen got about thirty foot away from the three horsemen, one of them stood up from his crouching position. There was something in the movement that lacked fear and shame. The others turned to look at their rogue compatriot in confusion and anger. The rest of them yelled curses and demanded he get back in line.

"What the fuck are you doing, whoreson?" one of them said to the standing man. Cuth and Sicga had no idea what was happening, but Carlnut understood every word.

"Get the fuck back into rank," another warrior pleaded, sensing something ill-fated was about to happen. The rogue just stood, silently fixated on Carlnut but slowly shifted his fingers round to the inner reaches of his leathers that actually appeared far too big for the man. The sea crashed either side of them whilst the plumes of smoke at Fortunes Well grew thicker and darker. Knowing time was of the essence, Carlnut charged, hoping the other two would follow. Sicga seemed to hate the strategy of running straight into a shield wall, but he carried on regardless. Seconds before the three crazed men tangled themselves in an outnumbering mess that would have surely meant their deaths, the rogue swung his hand axe into the neck of the man next to him. The surprised Northman dropped his shield and fell backwards clutching at the giant gash in his throat that leaked and leaked furious streams of blood and bile. The small wall then turned into a scene of slaughter and bedlam. Shields splintered as Cuth's axe struck them with an almighty blow and another broke into pieces when Sicga tossed his shield into the chaotic pile. The apparent traitor still made his way through the group chopping and slashing spraying blood across the sand in floods. Carlnut jumped over a low swing of a spear and parried a charging man, allowing Sicga to slice his belly open spilling stinking guts onto the sand-covered ground. The man screamed as he desperately tried to put his entrails back into his body, but his cries ended when Sicga allowed his sword to slice his neck open. Another man who held a shield that was more iron boss than anything else readied himself for Carlnut. He dropped his broken shield and picked up a fallen warrior's axe so that he wielded two small axes that could wreak havoc if allowed to hit the body. Both Carlnut and Sicga blocked his frenzy with their swords but both were caught on the back foot by the man's courage and skill. Carlnut looked into the berserker's eyes and saw a familiar sight that didn't bode well for his or Sicga's life. The black in the man's eyes were bigger than pebbles, and his sweat was almost green. There was a special type of mushroom that grew on harsh cliff faces that would send any sane man into a fit of fear-free anger and nerveless rage. Carlnut was certain the man's blood pumped with the mushroom's properties. His feet never faltered, and his eyes moved quickly from Sicga to Carlnut, checking each of their lunges. One strike cut down Sicga's chest, luckily only just drawing blood whilst another frenzied blow nearly sliced open Carlnut's neck. If it wasn't for Carlnut's reaction to move his head, he would have died there and then. After at least a minute of swinging and parrying blows, the double axe wielder had his back torn open. Carlnut saw the life fade out of his demon-like eyes as he sunk to his knees with his mouth wide open and face paling to a colour that only ever meant death. Cuth danced behind the dying man throwing his axe from side to side and chanting some gibberish in some phlegm-filled language. All six of the Northmen were dead, which caused their friends at the gates to smash harder at the wooden walls so they didn't have to fight men who had survived being outnumbered without so much as one death.

Six of the seven warriors were a pile of smashed bone and bleeding limbs. The rogue was looting the bodies for any scraps of coin and picking up their weapons, feeling their grip and testing their weight. Once he found a small blade that was tied to a dead man's waist, he dropped his axe and hung his new weapon on his belt.

"Who are you?" Carlnut asked, shocked at his boldness. The man didn't offer any sort of reply but the shake of a head. "This is my land, and it's being put to the torch; I am in no mood for games. If you don't tell me who you are, I will let my man slice you in two." Cuth seemed happy to oblige and straight away he walked forward ready to carry out his work. Still as silent as a dead man, the rogue warrior tugged at the straps that held his iron helm in place to reveal a bald head and a familiar face.

"Engelhard? What are you doing here? Where is Selwyn?" Carlnut said, feeling heavy with aching emotion. Engelhard pointed towards the burning scene of Fortunes Well and Carlnut gagged, his empty stomach being the only reason he didn't vomit. "Get on your fucking horses!" he screamed at Cuth and Sicga.

"Lord, we will never be able to get past that lot," Sicga suggested but allowed his words to fall on deaf ears. Engelhard jumped onto Sicga's horse, wrapped one arm round the nobleman and readjusted his helm with the other so that the shining iron plate hid his bald head once more. Before the others were ready, Carlnut was already several paces in front of them leaving clouds of dust to float and obscure his men's vision. Sicga looked nervously towards the raiders who were all still too focused on breaking the gates. Carlnut and his horse seemed to fly like a bird straight past the Northmen dodging arrows from above and the odd swing from men who hadn't noticed him pass. Arrows continued to rain down from above, but they soon subsided when the archers realised they did nothing but thump into wood. The raised shields fluttered with over one hundred feathered arrows jutting out of them. Sicga prayed to God for strength as he kicked his horse to follow the same path his Lord had just made. Some of the men screamed curses at the riders when they passed at the length of just ten swords. One who must have eaten the same mushrooms as the berserker charged like a hungry wolf, throwing his weapon to try and catch the rear leg of Cuth's horse, but luckily the point skidded across the ground and lodged itself in a pile of sheep dung.

It only took a few minutes to get to Fortunes Well, and during those moments Carlnut's head swam with a thousand images of what he was about to see. He half expected Arnum to be leading a force of forty men rounding up the raiders and binding their arms ready for the Lord's justice. He also hoped there were fewer wild warriors in Fortunes Well than were at the gates of Portland. But after all the fancies, what he did see forced him to rub his eyes. There was a scene of terror unfolding and unfolded in front of his eyes like some kind of dream that would cause sweats and sleepless nights. Fire raged like wild beasts from huts as men and women lay crisp and dead outside clutching onto small unbreathing children. There was a blackened carcass of a man or a woman, Carlnut could not be sure, as its burning flesh still smoked and bubbled in places. The separate infernos were all outmatched by the roaring flames of a boat that bobbed on the rising tides next to two similar-looking ships. Carlnut had never seen vessels like it; they were magnificent, and a part of him felt a twang of pride that his people could have made something so beautiful. Amidst the chaos, purple-clad soldiers and other weapons-wielding men were trying desperately to keep themselves alive. For every Wessex man there were two or even three savage warriors, but even so, they all appeared to be beginning to head back towards their ships. Carlnut thanked the man or men who managed to set alight one of the attackers' ships causing them to swap their want for women and treasure for their desire to return home. His smile lasted seconds as the desire to see Selwyn alive and struck him like a spear to the throat. Carlnut dismounted his horse and charged down the weaving path to the village, passing gorgeous blue flowers and horribly disfigured bodies. Cuth, Sicga and Engelhard flew down the path with him all failing to keep up with their Lord's supernatural speed.

"Selwyn!" Carlnut called when he got to the bottom of the path and closest to the first flaming house. Two more charred bodies lay still steaming at its door, and Carlnut's stomach whirled like a storm. The fire burned red and blue, creating disturbing shadows that danced across the path. A wave of heat stung Carlnut's face and forced beads of sweat to drip from his forehead. A crazed warrior carrying a heavy pouch and a spear appeared from an alley. Engelhard was alert to the danger and threw his blade straight into the man's forehead causing him to jolt backwards with powerful force. The mute pulled the blade free and disappeared down the alley, also desperate to see the woman he had sworn to protect alive. The smoke was horribly dense and filled their lungs with burning hot vapours leading to terrible coughs and annoying splutters.

"If Selwyn is anywhere she will be with Luyewn in the chapel," Carlnut shouted over the cracking fire that grew bigger and bigger beside them. Sicga led Cuth in one direction after a line of fur-clad silhouettes ran past in front of them carrying full sacks and speaking a language only Carlnut could understand. "They are heading to the boats. They are retreating!" Carlnut said helplessly as his words were absorbed by the thick scorching fog.

Eventually, after crouching his way through sandy alleys and climbing over lifeless bodies he saw the chapel. Somehow not a single spark had touched the few buildings surrounding it, and Carlnut sighed in relief. The hidden breath of the sea kept the air clear of smoke and debris; for the first time since he landed in Fortunes Well, Carlnut could see. Behind the unmarked chapel a whole host of Northmen scurried back carrying whatever they could to load their boats with. Some men carried chests and others carried bundles of cloth, but none of that mattered to Carlnut. His whole body began to shake when he saw a few had women draped over their thick shoulders. Ignoring all his better instincts, he burst into a sprint towards the retreating men, but they already had too much of a head start on him.

"Selwyn!" he cried at the top of his voice causing a terrified echo to bounce off the surrounding cliff faces. "Selwyn! Answer me, it's Carlnut!" Only one man on the entire beach responded, and suddenly they were the only people in the world. Carlnut was still over one hundred feet away from the man who had stopped at the sound of Carlnut's name. He was carrying a woman over his shoulder and ran with an awkward limp from a troublesome wound, from which blood dripped down his entire leg. The Northman's most striking feature was his long blonde hair that formed a carefully braided ponytail at the back of his head. No words were fashioned in Carlnut's mouth, and it felt like he had just swallowed a barrel of salt. Both men looked at each other for only a few seconds, but those tiny moments of realisation lasted as long as time itself. The sun had disappeared behind grey clouds, sending a chill breeze across the bay, disturbing the calm sea and turning it into one that could frenzy into chaos at any moment.

Solvi handed Selwyn to a thin, bow-carrying warrior beside him and walked towards Carlnut. All Carlnut could think of was home. "You will return to Hordaland" were Solvi's last words to him and maybe this was his prophecy.

"How can this be? The gods are cruel creatures," Carlnut said to himself as Solvi unsheathed his sword and limped closer to his brother. Carlnut was torn in a hundred pieces; he wanted his woman back, and his brother had stolen her and burnt his land but Solvi was his kin. He could not kill his kin.

"How can that be you, Brother?" Solvi said with tears in his eyes and the wind throwing sand into his face. "Come home." Carlnut turned back to the burning hell that was Fortunes Well; he felt the coarse sand swelling round his toes within his boots and heard the multitude of nesting gulls that shrieked on the cliffs.

"This is my home," Carlnut said, feeling strangely weak and defeated. Solvi froze and raised his sword, but he wasn't looking at Carlnut and instead pointed his blade in the direction of Sicga.

"I have had more visions and dreams, Carlnut, than you can even imagine. I remember one where you banished me from the halls of Valhalla, but I realise now I was not looking into Odin's great halls, but instead I was looking into the boring place you Christians call heaven. That is it, isn't it, Brother? You have been tainted by Christians! Are you a fucking Christian?! Do you kneel and sulk in white robes crying tears and drinking wine in front of a nailed bitch? How could I have been so–?" Solvi keeled over as if his wound had just doubled in size and ripped his skin in two. "How could I have been so stupid as if to invite you back to Hordaland? You will never return, Brother, because I will kill you right here and now." With that he charged like a wild beast towards Carlnut, seemingly forgetting his deep-set cut. Sicga tried to push past Carlnut to try and protect his lord but instead he was pushed over onto the wet shingle by Carlnut who had a wrath bubbling inside him. Solvi's first swing was a predictable one. He struck down in a hard furious blow that would have cleaved an unprepared skull in half. Carlnut met the blow with Karla, and for a moment he was transported. They had sparred as children since they were strong enough to wield any kind of weapon. Solvi was an intelligent fighter whilst Carlnut was all about power. Carlnut remembered the day that their Father Hrolf presented them with their swords mainly because of a scar he had on his hip where Solvi had become a little too wild in his swings. A similar strike came next. Karla sang as she parried away Gutstretcher, which was just a finger's length away from splitting the old scar open and spilling Carlnut's blood all over the beach below. Solvi was panting; he had raided and travelled and killed and every breath looked like it took an age to take in. Carlnut tried to hack into his brother's neck, then his leg and then attempted a low swing to split his shin, but Solvi was far too quick. For an injured warrior he had the reflexes and movement of a wild cat, always watching and anticipating. Solvi held the blade even, a perfect, undaunted horizon, always level with his bloodied nose, just as their father had taught them many years ago. Carlnut had stalled Solvi's strike but watched a wretched, stained grin split his brother's lips as Karla shivered under the brutality of Solvi's compelling strength.

"Weapons do not belong in the hands of Christians," Solvi throatily crooned, pressing closer to his face. Gutstretcher flashed as Solvi brought it over his head and hummed a low, swift tune when he brought it down again. A splintering pain pulsated through Carlnut's body as if he had just been split in two. He could feel the warmth of blood begin to flush down his chest and a sad weakness start to overcome him. Searing fiery bursts pulsated around the wound, intensifying with each dragging movement, jarring and brutal. With every attempt to move his arm the pain amplified, the bloody muscles quivered and his consciousness ebbed. Black mists swirled at the edges of his mind, drawing Carlnut into a sweet dark sleep. With one momentous effort he tried to lift his sword arm to parry another blow from

Solvi, but his shoulder would just not allow any movement. Carlnut was certain a death stroke was about to end his life. The horrid tang of blood washed around his mouth. His senses swam, blurring his vision and weakening every single muscle he had. Somehow in the time it takes for a fly to take flight or a bird to slap its wings, Karla whipped across his own face and blocked Solvi's attack. Carlnut was on his knees, but he felt a strange energy from the ground as if it was vibrating and willing him to fight, not just for himself but for Selwyn too.

Solvi turned to look at his small fleet and growled when he saw one of the ships was completely blackened and ruined by a wild blaze that had somehow taken its life. He was the only Northman left on the beach and Carlnut managed to make out the signs of a grimace forming on his face at the sudden realisation of being outnumbered. Cuth and Sicga must have both also seen the worry in the Jarl's face and decided to intervene instead of letting Carlnut either die from his wounds or from exhaustion.

"No! He is mine to kill! Go and save Selwyn!" Carlnut yelled as he finally managed to get back to his feet. Out of loyalty or stupidity the two huge men ran for the two boats that were being heaved into the deeper water by tired grinning warriors.

"Do understand, Brother –" Solvi said, wiping away some blood-infused salvia from his cheek, "– you have to die today. Even if you are not Christian, if you stay here for too long, then you will be. Our father will be watching every single path you choose and right now he is worried."

"I have people to care for, and Selwyn needs me," Carlnut pleaded behind strained blood-shot eyes.

"Do you mean that fire-red bitch that is now being eyed up by my men? For you, Carlnut, I promise I will not touch her even though she is a pretty one. However, how could I deny my hardworking men such a wondrous prize?" Solvi laughed, which made him scowl from some unwelcome pain. "When you are lying cold on this ground you will forget the Christian whore and will be ready to sheath your tiny sword in any women you like in Odin's halls." Carlnut's face reddened to the colour of a dawn's sun, and he felt like he could have torn his brother into two whole pieces. All the love he had ever had for Solvi had drained, and he found himself as empty as his hands now were. Karla dropped onto the sand, and surprisingly, Solvi did the same with Gutstretcher. Carlnut took a moment's breath in relief as he only dropped his sword because his right arm had become completely useless. Solvi jumped on Carlnut and unleashed a volley of earth-shattering punches and scratches that should have completely obliterated Carlnut. Even before Solvi struck, Carlnut already felt dead. He knew all he could do was try and survive for a few more minutes just in case Sicga and Cuth managed to save Selwyn. But Carlnut accepted they would die too, and all of them would either dine in Valhalla or Heaven; he didn't know nor did he even care.

Only a month ago he was begging in Ealdorman Osric's court to die with a sword in hand so that he could feast with Odin and Thor and his father, but all that hope and belief had been beaten out of him the moment he saw his burning home. There was a brief moment when Solvi just stared at his own hands; the blood had concentrated in the folds of his knuckles, making the usually pale creases dark. The congealed red-brown fluid had become caught in the webbing of his fingers, whereas the rest had been washed clean by relentless gushes of sweat. Carlnut managed to catch one of Solvi's punches and use the force to pull his brother to the ground. He held his face down deep into the damp sand and watched Solvi squirm like a beached fish trying desperately for breath. Carlnut punched Solvi's still bleeding wound sending him into horrible sakes and jitters of muted pain.

"This is the end for you, Brother," Carlnut whispered in Solvi's ear as his brother continued to struggle for even the small sip of air that would refresh his lungs and give him the strength to easily overpower the almost dead Carlnut. A glint caught Carlnut's eye, and at first he thought it was the sun shining off Karla, which looked so wonderful in the light. Instead of Karla it was Cuth's axe that drew Carlnut's attention away from killing the man that had destroyed his life. For some reason Cuth and Sicga were running away from the ships. They were running as fast as wolves to their prey and for a awful moment Carlnut had no idea what was going on. He turned to see what Sicga was pointing at.

All of a sudden a thunderous stomping noise charged in from behind Carlnut, and it wasn't until it was too late that he knew what was going on. The crew members that had been hammering the walls of Portland were storming back to their boats desperate not to be left behind in a strange land where they would be rounded up and butchered. The first two darted past Carlnut and Solvi not caring at all about their presence. He looked at Cuth who had the sea behind him and was engaging in a fight with a Northman. Two men stumbled into Carlnut thus releasing Solvi. The whole air around them seemed to become light as Solvi was finally able to breathe again. Carlnut was facing the sea where on either one of the two boats, the only good thing in his life was scared, frightened and alone. Meanwhile, Solvi staggered back to his feet and faced the retreating crew that had all but saved his life. The two brothers were almost back to back. They both panted for breath that just would not come and stared at the other's new life.

Another few warriors with nothing but full sacks pounded past like wild things drunk on plunder. The last person to pass was also the only one who seemed to notice Carlnut. The very slender warrior grabbed Solvi by the arm and started to drag him back to the boats. To Carlnut's surprise he saw that the warrior was in fact a woman. She carried two axes bright with blood, and she laughed back at him.

The world began to spin. Waves of heat coursed through his body. The sea turned upside down sending giant sprays crashing over the burning ship and blurring everything else. Bird calls went from being the loudest thing to the quietest. His eyes felt sunken and his skin pimpled; everything ached, everything sagged. The once gentle sea breeze felt like a storm and his entire body became a weight that no man in the entire world could sustain. A warm thick liquid heated his back and thickened his hair and the more he felt its stream, the less he felt like his feet were there. A sudden realisation of every movement he could or couldn't make swirled in his memory forcing him to forget the simple things in life. Carlnut's knee's hit the ground. His head followed with a moist bang and seconds later the world was black.

Epilogue

"Are you ready, Jarl?" Smaragus whispered to the bandaged Pintojuk Bergison.

"I've been ready ever since that upstart usurped my position. And I couldn't be more sick of calling you Athelstan," Bergison said, holding a hand to the bandages that hid his missing ear from the world. The stinking linen had been Smaragus's idea as had most of the past few months. Frosti's old tent was spacious enough for the two of them, but Bergison was always staring at Solvi's grand longhouse that still stood above the spot where King Sigfred had saved him from the Blood Eagle. The night was getting thicker and the snores and groans of drunken men were growing louder. Bergison knew the moment was almost upon him and he shuddered in part excitement and part fear.

"Can I not just take these fucking bandages off?" The Jarl asked, stretching his neck and arms to avoid the terrible itch the unwashed cloth caused.

"No, no, no. We must remain as we are for now; simply as Athelstan and Tojuk. Not long to go, Jarl. We are just waiting on one thing," Smaragus reassured him as he peeped out of the tent looking for movement. All he saw was a grey squirrel jumping around in a thorn bush and two bats overhead competing over a piece of dripping fruit. After another hour of silent waiting, a large silhouette appeared on the tent fabric being created by a dying torch so the peculiar-shaped shadow appeared to be dying as well.

"Come in, come in," Smaragus said, whilst he wrapped a great cloak round the pregnant Aesa. Her belly had swollen almost to bursting, and Smaragdus predicted she would give birth within the next month. The Christian monk continued to talk about her health and the mixes of herbs she could use to ease the pain. Regardless of Smaragus's efforts, neither Aesa nor Pintojuk Bergison listened to a single word. She waddled over towards her husband and desperately unwrapped his bandages, wanting nothing more than to see and touch his face again after months apart. He let out a huge sigh of relief as the cool air soothed his face. Lines weaved across his cheeks and over his forehead, which gave him an old wrinkled appearance, making Aesa look twice to see whether the man she loved was truly in front of her. Pintojuk ran his wrapped hand across her belly, smiling. Suddenly he pulled away as if her flesh had somehow turned to boiling, but they both laughed as she reassured him that it was only a kick.

"I have promised to call him Hulfdan. Hulfdan Sigfredson," Jarl Bergison said as he rested his only ear against her stomach hoping to hear his son's heartbeat inside.

"Sigfredson? Not Pintojukson?" Aesa asked, shocked by her husband's decision but decided not to push the question when he ignored her and started to attach a sword belt to his waist. "Eddval is sleeping; I've made sure of that. He's had far too much wine," Aesa told Smaragdus and Jarl Bergison as they left the tent. Smaragdus tried desperately to keep up with the bounding strides of Pintojuk, but his limp hindered any desperate progress. All his normal pain had subsided, and he thanked his God that he chose this night to relieve him of his agonising shooting pain that normally made the slightest movement an effort.

Bergison halted in horror when a small group of men walked into his path blocking his way to Solvi's longhouse. He could almost smell the stench of the stinking wine pouring from Eddval's breath. His hands twitched under the bandages in frustration. He searched the faces of every single man in the crowd but recognised not a single one. The man in front of them all had a set of finely trimmed whiskers and a beard that hung in several small braids. He had a mountain of fur pelts clinging round his neck that were much too thick for the summer night, however, he didn't seem to mind. The otter pelt he wore round his neck still had its mouth wide open showing its yellow, snarling teeth. Bergison's shaking hand reached towards his sword hilt, but the pelt-covered man just held out two rope-battered hands.

"This man is Finlit Hafgramr, Jarl," Smaragdus said in a loud whisper. "He is with us." All of a sudden Bergison was alive again, and his feet found a whole new source of energy. Finlit, Smaragdus and Bergison all entered the wonderfully built hut as silent as mice whilst the rest of the group remained like statues outside. The hut was awash in furs and cloth which stunk of clinging smoke that was being spat out by a dying fire. The hearth was in the middle of the great room. The pit was surrounded by carefully laid stones that trapped the ash from scattering to the floor. Four empty benches surrounded the hearth as well as dozens of damp empty cups. It was then that the trio realised they didn't have to be silent. They could have sung an entire verse of a booming war chant without Eddval ever waking up. Instinctively, they all straightened their backs from the strange crouched position they had adopted as they lightly stepped around the room. They found Eddval passed out on the floor between the huge hearth-room and the bedroom. His half-naked body was covered in a few rags whilst a puddle of vomit slowly matted itself in his long blonde hair.

"Shall we kill him?" Finlit asked, already getting a small knife from some pouch hidden deep within his furs.

"We will see," Pintojuk Bergison said as he sat down on a huge, wonderfully carved chair near the flickering embers. "We will see."

***

"We could do it," Osbert the Steward said to Bedfrith who searched nervously round the damp room wondering if they were alone. "It would be so easy. All it would take is another small cut to the wound, and the blood loss will do the rest."

Carlnut lay unconscious on the straw bed as he had done for almost two weeks. His sheets were blood stained and covered in various other staining liquids. Sicga had carried his Lord from the beach all the way to Portland and ordered that servants watch over him day and night. However, whenever Sicga was away tending to the reconstruction of Fortunes Wells, Osbert would limit their visits.

"The Ealdorman Osric has already sent me two letters ordering for the capture of Carlnut, but I know if I hand him to them they will take Portland too. Portland is mine," Osbert said defiantly.

"Is that your plan then? Kill Carlnut and take his lands? I am sorry to be the carrier of bad news, but he still has friends here and those friends surely won't follow someone so young," Bedfrith warned his new ally. "Arnum is in the cells still; Sicga is walking round like he owns the place and those two dogs Cuth and Engelhard are everywhere I turn. I would happily swap all their lives to have Selwyn back." During the raids the Northmen burnt and pillaged most of Fortunes Well but also breached the walls of Portland and stole gold, cloth and other treasures from wherever they could find them. Osbert had ordered all the soldiers to stay inside the hall with the women allowing zero resistance to the chaos that swarmed outside. A few men tried to resist the attack and died, including Ordmaer the blacksmith and Beric the old steward of Portland. A few days after the heathens' two remaining ships sailed off back into the sea a funeral service was held for all who lost their lives. It was discovered that Engelhard had set one of the boats on fire, and Osbert knew he owed him his life but he would never admit it. The funeral took place in Portland's great hall, which seemed empty without its Lord and Lady. Father Willibald ran the proceedings, but the whole event was continuously interrupted by the unusual spasms the man seemed to have every few moments. At one point after mentioning Father Luyewn, he was ushered out of the room because his flowing tears aggravated his new condition so much that all his words were high-pitched tics.

"Do you have a blade on you, Bedfrith?" Osbert asked.

"No, but I think I saw Carlnut's sword in the other room," the harpist suggested. "Karla I think he calls it. What kind of ridiculous man names a sword?" They both laughed, sharing their varied hatred for their Lord. The room they were in was large enough for a large family and other than the hall, it was the biggest room in Portland. Osbert nodded his head towards the door as if to silently command Bedfrith to get Karla, and he responded with a look of shocked horror.

"Do you not think I can do it? Ealdorman Osric and Earl Cynric will be here in a matter of weeks I imagine, with god only knows how many armed men with them. If we are found protecting Carlnut then we will be deemed traitors. Do you not understand? He is wanted by the King, Bedfrith, the King wants his head on a pike, and you hesitate to kill him." The harpist realised he had no other choice, and his head dropped as if a large weight was draped round his neck. Bedfrith left the room and Osbert smiled, crinkling his pox-scarred skin over his cheeks whilst he leant in towards Carlnut's ear. "Soon you vile piece of shit I will have the pleasure of sending you to the burning pits of hell. Osric's letters said nothing of your condition, but I know what you are, and you disgust me."

"Good," Carlnut croaked. Suddenly Osbert was on the other side of the room stumbling over a pot of cleaning water. The rattling pot seemed to spin forever sending water everywhere as the two men looked at each other.

"Lord, you are alive; it brings me such joy to—"

"Shut your traitorous mouth. I've heard every single word you have said today and—" a surge of pain interrupted Carlnut's speech, and he found himself grabbing the back of his head so hard that he was sure he was going to crack his own skull. As his hand pressed into the small of his neck his entire arm shook and fell limp. His head thumped, his shoulder shrieked with pain and his heart throbbed.

"I am afraid, Lord, you have no strength whatsoever. Your words cannot hurt me, Pagan. They are vile, you are vile, and I think the almighty Lord will bless me for eternity for removing you from a world that is too good for men like you." Osbert gained an abundance of confidence from Carlnut's miserable state of health. "In a few moments' time your precious Selwyn's lover will come through the door with Karla, and I will use it to end your disgusting life." The mention of Selwyn made Carlnut's body shudder. He remembered the beach and her unconscious limp body draped over his brother's back. With this memory he fell back onto his blood-stained sheets.

"Before you kill me, could you please tell me why you arrested Arnum and let that whole village burn? You let Selwyn get captured! You let Eafled and Luyewn die!" Each word got more and more tangled with a lash of rage. "They were good people, and you just sat on your chair doing nothing!" Carlnut screamed before another surge made him wince. There were times during Carlnut's worst moments of injury that he dozed in and out of consciousness. When his ears were awake he often heard Sicga talking to a maid or servant but sometimes the nobleman talked directly to Carlnut. Carlnut wanted to respond in any way, but his body would not allow it. He remembered his eyes being horribly dry when he heard about Luyewn's death.

"I do admit that Eafled's and Luyewn's deaths were upsetting, and I even shed a tear at their funeral; however, I would kill the King if it meant I had my own fort and land." Osbert laughed. The steward looked towards the door as a torch's light flickered underneath it and the sound of footsteps echoed through the cracks. Carlnut coughed furiously into his hands and noticed splatters of blood mixed in with his saliva but wiped the evidence away before Osbert could see more of his vulnerability. Bedfrith opened the door nervously, washing the room in a bright yellow light that made Carlnut's eyes water and wince. The harpist was not alone nor did he carry Karla. Instead, Karla was pressed into the arch of his back by the giant figure of Sicga. It seemed that Sicga had come to Carlnut's rescue once more. The Ealdorman's son had saved Carlnut's life in Wareham a few weeks earlier when his father wanted Carlnut's head, and he was fast becoming Carlnut's greatest friend. Carlnut became stronger somehow when he saw the big man's curling hair and stern face. Once again the balance in the room shifted in Carlnut's favour and Osbert found himself on the defensive again.

"I think if you were in my position, Lord, you would have done the same. I kept the women and children safe–"

"You didn't keep Selwyn safe!" Carlnut screamed from his bed, wanting nothing more than to jump on top of the man and strangle the breath from his body.

"I assure you I did everything in my power to protect Portland," Osbert said whilst his eyes rapidly looked from Carlnut to Sicga. Sicga was the only one in the room armed, and Osbert had already begun to regret leaving his own sword in his chambers.

"Get out," Sicga said to Bedfrith who was sweating like a small child about to be beaten. "Get out of this room, get out of Portland and get out of Dorchester! And I promise if you run to that ginger prick Cynric then I personally will cut you open like a deer." The harpist didn't hesitate at all and ran out of the room immediately. However, Carlnut was certain he would run for his harp before he would go anywhere else. Osbert also tried to dart out of the room but was blocked by the outstretched Karla.

"Please, Lords, have mercy, I promise I will leave. For god's sake, I will run to Northumbria or even Alba if that's what it takes," the steward pleaded.

"Athelhild!" Sicga shouted at the top of his voice, sending the young maid scuttling into the room like a flash as though she had only been a few steps away. "Tell them to come in now," he said, and she understood exactly what he meant even if Carlnut and Osbert did not. Bedfrith had left the torch in a rusty iron casket on the wall, and suddenly Carlnut was reminded of Selwyn's house where she and Luyewn had lovingly nursed him back to health. The flames leaped and hissed teasing his shadow. The orange blur turned blue then red then orange again warming the room but staying far enough away from Carlnut that his skin still pimpled. He closed his eyes and imagined home but nothing but darkness filled his mind. A rabble of men interrupted Carlnut's daydream, and he opened his eyes to find the room become suddenly cramped. The first man he saw was Arnum. It had been weeks since he last saw his friend, and the soldier jumped at the chance to embrace his Lord. He had grown a beard since they last met, and he wore it splendidly even if it was rough to touch and probably teeming with lice. Carlnut winced as Arnum's arms wrapped round his weak body, and a tear came to his eyes when he truly realised how weak he actually was. As well as Arnum, Engelhard had shown up; he showed no emotion and instead hung towards the back of the group on the threshold offering only a simple nod. Carlnut's stomach cramped at the sight of him, but his anger refused to bubble until it was ready. Cuth walked up to the bedside and knelt on one knee. He was a huge man, even bigger than Sicga, so even though he knelt he was almost the size of Osbert who stood shaking in the corner of the room.

"My Lord," he said in his fierce accented tone. "Lord Eafled is dead. I have no lord now. I will be your man if you will have me."

"Yes, Cuth, you have earned a place by my side. That and so much more," Carlnut replied, trying again to hold back more tears.

"Thank you, Lord," Cuth said. The beast took a few steps back and Osbert went to speak but thought different of it.

"Osbert," Carlnut said, bringing the steward's attention back to reality. "It would give me so much pleasure to kill you now, but I am far too weak. Soon I will have the pleasure of sending you to the burning pits of hell," Carlnut said, mirroring the words Osbert had said to him when all seemed to be going perfectly for the steward. "I am a Lord, and I think I must treat you the same as any other traitor. Sicga, get the men to set up the gallows. Arnum, take this man to the cells where he allowed you to rot. He will be hung in the morning." Osbert burst into a wail of tears and pleas, but every man in the room allowed them to fall on deaf ears. "Cuth, make sure Bedfrith makes it out of Portland alive; he was a friend of Selwyn, and I must do what she would advise me to do." Everyone had begun to dismiss themselves until Carlnut raised a shaking hand towards Engelhard. "You stay here!" Everyone else shuffled away including Athelhild who closed the door behind her, trapping Engelhard and Carlnut in the stinking chamber. They stared at each other for what seemed to be an age. Engelhard's face remained fixed as if its very features were made of stone. Thin bristles of hair had begun to grow again on the top of his head, and his hands lay still at his side until the fire drew his attention. He ran a hand through the flames making them jump and whistle, but if he did feel the burning, his face did not show it. Finally, Carlnut spoke:

"You swore an oath to Selwyn. You swore to protect her till the death but here you are alive and she is somewhere in the sea frightened and alone and quite possibly dead." Carlnut held back the urge to sink into a frenzy of despair. "Tomorrow I will make sure there is a boat and a small crew ready for you." Engelhard tilted his head in confusion. "I do not want to see your face until Selwyn is safe with me. I don't care how you do it, I don't care how long it takes, just find her! Go." Carlnut waved a hand to dismiss Engelhard, and as he went to leave the room the mute turned to face his Lord. His mouth wavered as if he was about to speak, but he turned away before his voice could make a sound.

The room felt empty and even the flickering torch seemed to subside as the passing hours tore and pulled at Carlnut's muscles. A sharp pain was interrupted when Arnum ran in panting like a hunting dog.

"An army, Lord. Our scout says Osric is marching here with an army, and he is carrying his banners along with Earl Cynric's!" Carlnut looked towards Karla who lay on a table beside his bed. His hand stroked her hilt, and he felt her heart racing in his palm.

"I promised you their deaths. I do not break promises," Carlnut whispered with a hint of excitement.

Historical Note

Note on Characters.

There are many characters within this book and throughout the series that were real people. I have tried my best to see through their eyes. The beauty of writing Historical Fiction is it is like playing a game of dot to dot, there are known facts and dates but not much knowledge of what went on in-between. My passion is to connect those facts with story and create a novel that both excites and informs.

The five kings of England that I have included were all real monarchs and I found it very hard not to give them bigger roles. Offa of Mercia, who was one of the greatest Kings at the time, will show up in the proposed sequels. King Cynewulf of Wessex the man murdered by a mad ealdorman named Cyneheard really did die in such a manner but for the benefit of time I had them both die at the scene. Most of the ealdormen and nobles like Eafled and Cynric are fictional however both Osric and Sicga have been mentioned in the Anglo-Saxon Chronicle, the latter being quite an important figure in early medieval history. The part of them being related is not true however I felt it added more depth to the characters. I must also add that Father Luyewn's name is not truly original and derives itself from Maester Luwin a character in George R.R Martin's Song of Ice and Fire series. The names for my 'British' characters are accurate of the times apart from Cuth. This is because Cuth is from Cornwall, which was still very tribal and somewhat pagan at the time.

For Solvi's character I was doing some research and I found the name Solvi Hrolfson who was a Jarl of Hordaland. Other than that fact there was no more information on him. So I worked with that. His father would have been named Hrolf and I added the name Carlnut as his brother because I liked the way it sounded. It is such a freedom when nothing but a name is presented to me as it allows me to create story for the character. Most of Solvi's crew is fictional but the friendships between them all are not. Crew's would have treated each other as a family and one loss would be felt by all. It is much more difficult to find real people in Scandinavian history at this time as not much is recorded like in English history. A lot of what we think we know was told by Snorri Sturluson an Icelandic historian, poet, and politician born in 1179 (Over ten years after the end of the Viking age). There is some knowledge regarding Kings and legendary characters. King Sigfred is one of those men. He is recorded as being a King of Denmark and not much else; I do think though that a man being harried in the south will look north for more lands. Smaragdus, the monk working with Bergison is based off a man named Smaragdus of Saint-Mihiel. He was a Benedictine monk in service to Charlemagne and his successors.

There was one contentious thing I did that kept me worrying at night but I felt like I had no choice. Gudrod the Hunter was born in the 770's-780's at best guess so that would make him a preteen at the time my book is set. Such a decision to include him before his time was a difficult one but he and his family are just too interesting to avoid. His line includes such men as Halfdan the black (Mentioned in Broken Tides), Harold Fairhead and Eric Bloodaxe. It is impossible to truly know birthdates during this period so I will continue to use that defence if any historians passionate about Viking lore want to question my intergrety.

Note of Locations.

Wessex was one of the Kingdom's on the isle of Britain as well as Northumbria, East Anglia, Mercia, Kent, and Cornwall. Modern day cities and towns such as Exeter, Southampton, Wareham and Glastonbury, would all now fall under the rule of Wessex. In 800AD Mercia under the rule of

Offa was the most powerful Kingdom and Wessex were used as a puppet domain.

The isle of Portland features pronomantly in Broken Tides. The reason for that is; Portland was where the first Northmen attack was recorded. Most text books will tell you that the first attack took place on the holy island of Lindersfarne in 793 however the Anglo-Saxon chronicle states that: During the reign of King Beorhtric of Wessex three ships of Northmen landed at Portland Bay in Dorset. It then goes on to say that a local reeve mistook the Vikings for merchants and directed them to the nearby royal estate, but they killed him and his men. The detail at the end I have tried to tell with the death of Earl Eafled as a reeve was in similar standing to an Earl. If you ever get the chance to visit Dorset I do recommend it, especially the strange isle of Portland.

According to what modern historians know, the three ships that invaded Portland were from Hordaland. The fleet I created started much bigger than that but I maliciously had twelve vessels sunk by a storm. The North Sea is still known to be a horrific crossing with storms a very common thing. The Roman's once had half of their fleet destroyed by the weather as they crossed the North Sea so I did not see it implausible for it to happen to Solvi as well. My descriptions of Hordaland are based of research and map studying as I have not had the privilege to visit yet but I am assured that I have set the scene somewhat accurately. The Bjornafjorden features prominently as well and I recommend having a look at aerial photos of it as that body of water is enormous. Solvi and his crew see it as a place of power and I can see why they would. The water is huge and would have looked breathtaking with the sea's current and moons light. As well as its spiritual properties it would have created a way of life for the people of this region, providing food and access to trade.

I have definitely exaggerated the conditions of the north of the region. I described the northern camp in a kind of dormant volcano setting but as keen geologists would know, no such a place exists. However there are a number of large mountains in the area and such places could have had volcanic activity far underneath the surface changing the ground temperature somewhat. The coldness would be intense that far north but perhaps I am guilty of exaggerating the difference in climate a tad too much.

Note on Events.

The story starts with Carlnut's shipwreck but then, by Solvi's third chapter, two years had passed. The reason behind this is that I needed Carlnut to learn English. I hadn't the time to have endless chapters of him learning and I feel the two year jump adds more realism to Solvi's hatred of Bergison.

As I have already mentioned the assassination of King Cynewulf is a key event in Broken Tides. Cynewulf became King after his predecessor, Sigeberht, was deposed. Cyneheard, the assassin was Sigeberht's brother and he rode to Merton (Merantune) with a number of men to kill the King. After the fight and Cynewulf was slain, Cyneheard ran away and offered the King's ealdormen money to join him. However Osric rejected and destroyed all of Cyneheard's men and killed the assassin.

Revolts similar to Jikop's revolt would have been a very common occurrence for Jarl's such as Solvi. The hierarchy system was set up in such a way that Chief's (Karls) could become very rich from individual raids and trades thus making them powerful. Jarl's would often have to crush Karl's that became too powerful in order to remain in charge.

King Offa of Mercia did in fact create his own archbishop to increase the power of his Kingdom and to stop relying on another Kingdom's archbishopric. Hygeberht was the first Archbishop of Lichfield. I had Hygeberht crown Beorhtric as a symbol of Offa's power over Wessex and in my opinion such an event may have taken place as all three of them knew each other quite well after meeting at the Synod of Chelsea.

In 787, three Hordaland vessels raided Portland and killed a shire reeve. The sight must have been chaos and terribly one sided. Luckily, in Broken Tides, soldiers are already at the scene for other reasons. The reason for this is that I can see no other excuse, but defeat, for the northmen to not attack British soil soon after. Instead the next recorded raid was six years later in 793.

Note on Sequels.

I have planned another three in the series with characters such as Charlemagne, his sons, and previously mentioned Kings becoming important players in the story. The next book is titled: Broken Tides: A Tale of Exile. The story is split across more locals with even more points of view including Selwyn in Frankia and Pippin the Hunchback in Charlemagne's court.

A Huge Thankyou.

I couldn't be more grateful for all the help my Kickstarters provided to make my dream of becoming an author a reality. So thank you to:

C. Nuttall.
C. Bates.
E. Barnet.
B. Darby.
M. Bamford.
S. Howard.
K. Beale.
A. Chaudhary.
A. Hall.
A. Peat
S. Bradley
A. Houghton
M. Harris.
D. Baer.
S. Schulte.
Z. Murphy.
D. Kenny.
C. Mitton.
M. W. Jevon.
M. Lees
D. Stack.
S. Kenny
C. J. Kenny.
C. Kenny
D. Marney
T. Marney
F. Elmslie

Made in the USA
Charleston, SC
03 January 2017